Crown of Horns

Written by F. David Schultz
Illustrated by Audra Balion

A novel set in Balion's Flight Nineteen *world.*

Published by Audra Balion Art & Design © 2025

4-115 3rd Ave S
Saskatoon, SK
S7K 1L6

audra.balion.ca

Dedicated to my amazing partner, Audra Balion,
who let me into her world—both real and imagined.

With special thanks to Sarah Rowe, who encouraged me to
keep going, and to my dear friends who have supported me in
the creation of this book.

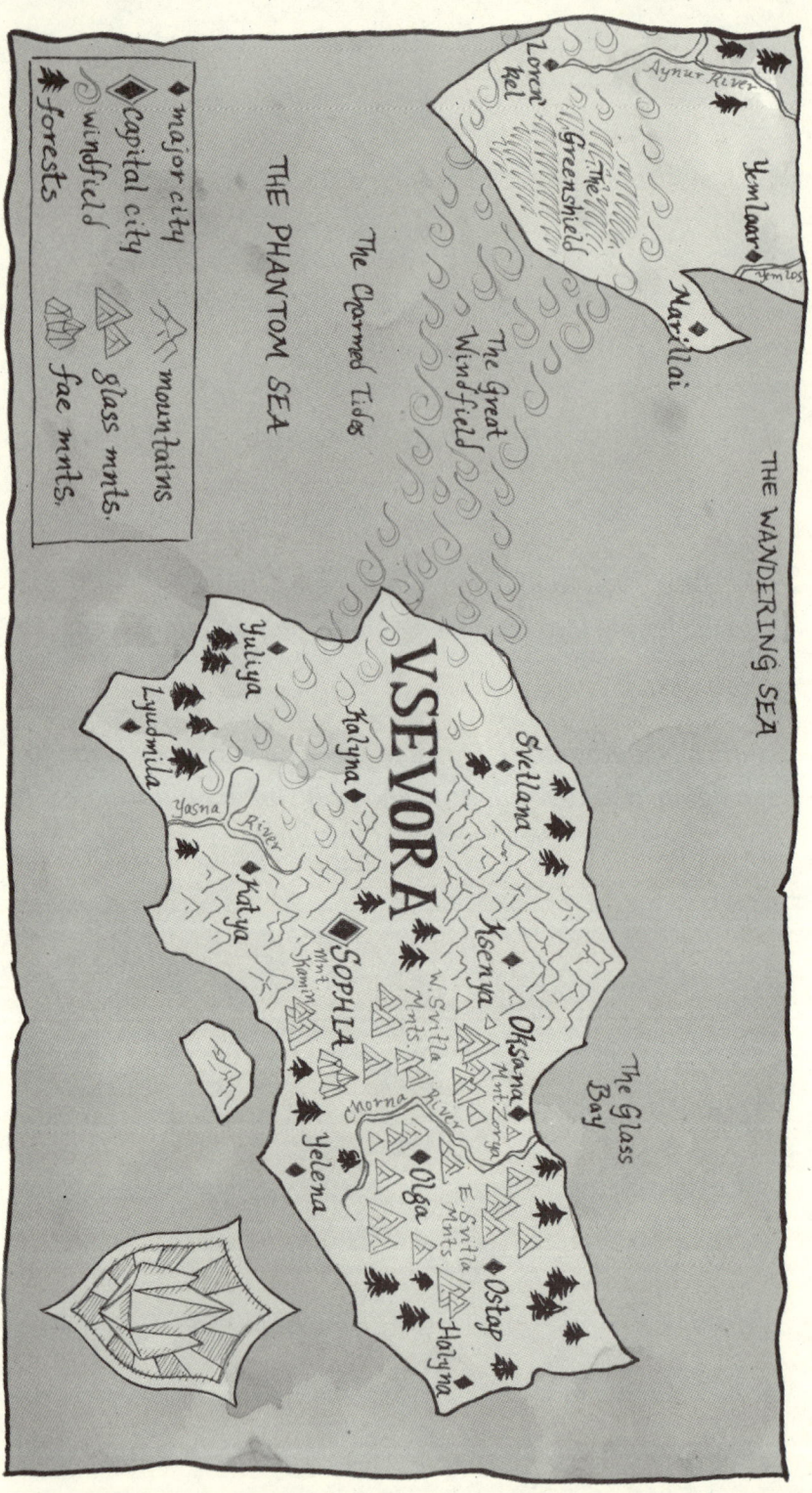

The nation of Vsevora has been plagued by war and conflict fuelled by racial prejudices. It has become a place where one's value is determined by the shape of one's horns.

Ishkara, a refugee with a vision for unity, seeks to bring peace to the fractured nation. She enlists the aid of a constable, an artist, and an outsider, but even the best of intentions can be corrupted.

There are no benevolent dictators.

Table of Contents

Preface

Crown of Horns is rooted in the culture and struggles of Ukraine. Although I am not Ukrainian, I feel as though I have been adopted into its culture. My partner, Audra Balion, traces her heritage back to Ukraine, and its culture is a significant part of her and her family's daily life. Thanks to her, I began to learn, appreciate, and participate in many aspects of the culture.

In 2013 and 2014, the Euromaidan protests caught my attention. The stories of police brutality broke my heart and that's when the first ideas for this story arose.

Around this time, Audra began creating a graphic novel: *Flight Nineteen*. It was a silent comic set in a world of mutants, hybrids, and oil. She developed a robust world and I worked with her on adding to it. With her blessing, I began to create characters, build an outline, and draft preliminary scenes set in her continent of Vsevora.

The project fell by the wayside. Come 2020, the pandemic put many plans on pause, including a trip to celebrate Audra's and my wedding anniversary. With the time booked off, I proposed we do something creative: write and illustrate a book.

I poured myself into the work. As I wrote, the Black Lives Matter protests erupted in the United States. Watching the brutality and violence was a sad reminder that history repeats itself. Consequently, themes of racial prejudice worked their way into the story. In the end, I wrote the first draft of *Crown of Horns* in two weeks.

As authoritarian and right-wing extremists continue to rise around the world, and as Ukraine continues to fight against invaders who would erase their culture, the story of *Crown of Horns* remains, sadly, poignant.

I hope this story speaks to you and serves as a reminder that preserving freedom requires vigilance, skepticism, and determination.

From Audra, illustrator & world builder

Flight Nineteen, was built by drawings and later strung together into stories. Images created the world, which is why David asked me to illustrate his written work.

The story of *Flight Nineteen* is set in only a few places but I happened to build an entire world map. It includes several continents, each with its own culture. Vsevora was inspired by my Ukrainian heritage. All of its cities are Ukrainian proper names. However, the cities of Olga and Ostap are of exceptional importance, being named for my grandparents. (I should note, they didn't fight like the cities do in this book.)

My Baba Olga, and late Dido Ostap, taught me so much about my Ukrainian heritage, and I grew up with the culture both at home and at school. It is so important to me to learn, cherish, and share our culture, especially now, as Russia tries to erase it.

I am proud of the story of resilience that David has written in Vsevora, in honour of Ukraine's struggles. It has been an honour to build this world with him, and to illustrate *Crown of Horns*.

Слава Україні! Героям слава.

Prologue:
The Death of Iryna Trembatya

Through sweat and blood and fire
We are reforged and born anew.
Let go of that which once was.

Through sweat and blood and fire
We grow and rise with the dawn.
Let go of fear, doubt, and shame.

Through sweat and blood and fire
We see ourselves and take to the sky.
Embrace what you have become.

— from "The Vinnya" by Tibor of Oksana

Iryna she/her

When I was very young, I asked my mother what my name meant.

"It means peace," she told me. "Iryna Trembatya, you shall play the songs of peace and carry them down the mountain."

There were no thoughts of peace when I looked into my mother's lifeless eyes, stained my dress with her blood, and wept over her body.

I remember dirt and blood and ash. I remember my father screaming and the sound of heavy footfalls drawing closer and closer. I remember him prying my shaking hands from my mother's body as a river of tears scoured my face. War forced us from our home and tore our family apart.

"We're going to Oksana," my father told me as we trudged through the snow. There were some two hundred of us all beaten and broken—all except my father. He spoke with optimism and tried to brighten my spirits:

"I went there, once, when I was about your age. It gets hot there; you won't need your big coat. And the mountains are like nothing you've ever seen. They call them crystal mountains. They're made of glass—like a mirror!"

My father's bolstering did little to ease the journey. We fled the snowy peaks of Ksenya, our once-beautiful home, and travelled through deep forest before clambering up sun-scorched trails. After several days of hard travel, we beheld Oksana's splendour.

Great crystal mountains stood guard around a verdant valley. The sun radiated its light and warmth off the mirror-glass in a dazzling sparkle that stretched across fields and villages all the way to a grand city by the shore. The city was surrounded by glass walls and a legion of windmills. High above, skyships gently hovered across the clouds, and out on the sea, sailing ships of all kinds drifted to and fro.

It was breathtaking. But it did not take away the hurt that brought us there. Our suffering had only just begun.

We were greeted with suspicion and ire. To the Oksanans, we had "invaded" their home. They offered us a place within their walls, but they vandalized our houses and terrorized our communities. The authorities turned a blind eye, blaming *us* for the Oksanans' cruelty. We were insulted, threatened, and spat upon. They hated us and they taught their children to hate us.

I hated them just as much. But to survive, I put on my best face and behaved. I learned quickly how to impress them with a humble tone and gracious demeanour.

"You're not like other Ksenyans," my teachers would say, "you're so courteous and polite." I would smile back at them, even though I wanted to scream.

I only had one friend amongst the Oksanans: Vitaliya. We made for an unusual pair; the two of us looked almost nothing alike. Oksanans tended to be tall, tanned, and lithe with bright amber eyes and round, focused pupils. By their teenage years, they had a pair of horns that started together at the top of their forehead in a 'V' and then spiralled straight upward at least a foot and a half. To me, Vitaliya and the Oksanans were like a rope that had been pulled tight—straight and strong.

In contrast, I was much shorter with curving hips and stout, hoofed feet. My legs and arms were naturally strong, and my shoulders were much broader. Atop my head were a pair of horns of my own, but they were like trees: two thick trunks of horn with branches that grew out in great curls. A Ksenyan woman's horns are her pride, and they never stop growing. Before she passed, my grandmother's horns looked like a nest of brambles that encompassed her head. What set me apart most were my eyes. Unlike the Oksanans' narrow circles, my pupils were stretched horizontally in a rectangular shape that they found unsettling— "crooked" and untrustworthy. Thankfully, Vitaliya saw past our differences; she treated me with kindness and respect.

My only other solace was the old library. It was a cool, quiet place where I could escape into history books and immerse myself in a better time. I read all about the golden age of dynast-kings and queens: when Oksana, Ksenya, and all of the city-states in the nation of Vsevora were unified. But the last dynast-king's avarice destroyed it all and began the cycle of war that destroyed my home.

I spent most of my days in that library. Studying. Daydreaming. My father didn't care for it. He insisted I stop hiding away and instead "be a part of the herd." That's why, as I approached my sixteenth birthday, he told me I would partake in the *Vinnya*.

Each season in Oksana, those who were about to pass into adulthood were made to climb the tallest mountain to celebrate their coming-of-age. They claimed it taught the meaning of hardship and demonstrated one's preparedness for life's tribulations. The *Vinnya* was a high honour and one of their most important ceremonies.

I wanted nothing to do with it; it was meaningless to me. But according to my father, it was essential if I wanted to lead a happy life here.

"We must assimilate if we are to be accepted," he said "Do you remember what your mother taught you? Unity. That's what you need to strive for, Iryna. We need to unify with the Oksanans."

I protested. We would never be accepted. But I lost the battle of wills. I was forced to make the climb.

~ ~

With a blood-red dawn, the day of the *Vinnya* came. There were five of us participating in the ceremony; alongside me were Vitaliya and three local boys we knew well. They didn't care for me, and they were unimpressed to be climbing alongside a Ksenyan.

The four Oksanans had focused looks chiselled upon their faces as they stared up at the crystal mountain. They had spent their entire lives waiting for this ascent.

Standing before us was an old Oksanan woman draped in a heavy red robe. It was embroidered with golden straw that formed jagged points and wide curls; the shapes represented the mountains and phoenix fire.

"People of Oksana!" she bellowed, "as the days change from summer into autumn, we are blessed to celebrate the *Vinnya* with these five young people. They leave us as children, but as they climb the crystalline face of Mount Zorya, their journey will bring unto them a metamorphosis in spirit! When they reach the peak and peer into the mirror-glass on high, they shall be blessed with vision! And when they return to us, they will be as the phoenix: reborn into Oksanan society, worthy of adulthood and of all the responsibility that entails."

The sun climbed and reflected off the mountaintops. The heat was already unbearable, and yet there wasn't so much as a bead of sweat on the old woman. She kept talking, undeterred, reciting a poem about sweat, blood, and fire, before bidding us onward. The people behind us cheered, and the four pilgrims next to me began their march.

I remained in place, frozen. My legs were unwilling to move. *They shouldn't have to move. I shouldn't have to do this*, I told myself. The cheering died down and was replaced by concerned whispers. The pilgrims stopped and looked back; the boys snickered. I glanced behind me and my father's hopeful face sunk.

I looked to Vitaliya. Her eyes urged me forward. "Come on," she said softly, unheard by anyone but me. "You can do this. I know you can."

I drew a deep breath and then placed a reluctant foot forward. Then the next. And on until I was walking side by side with her.

The march was excruciating: blistering heat and unyielding sun reflected down upon us. It was agony. And with every bend, the trail grew steeper. Stone soon shifted to glass and my hooves struggled to maintain their grip. For hours, I slipped and stumbled up the path. Vitaliya slowed her pace and helped me across the worst patches, offering reassurances while I sputtered in the heat.

The boys slowed their pace as well, but only so they could take every opportunity to mock me. The harder I struggled, the louder they laughed.

The struggle, the heat, and the mockery got worse the higher we climbed. My blouse was soaked with sweat. I was gasping for breath. My skin burned. When at last I could take no more, I let out a strangled cry and fell to the ground.

A chorus of laughter followed. I stood up, seething, and pounded towards the boys, glass crackling beneath my feet.

"Enough! At least mock me to my face!" I snapped.

"Aw, come on. We were saying nice things, weren't we guys?" one of them cackled.

"Well, except for those eyes!" the second sneered.

The third piled on; his tone was crueller: "Her horns are uglier than her eyes if you ask me. We should cut them off her crooked head." He rose up, inches away from me, his spiral horns towering above. He swiftly put his hands on my shoulders and shoved me to the ground.

Vitaliya let out a worried cry as I staggered and slid across the glass. The second spoke up again: "Aw, worried about your girlfriend, Vitaliya?" He laughed derisively. "Don't be. She doesn't matter. She's a goat after all."

I could see Vitaliya from my periphery, but she was staring at the ground. Maybe, deep down, she believed everything these boys were saying. I glanced desperately between her and the boys, hoping she would intervene.

The second boy moved in on her menacingly. "Got something to say?"

She straightened up and looked him in the eyes. I held my breath, waiting for her to shout him down. Then her gaze shifted to me. There was no resolve in her eyes. Instead, I saw fear, doubt, and shame. She turned away from us and wordlessly drifted by. She left me behind and quietly continued the climb.

I didn't understand. Was it so shameful to befriend a Ksenyan? Had she reached the limit of what she could bear?

"Why?" I gasped. The boys' laughter was the only reply.

The first leaned in close. "You think you can become one of us? We don't want you. *She* doesn't want you. You've done nothing but make Oksana worse."

He grabbed my wrist and pulled me up, only to spin me and throw me into the side of the mountain. The glass cracked beneath me, knocking the air from my lungs. I looked at a dim reflection of myself with blood dripping from my mouth. Then a snarling face appeared in the glass and a powerful fist pummelled my back.

I screamed in pain, rolled across the glass, and tried to clamber away. Instead, I found myself trapped. Two boys stood behind while the cruel one blocked the path ahead.

The boy ahead snarled, "You're filth, Ksenyan. You should be thrown out... by the spear of our horns!"

The three closed in. They were ready to kill me. Maybe they were right to. I was weak—worthless. It was time to give up and let the suffering end.

Stop it, I told myself. *Don't give in to their lies.* I drew a deep breath and steadied myself. *I don't need Vitaliya. I don't need anyone else. I can make it on my own.*

I glared up at the boy blocking the ascent and pulled my chin down to my chest. With a great heave, I leapt forward, bashing into his chest with my horns. I felt the wind gush out of his lungs and the buckle of his ribs. He hit the ground with a heavy thud and I ran overtop of him.

I could hear him moaning and gasping while the others cursed and shouted, but I kept going, running as fast as I could on the slippery path. I hurried past Vitaliya without so much as glancing back at her. I ran until I couldn't go any further and I fell in a heap under the blazing sun.

I gasped for breath, drenched in sweat and tasting iron. I spat. For the moment, everything was quiet. Then I heard a distant voice; it was aggressive and getting closer. I couldn't stop yet. I tried to push myself forward into another run, but my legs gave out and I slid across the trail instead.

If not forward, then upward. I looked up the crystal mountainside and got back to my feet.

I jumped. My legs lifted me as high as they could, but it was impossible to grip the slippery face of the mountain. My skin burned against the hot glass and my sweat sizzled as I slid and crashed back to the ground. I steeled myself, tore two strips from my blouse, and wrapped up my hands.

I had enough strength for one more attempt. I jumped, pushing my legs with every last bit of their might, and propelled myself higher than before. As I came down, I threw all of my force against the mountainside. I screamed as my fists plunged into the glass, sending shards scattering around me and cascading down below. A shockwave of pain pulsed from my knuckles and through my arms, but I stayed in place, dangling above the trail.

Gripping into my newly-formed handholds, I pulled myself upward with one hand and reached as high as I could with the other. I pounded my fist into the mountain until the glass gave way. It scalded me and dug into my flesh as I dragged myself up. My hands bled with every new handhold, but I kept climbing higher.

There was shouting below, and as I looked down, I couldn't help but laugh. The cowards were unwilling to follow me—too afraid to burn or to bleed. I looked up and smiled as I forged my path.

Higher I climbed until my arms trembled with fatigue and my breath came out ragged and heaving. Just when I feared I couldn't push myself any further, I reached a ledge. I pulled myself up onto it. Here, I was alone and safe.

My skin pulsed and radiated from burns and my entire forearms were covered in deep cuts, streaming blood to my shoulders and back. Seeking a moment of reprieve, I crawled over to the mountain face. I marvelled at the polished appearance of the glass; it was like a perfect mirror. I moved in closer and gazed upon my reflection.

A withered crone stared back at me. Her eyes, rectangular like mine, were sunken and tired from a lifetime of enduring hate. Atop her mess of tangled grey hair were two sad and broken stumps from which a beautiful crown of horns should have grown. Her face was devoid of passion, ambition, and hope, and her lips quivered in a defeated frown. I gasped in horror at the face before me, for I knew that it was my own. This is who I was doomed to become in this wretched place.

I lifted my hands and pounded them against the mirror. Smears of blood streamed across the reflection, spilling across the crone's face, but the glass didn't crack. "This isn't me," I told myself. "I am Iryna Trembatya."

The face stared back, unwavering, mouthing the words, "I am Iryna Trembatya" back at me in silent mockery.

I hurled myself at the mirror, but it didn't yield. I pushed my face up against the hot glass; the defeated, lifeless eyes stared back into mine. There was no spark, no energy, nothing in her eyes. Just emptiness.

I spoke, my voice harsh and raspy: "No. This is not who I am. You," I said to the reflection, "you are Iryna Trembatya. I will not become you." The visage remained unchanged.

Who am I? I asked myself. I thought of my mother and her smile. *Will I bring the songs of peace down from the mountain?* I didn't want peace. I wanted to rain destruction! But it was destruction that brought me here.

I thought of the golden age: the dynasties that united Vsevora and the last dynast-king who tore it apart. His legacy had killed my mother.

"It's called *ishkara*," my mother said. "Some say unity now. It's the power of memories and love. *Ishkara* pulls us up and brings us together."

Unity. Not by succumbing to them, but by becoming myself. Memories and love. That is what needed to be done. That is who I needed to be. *Ishkara.*

I rose to my feet and looked down on the crone. She was weak, lost, helpless. I lifted up my hoof and hurled it down onto the mirror. It shattered and the crone broke away in a thousand flickering shards. Iryna Trembatya was dead.

Chapter One:
The Birth of Ishkara

Smoke rises over the mountains. It engulfs the north and the south. It chokes the east and the west. As the sky turns black, the city of Sophia must open her arms: hope's final bastion.

— *from* The Blight of War *by Kavya of Sophia*

Velodik he/him

~Ten years after Iryna's death~

No one expects their life to change while ordering soup.

All I wanted was a moment to rest as I stepped from the snowy sidewalk into the warmth of the Brazen Bull Café.

"Constable Velodik," an equally warm voice called, "so good to see you!"

I closed the door behind me, and I looked over to the counter where a young man waved cheerfully at me. We looked so alike, one would have thought we were brothers: light grey skin, thick grey hair covering our faces and arms, rounded black noses, and pointed ears atop our heads. It was the eyes that set us apart. Mine were bright yellow while his were a pale blue. As I reached the counter, I stared quietly into his eyes, losing myself in them for a moment.

"Klim," I responded at last when I realized that I had been staring too long.

"Anything I can get you?" Klim said with a bit of a laugh.

I stammered, "I'll uh, I'll take whatever's on special. Something hot. The snow hasn't been letting up." The Brazen Bull was my favourite stop on my patrol; it always smelled of delectable soups and made the rest of my trudge more bearable.

Klim nodded and got to work as I made my way to a table. I looked through the nearby window at the snow drifting through the air. When I first came to Sophia as a child, I thought the snow was beautiful, but now it was wearing me down.

I thought of the sergeants kicking back in the warmth of the station. For years, I had served as a lowly constable, trying to prove myself and struggling to work my way up. But here I was, still stuck out in the snow. People like Klim and me didn't become sergeants. Nonetheless, I imagined that one day I could be the one sending the constables out on patrol while I reclined by a fire.

A hot bowl of soup appeared on the table and I felt Klim's hand on my shoulder. I shook off the daydreams, grinned and thanked him before turning my attention to my food. It smelled delicious!

As I savoured my first few spoonfuls, I noticed someone staring at me. She was sitting alone with her hood up. I could tell there were horns hidden beneath it. She had fair skin, looked between twenty and twenty-five, and wore a concentrated scowl on her lips. She gripped a steaming cup of tea in her gloved hands. The gloves ran all the way up to her elbows and matched her cloak: a kind of faded rose colour. Most striking, though, were her eyes. Her rectangular pupils were fixed on me. She probably hailed from Ksenya, Halyna, or one of those other goat cities.

I couldn't help but think of the goats as weak. They made good enough soldiers and officers—following orders and falling in line—but they didn't have the kind of cunning that I did. And yet, again and again, it was always some goat that got a promotion over me. I tried pushing the intrusive thoughts away and focused back on my meal.

I was nearly finished eating when I looked up again. She was still staring at me. There was a fire in her eyes—something prideful and determined. As I ate the last bite of my soup, she stood abruptly and left. The whole event had been incredibly strange.

"Klim," I asked. "Who was that?"

"Not sure. She's been in a few times—doesn't say much."

"I see." I rose to my feet, leaving behind the coins Klim was owed, and hurried to the door.

Why had she been staring at me like that? I imagined what kinds of trouble a goat like her might be up to. Looking down the street, I saw her rose-coloured hood, still pulled up over her horns. I followed briskly. As she came to the end of the block, she glanced back, paused for an instant, and then darted off around the corner.

"Hey!" I shouted and gave chase.

As I whipped around, I saw that she had already put more distance between the two of us. I barrelled forward, trying to keep her in my sight. She was sure-footed as she maneuvered down the street and whirled left around another corner. I plowed forward, not noticing an icy streak, and slid into a garbage bin. There was a tumultuous crash and heaps of garbage spilled onto me. I felt ridiculous, but I pushed myself up and charged. The gap between us was rapidly widening.

She took another left far ahead, into an alley. As I panted around the corner behind her, my eyes adjusted to the dim grey. Two five-story buildings flanked the alley and white mist floated up in plumes from a nearby vent. As I stepped past the mist, I saw her hoofprints leading down the alley and then came to a stop, but she was nowhere to be seen.

"Why are you chasing me?" A voice called from above. I looked up, and she was standing overhead, leaning over the bannister of a fire escape. I followed the metal frame down and was vexed to discover that there was no ladder or stairway within my reach. Either she could fly or she was a strong jumper. I appeared to have underestimated her. "Why are you chasing me?" she asked again, unwavering. Even though she had run, she was not fearful.

"You were acting suspiciously," I replied, trying to remain calm and authoritative. "You kept staring at me at the Brazen Bull and then ran off like that—"

"There are no laws against keeping an eye on the officers of Sophia."

I narrowed my eyes. What was her angle? I said, "My duty is to keep the peace, and there are a lot of folks from outside Sophia, lots of people like you, that are trying to disturb that peace. Innocent people don't run from city constables for no reason."

"You can rest assured, Constable Velodik, that I do not intend to disturb the peace. On the contrary, I care deeply for peace across all Vsevora," she said evenly, almost rehearsed. She knew my name. How long had she been keeping an eye on me? "Now if you'll excuse me, I'm going home." She started climbing the stairs.

"Hey! Get back down here!" I called up uselessly. She didn't pause for a moment. She climbed all the way to the top until she was at the roof. I watched as she leapt across the alleyway to the other rooftop and then disappeared. I figured that was the last time I would see her and endeavoured to push the whole embarrassing incident out of my mind.

The next day, I walked into the Brazen Bull to find her sitting in the exact same spot. I grimaced and she gave a hint of a smile as she glanced up at me. I grunted an order to Klim and then sat down, this time directly across the table from her. Her hood was down now, revealing branching horns that wound over her head.

"Constable," she greeted.

"Is this a game to you?" I asked.

"A game? I'm just here to have some tea," she said matter-of-factly, her eyes fixed on me.

"What do you think you're doing?"

"I told you. I'm here to have some tea."

I let out a frustrated growl and then we sat in silence. Klim came over and placed a bowl in front of me. He lingered for a moment and asked if everything was alright. I nodded and waved him away dismissively.

"What's your name?"

She leaned forward, her eyes locked onto mine with a fiery intensity that shook me. I blinked, straining to maintain eye contact. I wanted to look away, but to do so would have shown my weakness. We stayed there in silence for a long moment and I began to wonder if she even knew her own name. Perhaps she was debating whether or not to give me the right answer.

"Ishkara," she said at last with a depth and intensity that matched her gaze.

"Any last name?"

"Ishkara. That's it. That's my whole name."

"You're not from here," I said as though it were a fact, but it was more of a question.

"That's right."

I paused for a moment. I considered saying something else, but I reached for my spoon instead. "You're not going to run again, are you?"

"Do I need to?"

"No."

Ishkara's gaze didn't shift. Had she even blinked the entire time? There was something about the way she looked at me, like she was assessing me.

"I'm sorry about yesterday," I said. "You have to understand, I have a job to do."

"I understand. You need to uphold law and order." She lifted her cup and took a slow sip. "I think you will do a fine job, Constable Velodik." She finished her tea, rose, and left the café without another word. I didn't follow.

~ ~

A strange sort of friendship formed between us. Every day, while I took a break from my patrol for lunch, Ishkara was there. At first, I did most of the talking, but eventually she opened up and the unusual circumstances of our first meeting were forgotten. We enjoyed many cups of tea and bowls of soup together at the Brazen Bull.

One day, though, our meeting was not filled with idle chat and pleasantries. I burst into the café, fuming. I slammed the door behind me and stamped over to the table where Ishkara quietly sat.

"What's wrong?" Klim asked.

"Nothing," I snapped

He drew close and stammered, "Could I get you a tea, Velodik? On the house."

"I need something harder than tea!" Klim looked down uncomfortably. I sighed as I realized my harshness. "I'm sorry. Yes. Tea would be perfect."

"A bad day, Constable?" Ishkara said, unfazed.

I growled. "I'm going to get passed over for yet another promotion! Some Yuliyan who's been doing the job for half as long has caught my commander's favour."

"I see," she replied. Her expression gave nothing away.

"What?" I barked.

"It's just... I can understand why you might be upset if you were passed over by a Yuliyan."

"What? No! That's not the problem." I crossed my arms and glared. I didn't care for the implication.

"You were already in Sophia, then, when they attacked Lyudmila."

"No," I replied, startled. I didn't expect a Ksenyan to know anything about my home city. I leaned forward and my tone became quiet and solemn without my noticing: "I was there. Just a child. It wasn't until much later that I really understood what had happened."

She stared back at me intently. "What do you remember?"

I shook my head, but I felt compelled to answer. Like there was something that had been waiting for the chance to let the words out.

"Little fragments—tiny memories of fear and pain. I was woken up by my mother's screams. Then we ran. All through the night. We just had the clothes on our backs. Everything had been left behind—destroyed in the fires."

My hands shook as I dredged up the memories that I had long-since locked away.

"When we finally made it to Sophia, there wasn't anyone here like me. The Sophian schoolboys... Horned bullies... They'd shove me, yank on my tail, rip out my fur—they laughed while they did it."

Ishkara nodded knowingly. "There are hundreds of stories like that all across Vsevora." She paused for a moment. "Meet me after your patrol, Velodik. At the library."

I was puzzled, but I knew better than to ask why.

I rarely visited the National Library of Vsevora. It stood only two stories tall but extended across an entire block. The old building was painted white and gold. At its entrance were three great arches and massive columns that framed them. Inside was even more impressive with row upon row of massive oak bookshelves. I called out softly into the vast space, wondering how I was to find Ishkara amongst the maze.

She appeared from around a shelf and approached with a wide smile—a rare sight. "I've seen *you* on the job, Constable, now you get to see me at mine."

"What did you want to show me?" I asked.

She simply gestured for me to follow and hurried off through the rows of books. I felt like I was chasing her through the streets again. She wove left and right, deeper into a sea of books with no end. Suddenly, she stopped and I skidded to a halt next to her. We were in a quiet corner; there was a table with stacks of books laid out and a ladder nearby to reach the top shelves.

"What is going on, Ishkara?" I gasped.

"Your story," she said as she sat down and picked up an old brown tome. She gently ran her gloves over it. "I was a refugee, too."

"I'm... sorry," I replied awkwardly.

"Do you know why we're refugees?" she asked. I was uncertain how she expected me to answer, but she didn't wait for me to come up with one. "Life used to be better in

Vsevora. For generations, the dynast-kings and queens brought us together across all walks of life."

She laid the book open to a drawing of a handsome-looking man with the eyes of a charlatan. "The Umbral Prince," she said. "He ruled for thirty years. They say that with nothing more than his wit and charm, he convinced the Sky League of the north to give him a fleet of ships! His cunning opened up Vsevora to the world."

I drew closer and watched intently as Ishkara flipped through the pages. She revealed an older woman in a long, elaborate gown lined in gemstones.

"Who's that?" I asked.

"Queen Vekara. Perhaps the greatest dynast to ever rule. She uplifted the Ksenyans, called for the Golden Trail between Yuliya and Lyudmila, and calmed the Oksanans to bring them into Vsevora. She is the one who truly united us. She led with an example of love... one that has long-since been forgotten." Ishkara shook her head and turned the page to reveal an array of beautiful royal dresses. With a sigh, she read: "'Each intricate dress took over one hundred hours to craft, and it's said that Queen Vekara never wore the same gown twice.' For everything she did, most only remember her clothes."

"I don't understand," I said. "What's the point of this? What happened to these people?"

"Hekar," she said with a dark growl. She turned to an illustration of an emaciated-looking man. He had sunken, black eyes that shot hateful daggers off the page. I shuddered just at the look of him. "The last dynast-king. He saw unity as weakness. And even though he was the most powerful man in Vsevora, he turned the city-states against one another in his quest for more. He brought hate to the nation. And that hatred is a dark shadow over us still."

Ishkara took my hand in hers and held it tight. "We have both suffered. Hundreds—thousands of people have suffered. And it will continue. Peace between the city-states stands on the edge of a precipice, and the cycle of war is waiting to start again. The Ransacking of Lyudmila, the Scourging of Ksenya, and horrors just like them will happen again and again. It doesn't need to be that way."

I stared at her with admiration. I understood, first-hand, what she must have had to endure, and that no one could make it through such violence without deep scars. Yet, despite her past, her wounds, and her cold exterior that sought to hide them, a fire of hope still burned inside of her.

Chapter Two:
Self Portrait

Mother.
Sweet roses.
Gentle blooming.
Firm hugs, warm smiles.
A hand that guides me
Ever forward until
I must stand
Alone.

— Tibor of Oksana

Siranna she/her

~Thirty years after Iryna's death~

I loved Oksana. Really.

The way the sunrise glinted off the mountains. The fresh scent of wildflowers. The hot sun against my skin as we played olenball. As much as I loved it, I couldn't stop thinking of leaving.

Ours was a quiet village in the Oksanan countryside where life was simple—idyllic, some might say—but I felt trapped. The *Vinnya* was meant to mark my independence, but instead it had locked me away in a prison of obligation. And its foreman? My mother.

"Siranna! Hurry! We're going to be late," she beckoned.

I stared at myself in the mirror and sighed. I felt clownish. My cheeks were painted bright and rosy, my brows were heavy blocks, and my lips were shining pink. My mother insisted I decorate myself like this, but I hated it. I felt fake—like a doll.

"Siranna, did you hear me?" my mother shouted again, barely waiting for my answer.

"I'm nearly ready," I called back. I sighed, drew in a ragged breath, and kept staring into the mirror. Just over my shoulder, another face looked back at me. I turned around to face her. It was me—a self portrait.

I had painted her when I was twelve. The technique was sloppy and brushstrokes were childish. But despite that, I loved her. She was the person that I thought I would become after I completed the *Vinnya*—the person I wanted to become. As I looked at her now, I still felt that way.

Her sharp, yellow eyes were full of determination, and her wide smile shone brightly with happiness and excitement. She wore flowers in her auburn hair, tucked behind the horns that spiralled up from her forehead and into the sky. She held a paintbrush in her hand, and from its tip the flames of a phoenix arose. She had a strength that could persevere through anything.

Somehow, I had fallen short. Standing before her, I felt like I was more a painting than she was. Contrary to her, I was nervous, weak, and sullen. Bridging the gap between us seemed an impossibility.

I thought back to the words of the high patron when we were about to make the climb: "Together, you make for the sky—like the phoenix—and you will be reborn. Some would deny you this rite, but it is a sacred passage." He had lifted his red-robed arms up high and called out with such passion. I was hopeful when he spoke. "Embrace what you will become at the journey's end. Embrace your new life, your new responsibilities: to yourselves, to your families, to Oksana."

My trek up the mountain had not transformed me. Worse still, it felt like the "responsibilities" I was meant to embrace were smothering me instead.

With the *Vinnya* behind me, it was time to arrange my suitor, and my mother had been quite insistent that Sylchiv was the man for me. He was two years older than I and looked to be made of chiselled stone from head to toe. Unfortunately, he also had all the personality of chiselled stone.

Mother would advocate for him constantly. "He comes from a good farming family," she'd say. "He will be able to support you and your future children!"

He seemed kind enough, but every time I talked about art, or books, or music, all I got in return were blank stares. His interests began and ended in the field. He could make someone very happy—I was sure of it—but that someone wasn't me. He certainly wasn't the kind of person that the woman in my self portrait would have married.

I turned back to the face in the mirror. Who was she? She was someone who always did as her mother asked. Who put on her makeup and batted her eyelashes and smiled her painted smile so that she might please her mother and enchant Sylchiv. Then what would she do? She would run away to a farm, and let all of her dreams and ambitions melt away.

I looked into the sad yellow eyes that stared back at me from behind the paint. *This isn't me*, I thought. *That isn't the life I want.* I felt a spark of determination and my face lit up.

I picked up a damp cloth from my dresser and pressed it to my cheek. I hesitated. What would mother say? She'd be livid. She would yell. I felt my heartbeat quicken and my breath sharpen just at the thought of it. I looked at the portrait behind me again, at the flowers in her hair, and the flames of her brush.

"It's okay. You can do it," she seemed to say.

I tried to steady my breathing and pressed the cloth against my face. It felt cold and rough, but refreshing. I rubbed away at the paint that caked my skin. I worked quickly, scrubbing away until I was clean.

I looked again in the mirror and smiled at the new face I saw. My tanned skin shone with its natural colour. My brows and lips were thin but happy. I gathered up wild-flowers from a vase and slipped them into my hair, tucking them around my horns. I grinned and my eyes seemed to sparkle as I did. I hurried out of my room and to the front of the house where my mother waited impatiently.

We didn't look much alike, but I was told I was a spitting image of her when she was young. I wondered if that's why she was so surprised that I didn't want to follow her every instruction; because she felt like she was talking to some version of herself and couldn't comprehend why it didn't behave as she did.

Now, her face was marred with heavy wrinkles that formed a perpetual frown across her whole face. Her long, grey hair was always wrapped up tightly and neatly around her horns in a thick braid.

As she turned to face me, her ever-present frown shifted to incredulity. "Siranna Ankova! What have you done?" she gasped. She stared, unblinking, at my bare face.

"You told me to make sure I looked nice," I replied, inno-cently and nervously.

"Child!" She let out an exasperated noise, something be-tween a sigh and a grunt. "What will Sylchiv think if he sees you like this? Don't you want to impress him and his par-ents?"

A knot formed in my stomach. I kept thinking of the fire rising up from the paintbrush in the portrait. I trembled slightly. I felt the phoenix's flame growing within me. I planted my feet, holding my ground. The knot gave way and I conjured the courage to speak:

"If they aren't impressed with me as I am, then no, I don't want to impress them."

I could tell that a fire was burning within my mother as well. She was confounded and enraged. She clenched her fists and then let out a long exhale through her nose. The tension tentatively fell away.

"Fine," she gasped. "If that's how you feel, then stay here. Your father and I will tell Sylchiv that you're unwell. Clearly you need some time to reconsider what you're doing."

"I don't need time, mother," I bit back quickly. "I know what I want, and it's not to be tied down to some man I don't even care about. I want to be an art—"

"Silence, Siranna! Enough!" my mother screamed. All of the tension and rage came surging back. Her steely eyes burned hot and she gripped me around the shoulders; her whole body was shaking. "No man wants to take care of some transient—some artist!" She spat out the words in disgust, as if just saying the word artist was repugnant, let alone that her daughter aspired to be one.

"I don't need to be taken care of. I completed the *Vinnya*. I climbed the crystal mountain and tasted the heat of the sun! And I did it on my own. I *can* take care of myself. I don't need you, or father, or Sylchiv, or anyone else to do it! My path is my own, and I know it might be hard for you, but that path isn't the one that you make for me."

Silence hung in the air. Even the breeze and the birds outside held their breaths. I expected her to keep yelling, to tear me apart, and to bash her fists against the counters. Instead, mother's voice was barely above a whisper.

"Sometimes, we cannot choose the direction of the path, and sacrifices must be made to keep from falling off it," she said softly. "Go to your room. Stay there and think long and hard about this path you wish to take." Her voice was eerily void of anger; it was void of any discernible emotion. "You may think you are strong now, but the world is heavy and it will crush you beneath its weight. I do not think you are strong enough to carry it alone, Siranna. Goodbye." She turned from me, opened the door, and slid out without looking back.

Her words were cold and laced with malice, and they pierced right through my heart, through my stomach; they tore me asunder. My legs trembled and my head grew hot. I felt fuzzy, almost dizzy, as tears streaked down my cheeks. I stared at the closed door—the black void through which my mother passed and left me behind.

I didn't know what to think. I nearly forgot to breathe. A deep, retching moan escaped from my throat as the tears came harder and faster. I stumbled back into the dining room table and fell to my knees. My head grew hotter and hotter; the heat wrapped around my skull and spread through my ears, my face, and my neck. I felt queasy; my whole stomach rolled around on top of it itself. I wrapped my arms around the twisting in my stomach, tried to shake the heat out of my head, and cried until my throat was raw.

Slowly, I regained my composure. The heat and the churning subsided. I wiped my face against my sleeve and I swallowed hard—it hurt to swallow. I pulled myself back up to my feet. I struggled to find my footing; I felt exhausted. When I finally steadied myself, I ran to my room.

I had no intention of remaining there. I scrambled around, digging through my possessions—searching, sorting, and planning. I picked up a heavy pack and started to fill it with everything I could: brushes, paints, and garments. I hurried through the house to gather food, a waterskin, and a clean towel.

I couldn't stay. How could I? With every item I added to the pack, I felt the knots within my stomach and the heat in my head build up again. I heard my mother's words over and over, ringing through my mind. But with every word of discouragement that echoed in my ears, my determination rose. I knew that this was what I needed to do.

I filled the pack with as much as I could carry and heaved it over my back. My knees almost buckled from under me. *The world is heavy...*

"I will not be crushed," I hissed through gritted teeth. I held my ground. The weight settled in and I started to move. I could manage. I could carry it on my own.

I marched to the door and reached for the handle. I paused and drew in a deep, quavering breath. I stepped back, then turned around. Slowly, uncertainly, I made my way back to my room.

I stopped in front of the self portrait. I stared. Tentatively, I reached toward her and ran a finger along the frame of the canvas. I shifted uneasily from foot to foot, feeling the weight of my pack on my back.

"I can't carry you with me," I told the face in the painting. She looked back at me unchanging, just as determined as ever. I turned around, facing myself in the mirror, and looking into my eyes. "But I will see you again."

Without hesitation, I stepped out of my room, left the house, took to the road, and left Oksana behind. Whatever the weight in my pack, I had never felt so unburdened.

Chapter Three:
Confined

We saw them out in the mists: faceless vampires that lurked at the edge of our camp. We were not welcome.

*— from the account of Laeti,
sole survivor of The Grassland Expedition*

Kalrevi she/her

~Thirty years after Iryna's death~

"To the rest of the world, we are myths—monsters told in stories to keep children inside at night. They do not know that we exist and we do not tread beyond our homeland. That is how it has been for hundreds of years." And that is how my father would have it for as long as our people live. He had given this speech countless times during our walks along the Greenshield. I sighed heavily and he came to an abrupt stop.

My father, Surrendra, was a tall and imposing figure. He looked down at me with patient eyes and then up at the massive blades of grass that towered above us: the Greenshield. It stretched out farther than I could imagine, forming an impenetrable barrier between us and the outside world. My father called it protection, but I called it a cage.

"We are safe here, Kalrevi," he continued, as if he could read my thoughts. "The Greenshield protects us from the world. Our traditions and ceremonies remain our own. We remain unscathed by that which would try to corrupt us." He ran three of his six powerful hands along one of the lofty blades of grass. It stood at least ten metres high and swayed gently back and forth. My father often described the movements as tranquil and peaceful, but I felt like the grass was looming over me—an imposing and indomitable presence.

"We're not protected. We're trapped. We're afraid. You're afraid—afraid of changing anything! And so you force us to wallow behind the Greenshield," I lashed back at him. My words might have seemed severe, but we had this discussion often, and I needed him to truly listen. More and more we had been arguing, and yet he always said the same thing, as if the repetition alone would convince me to conform.

This time, his argument shifted: "I have fought the destroyers that lurk beyond the Greenshield and watched friends die to those whose cruelty and avarice rend soul from flesh. They would tear apart these lands, force us from our homes, and rip off our masks." Despite the vivid harshness of his words, his tone was even and inscrutable, just like his face. Of course, I never saw his face. It was hidden behind an expressionless mask. Mouthless. Pure white.

To the Feras, our people, the mask is the final rite when one has ascended to true personhood. It is a symbol that one has taken their place in society. When a young Feras has found their calling and they at last grow from apprentice to master, they adorn the same mask that has been worn by every Feras. Forged under the light of the moon and first donned on a moonless night, the mask becomes the face of Feras society. From that moment onward, the mask is never removed in a public place. Only in privacy and solitude is it to be taken off. I have heard that even among spouses, the mask is worn at all times. From the moment a Feras enters society, society no longer knows their face. Under the mask, the Feras are as one.

I took a moment to respond to my father's warning. "That was a long time ago. The world beyond the Greenshield could be different now," I reasoned.

He stared at me with wide eyes for a moment. He began with his carefully measured tone, but became more irate as he continued. "These things do not change. The savagery of the outsiders does not fade with the rising of the moon or shift like the seasons. You think I fear change for our people, but it is the unchanging malice of the outside world that we must be cautious of. Be thankful that you did not need to fight and know the suffering of your forebears!"

"One thing certainly won't change. You. You will always be stubborn and close-minded."

"Kalrevi! I grow weary of this. I wish you would try to understand, but you only argue. What would your mother think if she saw you like this?" My father turned away from me to look to the Greenshield. I could hear his voice crack, the way it did every time he mentioned my mother.

He was too set in his ways and unwilling to listen. I saw that his breathing was becoming laboured as he pushed whatever anger and sadness he was feeling deeper down inside of him. Few in our community had seen him lose his composure like this. He believed that as our leader, he needed to remain strong. And strong meant stoic and devoid of "weak emotions" like anger, sorrow, and regret.

He was always proud of me in my youth, boasting of my wit and skill, and spoke of how I would contribute my ingenuity for the betterment of the community. But as I learned more and my skills improved, my curiosity for the world beyond the grass sea only grew. He believed that after I adorned my own mask two months ago, I would finally begin to see things his way and conform to Feras life. To his disappointment, that had not been the case.

I had developed my skills as a tinker and a builder, and he imagined that I would discover new innovations in irrigation or in harnessing the power of the wind. Instead, my "foolish" obsessions had only increased, and I spent much of my time seeking out the knowledge of our ancestors.

They had fashioned rafts that could ride across the top of the Greenshield and sail with great speed over vast stretches of water known as "the ocean." They explored the great beyond and then went further still. I wanted nothing more than to rebuild one of those ancient craft and take it on a grand adventure.

My father turned back to me, still composing himself. "We should go home. In time you will understand. I will be patient with you."

I scowled and crossed my arms. Like most women of the Feras, I only had two arms. I drew a breath to speak, but was interrupted before I could continue.

"Surrendra! Surrendra!" a frantic voice called out. A four-armed man was running towards us. I could see the worry behind his mask. He was muscular and wore four swords on his back. He was one of my father's scouts who "protected" our lands. I did not see much of what they did as protecting when there were no outsiders entering our borders. "Surrendra, you must come quickly!"

"What is it?" my father asked earnestly. All aspects of "weakness" had disappeared and he stood tall and stern. The muscles in his arms were tense.

"An outsider! An outsider in a machine!"

"What?" my father and I spoke in unison, equally incredulous. Although my tone was certainly more enthusiastic than his.

"There was a great thunderous blast and a streak of smoke across the sky that fell into the east marshes!" the scout continued. "We investigated and discovered a bulking machine—a skyship—and found the outsider within. He is alive, but unconscious and badly wounded. He has been taken to Doctor Lakira. Surrendra, what do we do?"

"Take me to him," my father said without hesitation. In a moment we were running back toward the village. My father didn't even realize that I was keeping up with them. My heart raced with excitement and I wondered at what this would mean for us. Perhaps it was the first sign of a new moon rising for the Feras.

He was unlike anything I had seen before. Golden hair adorned his head and he had a pair of tiny horns peeking out from among the strands. There was a deep gash on his face that ran from the top of his forehead down to his left eye. There was bruising across his face and I saw a set of mangled goggles nearby. They must have been the only thing to have saved him from losing an eye.

The doctor was stitching the head wound with two hands and carefully feeling the outsider's abdomen with the other two as we entered. She paused and turned her attention to us. Doctor Lakira was the only woman I knew with four arms. She was far taller than I, almost as tall as my father. Her posture revealed her deep concern.

"There's internal bleeding. If I work quickly, I may be able to help him, but I can't be certain that he will make it through the night," she said solemnly, her voice low and serious.

"Do nothing," my father said callously. "Ease his suffering, but no more. Make sure that it is a painless death."

Doctor Lakira's hands paused, frozen in place. She stared at my father, deep contemplation in her eyes. She looked down at the outsider and nodded solemnly. "Of course, Chieftain. I can ensure that he does not suffer." She drew back her hands and turned away, looking to a cabinet filled with tinctures and medicines.

"What?" I gasped. "Father, you can't be serious. Doctor Lakira, you have to help this man!" The outsider lay there, his breathing laboured, and I stared at his quiet, maskless face. I wondered at who this man was, at how he had come here and why. What secrets did he hold? What world had he come from? What family had he left behind? He had a life and it was worth saving.

"Leave, Kalrevi! This does not concern you!" My father gestured to the scout who had followed us in, and I felt four powerful hands grasp my shoulders and my elbows. I tried to pull away, but the grip did not relent.

Doctor Lakira's upper-right hand traced its way along the bottles and flasks within her cabinet. She grasped one and carefully inspected it, oblivious to the commotion the rest of us were making.

"Doctor Lakira, please! Aren't you sworn to protect and heal? Is that not what you promised when you looked up to the sky of stars?"

She paused and placed the tincture back upon its shelf. I saw her shoulders rise and fall with a heavy breath and then she turned. She looked at my father first, then to me.

"It has been many moons since I first put on this mask," she said. She was as serious as before, but there were many other notes within her tone: introspection, compassion, and perhaps even a hint of grief. "But you are right. I am bound by it to heal those who have been harmed."

I drew a hopeful breath. "Then you won't leave him to die. You'll save him!"

"Kalrevi," my father rumbled. He took a step closer and I felt the scout's grip tighten upon me.

Doctor Lakira raised a hand. "Surrendra, please." She stepped closer to me. Her eyes flickered behind her mask with an intensity that matched my father's. "My oath is to this community. And your father is the one who decides what this community needs."

"No. His will is not the only one. Think for yourself!" I cried. I tried to pull myself away but I remained trapped.

"The Chieftain sets the course for all Feras," my father said solemnly. He gestured to the scout and I was released, but my father quickly closed the gap between us. Six gentle hands ran down my arms and he leaned in close. "Kalrevi, I ask that you trust me. I do not make this decision lightly."

I shoved his hands away and pushed past him. "Doctor Lakira. When you put on the mask, what did you hope for your life? Was it this?" I pointed toward the dying man with a quivering hand. My whole body began to tremble. "To let someone suffer because of an old man's close-minded ways? You can't just let him die!"

She shook her head and crossed her lower arms. With the other two, she reached forward and gently brushed away the strands of disheveled hair that had fallen in front of my mask. "You wear the mask, Kalrevi. But I think you are still learning what it means. One day you will understand." With that, she returned to her cabinet.

I cried out and leapt toward her, but my father caught hold of me. "Take her home!" he exclaimed and the scout swept in to pull me away.

I screamed, thrashed, kicked up my feet, and threw my head back, but I couldn't break free. As the scout dragged me out of the room, Doctor Lakira produced a tonic from the cabinet. It would ensure the outsider never awoke—that he would dream a pleasant dream until he let out his final breath.

The scout didn't release me until he brought me home and escorted me inside. I spun around and thrust a fist into his abdomen, but he was unfazed by the assault.

"I will keep watch on you here until your father returns," he said plainly, crossing all of his arms across his chest. He stood imposingly in the doorway.

I turned away and retreated to my room. Once there, I pounded the walls and seethed. "There will never be a new moon for the Feras. Not here."

I took a deep breath and began to compose myself. *There will never be a new moon.* The realization struck me and I knew that I could not remain here. The outsider was doomed. But the skyship. Perhaps I could decipher that. I gathered my tools.

Chapter Four:
The Gala

Crystal and amaranth.
She was vested in crystal and amaranth.
Glorious and beautiful and wondrous.
And then she fell.

— *from* The Fall of Vsevora *by Orianna, knowledge keeper*

Velodik

~Ten years after Iryna's death~

It was a weary morning. I groaned as I sat in front of my locker at the station, put on my uniform, and quietly dreaded going on patrol. Every day it seemed my commander was showering more praise over my Yuliyan comrade, and every day my motivation fell further.

I sighed as I put on my boots and dragged myself up to my feet. I wrapped my long, sash-like belt around my waist, then folded it so its end hung slightly to one side. It felt loose. I undid it and adjusted. Still not right. I tried again. And a third time.

I stopped. I drew in a deep breath, held it, and let all of my thoughts rattle through my head for a moment. Then I pushed them all out as I exhaled. I paused and everything settled. I stepped out of the station, ready to begin my day.

"Are you excited, Velodik?"

"What?" I looked around, startled. Zradya was coming down the stairs behind me. Zradya was the Yuliyan my commander had taken such a shine to. We were both up for promotion, but it was practically a guarantee at this point that she would get it instead of me.

She had a cocky smile—as always—and she made sure to stop a few stairs above so that she could lord over me. Otherwise, she would have been a head shorter. She had thick, curly black hair and two great horns that wound back near her ears. Her complexion was unique; she had deep brown skin, but it was marred by patches where the colour had drained away. Her eyes were dark, and they glimmered with a duplicitousness that made my hair stand on end.

"I asked if you're excited," she said impatiently.

"And I still don't know what you're talking about!" I snapped back.

She laughed and leaned against the bannister. "Did they not tell you about the gala? I guess you weren't invited."

I shook my head. I didn't want to deal with this. "Maybe I'm not. Just leave me be, Zradya. It doesn't matter."

"Oh, but it does. A few constables have been hand-selected to attend. Did you not get an invite in your locker?" She held up an envelope and her cocky grin grew wider. "An evening of opulence! There will be senators, the chancellor, and some of the most important members of the constabulary. I guess that's why you weren't invited." With that twist of the knife, she brushed past me down the stairs and carried on down the street.

I clenched my fists, let out an angry huff, and glowered at the back of her head. Slowly, I started down the block in the other direction, defeated. I didn't relish living out the rest of my days on the same sad patrol. There had been no invitation laid out for me... Or had there? I hadn't paid attention. I turned back.

I rushed to my locker and tore it open. There! Down at the bottom, crushed under my discarded shoes, was an envelope. I grabbed it hastily and pulled out its contents: an invitation! I pounded my fist against the locker door in a joyous crash. I still had a chance: this gala was my opportunity to secure my promotion.

I carefully read through the invitation. I was allowed a single guest—another opportunity. There were a few men in my life that I could bring, and such a high-class affair would have made it easy to woo one of them to bed afterwards. Perhaps even...

I hurried out on my patrol, excited for my stop at the Brazen Bull.

The café was full and Klim was busy with other customers when I arrived. I made my way to the usual spot where Ishkara was already sitting with her cup of tea. I set down the invitation in front of her and told her about how I was hand-selected for the regal affair. Her eyes lit up immediately with a keen understanding that I hadn't expected. Her reaction reminded me of the intensity and passion she showed at the library.

"Did you already know about this gala?" I asked.

"Of course! This gala is the celebration of years of effort."

"I, uh, had no idea," I mumbled.

She appeared astonished at first, but gradually she settled. Her tone became slightly more professorial. "This gala commemorates the newly-signed peace accords between Sophia and Olga. It's a historic moment. The two city-states have been at odds since the time of Hekar. While it's been many years since there has been outright violence, the war between them never officially ended."

History and politics were not what I had hoped we'd be talking about. As she dove into the intricacies of the relationships between the city-states and implications these accords would have across Vsevora, I let out a heavy sigh. Not out of boredom—well, perhaps a little bit—but out of realization.

I realized that there was no one in the nation outside of senators and delegates that knew more about these accords than Ishkara. And that meant that there was no one better to bring with me to the gala. I looked over her shoulder, gazing longingly at Klim. Another sigh.

"Ishkara," I said, interrupting whatever fact about Olga she was discussing. She paused and furrowed her brow. "I can bring a guest with me to the gala. I think that you should join me."

Her smile grew and her eyes flickered with life. She was overjoyed—in the kind of demure and measured way that she often expressed herself, but overjoyed nonetheless. "I would be honoured!" she said.

~ ~

On the night of the gala, I waited outside of the palace. The royal palace of Sophia had once been the seat of the great monarchs of old and would now be hosting the grand event. I paced about, uncomfortably tugging at my dress uniform, wondering why Ishkara was so late.

I heard the gentle sound of hooves as a carriage pulled up, drawn by two massive, feathered beasts. The door to the carriage swung open, and I stared, slack-jawed, as Ishkara stepped out.

She wore a flowing blue dress lined with fur. Elegant, matching gloves stretched from her forearms to her fingertips. She wore shimmering rings, two on each hand, and three chokers encircled her neck. Strings of beads cascaded down from her horns like falling stars. Her lips were an icy blue, but bore a warm smile. Gone was the cold exterior and measured joy. Her eyes glowed with an unfamiliar, genuine delight.

"Well," I stammered, still taken aback. I had never seen her so warm or so beautiful. "You look like you're ready for a good evening."

"I most certainly am," she chirped. Ishkara stepped up next to me and placed her arm in mine. "Let's go."

Inside the palace there were dozens, perhaps even hundreds, of people. I had never seen so many jewels and fine fabrics as it seemed that each and every person was covered in them from head to toe. My dress uniform, even though it was meant for special occasions, felt plain compared to everyone else. Ishkara fit in perfectly, though.

We wove through the crowd into an elegant ballroom. The walls from floor to ceiling were covered in intricate designs, etched in gold. Shapes representing branches, horns, and leaves curved above archways and extended up into the ceiling, trailing and meandering their way to an enormous crystal chandelier that hung overhead.

I felt overwhelmed by it all. Then I noticed some of my colleagues. We hurried toward the familiar faces and slipped into their circle as they chattered. I couldn't fully relax, though.

"Velodik! So good to see you here!" Zradya's voice shrilled above the others', oozing with fake friendliness. Of course she was already here. "And you brought a friend with you. How sweet. Couldn't find a man who'd want to join you for a date?" The jab sent a chuckle through the group.

I glared back at her, then shifted my attention over to Ishkara who had, to my surprise, burst into laughter.

"Oh, you should have seen him," Ishkara began, pulling me in closer. "He had two suitors vying for his attention—practically fighting over him, claw and horn!" She looked up at me, her eyes still glowing warmly. I was so confused. "Velodik, here, is such a sweetheart, though. I've been talking about this gala for weeks and he brought me along."

"Oh, well, that's uh, very kind," Zradya stammered. She was about to start on some other topic, but Ishkara quickly jumped in and began chatting up the others.

I appreciated Ishkara's quick defence and enjoyed the way that she had stolen the wind from Zradya's sails, but I found the whole situation jarring. She was personable and quick—quite unlike the person who glowered down at me in the alleyway when we first met. I had expected her to treat my colleagues similarly, but she was warming up to them without missing a beat. What was it about me?

"I think I'll get some ice wine," I said and stepped away to clear my head. It took some time to navigate the maze of people and endless expanse of the ballroom, but when I finally returned, two glasses in hand, Ishkara was gone.

"Where's Ishkara?"

"Oh, your little friend? No idea where she got off to," Zradya replied. "You should go look for her." She turned away from me and that's when I noticed that our commander had arrived. Before I could say or do anything else, Zradya focused in on the commander.

I hesitated for a moment and growled. There was no sense trying to talk to the commander now—not with Zradya already stealing her attention. With a terse sigh, I slipped away to search for Ishkara. I swam through the sea of bodies, trying to catch a glimpse of her amongst the glamour to no avail.

The evening was wasting away. I found myself guzzling down both glasses of ice wine, and grabbing two more to drown my frustrations. That's when I finally spotted her.

She was chatting with someone in a suit and playfully patting their arm. As I made my approach, I realized that she was speaking with Senator Dazbov, a relatively small player as politics went, but a senator nonetheless.

"You know, Senator," Ishkara said in a vibrant and charming tone, "I have to say that you're really quite clever. The recent changes you introduced to grain tariffs must have been what secured Olgan support for the accords. The tariffs have always been a sore spot for their farmers, and your astute recommendation would have provided the rural support that was so desperately needed."

The senator appeared flabbergasted. I winced. Ishkara had pushed her luck too far, trying to flatter her way up beyond her station. I was about to rush in to pull her away when Dazbov wrapped an arm tightly around her and gave a hearty shout.

"My my my! I don't know if I've met anyone with such keen insight—even amongst the Senate!" They guffawed loudly and shook Ishkara in a merry manner. "What do you do young lady?"

"I'm just a librarian, Senator."

"What? You're just squirrelled away with a bunch of books all day? I don't have a single page with half the brains you have. You're going to work for me. I insist!"

I stood there, mouth agape for the second time that evening. Did I even know who this woman really was? This person who was so stern, stubborn, and severe when I first met her was suddenly a charismatic charmer, wining and dining with the political elite. I knew that Ishkara had a keen wit and was knowledgeable about politics and history, but to swoop in and win over a senator? I quickly swigged down my second round of ice wine as I struggled to comprehend what was happening. I was lifted out of my daze by Ishkara as she sidled up next to me.

"Ah, Velodik, glad to see you're having a good time." She smiled wryly as she flicked the empty glasses in my hands.

"You know," I started, "I invited you because I knew you'd enjoy yourself, but I didn't expect that you would disappear for most of the evening. And then when I do find you, you're getting job offers from Senator Dazbov!"

"Isn't it exciting?"

"Yes, of course! But tonight wasn't about getting you a job. It was my chance to talk to my commander and secure my promotion!" My temper grew the more I talked. My only saving grace was that the din of the party kept my yelling from standing out. "Now I've lost that chance. He's probably handed it over to Zradya by now."

"Velodik, relax. It's fine. I spoke to your commander already."

"You what? How? I didn't even introduce you to her." I felt my stomach sink as I imagined what kind of trouble she had gotten me into.

"That's all right. The mayor introduced me."

"The mayor? You spoke to the mayor, too? Who haven't you—"

"Shush. It's all right," she replied with a smile and patted my cheek. "Your commander had very nice things to say about you. You'll get the promotion."

"Ishkara, I didn't need you to ask on my behalf."

"I didn't ask. I only talked about you and your service to Sophia. She's ready to give you the promotion."

I squinted and shook my head. "What about Zradya?"

Ishkara chuckled and waved a dismissive hand. "Zradya's too conniving. Just be authentic and straightforward. All you need to do is ask and the job will be yours."

"She told you that?" I asked incredulously.

"No. But I can tell."

"Oh." My ire had faded quickly. "Well. Thank you," I said awkwardly.

"Happy to. Now where can I find a glass of that ice wine? Or did you drink their whole supply?"

The rest of the evening flashed by in a blur. I found my commander and just as Ishkara said, she was happy to promote someone with my drive and authenticity. After a brief chat, she told me that the paperwork would be finalized within a week.

From there onward it was ice wine, Ishkara's charm, a flirtatious conversation with a bartender, and more ice wine. My head was spinning with joy as the night was drawing to a close, and Ishkara and I sat at an empty table.

"Ishkara. This was something else. Thank you!" I slurred as I clinked my glass into hers. "Sergeant Velodik. Now that has a ring to it. There will never be another gala like this."

"There will be more galas," Ishkara said, her tone returning to its familiar evenness and calm. I stopped mid-drink and set down my glass. There was a sudden sombreness that, for the moment, sobered me up. She continued: "I won't be so readily accepted at each one. I'll need help." She placed her hand on mine and our eyes locked. "I can help you along the way, too." I was confused, and my face said as much. "We can become more than the lives we left behind."

She meant it. But I didn't realize just how far she intended to go.

Chapter Five:
Restless

Shadows fall and sorrows rise
Nightmares fill your heart and mind
Rest my dear
Close your eyes
When morning comes
The light will shine

— Vsevoran lullaby

Siranna

~Thirty years after Iryna's death~

Leaving home wasn't easy. There was no part of it that was easy. The journey out of Oksana drained everything out of me. While I could find a warm bed in the little villages and towns along the road, I rarely found rest.

It was hard to sleep. Each night, my breath came in and out in heavy sighs and I rolled left and right. *What if I made a mistake?* I thought. *What about my responsibilities? Have I been reckless?* I thought about my mother. I thought about Sylchiv. I thought about the self portrait.

There I was, far from home, in an inn on the edge of a beautiful forest. There were fireflies dancing outside my window and hot tea on my nightstand. I should have been delighted. Instead, I rolled onto my stomach and buried my head in a pillow, bombarded by a steady stream of doubt.

I pulled myself back up to the edge of the bed and tried to steady my breathing. I drank the last of my tea, let out an even, controlled breath, and laid back down, letting my thoughts drift away with the fireflies.

This isn't a mistake, I told myself. *I need to do this.* I repeated the words until I found a moment of stillness, and with it, I finally drifted off to sleep.

I slipped away, down into deep darkness. And then into hazy orange-red light. I saw the sunset reflected off Mount Zorya. There was cheering coming from a happy gathering from the village, all smiling proudly. My mother's smile was widest of all.

She wrapped her arms around me tightly and pushed the breath out of my lungs. I laughed. *I've just endured the Vinnya, only to fall to my mother's embrace!*

The high patron was there. The golden straw woven into his robes flickered and danced—alight with phoenix fire. He patted me on the back and made his way around to each of us who had completed the trek.

My mother pulled back from the hug and the crowd began to disperse. She didn't move. She gripped my shoulders and held me there, smiling still. Then she gestured for me to wait.

Strange shapes danced and clattered around us. I heard a jingling sound that transformed into the cry of a bird. The mountain, the shapes, the sounds, they all faded away and my mother and I were alone together, bathed in warm light.

She produced a small bundle and placed it into my hands. It was heavy and wrapped in a kerchief of red and gold.

"What is it?" I asked.

"Open it!" she exclaimed.

I pulled back the fabric and discovered a small pile of coins. I stared at it with wide, knowing eyes, then looked up at my mother. She nodded gently.

I pulled at the coins and revealed the strands that connected them all together in three rows of shining golden medallions. "Your necklace!" I exclaimed in a whisper.

"No. Your necklace," she replied. "My mother gave it to me when I completed the *Vinnya*. Just as her mother gave it to her. Six generations it has been passed down... Seven now."

I held the necklace tight as happy tears welled up in my eyes. I wrapped my arms snugly around my mother, squeezing hard, before standing back and putting the necklace on. It was heavy, but it felt oddly balanced.

My mother faded out of my embrace and the warmth shifted into pale moonlight. I stood alone in darkness. There were voices echoing around me. My parents. Little half sentences and broken memories vibrated through the void.

"It's time," my mother said. "We... need to choose."

"...you sure?" my father asked.

"Of course! She can't... *Vinnya*... It's up to... needs a husband."

"You're right."

I felt a quivering in the pit of my stomach and I gripped the necklace at my throat. As my fingers fidgeted nervously along the medallions, the weight around my neck seemed to grow.

Seven generations had borne this necklace. How many more would carry it still? Another pang in my stomach that ran up to my head. I tried to shake the feelings and the thoughts away, but they just radiated further.

I took off the necklace and it floated in front of me. It spun around, growing larger and larger. The strands spread out and began to wrap around me, binding my hands, my arms, and wrapping around my head. The coins covered my eyes and I was carried up into the darkness, flying higher and higher until suddenly I fell.

With a thud, I hit a hard surface. As I sat up, the necklace came loose and wound around until it returned quietly to its place around my neck.

There was bright light all around me and as my eyes adjusted, I realized I was on Mount Zorya. But I had never walked this trail before.

I got to my feet and made my way to a nearby ridge. As I scrambled over it, I slipped. I slid down the smooth mountain glass and crashed into a wide, sheltered basin. High peaks towered all around me and there was a crystalline glow that filled the entire basin—the reflection of the sun's light refracted in all directions.

The light danced around me and seemed to carry me forward to the centre of the basin where I came upon a mass of tightly-knit brambles: a nest. It was as tall as I stood from toe to horn-tip. As I examined the impenetrable wall of the nest, I wondered how I could see what was inside.

I turned my search to the surrounding area and discovered that there was some rock that overlooked the nest. The outcropping of stone and glass looked easy enough to climb. I pulled up my sleeves and carefully pulled myself up until I stood atop the outcropping. Gingerly, I crept my way to the edge and gently leaned forward to peer down below.

At the nest's centre was a massive egg; it must have been at least as long as my arm. It was a gentle yellow-orange colour, with darker red spots near its round bottom. I stared at it in awe, leaning further and further forward along the thin edge to get a better view of the egg. I heard a gentle crack of crumbling rock and splintering glass.

I lost my footing and tumbled down into the nest. I crashed amongst the brambles and rolled into the egg, slamming hard against it. I cried out in a panic and scrambled to my feet, staring in horror as I looked over the egg, hoping I hadn't harmed it. A sharp crack now marred the shell's surface and my heart sank. *What have I done?* I thought. Then the egg started to tremble. I gasped and gazed forward, dumfounded, as it shook and the crack grew wider. *Is it hatching?*

A deep shadow overtook me followed by a wave of heat. I looked up. A great bird with four great wings formed a silhouette up above: a mother phoenix. My heart started beating fast as fear overwhelmed me. I scrambled away from the egg and climbed out of the nest. I lifted myself back onto the outcropping and back onto my feet, desperate to escape, but as I started to run, I stumbled and toppled forward with a heavy thud. I rolled onto my back in time to see the tremendous bird swoop down toward me. I scrambled backwards, moving away from the nest, until I felt my back pressed against the glass face of the mountain and I could go no further.

The phoenix came down with a fiery beating of her forewings, and she landed on the edge of the outcropping, facing toward me. Fire rippled from her feathers, radiating intensely with heat. I could hear my heart racing in my ears as her eyes locked onto mine and she stepped forward, her mighty forewings spread out threatening before me.

Her hindwings were actually her legs, thick and powerful with massive red feathers that rippled and fluttered as she drew closer. The phoenix's talons were long, curved, and sharp, leaving scars in the stone beneath her with each step.

I trembled as the mother phoenix towered above me; the great heat that emanated from her flowed through my body and into my head. I felt dizzy and weak.

She leaned forward, lowering her great head down to the level of my own. Her face was beautiful and terrifying. Her head was covered in smooth, red feathers, but there were a few additional feathers that stretched out like thin quills from the top of her head and ended with fiery feather-petals that gently bounced as she moved. Her beak was long and sharp. She could rip me apart in an instant any moment that she wanted. She leaned in close, her face just in front of me. Her yellow-red eyes were alight, like the rest of her.

My breath quavered with fear and I stammered, "P-please... I didn't mean to harm your egg." My mind raced as the heat continued to flood through my head. I thought of the egg shaking and the crack spreading. "B-but I think... I think it might be time for it to hatch," I gasped out. I hoped beyond hope that she could understand me—that she would believe me.

The phoenix stared at me, as if considering my words. I saw my reflection in her eyes: my face was contorted in fear, my auburn curls were matted to my skin with sweat—even my spiral horns seemed to quiver before her. I saw the reflection shift as she turned her eye to my necklace; the golden medallions shone within her eyes. I gripped the necklace and she let out a sharp, shrill sound that made me jump and press myself even tighter against the mountain behind me. She rose back up and turned, hopping down from the outcropping and into the nest.

I slowly moved forward, crawling on hands and knees, and peered down below to watch. The mother phoenix let out another cry as the egg continued to shudder. A blazing flame erupted from around her beak and she lowered it down to the egg, tracing her beak along the crack. As she moved her beak along the egg, the crack sealed back up. It was as though she had cauterized a wound. When the egg was healed, the fire from her beak dissipated, and the phoenix gently strutted around the nest until she settled and sat upon the egg, the fiery warmth of her feathers embracing it tightly.

And then I awoke. I lay in my bed, my body sticky with sweat and my heart beating fast. I had left my necklace on the nightstand, but I discovered that I now held it tightly in my hands.

I looked out the window at the flickering light of the fireflies and the cool glow of the moon. As I gently released my grip on the necklace and held it out in front of me, the shifting light caught it and shimmered throughout the room, refracting like the lights of the crystal basin.

I felt hot. Was it phoenix fire rising up within me, or was it a great flame sealing me away? It took a long time to fall back asleep.

Chapter Six:

Finally Free

We didn't just lose our friends out there; we lost ourselves.
Never again. Lest we lose it all.

— Surrendra of the Feras

Kalrevi

~Thirty years after Iryna's death~

Dusk had fallen as I reached for my window. I would slip toward the marshes under the cover of darkness and when I found the skyship... Well, I wasn't entirely certain what would happen next, but I was confident that between my tools and my years of study, I could uncover its secrets. I pulled myself up.

"What do you think you're doing?" My father's voice bellowed behind me. I closed my eyes and froze in place, wishing I had been faster. My father continued: "You're trying to escape? Trying to crawl back to Doctor Lakira? What did you hope to accomplish? Kalrevi, look at me!"

I stepped down from the window, but I kept my back to him. I hung my head disgracefully and clenched my fists. He gripped my wrists and turned me to face him. I averted my gaze. Two hands reached under my arms and four at my waist. He lifted me up to meet him at eye level. I could see the bloodshot anger and shame behind the mask.

"Put me down. I'm not a child anymore," I fumed.

"Perhaps if you did not behave like one," he replied coldly. Nonetheless, he lowered me back to the ground and eased his grip, keeping only two hands at my shoulders. I looked up at him, unblinking.

"The outsider is worth saving, father," I said obstinately. I knew his fate was out of my hands, but part of me still yearned to try—to convince my father to allow Doctor Lakira to heal and awaken him.

"It doesn't matter, Kalrevi. The outsider is dead." The words were like a punch to my stomach. I wondered how my father could be so cold and cruel. "Even if Doctor Lakira had acted, there was nothing that could be done for him. He was dead the moment his skyship brought him here."

"You don't know that," I growled.

"You bear the mask of the Feras. You are of our people, and you must accept your place among us. You cannot pass the Greenshield and outsiders must never be allowed to pass into it. Everything that has happened, everything that is, these things cannot be changed. The outsiders do not change. Perhaps, as you say, I do not change. I hope you can understand that despite all of that, I love you and only want what is best for you. As I do with all of our people."

I said nothing in response. We stared into one another's eyes. In his, the anger had faded. He showed no remorse for his actions, but there was some other kind of sadness there: disappointment, shame, and even defeat. He turned away and left me alone.

My father, Surrendra, leader of the Feras, always stood tall and strong. Only on the days leading to my mother's death, when he knew he was losing her, did I see that strength slip away. He was grasping for it again here, but he could feel me drifting away. It pained me to see him like this, but I couldn't live this way any longer.

I reached again for the window and pulled myself up. I paused for a moment, thinking of everything that my father said. "Things change. I hope that you change, too. Forgive me." I jumped out and didn't look back.

I moved silently, just as my father had taught me when I was a child. Back then, he hoped that I would grow up to be a warrior like him and take his place as leader. While that never came to pass, everything he taught me about how to move and strike as the shadow had proven itself useful.

Cool, grey mist clung to the ground of the east marshes. I moved softly and swiftly so as to not sink in the damp ground. I could smell smoke, and the smell grew stronger as I travelled deeper into the marsh. There would be a scout at the machine standing watch, and others might be out searching for anything else unusual coming from the crash.

I pressed on, brushing through thick tree branches, as the mist grew thicker and the path denser. I felt a sudden shock up my leg and with a thud I hit the ground. I looked up and saw someone staring back at me through the mist.

A pair of yellow eyes with bright red pupils swung out of the depths and peered into mine. I didn't know who or what was looking back at me, but to those eyes, my face was the expressionless void that my mask displayed. Behind the mask I stifled a terrified scream. The mists shifted and I realized what I beheld.

Creeping vines. I pushed myself back to my feet, kicked at the loose roots I had tripped over, and cursed at myself under my breath. The eyes were attached to a pair of vines that hung down from a tree branch, and I promptly shoved them out of the way. I hated the way that creeping vine stared and lingered. I could feel the eyes turn and watch me as I continued toward the smell of the smoke.

At last I found it: the skyship. It was a massive black hulk in the dim starlight. I thought back to everything I had read. Those old books had sketches of sleek little rafts with great sails racing across the top of the Greenshield; but this was a single, encapsulated machine with metal sails spread out at its sides. There wasn't much damage that I could see from out there and it appeared that the skyship had made it through the crash better than the poor outsider had.

There was a single scout keeping watch. I kept moving through the vines and caught a few more looking at me, but as long as the scout didn't notice anything, I was fine. I crept up to the skyship and saw a hatch at the back lying open. I made a dash for it and swooped inside.

It was cramped—only big enough for one person. As I examined the craft's cabinets and control panels, I was surprised to see how similar it was to other sketches and schematics I had read. While it wasn't like the Feras rafts of old, I noticed similarities with our harvesters and wind turbines.

I can do this, I told myself, *I can make this work.* I understood what needed to be repaired and what I had to do to get airborne again— at least I hoped. It just needed to fly long enough to get past the Greenshield.

There wasn't much time. My father probably didn't expect me to be so brash as to try to escape on the skyship, but he wouldn't leave me alone all night. Once he discovered I was gone, he would be on his way. I laid out my tools and got to work.

Tinkering is an easy task when you can loudly bang pieces together and yell when it doesn't work. Tinkering under subterfuge—that's a whole different matter. I needed to be careful not to drop anything, and focus my strength with every piece I connected and tightened. Most of all, I couldn't let my frustrations get the better of me as I patiently worked through the repairs as quickly as I could.

As I worked, sweat built up beneath my mask and my arms strained to reach into each awkward nook. With each twist of a screwdriver and every gentle attempt to knock something back into place, I could feel a toll being taken. I worried that my strength wouldn't last. And even if it did, would the ship even fly?

The damage to the steering was most extensive. The outsider must have slammed against it during the crash. It was a challenge, but I told myself that my toil would pay off. Everything was reconnected and it appeared to be functional, but something wasn't quite right. The yoke was getting stuck. After carefully reassessing my work, I decided the problem was likely with one of the metal sails.

I crept outside of the craft to investigate. So far, the scout hadn't taken any notice of me. I gingerly climbed up the side of the machine, careful not to make a sound. I crawled on my belly across the top from sail to sail, inspecting each one. I soon discovered the trouble—a faulty hinge—and got to work to make the repair. I had only just begun when I dropped a screwdriver and it clanked and banged along the skyship before hitting the ground.

The scout called out and ran toward me.

I had to think fast. I grabbed a wrench and whipped it at the scout. It cracked into his mask and he hit the ground.

I winced. "Sorry." I hurried back to work, hastily finishing the repair before the scout came to.

"Kalrevi!" A powerful voice echoed across the marsh. My father had arrived and, as expected, was not pleased with my decisions. I jumped to the ground as my father stepped into the clearing with two warriors at his side. The white of their masks stood out against the darkness. My father stood still and opened all his arms toward me. He pleaded, "Stop this foolishness, Kalrevi."

"It's not foolishness. It's freedom. I have to do this, father." I turned and ran as quickly as I could.

I leapt into the skyship and scrambled to close the hatch. My father was right there. I strained against the hatch with my work-wearied arms as my father reached inside. I pulled as hard as I could; with a heave, my father fell back and the hatch slammed shut. I thrust the lock into place and my father hammered loudly outside.

I ducked into the cockpit, gripped the yoke, and hoped that I had done enough. I turned my focus to the controls, but my thoughts were quickly broken by a new cacophony. As far as I could tell, father's two warriors were clambering along the skyship, perhaps trying to find another way in— or to make one.

Then I heard a muffled shout nearby. I looked out the window and saw my father looking back at me; he waved his arms desperately, beckoning me to stay. I paused for a moment. I wondered… Another clang from the warriors.

This was it. Now or never. I flipped the ignition. There was a great burst of sound and a shudder throughout the entire skyship. There was a startled shriek and the warriors backed off fearfully. I closed my eyes and gripped the yoke as the machine rumbled. The vibration resonated through my whole body. I drew in a deep breath. No time for fear. No second guessing. I had to trust myself. I opened my eyes and looked to the sky.

That first exhilarating moment as the ship burst up off the ground—I knew I'd never forget it. It was a pang of terror and unhinged delight that rolled its way across my body. The skyship shot up and barrelled into the sky. It shook and tossed me about violently as it broke through the treetops of the marshes. I cried out in a mix of fear and celebration, frantically familiarizing myself with the controls.

There was no going back. Onward, upward, higher, faster. My knuckles were white-hot as I clung to the yoke and steered the skyship over the trees, and I hoped beyond hope that I would not meet the same end as the outsider.

I looked out at the treetops below and I trembled—not from the rumbling of the machine, but from the exhilaration that coursed through me. I laughed. It was an uncontrollable surge of emotion that tumbled out of me.

Gradually, the shaking faded and a feeling of comfort took hold. It felt right—natural. I thought of the Feras of old and their ancient rafts. Like them, I looked to the stars for guidance.

Instead of stars, I saw a great looming blackness ahead. The Greenshield! Its blades swayed even higher than the tallest trees. Fear rose up once more as I pulled on the yoke and the skyship groaned. Had I done enough? Could it manage?

If I crashed, then the Greenshield would devour me. I'd be dead or doomed—doomed to spend my days trapped under my father's vigilant gaze.

Neither of those options were acceptable. I had to make it. There was no other choice!

I pulled hard and drew the yoke in close. It creaked with the effort and I thought for a moment that it would snap. My weary muscles trembled. I stared forward, unblinking, and hoped with every bit of my being.

The skyship shot straight up along the dark wall of the Greenshield, but something was wrong. The ship's ascent was slowing. If I didn't act fast, I would tumble back down.

I grit my teeth and adjusted the yoke, turning the sails so they might catch enough of the wind to carry me higher.

With a shudder, the skyship climbed up, overcoming the dark wall and reaching the tops of the blades. I could see the fullness of the sky above. It was boundless. As I stabilized the craft, I was hit with a wave of relief.

Like my kin, I was now sailing over the Greenshield.

I flew east and I reached the far edge of the towering grass—an edge I had only ever imagined.

The night was full of glistening stars to guide my way. There was no moon out tonight. A new moon. A new cycle. A new beginning.

Chapter Seven:

The Fire of Her Will

She will use her power to deny my place on the throne. But I will take what is mine by right, even if Vsevora itself must burn.

— from the diary of Hekar, the last dynast-king of Vsevora

Velodik

~Twenty years after Iryna's death~

"Velodik, let me in." The words shook me out of a stupor. There was a gentle but fervent knocking at the door.

"Wh-what?" I gasped, trying to get my bearings. It was dark and the stink of alcohol and sweat stung my nostrils. I had been celebrating. Perhaps a little too much.

Almost ten years had passed since that first gala. Just as Ishkara said, there had been many more. And at each one, there were senators, diplomats, and ministers ready to be enthralled by her wit and candour. One by one, Ishkara grabbed hold of each new opportunity. With each one, her influence grew. And so did mine.

I had just become Commissioner of the Sophian Constabulary. It was certainly something worth celebrating, but as my head pounded in time with the incessant knocking, I began to question my choices.

I tread carefully through the dark room, grasping in vain to feel my way forward. *Crack!* A sharp pain shook my knee as it collided into something. I hobbled to the door and opened it slightly. As soon as I did, it was thrust open and I was shoved back. A storm of horns and azure fabric barrelled past me.

"I need you to do something for me," the storm said firmly before a blinding light erupted from above. I recoiled from it instinctively and moaned. The light seared into my eyes and burnt through my entire brain.

Ishkara had flicked on a light switch and the mess of my flat was laid bare. There were liquor bottles scattered everywhere and two men passed out on the couch. She was unfazed by all of this.

"I need you to do something for me," she said. "Let's speak privately." She gestured with her spiralling horns to the unconscious men, then looked me over. "And put on some pants."

It was a struggle, but I got dressed and kicked out my guests; although they weren't happy to be woken up so abruptly either. I poured a glass of wine to settle my headache and sat down across the room from Ishkara.

"What's so important that it couldn't wait?" I sighed.

"Dazbov was arrested," she said.

"What? Really?"

"I'd expect the Commissioner of the Sophian Constabulary to be better informed than I."

I shot a glare at her. "Why were they arrested?"

"Illegal gambling racket out of their house," Ishkara replied with a smile.

I scoffed, "Like that matters. Dazbov is rich; they can get around the fines without a problem."

"True," she replied, "but people may not be so pleased with the hypocrisy since they're the one who put forward the bill to outlaw it in the first place."

"Right. So now's your chance to get them out of the way."

"Exactly," she said. "With Dazbov gone, their Senate seat opens up."

"And who better to fill the role than Prefect Ishkara? So why do you need me?"

Ishkara leaned back into her seat, a thoughtful smile on her face, as though she were daydreaming. "Dazbov will assuredly try to hide all this and expunge the records. But if the newly-minted Commissioner were to get me the files and help me expose this..." She trailed off and the smile turned to a full grin.

"Hold on one moment," I said, rising to my feet. My head started spinning again, and not from the wine. "Ishkara, I just became Commissioner. Exposing a Senator like that? It'll paint a target on my back and I'll be dropped back down to Constable. Hell, I could be thrown out of the city!"

Ishkara's smile vanished and her posture became rigid and imposing. "Remember, Velodik, that if it weren't for my recommendations, you wouldn't have spent the night celebrating."

We locked eyes and she stared me down. It was the same burning stare from the day we first met. I gulped down my wine and put down the glass hard enough that I was surprised it didn't break. Her eyes didn't falter.

"Fine. I owe you. But you'd better have my back."

She did, of course. After I exposed Senator Dazbov and Ishkara replaced them, she made sure that I was well protected. It wasn't the last time that I used my influence and authority to help her, either.

~ ~

"Senators, it is time for us to act." Ishkara stood at a pulpit, looking out at the assembly. I watched from the public gallery above, leaning in. Her expression was firm and focused. She spoke in a clear, earnest way that captured the attention of the hall.

"Yet another incident in Oksana of all places, our crystal treasure on the northern shore. But it is something we have seen all too often—in Sophia, in Olga, in Ksenya. Another failing of the local constabulary to protect its citizens."

There was a soft murmur throughout the hall. Ishkara spoke of a recent fire—an arson. A Ksenyan bakery was burnt to the ground by some xenophobic Oksanan, and the constabulary had turned a blind eye; they refused to investigate.

Ishkara asked me to send in a few of my people. I obliged, of course, and my inspectors uncovered more than a lazy constabulary. They discovered a chain of corruption linking the xenophobe all the way up to the Oksanan commissioner. It was a disgrace.

"As a Senate, it is our duty to protect the people of Vsevora," Ishkara said. "We can no longer trust the local jurisdictions to fulfill that duty. And so, I propose the formation of a new ministry to oversee and guide our constabularies across the nation: the Ministry of Public Security."

There was another gentle murmur. The idea gained traction quickly and soon the ministry was forged. When it came time to appoint its Chief Minister, Ishkara made sure that I was prime candidate.

In a way, it felt like we were enacting justice. She had an uncanny skill to root out the rot around her and together we purged it. Bribery, embezzlement, and fraud—bit by bit we stomped out the corruption that ran rampant throughout Vsevora.

Alliances and agreements; concessions and compromises; subterfuge and sabotage. Through them, Ishkara's status rose and mine followed soon after. At times, I questioned her. Especially when her tactics called for unsavoury methods.

~ ~

"The end justifies the means," she told me one night as we discussed tearing down another senator.

"She has a family, though. Children who look up to her. I understand that such, such," I struggled to find the right word, "substance abuse is unbecoming of a senator, but imagine how this discovery could tear them apart." I didn't want to admit that exposing a senator's drug use made me so uncomfortable. After all, I had done so myself—only once or twice—and there was never any harm or misuse. It felt hypocritical to destroy someone's livelihood over so small a thing.

Ishkara leaned close. Her expression showed empathy, but her eyes held something deeper. I pulled away from her. I felt as though she could read my every thought.

"Remember, Velodik," she said, "that she was one of the most vocal advocates in increasing the penalties for such substance abuse. How many families has she torn apart? How many people have been sent to Kamin Prison over one mistake? And yet not only is she a hypocrite, but she also aids the black market by purchasing and consuming such substances. I know it is difficult and painful to have to hurt her and her family this way, but in doing so, we will bring justice to countless others."

As ever, she was right. The end justified the means.

~Thirty years after Iryna's death~

For over ten years she served as Senator where she peti-tioned heavily for change. While her seat of power was lim-ited to Sophia, she became a shining example of someone who fought for the rights of people across Vsevora. So much so, that when the time came for the Senate to appoint a new Chancellor, her name rose to the top of the ballot.

The night before the election was tense.

"I don't know if I'll make it," Ishkara said nervously, pac-ing across my flat. She wrung her hands together and sighed. She was nothing like she had been earlier that night.

Just a few hours before, Ishkara had stood before a crowd of people outside of the Grand Hall. She wore a dress that was much like the one she wore the night of that first gala. She was draped in starlight. She spoke optimistically and with a commanding voice.

"My friends, we have been at war with each other for too long. I do not mean bloodshed. It has been many years since a city-state has raised up arms to another. I mean a war against one another—person to person.

"Three generations ago, the last of the dynast-kings taught us to hate one another. Through his greed and treachery and wrath, Vsevora was torn apart. And for three generations, those feelings have been allowed to fester and boil. Ksenyan and Oksanan, Lyudmilan and Yuliyan, from mountain to vale, for three generations we continue to hate! The war must end.

"That is what I aim to accomplish. For years, I have served within this hall as a representative and ambassador of Sophia to the rest of Vsevora. If I were to be named Chan-cellor, it would be my duty to oversee the entirety of the Senate, and to ensure that all peoples of Vsevora are repre-

sented here. It is a duty that I would fulfil with honour...
With memories and love."

The speech had been a rousing one, given by someone
who was confident and assertive. Now she appeared meek
and sheepish, wrapped in a heavy blue-grey dress, and pac-
ing relentlessly. I could hardly recognize her. She was nervous, uncertain—nearly afraid! I had never seen her like
this before.

"Relax, Ishkara," I soothed as I poured her a glass of
wine. "The Chancellor doesn't hold true authority. It's just a
fancy version of your current job." She stopped at the window; I could tell she wasn't in the mood for levity. I tried for
sincerity: "You just need to wait. You've done everything
that you can." Her reflection in the window looked back at
me; the sight of her burning eyes sent a shiver down my
spine.

"Not everything."

I gently put the glass of wine down on the table. The quiet hung between us uncomfortably and I realized I had
been holding my breath. I slowly exhaled, but I said nothing.

The next words she spoke came out almost inaudibly,
just above a whisper, as if each word that she said were forbidden. "We can make sure that I win. You can make sure."
She gradually turned her head and looked at me directly.
"Public Security oversees the ballot boxes, do they not?"

I stood. "Ishkara," I hissed, "I don't like what you're im-
plying."

"All I'm saying is that it would be well within your rights
as Chief Minister of Public Security to ensure that the ballots were counted correctly."

"No, Ishkara."

She snaked closer to me, picking up the glass of wine as she approached. "If I am set to win, as you say, then there's no trouble. You check the ballots and you get to be the first to confirm my victory." I glowered at her, our gazes locked. She continued: "And if it should happen that my name appears on more ballots than expected... Then perhaps the new Chancellor could repay your diligence. Senator Velodik has a ring to it, doesn't it?" She stood inches away from me, a dark smile on her lips as she took a drink.

"I owe you a lot, Ishkara," I said softly.

"One could say you owe me everything," she replied. "From a simple constable to the Chief Minister of Public Security. It's a difficult mountain for anyone to climb. Especially for someone with so many... indiscretions." She gently pressed a finger to the tip of my nose. I winced.

"Yes," I whimpered. "You could say I owe you everything."

"Remember, Velodik." She pressed her face up to my ear and whispered. The combination of her warm breath and icy tone sent another shiver through my whole body. "The end justifies the means."

I staggered back. "I-I can't do what you're asking of me. If I'm caught... I lose it all. *You* lose it all. I'm sorry, but trust me when I tell you, I believe in you. You don't need me to steal this for you; you can do it on your own."

Her smile trembled and she broke her gaze away from mine. She stepped back and took a seat, setting down her glass. She reached for her bag, and I stared at her silently. In all our years together, my will had never won out over hers, but this time I had done it. I sighed with relief, thinking that the madness had passed and that her nerves had just gotten the better of her.

"I didn't want to do this," she said softly, and the tension returned. She took a sepia photograph from her bag and placed it down on the table. I picked it up. It was me, passed out on the floor of my flat. There were two tiny vials next me and white powder dusting my nose. I tossed the photo back down on the table.

"How dare you," I snarled.

"It's not like you're leaving me much choice," she replied calmly. "And before you think of destroying that one, there are copies. They'll be released to the press tomorrow morning and then the Chief Minister may soon find himself without a job. But of course, I can stop that from happening."

I started shaking. Anger bubbled up inside of me. I bared my teeth and I felt the hair along my arms standing up on end. She just stared back up at me. The same stare as ever. The curling horns around her head were like a demon's and I wished that I could banish her back to whatever hell she had crawled up from. I wanted to be rid of her from my life forever. Her eyes continued to bore into me.

What choice did I have?

The next day, Ishkara was appointed as the Chancellor of the Vsevoran Senate. She was dressed in all her royal blue regalia and beaming with pride as she addressed the nation:

"I cannot fully express how I feel right now. Here I stand, a Ksenyan, a refugee, a woman with no family name. By all measures, I should not be here. Yet here I stand in Sophia's Grand Hall, uplifted as Chancellor.

"For many years, I have served in this Senate Council. My seat was in Sophia. My blood came from Ksenya. But my heart is for Vsevora.

"When we look back at times long since passed, we were unified. Vsevora stood strong. We worked together, helped each other, and built the most powerful nation the world has ever known.

"We can do it again. As I tell you this, know that I believe it from the bottom of my heart: we can do it through memories and love. We shall build a Vsevora that draws from the memories of its roots; a Vsevora that believes in love over hate; a nation that is joined in the bonds of unity!

"As we look out at one another in this hall, we may look into the eyes of Ksenyans, Oksanans, and Lyudmilans. But it does not matter. Their eyes are our eyes. Their flesh is our flesh. We are one nation. We are one Vsevora!"

The Senate burst to their feet with applause. I could see tears in the eyes of old and young alike. In that moment, I believed in everything that she said. I believed that she was the right person to set in motion a new beginning for Vsevora. I grinned and cheered with all of the others as Ishkara smiled brightly at the crowd.

Then her gaze shifted onto mine. I stopped applauding and the world stood still around us. All of the charisma and charm and allure melted away until there was only the burning of her gaze—the fire of Ishkara's will. It was the same fire in her eyes the day we met at the Brazen Bull; the same fire that plotted over each politician we exposed; the same fire that burned in her reflection the night before.

Vsevora would come to know as I did what the fire of Ishkara's will could do.

Chapter Eight:

A New Life

Strong legs, strong back, strong arms.
Have those and you're fine.
Strong mind and strong heart?
Those get you into trouble.

— old saying in Yelena

Siranna

Sophia was overwhelming. I had left the village before, saw the city of Oksana proper, but it was nothing like Sophia: massive buildings, lengthy streets, a constant flow of carriages, and people—so many people.

As I arrived, I immediately questioned every step that brought me there. Everything was so different. Sophia was an industrial city. It ran on steam, soot, and sweat. The air was dingier, the mountains didn't shine from the sun, and even the shapes of the buildings were more foreboding. As I choked on grimy air and pressed my way through a busy market, I wished I were standing on a peaceful hillside, watching the windmills turn in the breeze.

The people looked so different, too. Back home, almost everyone was Oksanan. There were others, of course: Ksenyans, Halynans, Ostapans, and more, but they were mainly found in the city in their own little neighbourhoods. Here in Sophia, every possible person from across Vsevora could be found, all milling together. I struggled to find any familiar spiral horns poking out from the crowds.

Sophia had been Vsevora's capital since it had been ruled over by kings and queens. As the nation strained with conflicts, Sophia continued to be a place where people migrated. Whether they sought refuge or new opportunities, the grand city opened its arms to people from across the nation. Now I was amongst that number seeking out a new life.

As I made my way through the bustling streets, I became keenly aware of a growing ache through my back. The weight of my pack was taking its toll, and the words of my mother invaded my mind. As I trudged forward, she kept repeating herself: "The world is heavy and it will crush you beneath its weight."

I was so lost in my thoughts, I didn't notice as I stumbled into someone. With a jolt, I staggered backwards and lost my balance. My pack nearly pulled me to the ground, but I managed to steady myself. I looked up at a tall, hairy man with short, bullish horns that angled forward in a threatening fashion. He glowered down at me.

"I'm so sorry, I was—" I began nervously, but I was swiftly cut off.

"Watch where you're going, you clumsy awk!" he snarled and pushed past me.

I stood dumbfounded for a minute. I had never been called such a thing before. But the venom with which he said it cut through me.

I tried to shake it off, but that night, as I curled up in a bed at an inn, I still couldn't get the incident off my mind. Reality was setting in. I had left everything about my old life behind me.

I didn't have very much to get by, and I certainly wasn't about to become a renowned artist overnight. I needed a place to stay—a place where I could work on my craft—and in order to do that I needed a stable job.

Finding work wasn't a challenge if you were willing to put your back into it. Sophia's mining industry was booming, and they didn't care about your past experience if you could use a pickaxe. To say I regretted signing on for the work was an understatement. I barely survived my first day.

I stood nervously in front of the black entrance of the mine, pick in hand, holding my breath. My knees were shaking. This wasn't what I wanted to do. I wanted to paint. But I needed to support myself. I gripped hard onto the pickaxe, summoning my courage. *You can do this,* I told myself. *You've climbed the crystal mountain. You can bore into one, too.*

As I tentatively took my first few steps, I was shoved from behind with enough force to send me stumbling. I couldn't steady myself and I hit the ground. I groaned and looked up at a set of rectangular eyes glaring back at me.

"Come on, ya stupid awk. Time to get going." It was another miner. He was a heavy brute with short, curly horns. He stamped past me with a laugh and called back: "You're with me, awk! I'll be the one showing you the ropes. Bet you don't last a day, though, with those spindly arms."

The worst part was that he was right. I had scrambled into the mine after him, determined, but my determination wasn't enough.

Thick clouds of black dust kicked up all around us as we dug, and the brute had a good laugh every time I needed to stop due a coughing fit. The dust seared my lungs. As the day wore on, a terrible headache set in.

I made it through the day, but only barely. I was covered from the tip of my horns to the tip of my toes in heavy, black dust. I was gagging and gasping for fresh air by the time we got out. Getting out was hardly a relief, though. The foreman tore into me and told me not to come back. As I struggled to hold back my tears, the foreman just sneered and the brute laughed nearby.

When I returned to the inn, I stared at myself in the mirror. The only parts of me that weren't blackened were where my tears had washed away the dust. I thought of the moment I had cleaned the paint off my face and left my life behind. Sylchiv was far kinder than anyone in Sophia.

I couldn't think about that. Although my mother's voice continued to ring in the back of my mind.

I struggled desperately that night to wash off the dust and purge the misery of the day. The dust had mixed with my sweat and caked onto my skin, refusing to wash away without a fight. I spent hours scrubbing every inch of my body and then collapsed onto my bed, exhausted. By that point, I was too tired to cry, and I quickly fell asleep.

Thankfully, I had still been paid for my one day of labouring in the mine. Unfortunately, I needed to find a different place to stay—one where I could stretch my dwindling means a little further. I felt like I was running out of time.

I came upon the printing press a bit by accident. I had heard of some boarding houses in the industrial quarter that offered inexpensive, if somewhat cramped, lodging. While trying to find my way there, I had gotten myself quite lost through Sophia's endless streets. As I wearily trudged past a massive factory, I paused as a poster on its wall caught my eye.

"Seeking hard workers for the steam engines and other tasks. Inquire within."

It has to be better than the mine, right? I thought. I went inside.

The facility was hot and humid—it reminded me of home, but I had never seen anything like it back in Oksana.

There was an incredible racket: constant, rhythmic clanking sounds, each overlapping and slightly out of time from one another. People were shouting over the noise in order to communicate, and they were tending complex machines with massive gears that turned heavy drums. I stopped in my tracks and stared for some time, until someone finally approached.

He was a broad, thick man, with coarse hair and dark brown skin. His horns were bullish, his nose was wide, and he wore a curious, friendly expression. He was well-dressed; clearly he wasn't one of the labourers. I found my-self standing up a bit straighter in his presence.

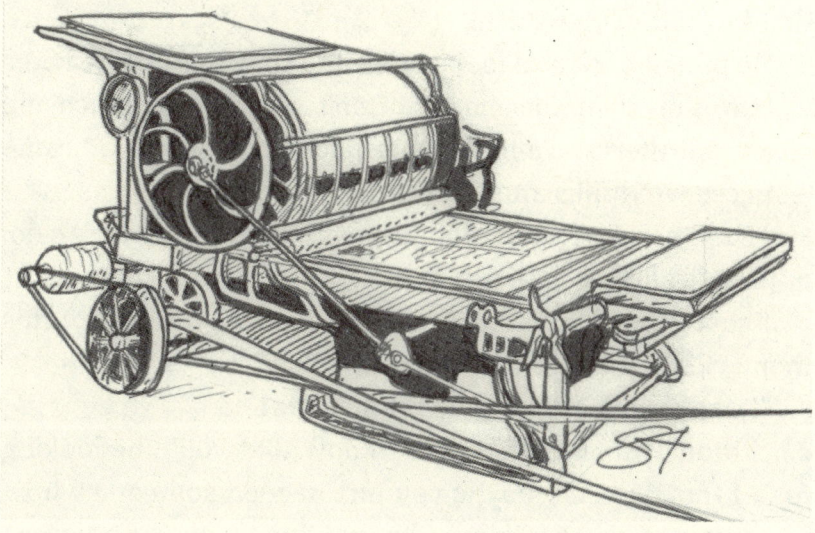

"Are you lost, miss?" he asked, warmly. His voice was deep and while he didn't appear to be speaking very loudly, the sound of it resonated over the cacophony.

"Uh, actually, yes, but also, maybe not?" I said. I could tell he couldn't hear me. I started to shout, "I uh, I saw the poster! The one outside!"

He nodded knowingly and turned, beckoning me to follow. He led me up a set of stairs; I could hear his hooves clacking lightly over the noise as he climbed each step. We then stepped into an office that overlooked the printing facility. The noise softened to a din as he shut the door behind us.

"Have a seat," he said kindly and gestured to a chair by the desk. I followed his instructions and he sat in a large, comfortable-looking chair across from me. We exchanged introductions cordially; he introduced himself simply as Mr Pravda. He leaned over the desk and looked at me carefully. "Tell me, what's your experience with steam engines?"

"Oh, uh, my experience," I stammered. "Well, I should say that I uh, I don't have any."

He pulled back and looked perplexed. "None?" he asked.

"No. I'm from Oksana. We don't really have much uh, steam out there." We had power back home, but it all came from the windmills and the sun.

"Then perhaps you're familiar with type setting," he said, optimistically.

I shook my head. "No. We didn't have anything like this in my village."

"I don't think I quite understand, Siranna."

"I didn't think. I, uh, I didn't know that you'd be looking for... I thought that maybe you just needed someone who.... I'm quite strong, you know. I know I don't look it, but I'm no stranger to labour. A-and I'm willing to learn, sir."

"I see," Mr Pravda said softly, leaning back in his chair. "I suppose we should have made it a bit clearer on that poster. We really are looking for someone who understands steam engines or how to work a printing press. I'm sorry, Siranna." Mr Pravda frowned and pushed himself up from the chair.

"Wait, please!" I shot to my feet and held up my hands. "You don't understand. I'll put in the work, sir. I'll do whatever it takes. Trust me, Mr Pravda, I will. If you'll just give me the chance, I'll prove it to you."

He furrowed his brow and stared me down, scrutinizing me in silence for some time. I held my breath, meeting his gaze. At last, his face softened and he gave a slow, thoughtful nod.

"Very well," he said softly, his voice just barely carrying over the din of the machines below. He repeated louder, "Very well! You're hired, Siranna. But I'll be keeping a close eye on you."

I was elated. "Yes, of course, sir! Thank you, Mr Pravda!"

"You'll start bright and early tomorrow morning. Shifts run from ten to twelve hours. Come dressed for the heat and be ready to work hard. We're under some tight deadlines, so if you can't cut it, we'll be forced to let you go," he said sternly. Despite the tone of warning, there was a friendliness in his voice that gave me hope.

"I understand, sir. I'll be here, and I'll be ready."

~ ~

Saying that the work was hard was putting it lightly. It was gruelling. Long hours, hot fires, and heavy lifting. Most of my work was centred around tending the steam engines: preparing and loading the fuel, ensuring the fires stayed lit, stoking the flames, and cleaning the ash. I'd also need to haul things, parts or paper mostly, throughout the facility. It was back-breaking. But despite that, it wasn't nearly as bad as the mine. And the people were kind-hearted enough.

Mr Pravda was far kinder than the foreman of the mine, although that was not a difficult standard to exceed. He spent a lot of time on the floor, keeping a watchful eye on the work being done. But he also took the time to talk to people and to teach as well. It seemed as though he knew about every task that needed doing, and he knew the best ways to get them done, as though he had done them all personally at one time or another. I knew that he was the owner of the facility, but I often wondered how he got started. Had he been a labourer like I was, and worked his way up?

I imagined how I might rise up as well. The work paid well enough that I could afford a tiny apartment for myself and I started to amass a small collection of supplies so that I could paint. Sadly, the long hours left me with few opportunities and little energy to paint as much as I liked. But that didn't stop me from dreaming of how I would create something that could take me away from the printing press and propel me toward greatness.

As time went on, Mr Pravda insisted that I be taught about more functions around the facility. He wanted to make sure that each worker had at least some understanding of each job. I was taught how to maintain the machines and was even given opportunities to prepare the machines for print. Typesetting was a welcome reprieve from the engines, but no less difficult. It required a careful focus and meticulous attention to detail. I found, though, that I had a bit of a knack for it, and could work quite quickly when the opportunity for typesetting presented itself.

Then, one morning, Mr Pravda gathered everyone on the floor. He stood up at the top of the stairs overlooking everyone and exclaimed, "Good news! We have been officially named a sanctioned printing press!" There was a roar of applause. I clapped along, as "officially" and "sanctioned" both sounded good, but I didn't really understand what that meant.

Mr Pravda continued: "We'll be seeing some exciting new jobs coming in from the office of Chancellor Ishkara herself. I expect everyone to be at peak performance. What we print here will be distributed across all of Vsevora. Let's show the nation what we here at Pravda Press are all about!" Another cheer followed by a quick dispersal as everyone hurried to their duties, motivated by this news.

As I got started on preparing one of the engines, Mr Pravda appeared next to me. I didn't notice him at first and I cried out in surprise. He laughed.

"My apologies, Siranna. I didn't mean to sneak up on you like that," he said with a grin across his wide face.

"It's okay, sir," I replied as I caught my breath. I started to pile some coal into a small cart.

"I thought you might be interested in something," he said coyly. I stopped what I was doing and gave him a puzzled glance. I saw that he had a piece of paper in hand. He offered it to me. "This is one of the jobs we've been commissioned to print."

I took the paper and read it over. It described some posters that would be distributed across Vsevora advertising for the Gallery of Sophia. It was for an exhibit: *Creating a New Vsevora: Emerging Artists in a Nation Renewed*.

"This sounds really interesting. I'll be sure to go to the gallery to check it out." I smiled at Mr Pravda's thoughtfulness. We had spoken a few times, and I had mentioned my aspirations. It was very kind of him to let me know about the exhibition. It would be exciting to see what kinds of work other artists were creating.

"You should look closer, Siranna," he replied. "The show isn't up yet."

I looked back down at the brief and read closer. My eyes widened as I realized. "It's a call for submissions," I gasped.

"That's right. I thought that you might want to put something together for it."

My thoughts raced and the possibilities flashed through my mind. The moment of wonder quickly turned into agony as I realized how little time I would have—the long and arduous hours left little time to follow my passion.

Mr Pravda read my expression like a book. He placed a gentle hand on my shoulder. "There's time," he said softly and he took the brief back from me. "And now you know about the exhibition before any other artist in Vsevora. It gives you a bit of a head start, I'd say."

My worry faded and I smiled up at Mr Pravda. "Of course!" I exclaimed. "Thank you. Thank you so much for telling me!"

"Happily, Siranna." He walked away and I jumped into my work, excitedly imagining what I might soon create.

Chapter Nine:
The Cost of Freedom

How much is a life worth?
What have you got in your pockets?

— a merchant creed

Kalrevi

It was another cold, grey day. Clouds hung in the sky, waiting to rain down on the dreary city below. I shuffled slowly, aimlessly, down a dingy street, and paused to lean against an overfull bin of rubbish. I was hungry, my clothes were a drab mess, and I was so, so tired.

I reflected on how I wound up in this situation. Many seasons had passed since my flight across the Greenshield. Nothing had been as exhilarating or as freeing as that day.

The skyship had taken me into a world I had never seen before. From up high, I could see a distant city; it seemed a massive place that could have housed all of the Feras a hundred times over. And then there was a wide expanse of water: the ocean. I had read about the ocean before, but to actually see it as the morning light sparkled off its crystal-blue surface... I was elated. But it all came crashing down.

My repair to the sail's hinge gave way and I lost control of the ship. It was a small miracle that I managed to hold the craft, and myself, together long enough for a rough landing along the beach. I was alive and in one piece at least.

I collected my wits and trudged along the shore toward the nearby city. A myriad of thoughts raced through my mind. I questioned what I had just done. There was no turning back now that the skyship was well and truly ruined. But for every question or doubt, another thought sprang to the forefront of my mind: I was free. My life was mine to do with as I pleased.

When I arrived in the city, I discovered that they were not violent marauders as my father believed. But they did not welcome me, either. They feared me. One look at my mask and they backed away or quickly turned from my path, worriedly muttering amongst themselves. From their whispers, I could tell they had heard stories of the Feras. Vampire, they called me. Demon. Soul-sucker. We had become twisted into the villains of their myths.

Despite this, I tried to integrate myself into the city—to create a new life for myself. But I was an outsider. They wore no masks to cover their faces, and those faces looked so strange and different to me. Their whole way of life was nothing like my home.

I saw people working—toiling on the docks. There was no joy in their labour. For hours they wore down their bodies and I saw that at the end of each day they were handed a small bundle filled with coins that they exchanged for hot meals and foul drink.

We Feras did not use money in payment for labour. We did our work because of our callings and for the good of the community. In this place, no one seemed to care about those around them. I didn't understand.

I tried to do as they did—to work and earn money—but I was turned away everywhere I tried. They had never seen anyone like me before, and they didn't trust me to build or to fix or even to toil. I had nowhere to turn.

I took shelter in alleyways and under trees. I foraged as best I could, but there was surprisingly little growing in the city. I had found an outdoor market where I could purchase my goods. That's where I met a sly-speaking merchant with hunched shoulders and a fake grin. Lucien was his name.

He had a large stall with jewelry, clothing, and trinkets of all kinds. He wore a long, striped robe of grey and green, and a goldenrod sash wrapped around his waist. Upon his head was a round headdress; it covered the top of his head and rested just over his forehead, matching the colours of the rest of his attire. Most distinctive about him, though, were his long, grey whiskers that extended nearly all the way from his nose to his shoulders.

To get the money I needed, I sold what few possessions I had. I started gradually: a piece of jewelry, then a tool that I didn't have much use for. Before long, I had nothing left. My situation had become dire, leading me to where I was now: leaning against a pile of trash.

I stared up at the clouds, waiting for the rain to come. There was a stabbing pain in my stomach; I hadn't eaten for days. I could hear the bustle of the market echoing down the street. I needed to do something, so I stumbled weakly toward the sound of the crowds.

The market was alive and energized as people hurriedly gathered their goods before the rains. I tiredly scanned the area and noticed a few suspicious onlookers eyeing me closely. I had become a regular sight here—and an unwelcome one. It didn't matter. I pressed onward to Lucien's stall.

"An excellent choice, sir! Your wife is certain to love it! Let me wrap this up for you." The merchant had just finished up a sale. I recognized the golden cuffs in his hand as the ones that I had sold him. They had been my mother's. It pained me, but selling them had sustained me for many weeks. I knew that she'd have rather seen me live than keep them.

As Lucien's customer walked away, glancing uncomfortably over his shoulder back at me, Lucien greeted me with a warm and toothy grin. "Kalrevi, my sweet! You don't look well. What can your old friend Lucien do for you, hm?"

I sighed, "I need to buy some food, Lucien."

He chuckled callously. "Well, you'll need to pick a different stall! You know I don't sell that here."

I sighed heavily. "No. You know what I mean. I just... I need a bit of money for food."

His smile widened. "Ah, here for business! What do you have for sale today?" He rubbed his hands together and his whiskers twitched excitedly.

"I don't have anything left, Lucien. But maybe something to tide me over. Or... or maybe you need help here at the stall. I could earn my keep."

His smile vanished and his whiskers sank. "Kalrevi," he said seriously, "take a look." He gestured out of the stall where there were several onlookers staring in and muttering. "You'd be bad for business. You start working here and I'd have no customers. You should be happy I take your business at all."

"Please," I said, a desperate and sorrowful lump building up in my throat. "Y-you just sold my cuffs. I saw. Perhaps a few coins from that sale..." My voice trailed off as his frown grew deeper.

"I already paid you for those cuffs. I don't do handouts, my dear."

I stood quietly before him. I could hear harsh whispers from the onlookers outside the stall. My stomach knotted. I gave a slow nod, turned away from Lucien, and started to stagger away.

"Just one second. There's one thing, Kalrevi," he said and paused. I turned back around to face him. He was staring intently into my eyes, a hint of a smile creeping back onto his face.

"What about that mask of yours? It's really quite extraordinary. I would pay you quite well for that." There was something sinister about the way he spoke, or perhaps it was the horror of the suggestion itself that made the words sound so vile.

Despite having left the Feras behind me and despite the fear and distrust that the mask struck into those who saw me, I never took it off—save for moments of solitude. Something told me that I still needed to wear it. Was it the voice of my father lurking in the back of my mind, telling me that I had betrayed my people? Was I clinging to some piece of my past that I didn't want to let go? Did it even matter?

I stammered, "Wh-what? My mask? Why would you want my mask?"

Lucien moved in close. "A Feras mask is quite the prize. There are only a few out there, and none in such beautiful condition." His hands stretched greedily up toward my face.

I staggered away from his clawing hands, bumping into a display of various colourful garments. My thoughts were racing.

Giving up my mask was unthinkable. But what had it done for me here? Ever since I arrived, it had only caused distrust and suffering. Without it, perhaps I could finally find a place within this new world—perhaps I wouldn't need to suffer any longer.

Was that freedom? Was it giving up on my people and my traditions? Had I already given up on them when I left the shelter of the Greenshield?

I had let the past go. But I hadn't let go of myself.

"No," I said softly, and then repeated it louder and firmer: "No! The mask is mine. Thank you, Lucien. Goodbye." I hurried away from the stall, dashed past the on-lookers, and down the street.

I ran until I reached a quiet alleyway and collapsed. I lay there, breathless, gripping my aching stomach. The strap that held my mask in place felt like it was burning into my skull. I bashed my fist against the ground. Then the rain started to fall.

I wasn't sure how much time had passed. I just sat there in the gutter, shivering weakly as rain pelted down on me. My head started to ring. Bells. Gongs. My death knell.

I let myself fall to my side and sink into the cold, wet stone. The ringing in my head continued and I closed my eyes. I imagined a warm fire at home and the smell of my father's cooking. I pictured his stern, patient eyes, and the hurt I saw in them whenever he thought about my mother. I wondered what hurt now lived in his eyes when he thought of me.

The toll of the bells didn't stop.

No. It wasn't my head ringing. I knew those bells. They were ringing down by the docks. A ship was preparing to depart.

My eyes shot open and I leapt to my feet as if I had been pulled up by some unseen force. An idea had sprung to life and adrenaline was taking over. I darted through the streets and burst out into the port.

There it was: the boat. The last few passengers were hurrying aboard. "Leaving for Vsevora!" a voice cried out over the sound of the bells and the rain. There was no time to waste.

I ran. Just like my father taught me. Swiftly. Silently. Like shadow. The boat began to pull away. I ran down to the beach, over to the pier, and then leapt up through the pilings, over the beams, leaping from truss to truss.

I couldn't be seen. But I couldn't miss my chance. *Jump, Kalrevi!* The boat was slipping further and further away. *I can't make it. I'm too weak,* I thought. *No. I have to try.*

My body screamed. I catapulted myself toward the boat. I crashed into the side of it and began to slide down its edge. I scrambled, grasping uselessly. Then I caught the lip of a porthole. With the last bit of strength I could muster, I climbed up and heaved myself onto the deck of the ship.

As I tried to catch my breath, I couldn't help but think that my fate was to keep escaping. I was tired of running. Leaving for Vsevora, they said. I had no idea what or where Vsevora was. I could only hope that I could finally stop running when I got there.

Chapter Ten:
Propaganda

In his bid for power, my son thinks he can turn the people of Olga and Ostap against one another. He does not realize that their memory runs deep and their love for one another cannot be swayed.

— from the diary of Queen Vekara, dated three days before the outbreak of the first Olga-Ostap Conflict

Velodik

One more day. I just needed to survive one more day. And then... freedom.

I was looking forward to my trip. I had never gone sailing before and the idea was absolutely whimsical. My parents used to tell me stories of the sea. I think they had used them to try to scare me —they always dealt with cold-blooded pirates or faceless monsters that rose up from the deep. Those were the stories that excited me most.

Since I had become a Senator, I had been granted new authority, responsibilities, and benefits! Ishkara called the trip a mission of diplomacy and an opportunity to showcase Vsevora's advances in its efforts of unification. She wanted the nation to be a shining gem—an envy to all peoples. I would certainly do what I could to fulfill that duty, but it didn't mean I couldn't have a bit of fun while I was away.

The anticipation was killing me, and my present responsibilities weren't making it easy! The Senate was in session and I swore they had lined up the stodgiest bunch of senators and asked them to take up as much time as possible on absolute tedium.

I had lost track of what was happening. Another dull discussion—a senator from Olga was droning on about something inconsequential. I had to do everything in my power just to keep my eyes open. I slumped forward. I just wanted the damnable session to end. Perhaps I could sleep through it and end the suffering.

"Thank you, Senator. Now, to our final item," Ishkara said as the Olgan senator took their seat. I perked up at the mention of final. "The floor recognizes the Senator from Oksana."

"Thank you, Chancellor," a middle-aged man responded as he rose to his feet.

I groaned quietly and closed my eyes. The Oksanans were always complaining about something. He'd probably blather on about the lack of windmills in central Vsevora for the better part of an hour. I drew in a deep breath, held it for a moment, and exhaled. *Patience. It will be over soon.*

The Oksanan began his wearying speech: "Chancellor, I would like to raise our concerns over some of the reforms you have recently proposed. In particular, your new prohibitions on literature, art, and culture."

Blah blah blah, I thought with an exasperated sigh. *Such a waste of time.*

"You have put forward an outright ban on the

works of several writers, including one of Oksana's greatest poets. Chancellor Ishkara, this is an insult. Not only to the Oksanan people, but also to the nation itself. For you to suggest that these writings must be censored is an injustice to the work of some of Vsevora's greatest artists. You treat Vsevorans like children who are unable to make their own choices. Oksana will not stand idly by and allow such a proposal to pass into law. By the spear of our horns."

I opened my eyes and sat up straight. "By the spear of our horns" was not some idle turn of phrase—it carried significant weight. In impolite company, it would be seen as a very clear and direct threat. Here in the Grand Hall, its threat was not so explicit, but its meaning was obvious. I looked up at Ishkara anxiously, uncertain how she might respond. I could see the kindling in her eyes, but her demeanour remained even.

"Senator, I suggest you mark your words carefully," she began. "You are a representative of Oksana and you disparage this entire assembly with your threatening tone. I shall forgive your discretions, but such remarks would be enough to expel you from this hall."

There was a low murmur of agreement from the other senators. I glanced over at the Oksanan. He was stone-faced. His beady, yellow eyes were focused straight on Ishkara's. He was not intimidated.

Ishkara continued: "As for my proposal, I believe that you are intentionally misinterpreting and misrepresenting what it sets out to do. Vsevora is at a turning point, Senator. We are approaching a new golden age, where Vsevorans solve problems together. Where we settle our differences not *by the spear of our horns*, but with the virtue of our ideas.

"There are a selfish few who do not see it this way. Their greed and appetite for violence blinds them, and they would pollute our discourse and spread disinformation so they may blind us as well. I do not suggest a ban on art and culture. What I seek is a prohibition on the radical, sectarian propaganda that threatens to divide us."

There was another murmur from the crowd: a mix of both approval and dissatisfaction. The Oksanan senator looked tense but firm. He responded with the same confidence that Ishkara possessed: "And yet, Chancellor, you consider the works of Tibor of Oksana a part of this radical propaganda. This is a slight against our people that we will not abide!"

Ishkara snapped back without missing a beat: "It was Tibor of Oksana who wrote,

'Cut the horns from their heads and raise them high—
A trophy that is earned by blood and might.
Then look them in their crooked eye
And cast them out from mountains' light.'

"But perhaps, senator, you are not as well-versed in his writings as you should be. It is clear of whom he speaks: the Ksenyan people." Ishkara's voice was a low, serious rumble that built up into a vehement tempest. "If Tibor were alive today, he would not stand for a Ksenyan woman presiding over this Senate. He would not stand for a united Vsevora. He would have us fight one another and eliminate anyone with *crooked eye*. Uplifting the works of a bigot will not lead us to a new Vsevora, Senator. We must purge such backwards thinking if we are ever to move forward as a nation.

This is the kind of propaganda that must not be allowed to spread."

Ishkara and the senator's eyes were locked on one another as the hall continued to chatter. I could tell that the senator was not ready to back down. I held my breath as he spoke.

"You speak of radical propaganda, as though Tibor is alive today, trying to tear down what we are building. You paint me as someone who wishes to destroy the dream of a united Vsevora. Far from it, Chancellor." The senator's words were sweet, but his tone still held the aggression and antagonism with which he began. "We must not wipe away the beauty to protect ourselves from the ugly parts of our past. Oksana's heritage is rich and storied, and we cannot accept any law that would tear it away. It is my hope to see the history and culture of Oksana become an important piece of a united Vsevora."

The hall grew quiet. Uncertainty hung in the air, but there was a sympathetic murmur for the senator.

Ishkara was not finished. "Senator," she said, "your heritage is Vsevoran." Her words hung there for a moment, and as she continued, her voice became forceful and fierce. "Without Vsevora, Oksana means nothing. It does not have a distinct culture. It does not have a history separate from Vsevora's. Our nation will not be held back by those who cling to the past, who celebrate bigots like Tibor, or who endorse barbaric practices like the *Vinnya*. We will put an end to radical sectarianism and destroy the blight that threatens this nation!"

Silence. Her rage could still be felt, reverberating through the hall. Her gaze shifted away from the Oksanan and over all of the other slack-jawed senators.

"This session is over."

Ishkara stepped away from the pulpit and stormed out. As soon as she disappeared, the hall erupted with chatter. The Oksanan senator stood still, defiant. The room was divided. Some approved of the chancellor's sentiment while others muttered their discontent. I slowly rose from my seat and followed after Ishkara.

Back in her chamber, Ishkara seethed and paced the room. "How dare he? Does he think he can intimidate me? 'By the spear of our horns!' The wretch."

I leaned back on a soft couch on the edge of the room. "You know," I sighed, "it was a good thing he decided to say something as stupid as that. If he hadn't, I think it would have gone a lot worse for you."

"Don't you start, Velodik!" Ishkara snapped.

"You need to be careful," I replied. "More outbursts like that, and you'll lose support. 'Oksana has no distinct culture'? You couldn't have chosen a worse target for a statement like that."

"It's true!" she growled. "Remember the Umbral Prince? Old Tibor would have been nothing without his patronage; he'd have died alone and forgotten."

I shook my head. "I've heard the murmuring. There's growing concern about your treatment of people's art and culture. There are many proud city-states, like Oksana, that treat all of that as part of their identity. To attack it is to attack the people."

Ishkara glared back at me but after a moment her eyes relented. She disliked it when I was right, but she was able to accept it at least. She sighed deeply and placed her gloved hands on her desk, leaning forward tiredly. Her head drooped down, as though she were unable to carry the weight of her branching horns, and she said something I almost never heard her say:

"What would you suggest I do, Velodik?"

The words caught me quite unaware, like being hit in the face with a brick. I shook the feeling off and sat up thoughtfully. The room was intensely quiet and from the silence an idea began to form.

"Well," I started slowly, "perhaps a bit of a spectacle. Something that will distract people. And you also need something that demonstrates that you're not out to destroy people's culture."

Ishkara slid into her seat. "What are you thinking?"

I got to my feet and paced about, as if to shake my own ideas out of some sleepy corner of my mind. "Maybe some symphony or a play... Something that brings people together from across Vsevora. Showing how our cultures combined are better than the broken pieces of each one alone."

A hint of a smile crept up and replaced her scowl. She nodded thoughtfully, considering her options. "Yes," she said. "We bring in people from each city-state—from every little backwater. But not music or theatre. It must be something timeless."

"An art exhibit, then," I suggested.

She beamed and her eyes lit up with excitement. "Yes. They'll be able to see it. We can distribute the images— plaster them up everywhere. People will see them every day. The message will be clear: I'm not destroying their culture, I'm creating a new one. Creating a new Vsevora..." Ishkara trailed off and she gently tapped her fingers together. I could see the plan was unfolding in her mind.

Chapter Eleven:
Creating a New Vsevora

The act of creation. It is a thing of beauty! Its fruit, while lovely, pales in comparison to the act itself. For it is through this act that one's spirit flows out and brings life to the void.

— Raman Bilhor, Yuliyan thespian

Siranna

"Chancellor Ishkara continues to aim her concerns at the Ok-sanan Council. Even as the propaganda ban remains hotly debated, she has added more fuel to the fire by calling into question their *Vin-nya* ceremony, stating that it—and customs like it—create cracks in a united Vsevora. The Oksanan Council responded by urging other city-states to join them in rejecting Chancellor Ishkara's proposed ban. Concerns mount as rhetoric grows harsher, leaving some to question—"

I turned the dial. Static. Even that was better than the endless rambling of politics. I didn't care about whatever was going on in the senate—I wanted to paint!

The static thickened as I adjusted the dial and fiddled with the radio antenna. The stupid thing never worked properly. Finally, the sound of a violin and a drumbeat—still marred by static, but good enough.

This was it. The one morning I had to myself. The one morning to work on whatever I wanted. The rest of my hours were spent at the printing press—not the most thrilling way to spend my time.

As the sun rose, I got myself some bread, threw some jam on it, and laid out my paints. I had two weeks left to complete this painting and submit it. And then maybe, just maybe, it would be selected to hang at the Gallery of Sophia.

Paintings and drawings were mounted on every wall: images of four-winged phoenixes rising from glass-crystal mountains; bare-headed people in fields of grass on one side, and then on the other, they scaled the face of a cliff, now adorned with spiralling horns; windmills decorated in gold and shades of red. I had dozens of finished works, any one of which I could have submitted, but I knew they would not be chosen.

Creating a New Vsevora: Emerging Artists in a Nation Renewed was the title of the upcoming exhibition, but my paintings were not the new Vsevora. They were stories, myths, and traditions of my home in Oksana.

This isn't what they want to see, I told myself as I shifted my gaze from piece to piece. For weeks I struggled. Despite everything up on my walls and the stack of sketchbooks riddled with ideas, I was unsatisfied. None of them were right. They didn't *feel* right.

Worst of all, time was running out. While Mr Pravda had given me a head start, the deadline was fast approaching and I felt no closer than when I began. My hands started shaking nervously as I finished spreading paint across my palette. I didn't know what I even planned on painting in the moment, I just knew that if I wanted to paint *anything*, I needed to set up.

I took a deep breath followed by a bite of my bread. *I can do this*, I thought. I chewed mindlessly, staring at the blank canvas in front of me. I tried taking a few steps back to adjust my view, but I bumped into a chair and stumbled, dropping the bread. It landed jam-side down. I sighed and softly cursed my tiny apartment.

My bed and night table were jammed right next to my easel, and a few paces beyond that was my "kitchen." I used the term loosely, as it was really just an extension of my bedroom and studio which just happened to include a wood stove. Almost every surface from wall to floor was covered with pictures, whether they were my completed works or the newspaper clippings I had laid out on the last few centimetres of empty space on the floor.

As I crouched down to clean up the mess, I imagined what it could mean for me if I could finish this piece. If it were accepted—oh, the doors that would open! People would want to see more of my work, they would recognize me, and before I knew it, the long days at the printing press would be a thing of the past. If I could just finish this one piece. And finishing it also meant I needed to start it.

I picked up the bread and sighed at the gooey jam on the floor. Next to it were a few pieces of paper stacked up in a loose pile. Under the pile was a picture of Chancellor Ishkara, but she was obscured—except for her horns. I found myself lost in the shape of them: branching, spiralling, and stretching out in a crown around her head. I saw pathways in her horns, each person making their own way, but all leading back from one place. All of Vsevora, united, but each city-state—each person—carving out their own path. That was it.

I forgot all about my bread and jam, and I picked up a pencil. I started sketching, my hands moving furiously. There wasn't much time; just one morning where I could focus entirely on this.

Hurriedly, I sifted through my brushes, gently feeling their bristles. I scowled as I realized I had left paint to dry on one of them. It crunched uselessly, the bristles stuck together. I hastily tossed it aside, picked up a clean brush, and put paint to canvas. My head was spinning with the images. My heart raced and I felt like I was flying, a smile etched into my very being as my hand danced to the staticky sound of the violin.

The white of the canvas quickly vanished as I applied layer upon layer of colour, becoming more and more vibrant. I had never worked so quickly and I soon became lost in the branching shapes of Ishkara's crown.

I stood back, letting out a rapturous sigh and grinned excitedly at the crown of horns. Flecks of opalescent paint shimmered like stars across the canvas and the brushstrokes gave the crown life and movement. It radiated with colour. I was thrilled.

Then I looked at the clock. I cursed and tossed my brushes and paints aside in a panic. I was late.

~ ~

A nerve-wracking eternity had passed before the letter arrived. It was sealed in wax, emblazoned with the crest of Vsevora. My hands trembled. I had just returned from an exhausting twelve hours at the printing press, but seeing the letter in my mailbox had been enough to reinvigorate me. My heart was pumping so fast I thought I would collapse.

I tried to steady my breathing as I sat on the edge of my bed, gripping the envelope tightly. I then panicked that the heat of my hands might somehow destroy the ink inside and I dropped it.

No. No. I can't do it. I can't open it, I told myself. If rejection awaited me, I wouldn't survive the anguish. All of my efforts would have been for nothing and I would toil forever at the printing press.

But what if it's accepted? I asked myself. It could change my whole life. I couldn't just *not* open it and leave it forever unknown. My thoughts were whirling around my head and spiralling out of control. I tried to steady my breathing.

This is it. I braced myself. *This is what you've been waiting for. Do it.* Gingerly, I pulled at the seal. The wax started to crack and I stopped. *I should preserve the seal, shouldn't I?* I looked for a letter opener, but every possible surface in my home was strewn with papers and every cubby stuffed with brushes, nicknacks, and paddiwacks—everything that wasn't a letter opener. *A knife! An ordinary knife will do fine.* I opened the cutlery drawer. No knives. My knives were all covered in jam. Even my cooking knife and my bread knife were both caked in jam. *Forget the knife,* I thought. *Forget preserving it. Just open it!*

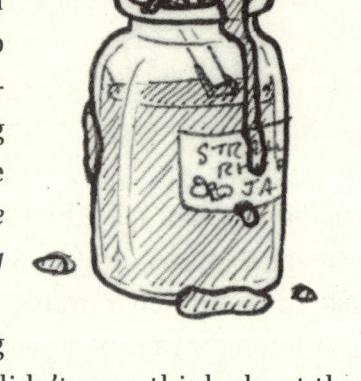

I tore into it hastily, shredding the seal and ripping the paper. I didn't even think about the possibility that I could be tearing apart the letter within—I just needed to get to the message inside.

"Dear Siranna Ankova," it began. "On behalf of the Gallery of Sophia, I would like to extend our gratitude for your recent submission to our exhibition: *Creating a New Vsevora: Emerging Artists in a Nation Renewed.* We received a large number of submissions, and the selection process was quite challenging. However, we have carefully reviewed them all and we appreciate the time and effort that you put into yours."

There was a stabbing pain in my stomach as I read. I tried to prepare myself for the worst. I waited for a "regrettably" or an "unfortunately." *How will I get my painting back?* I wondered. The base of my skull started getting warm. *Was it theirs, now? Doomed to collect dust in some basement forever? Or maybe they threw it out. They thought it was so terrible that they destroyed it—burned it!*

"Stop it!" I commanded, aloud. *Stop thinking and read.*

"We are pleased to inform you that your artwork, titled *Crown of Horns*, has been accepted—" I stopped and my hands shook. Accepted. It said accepted. I couldn't believe it. I read it again: "—your artwork, titled *Crown of Horns*, has been accepted by the committee and selected for inclusion in the upcoming exhibition. Your piece captured the essence of our theme and it will undoubtedly enrich our permanent collection. Details on your compensation are provided below. In addition, we look forward to meeting you in person, and cordially invite you to the exhibition's opening reception on..."

I stared at the paper and my jaw dangled like an empty swing. I lifted my arms in the air, gripping the letter in my quivering hands. Unable to contain my euphoria, I screamed in delight. I fell back on the bed, curling myself in a ball and then flailing my limbs outward as my scream turned to laughter.

Finally, I sat up, my mind racing. *What to wear? What to do? Could this be it? Can I quit after this? I need time off. Who do I bring? Maybe Mr Pravda. Bribe him to let me have the time. That could work, actually. What do I wear?* I tried to steady my breathing.

Chapter Twelve:
A Helping Hand

When you choose a dog, find the one that's half starved: the one with mangy fur and looks like it's been kicked around. Look it in the eyes. See how desperate it is. The more the better! No matter how you treat it, it'll thank you. And it will serve you finer than any pedigree.

— Senator Gavriil of Lyudmila

Kalrevi

I laid on the deck of the ship getting pelted by the rain, my hair strewn around me in muddy clumps. I gasped for breath, my muscles quivered, and my stomach roared: my body's reminder of how long it had been since my last meal and just how much energy I had expended to get where I was.

I got up shakily and looked around. There was no one on the deck—probably taking shelter from the rain. I stumbled to and fro as I tried to navigate; I had never been on a boat before, and so my grace and agility were not well adapted to its shifting movements. Nonetheless, I found the shadows and made my way below deck.

The boat was extravagant—more luxurious than anything I had seen since leaving my people. I crept along and found a closed door. It was unlocked. I peered inside to find a massive suite with fine, sculpted furnishings and a chandelier overhead. At its centre was a table spread out with delicacies that immediately made me salivate. There was no one there, so I ducked inside.

I immediately grabbed a hold of a thick, meaty bird-beast leg and ripped it from the carcass. The leg was massive and smelled divine. Without a care, I tore my mask off my face and let it drop to the floor as I dug my teeth into the seasoned flesh. My sharp canines rent the meat from the bone. I greedily devoured the first bite and then I opened my mouth wide. It stretched and expanded until I shoved the whole leg inside and then hungrily clamped my mouth shut. I pulled on the bone, scraping the meat off with my teeth, and threw it aside. I had barely finished swallowing when I reached my hand straight into some kind of buttery vegetable mash. My long, raven hair whipped around me and draped over bits of food on the table, but I didn't care as I continued to grab handfuls and shove them into my ravenous maw.

"Well, isn't this a surprise," I heard a soft voice say. My eyes shot wide open and I jumped. Quite literally. I jumped up and grabbed onto the chandelier above. I spun my head around and saw a wolfish man with sharp yellow eyes and a flat green hat. "That was quite the feat," he said with a smile. This was the first outsider other than Lucien that wasn't immediately afraid at the sight of me. "You know, I could use more people with that kind of athletic prowess back in Vsevora." He chuckled and stepped closer.

He knelt down and picked up my mask. I stared in horror as I realized I wasn't wearing it. My hands instinctively moved to cover my face, I lost my balance, and I crashed to the ground. My legs struck the table, knocking it over with me, and I was lost in a sea of vegetables and hot gravy. The hot mess scalded me and I flailed about like a wild animal. I got back to my feet and scurried to the nearest wall, pressing my back up against it and still holding a hand over my face. The whole while, this man's wolfish grin stared back at me.

The door opened and two more men burst into the room. They had horns with razor-sharp tips and when they spotted me, they looked like they were ready to gore me with them.

"Senator! Are you alright?"

"You there! You're under arrest!"

"Now now," the yellow-eyed man said, waving a hand dismissively at the two of them. "I think this young lady was just a little hungry and I startled her. That's all. You two get back to whatever you were doing."

"But Senator," one of them began, but was cut off.

The senator's demeanour changed from gentle to commanding. "That was an order. Leave us." The two horned men hesitated, but soon exited obediently. The yellow eyes turned again to meet mine. "My name is Velodik. What's yours?"

I said nothing. I just kept trying to push myself back into the wall and keep him from seeing my face. My eyes were locked on the mask in his hands.

His gaze followed mine and he nodded gently. He moved slowly toward me, holding the mask out at arm's length. "Here you are."

I snatched it out of his hand. If I were doing it properly, I would have turned my back to him in order to put the mask back on, but I wasn't about to leave myself so vulnerable. I pressed the mask up to my face and awkwardly fastened it back into place.

"I hope you're more comfortable now," Velodik said, stepping away and sitting on an elegant white couch. "As I was saying, my name is Velodik. Please, have a seat and join me. I would love to hear more about you." He gestured to a matching white chair across from him.

I glanced at the door. I could run for it, jump into the water, and swim back to shore. But how far had we travelled already? My arms would give out and I would drown before I could make it back. Was this boat really my bid for freedom or had I just imprisoned myself again? As the thoughts spun around in my head, Velodik smiled patiently at me. At least he appeared to be a cordial warden.

"Y-you're not afraid of me," I stammered as I cautiously made my way closer.

"Not at all. Should I be?"

"You're not from here."

"Quite astute. That's right; I come from Vsevora. Lyudmila to be precise."

I tilted my head. The names meant nothing to me; I knew so little of anything outside of the Greenshield. Velodik appeared to understand.

"Vsevora is a very large country across the sea. There are all kinds of people there; although, I must say, we don't have any masked dinner thieves like you back home. No, I suspect very few have even heard of the Feras, let alone have met one."

My eyes grew wide and I staggered back. At first, I thought that his kindness came from ignorance, but he understood that I was Feras. The words of the fearful city-folk ran through my mind: vampire, demon. He wasn't afraid like they were.

I thought of Lucien clawing at my mask and his greedy desire to sell our most sacred objects like trinkets. Was this man like Lucien?

Velodik continued to smile. He appeared to be warm and genuine, but I could tell there were other thoughts spinning behind his gleaming eyes. What was he plotting?

"What do you know of us?" I asked.

"Back in Lyudmila, we had stories of the Feras," he said, relaxing in his seat. "My parents would regale me with them as they sent me to bed. There were tales of heroic sailors battling the ghost pirates of the Phantom Sea; they described their void-white faces and relentless cunning. Or the story of Odarka of Lyudmila who fell in love with a Feras man and stole his face away from him. I had always imagined that they were more than just myths passed down from sailors, but I never expected to meet a real Feras." He was quite animated as he spoke and his smile never faded.

I had to admit, I was curious to hear more about these stories, but I couldn't let my guard down just yet. I stood still, the sway of the boat rocking me as I assessed everything that he said. My mind whirled with questions. Why was he being so kind? What was he after? Was he one of the marauders my father warned me about? Was he seeking out my people and planning to destroy the Greenshield?

"Why are you here?" I asked bluntly.

"I should be asking that of you, but all right. I came here for a bit of business," he paused to draw a deep breath, "and some pleasure. I was here as part of a diplomatic envoy. It's been mainly a dull endeavour, but there have been a few interesting highlights. This being one of them. But my business here is concluded, and we're heading back to Vsevora. If you were hoping to go back to the city after your meal, I'm sorry to tell you it's a one-way trip."

He didn't appear to be lying, but there was still something about him that made me hesitant to trust him.

"You weren't planning on going back, though," Velodik continued. "You look like someone who lost their home." I was surprised by his insight, but given my sad state, perhaps I shouldn't have been. I said nothing.

He retrieved a glass and a bottle from a cabinet next to his seat and poured; I could smell the fumes from where I stood. He spoke between greedy sips. "I'm a refugee myself.

I know what it can feel like to be alone. I understand how hopping aboard a vessel and escaping to a new life could be tempting, but there are dangers out there. Those who would lock you away for breaking the rules... who don't care for stowaways."

What was he getting at now? Was this some game?

He gestured again for me to sit and said, "I used to be like them. But I've come to realize that some rules are meant to be broken. Take this brandy. It's illegal, you know. Too potent, they say: unsafe for consumption. But I can make that choice for myself, can't I? And as long as no one else gets hurt, what does it matter?" He topped up his glass.

"You're welcome to return with me to Vsevora as my guest. And I can help you get back on your feet," Velodik said after a hearty draught of brandy, "but I want to know at least a little bit about the one who snuck into my cabin and spilled my mashed parsnips."

An uncomfortable silence followed. Everything he said was dripping with ulterior motives. Yet I felt that he was being honest and open. He meant me no harm, and more than that, he wanted to help me.

I thought over the seasons that had passed since I left the Greenshield—the hardest in my life. I certainly couldn't go back there. I had no one. I was alone. All I had left was this enigmatic man offering me a renewed chance at the freedom I had been running to for so long.

No; that wasn't all. I had myself. I had my mask. But that wasn't enough.

I spoke up at last: "My name is Kalrevi. I left home and have been lost ever since. I need help." All at once, I told him everything. I hoped this was finally my chance to be free.

Chapter Thirteen:
A Morning Stroll

The morning came. The sky was filled with smoke and the ground was covered in ash. In many ways, we only had ourselves to blame. We had hurt those around us, and it came back in the worst possible way.

— Baba Raisa on the Scourging of Ksenya

Velodik

I drew in a deep, happy breath as I awoke. The air had a scent of warm bread and dry sweat. I could always smell the morning baking from across the street. I rolled over in the sea of my bed and placed a hand delicately on the bare chest of the man next to me. It rose and fell steadily. He was still asleep. I sighed deeply, thinking back to the carnal delights of the night before. Before last night I had never known this man, and as I pressed my head against this stranger's chest, listening to his heartbeat, I felt a bit of remorse knowing that I likely wouldn't see him again.

With another sigh, I got out of the bed, wrapped a robe around me, and made my way out of the room. I paused at the mirror and looked at the glimmering yellow eyes staring back at me. I brushed a hand at the thick, shaggy grey hair on the sides of my face and then leaned forward. There were dark bags under my eyes. I frowned. Too many late nights? I looked back at the man still in my bed. I shrugged. It seemed like an even exchange. I quietly slid out of the room.

"Kalrevi," I called as I moved down the hallway. Her masked face quickly appeared out of the shadow and began to walk astride me. "When he wakes up, make sure to send him on his way. A little kinder this time. I do find it such a shame the way you tell them off."

"It's to keep them from coming back, Senator." Her voice was soft and airy, but not in a sing-song way. It was as if her voice was made from the wind itself. I often wondered if all Feras had this ethereal quality to them. She had certainly shown herself to be more charming than the first time we met; not that I blamed her then. She was hungry and afraid. I was happy to bring her under my wing.

"I understand. I just wish..." I trailed off. I didn't really know what I wished. It wasn't really practical for me to have some young man hanging off my arm at every function or event. It was far more convenient to just let them go and make it clear not to come cooing back at one of my offices. "All right. Send him away and give him a bit of a scare if you feel so inclined. Just be sure to wait until he's awake and dressed. The last time there was a naked man running off down the street, the neighbours got concerned."

"Understood, Senator."

"Kalrevi. Two things. First, a bit of humour. You can have a laugh once in a while." She stared back silently and I sighed as we came into the kitchen. I started grabbing some food. "Second, remember, just Velodik. I understand that we have a working arrangement, but I would like to do without the formality, even if it's just for breakfast."

"As you wish, Senator."

I stopped and scowled at her. I wished I could see her expression behind that mask.

"A bit of humour, Velodik."

I sighed and continued my preparations, waving Kalrevi away. "Just keep an eye out and then throw away my toy, all right?" *If all Feras are like her, I can understand why she was so eager to leave the colony,* I thought. *I'm going crazy putting up with just one of them.* I chuckled.

As much as I found her sense of humour to be a bit jarring, I rather enjoyed Kalrevi's company. And in the short time since I brought her to Vsevora, she had certainly become a valuable servant to me. Throwing out toys was only a small part of her duties. She had taken on the role of my own personal security. She had incredible skill in remaining unseen; she was quick and sharp—infinitely better than some brute trundling along anywhere I went. She had also proven herself useful in assisting me in certain tasks that I could not trust to any other Public Security officer.

The one catch was that I needed to buy another radio. I had caught her a few nights before in the midst of disassembling mine. She had reassembled it, of course, only to take it apart again the next day.

I had just finished preparing two plates of food when a scream came from my bedroom. A moment later, a shirtless man ran by, straight out the front door. I sauntered over to the open door and sighed as he hurried down the street.

"Kalrevi!" I called. Dutifully, her white visage reappeared at the edge of my periphery. "What did I tell you?"

"He was wearing pants at least," she replied. I could detect a hint of a smile behind the mask.

I shook my head and closed the door. "Let's take a little trip to the market together after breakfast." I gestured back to one of the plates. She nodded, took the plate, and flitted gracefully to her room.

I grabbed my own plate and stepped up to the largest window in the kitchen. I looked over at the nearby bakery. The scent of freshly baked bread was uplifting. I drew the curtain closed and pulled it together tightly to ensure the window was completely blocked. I glanced behind me. Alone.

I opened a nearby drawer; it was filled with polished cutlery made of pure silver. I then reached up into a secret compartment and pulled out a small vial half-filled with a white powder. I popped open the vial and gently sprinkled some of the contents of it onto one of the elongated nails of my hand. I snorted it up eagerly. There was an invigorating whoosh from my head to my toes.

As the shudder of pleasure subsided, I felt around the compartment and smiled. Two more little vials waited patiently for me for another day. Kalrevi had truly become a great asset to me.

"There's a grand art reception tomorrow night. I'm thinking of getting some new jewelry—something to make me stand out and attract attention."

"So I should be prepared to scare off another of your 'toys' I suppose," Kalrevi said.

I laughed, "You're figuring me out. Well done!"

We turned a corner to a street filled with market stalls and shops. Barkers beckoned people toward their wares, and there was a healthy bustle of activity.

There were more than a few intrigued onlookers gawking at Kalrevi as we approached. Some of the barkers even stopped mid-pitch as we passed—they were uneasy around her, even though we had been through the market several times before.

"Does it bother you?" I asked.

"What do you mean?"

"Their stares."

Kalrevi was quiet for a moment, then said: "I prefer the market at night. They don't see me then."

Another corner, another street full of shops, stalls, and spendthrifts. I spotted the shop I was interested in and started to beeline for it when I heard a sudden commotion.

"What's that?" Kalrevi asked. I was thinking the same. I shook my head and started weaving through the people to see what was happening. It sounded like shouting. A small crowd was forming.

"Stop the ban! Protect our culture!" There was a trio of Oksanans on the street corner shouting and waving flags. I looked around and noticed three more were going around to shoppers and rounding them up for their support.

Kalrevi moved in toward them. "Hold up!" I exclaimed but she ignored me. I growled and followed after her.

"Chancellor Ishkara wants to destroy our culture! She wants to ban Tibor of Oksana! We have to stand up and put a stop to it!" The leader was standing on top of a stoop and shouting as loudly as he could. He had a wide face for an Oksanan and dark, scraggly hair.

"Shut up you damn awk!" came a response from somewhere in the growing crowd.

The Oksanan crinkled his nose but otherwise didn't miss a beat: "It's not just our culture that she means to stamp out. The stories and music you all love, one by one, will be purged. We can't let that happen!"

I squeezed in next to Kalrevi. She stared intently at the leader as he spoke. "We should go," I hissed.

"What are they talking about, Velodik?" she asked.

"There's no time to explain. Let's just say they're overreacting. Oksanans are a melodramatic lot. Let's go."

"Please," she replied, "I want to listen. I want to understand what's wrong."

I sighed. I guess I couldn't blame her; she sought to discover the world beyond her monoculture. But I really didn't want to deal with these buffoons. Ishkara wouldn't take kindly to their actions, either.

I spotted a pair of Public Security officers on the edge of the crowd. As I approached, I noticed the second trio were still badgering people along the street. One interaction in particular caught my attention.

A young Oksanan woman with auburn hair was hurrying by. She appeared to be lost in thought, or perhaps ignoring the commotion. One of the trio closed in on her; he was much taller than she was and quite muscular. He blocked her path and she nearly stumbled into him.

"Hey! Come stand with us. We Oksanans need to stick together!" he said emphatically. I couldn't catch what the young woman said, but it was clearly a negative. The man refused to let her pass, and he continued his diatribe.

"Please, I don't have time for this. I have to get to work!" she exclaimed as she struggled to push past him.

I snarled as I watched the unseemly display and ran to the officers. "You there," I barked. "Put an end to this right now!"

The officers appeared to be shaken awake by my orders, but quickly sprung into action. One made their way over to the young woman and the malcontent while the other made for the leader.

"Enough! This is over!" they shouted. "Clear out!"

"You see? Ishkara's dogs silence us!" the leader cried.

I had enough. I stomped over to the leader, grabbed hold of him, and threw him off the stoop. I stood up in front of the crowd. "Disperse immediately! By order of Public Security, you need to clear out for your own safety."

The leader glowered up at me. I could see rage burning in his beady little eyes. I knew he wanted to get violent. Two more officers closed in from behind having heard the commotion as well. The leader looked over to them.

"Time to go," I said, my tone keenly serious. The leader appeared to be weighing his options. His bulky friend who had been harassing the young woman stomped toward us.

Then Kalrevi stepped in. She swooped in close to the leader. "Please. Be on your way," she said. There was more compassion in her voice, but with a grimness that put out the fire in his eyes.

The leader spewed out a curse and a few unkind epithets and then turned. He and his companions trundled together down the street, defeated. As I watched them disappear, I quietly hoped that tomorrow's art reception would bring the answers Ishkara needed to quell the likes of them.

"Well done, Kalrevi." I breathed a sigh of relief and stepped down next to her. She nodded her appreciation. "Come on. Let's get to the shop." I gestured to our destination across the street.

"You'll need to explain what that was all about," she said.

"It's complicated. I will when we get home. Let's just enjoy ourselves."

"What are we shopping for anyway?" she asked.

"Radios," I said. "I could use a few extras."

I held the door open. Inside were shelves upon shelves of intricate gadgets. As Kalrevi approached the threshold, her eyes lit up with wonder. I smiled and followed her in to help her pick out whatever she wanted.

Chapter Fourteen:
Golden Age

Peace rings true from the tops of the mountains to the depths of the valleys. Not because of me or my father before. Our peace is because of you: the people of Vsevora.

— Queen Vekara, the day of her coronation

Siranna

There I was at the Gallery of Sophia. The reception was packed. There must have been hundreds of people dressed in their finest clothes milling about. I hurried excitedly through the gallery to find my piece. It was hanging prominently on a long wall, flanked by two other stunning works.

Most stunning of all was that Chancellor Ishkara herself was there. She gave a rousing speech that kicked off the festivities, and she did it while standing right next to my painting.

"Thank you all for coming," she began. "I know that for some of you, myself included, the last number of weeks have been exhausting. So many artists came together from all across Vsevora to make this happen, and your efforts have been nothing short of extraordinary!"

The crowd applauded graciously and Ishkara smiled. She was dressed in a dazzling blue-violet—a colour richer and more vibrant than any of my paints seemed to be. She glistened with jewels and beads. I stared at her horns as they stood next to my painted crown. I glowed, now seeing her in person, excited at how well I had captured her horns.

"For many people across Vsevora, there has been growing concern. And I do not blame you. You have heard of the discussions within the Senate; you know of the changes we seek to make; you are worried about what is to come. Some believe that I would try to remove all that is beautiful from

Vsevora. I hope, looking around you here tonight at these beautiful works, you recognize that is not the case.

"Vsevora is maturing. Changing. In the past, we observed heartfelt traditions, we created majestic artwork, and we wrote great pieces of fiction. But as Vsevora changes, we must consider if these things live up to the values we aspire to today. We must ask if holding such symbols up to such a pinnacle only serves to hold us back.

"Instead of clinging to the harmful ideas of the past that turned us against one another, let us instead celebrate what it is that we can become. Let us turn to a new Vsevora. One represented here, tonight, by the talents and ideals of people from every city-state, from every background. The works on display tonight are a vision of a better world—a better life! One where all Vsevorans come together. Where we are joined in memories and love."

There was thunderous applause. I found myself taken aback by the passion of her speech. She painted a beautiful picture of Vsevora—one as lovely as any of the pieces that surrounded us.

Then, one by one, each of the chosen artists got a chance to meet the chancellor. We stood in front of our paintings as she gently moved from artist to artist. I shuffled nervously as she spoke to a Ksenyan artist next to me. I felt my stomach shifting and my breathing sharpen. I closed my eyes, trying to keep calm. When I opened them, there she was!

She was smiling warmly at me. Her eyes were filled with kindness, but they were sharp and intense. I was staggered by her presence; so much so that I couldn't speak. She didn't seem to mind, as though she had been through this exact scenario a hundred times before.

"I'm quite flattered, Miss Ankova," she said. "I think you really captured my good side!" She gave a gentle laugh and reached out to take my hand. "You've done a marvellous job. I look forward to seeing more of your work." She gripped my hand firmly and placed another warmly upon my cheek. Then she moved on.

I was dazed by the whole thing and only came back into reality when Mr. Pravda clapped a jovial hand upon my shoulder. I did end up inviting him, although not as a way to get time off. It seemed right; he was the one who helped me get where I was, after all.

"I'm impressed, Siranna. This is truly something special," he said in his soft, kind way. He beamed proudly at me as he gazed at my painting. "You have an incredible talent. I worry that it's wasting away stoking the fires at the printing press."

"I wouldn't have survived in Sophia if I weren't stoking them," I replied. "But thank you. I owe you a lot, Mr Pravda."

"I did nothing, child," he said with a bit of a chuckle. "It's your determination that got you here. I saw it in your eyes the first day we met. That's what made me give you a chance. That's what got you here, tonight." We smiled at each other for a quiet moment. His words warmed my heart. "Enjoy yourself, Siranna. Celebrate! You deserve it." He nodded and turned to leave.

I reached out and caught his wrist to stop him for a moment, and I gave him a tight hug. "Thank you," I said. When at last I released him, he wished me a good night, and left.

The rest of the reception flew by in a whirlwind: blurred faces of people I didn't know; tables full of fancy food; expensive drinks handed out for free; a parade of paintings that looked so much better than mine; dozens of compliments from people fawning over my work; feelings of pride and inadequacy all at once. It was surreal. As the night wore on and people began to filter out, I didn't want to leave. I wanted to live in that moment as long as possible.

This could be it, I thought. *Just a flash in the pan, and then back to everything as it was before: 12-hour days and a cramped apartment.*

I played nervously with my necklace, tracing the three strings of gold medallions that draped from my neck. I thought of the generations that had worn it before me. How much joy had this necklace been through? How much sorrow?

I missed my mother. I tried not to think of our final parting and instead remember happier times with her. Sometimes, during long shifts at the printing press or tear-filled nights alone, I wondered if I should have stayed. I wondered if I could bear the weight of continuing on my own path.

But I knew that back at home my path would have been fixed. I wouldn't have been able to hone my art the way I had in Sophia; whatever small pieces I could have created would have been lost in obscurity in that quiet village. I would have married Sylchiv. If not him, then some other man, a baker or a cobbler, and we would have had a child by now. Then I wouldn't even have that one morning each week to create. And I certainly wouldn't be standing next to one of my paintings on display for all of Sophia to see.

"Excuse me, Ms Ankova," a gentle voice pierced through my thoughts like the feeling of falling while on the verge of sleep—a sudden jolt that pulled me back into reality. A grey-skinned man stood before me. His face was hairy and peeking out from his flat green hat were a pair of pointed lupine ears. Back in Oksana, people would have called him a wolf-man or a lewd, but such phrases were impolite, to say the least. Even in all of my time in Sophia, I had never spoken with someone from Lyudmila before.

He continued before I could speak, "My apologies for startling you. My name is Velodik, Senator and Chief Minister of Public Security."

"Oh. Um. A pleasure to meet you, Senator. I'm uh... Siranna. You can just call me Siranna. No Ms Ankova required." I smiled and tried to be charming, but the expression on his face told me that I hadn't quite succeeded.

"Of course. It's a beautiful painting, Siranna. Elegant and regal," Velodik said, looking up at the crown of horns.

"Thank you so much, Senator. I truly appreciate your kind words. They're quite touching. Thank you," I replied, hoping to capture a balance between graciousness and respect. I had been floundering about like that all night, and this interaction didn't feel much better.

Another smile from the senator, and then he said, "Velodik is fine." I nodded. "The Chancellor has taken an interest in your work. She would like to see more of it."

"Wh-sh-really?" I stammered. I felt dizzy.

"Indeed she does. She thinks you have a true gift and that you captured her essence in this piece." We stood in silence for a moment. I didn't know what to say. He just kept his yellow eyes locked on the painting, carefully following the paths of the horns. "She asked me to extend an invitation. She would like you to come to the royal palace—first thing in the morning if possible."

"M-me? Chancellor Ishkara wants me? To come to the royal palace?"

"Yes. I hope you don't have any other arrangements."

"No! No. I mean um, I have no other plans. I would love to. H-how. Um. What do I—?" I continued to stumble over my words and Velodik turned to me with a laugh.

"Take this pass." He handed me a slip of paper with my name on it and the crest of Vsevora. "Give it to the person at the gate. They will instruct you from there. It was a pleasure meeting you, Siranna. Congratulations on your accomplishment." He gestured up at the painting again, turned, and began to walk to a group of well-dressed men and women, his furry, grey tail swaying gently behind him.

"Thank you, Sen, er, Velodik. Thank you!"

What is happening? I asked myself. I didn't know. How could I know? I barely slept that night.

Dawn's light sparkled behind the royal palace. I stood in awe, gripping my sketchbook tightly in hand, and I wondered if any of this was actually real. I didn't expect Velodik's instructions to work. Maybe this was all a sick joke. I gave the slip of paper to the person at the gate. To my amazement, the gate opened and I was escorted in by a burly woman with thick, pointed horns. I was brought up a marble staircase and into a gilded hall. There were blue satin drapes and indigo flowers filling the room. I felt woefully awkward and out of place.

"Ms Ankova! Such a pleasure to meet you!" a small, shrew-like voice echoed from above. A young woman with a tanned, fuzzy face made her way down the stairs, flanked on each side by a guard in a pristine, deep-blue uniform. I couldn't tell if she was incredibly small, if the guards were incredibly tall, or both. "I must say, that piece you made truly spoke to me. Simply magnificent! And it certainly caught the eye of the Chancellor as you well know."

"Thank you! When will I speak to Chancellor Ishkara?"

"Oh no, my dear," the shrew laughed kindly. "The Chancellor is far too busy to meet you, I'm afraid."

"Oh. I thought that's why I was asked to be here," I replied, confused and suddenly nervous. I wrung my hands together awkwardly and glanced around, looking for some hint at what to expect next.

The woman laughed again as she continued her descent. "Don't you worry! Everything is fine." She must have recognized my growing panic. "You will have an opportunity to meet with the Chancellor and spend some time together. Just not today. Come. This way, please." As she reached the bottom of the stairs, she made an abrupt turn. One of the guards that flanked her continued to keep pace while the other stopped and locked eyes on me. I stood there, frozen for a moment, until the guard gave a gruff cough, and I realized that I should follow the shrew.

I was led through a stream of hallways, past innumerable doorways, paintings, sculptures, and potted plants. We finally stopped at an unassuming and seemingly random door. The lead guard pulled it open and the shrew gestured for me to step in ahead of her.

I sheepishly stepped inside; it took a minute to comprehend what I was seeing. The room itself was at least five times the size of my entire apartment. Inside were wide, open windows overlooking a stunning floral courtyard. Dozens of blank canvases, easels, cabinets, and drawers were spread out across the room.

"What is this place?" I gasped. I gazed in wonder at the studio of my dreams. I had an anxious, excited feeling that I knew what was coming, but dreaded the response, knowing that what I imagined was too good to be true.

The shrew spoke in a measured and rehearsed manner, as if reading from a contract: "Chancellor Ishkara hereby extends an invitation to you, Siranna Ankova, to become the new artist-in-residence. The position is for the term of one year, which the Chancellor reserves the right to extend or terminate at her sole discretion. You shall be provided with room and board, a fortnightly stipend, as well as any necessary supplies. You shall, of course, be required to complete a few personal commissions from the Chancellor and from the Office of the Regency of Vsevora. You shall also have the option to work on personal projects as desired during your residency, and while approval is not required, the Chancellor shall have the right to review and approve of any such projects."

I couldn't believe what I was hearing. *I* was invited to become the new artist-in-residence?

"Yes!" I screamed. "Yes! Yes! Of course yes!" I smiled so much I thought my cheeks would fall off. I would have wrapped my arms around that svelte woman if it weren't for the guards menacing next to her.

"Wonderful," she responded coolly. "We'll draw up the paperwork and then show you to your room. We'll make arrangements to move and store any of your property. Welcome to the palace, Ms Ankova."

A whirlwind of joy blasted throughout my entire body. I wanted to jump up and down and shout out the window. I tried to contain myself as best I could. I was vibrating.

This is it, I thought gleefully. *This is the beginning of a brand new life. No more living by my mother's approval. No more 12-hour days breaking my back at the press. No more cramped apartment.*

I looked around the studio, imagining everything I could create. I saw mountains and phoenix fire. I saw the pathway of Ishkara's horns leading me to this paradise. I saw my self portrait—a new one—filled with flowers and sunlight.

This is the beginning of my golden age.

Chapter Fifteen:
Masquerade

I've learned one thing since I left the Greenshield: everyone wears a mask. I'm just the only one who shows it.

— *Kalrevi of the Feras*

Kalrevi

"It's a celebration, Kalrevi! You must come!" Velodik exclaimed.

"I don't understand. It has nothing to do with me," I replied.

"Yes, yes, I know, but..." Velodik let out a frustrated huff as he slipped on his dress coat. It was a deep green and had resplendent, golden clasps. He stepped up close to me and rested his hands on my shoulders. "You have begun to integrate yourself, now it's time to ingratiate yourself! You must make your presence known within the palace—your opportunities are boundless, Kalrevi!"

It was a strange dichotomy. He wanted me to be noticed, but much of my service to him was in secret—night-time shopping trips to procure vials of forbidden substances.

Velodik had told me a lot about his illustrious rise from constable to senator; he spent his life snaking his way into higher and higher authority. I concluded that he knew no other way, and so his default was to "help" me do the same.

"If you insist," I said with a sigh.

"Good! This is an exciting day," he continued as he turned and finished his preparations. "The propaganda ban has been put into place."

Vsevoran politics were confusing to me, to put it mildly. I didn't understand how so many people could all get into a room with one another, disagree on everything, and hope to accomplish anything. It seemed to move so slowly to reach any kind of decision. From what I understood, this propaganda ban had been discussed for months.

Behind the Greenshield it was clearer: my father was chieftain, and his word was law. Swift, simple, and absolute. Of course, I knew all too well the challenges and dangers that brought. Our community was beholden to a single voice, when instead, each of our voices should have come together to make a choice. The more I thought about it, the more I preferred the Vsevoran system. For all its complexities and conflicts, they were at least trying to bring all voices together.

Still, ever since Velodik explained this propaganda ban to me, there was something about it that didn't sit quite right.

"That's what those protestors were talking about," I said quizzically. "The ban that seeks to destroy their culture."

Velodik stopped in his tracks and turned to me, his face quite serious. "What did I tell you? That's not the case. It's about putting the old ways behind us. There's a lot of dangerous thinking that hurt a lot of people not so long ago, and if we allow it to go on, it jeopardizes everything that we aim to build today."

"I understand that," I replied. I understood, but that didn't mean I agreed. I dug in my heels. "But surely there are better paths forward than an outright ban. Why not focus on teaching people? Show them the errors and help them to understand."

"Kalrevi, stop!" He shouted louder than I had expected and his voice was severe. He glared hotly at me and once again closed the gap between us. He leaned in close. I stood my ground, but there was certainly something quite threatening about his sudden change in demeanour.

"Please," he said, much quieter and calmer now, "just stop. Don't speak like this in front of Ishkara."

I quietly considered his request. He hadn't lead me astray. "Of course," I said. "I'll be on my best behaviour."

Velodik smiled and the tension between us dissipated. He clapped me brightly on the shoulders. "All right. Let's get going then!"

"She's just going to stand there, is she?"

"What do you expect? She's my personal guard."

"That doesn't mean she needs to stand there. She's allowed to eat with us. I don't make Galva stand next to me awkwardly."

"She... she doesn't like eating in front of others." Velodik shot me a knowing look.

I stood in the corner of a lavish room; at its centre was a table laid out with a feast fit for royalty: vegetables lined up in a stunning expanse of colour; steaming roasts whose succulent aroma filled the air; custards and puddings aplenty; and an arrangement of decorative braided breads that served as the centrepiece of the table.

Velodik was greedily filling a plate. Sitting across from him was Ishkara. I stared at her hands as she gingerly pierced a cherry tomato with her fork, curious as to why she was still wearing her long, formal gloves. She glanced suspiciously back up at me, probably pondering the same thing about my mask. I couldn't help but feel that she was judging my appearance.

We were nothing alike. My dress, while vibrant red, was quite pedestrian: a plain form that flowed down to my ankles, where it streamed out in an intentionally tattered cut. Hers was fit for royalty in a deep blue-violet, with embroidery and fur. We each wore jewelry; I had golden bracers and anklets, although she had several jewel-encrusted necklaces and shining rings overtop her elbow-length gloves. My hair was a voluminous mess of black wisps while hers was cut short and neat beneath her curving horns. My mask showed no expression, while each line of her face and shift of her eyes showed a lifetime of rage, sorrow, and perseverance.

To Ishkara's right sat Galva: her personal guard. She had eyes like Ishkara's, but that's where the similarity ended. Velodik told me that Galva was Halynan; typically they had short, pointed horns like those of a goat and a coat of coarse brown fur. She was a broad beast of a woman.

She reached out with a thick, furry arm to steal away a large slice of meat from a platter. She moved so aggressively, I was almost certain she'd have rather gored the plate and ripped the meat away with her horns. I marvelled at her muscles and thought of my father. If there were anyone

who could beat him in a test of strength, it might have been Galva.

There was one empty seat remaining across from Galva. Back behind the Greenshield, we ate in private. It was a simple affair without the pomp and circumstance of well-decorated rooms, silver platters, or tight-knit gatherings for stories or songs. As such, the thought of sitting with anyone while they ate was disturbing to me.

"Just sit down!" Galva burst out suddenly. Her voice was rough and bitter. Ishkara shot her a glance and Velodik jumped slightly in his chair. A moment of silence hung in the room as all eyes slowly shifted toward me.

I expected, for a moment, that Velodik might say something. Perhaps he would assure them that I would be happier standing, or maybe he would dismiss me, or... anything really. But he said nothing. He just stared with the rest of them. He had this lackadaisical expression that seemed to suggest he wasn't interested in pushing things further.

Ishkara was more measured and curious. Her eyes were keenly focused on mine. I almost felt as though she could see straight through my mask. Galva was frustrated; a murky grimace carved into her fuzzy face.

I sighed. I didn't want to escalate anything so I stepped out from the corner and sat at the table. I placed my hands on my lap and stared across at Galva. She glowered back, snorted, and returned her focus to her plate. Ishkara glanced away from me and over to Galva, a bemused smile slinking across her face.

"Well good," Ishkara said, stabbing another vegetable with her fork. "I'm glad we're all comfortable now." She popped the vegetable into her mouth and bit down with a crunch. The others followed her lead.

I clenched my hand tightly as I tried to withstand the sounds of their chewing. I felt as though they were each leaning towards me, pressing their wet mouths against my ears, smacking their lips together and grinding bits of meat through their teeth, then lapping up pudding with their noisy little tongues. I felt my stomach churn. As delicious as everything smelled, all of this eating was making me lose my appetite.

"Let's take a moment to pause," Velodik began, and I breathed a sigh of relief that the noises would stop, if but for a moment. "A toast! To rallying the Senate behind a righteous cause!" He grabbed hold of a glass of wine and held it in front of him.

"Hear hear!" Galva shouted, bits of bread flapping out of her mouth as she spoke. She picked up her own glass and smiled broadly. She didn't smile often; I could tell by how strange and awkward it looked on her face.

Ishkara smiled as well, although hers was more natural. There was something else behind that smile—something in her eyes that I couldn't place. She picked up her glass and spoke with a practiced graciousness: "Thank you. It is a good day for Vsevora—another step toward a united future. The propaganda of our past will trouble us no longer."

The three gave a little heft to their glasses and all drank together. I shuddered at the gulping sounds as the wine squelched down their throats.

"All of the preparations are ready for the trip?" Velodik asked, setting down his empty glass.

"Yes, the arrangements have been made and we leave next week: a skyship to Ksenya, then off to Oksana before touring the east," Ishkara replied.

"Do you ever miss it? Your old home?"

Velodik's question was directed at Ishkara, but the words rang through me. It felt like an eternity since I had left the Greenshield. Somewhere, deep down, I did miss it. I missed wandering in the marshes. I missed sifting through the old records. I even missed the towering grass. But I wouldn't go back. Every time I thought about the things I missed, I remembered all of the things that drove me out— and everything I had discovered since I left.

The city of Sophia wasn't any different than the city across the sea, but with Velodik's help I could follow my own path. My service to him kept me out of the gutters, and I had learned about wonders that I had never imagined at home: radios, steam engines, and skyships as big as a house.

"No," Ishkara said, breaking me out of my thoughts. "I have no home outside of this place. I was so young during the Scourging. Whenever I go back to Ksenya... it means nothing to me." I had expected some twinge of sadness in her voice, but there was nothing. She sounded so matter-of-fact and cold.

Velodik quickly changed the subject before a silence could develop: "And you'll be bringing that new artist girl— Siranna. How's she faring?"

"She's doing exactly as we intended, as you well know," Ishkara replied with a grin. "She's obedient. We tell her what to paint, and she'll paint it. You saw the piece she did: 'Look to a future free of the violence from the past.' Coming from an Oksanan! It was perfect."

"Right from the reception, I knew just from looking at her: an unknown from the Oksanan countryside, poor—and desperate! Couldn't have asked for anyone better." Velodik laughed. "Bringing in an Oksanan as the artist-in-residence has put the Senate at ease. I don't think the propaganda ban would have passed without her."

"Except she can't paint Ishkara worth a damn," Galva muttered.

"What?" Ishkara asked. Her face became uncharacteristically warm and lighthearted as she turned her attention to Galva. "I thought she's been doing quite well. She knows how to capture regal authority."

Galva snorted again. "Her paintings look too sharp. You're softer than that."

Ishkara laughed, "Well, then she's doing a perfect job. I don't want to look soft. I need people to look at me and think of confidence and strength."

"Soft is important, too," Galva said. It was a surprising statement from a beast of a woman. I scoffed softly and caught a subtle glare from Velodik in response. I was glad to have my mask, so they wouldn't notice my incredulous smile. Galva didn't seem to care. Still focused on her plate as she kept shovelling food into her face, she continued: "You want people to feel safe. They should be comfortable with you and your decisions. Soft isn't threatening."

"I suppose," Ishkara said thoughtfully. "What do you think, Velodik?"

"Depends on who you're showing the paintings to," he replied. "An Olgan? Those bruisers want strength. The Oksanans, on the other hand, need to see a softer side of you."

Ishkara waved a dismissive hand toward Velodik. "The Oksanans will be fine. They've been eating up everything we feed them since Siranna was chosen. By the time our national tour is over, their council will be lined up to throw old Tibor's books on the pyre."

Velodik leaned in close and his tone grew more serious. "You've been pushing hard on them lately, Ishkara. First Tibor's poetry, and then you start ranting about the *Vinnya*. You may have gotten your ban, but push any harder and even this tour with Siranna won't help. You need to build up more trust."

Ishkara furrowed her brow. "I don't think I've gone too far on the *Vinnya*. It's a wretched tradition that endangers the lives of children."

"Children? I thought it was about becoming an adult," Galva muttered with a laugh.

"They're children!" Ishkara bit back harshly. "But the Oksanan Council doesn't see it that way either. Three youths nearly died just this year while climbing their forsaken peak."

The table grew quiet again except for the deafening cacophony of chewing. I could no longer withstand the noise, and so I spoke up. "What's the *Vinnya*?" I asked.

"It's an old tradition," Velodik said.

"It's a death march," Ishkara interrupted, solemn and intense. "Every season, the Oksanans send their children, unguided, to climb their tallest peak. The sun beats down, its light reflected by walls of glass. With no shelter from its onslaught, it grows hotter and hotter—enough to sear flesh! It's a brutal climb and barbarism of the worst kind. They torture their children for no other reason than that is how it has been. No one should be forced to make that climb." The room became silent. Even the chewing had stopped. I held my breath and stared at Ishkara. Her hand was gripping her fork so tightly that it was trembling. She was staring intently, focused, but she didn't seem to be looking at anyone or anything in particular.

She continued, her voice drained, but darkly serious: "It needs to stop. It needs to be purged. The *Vinnya* and anything like it will do nothing but hold Vsevora back. I won't let it continue."

Silence again. I saw Surrendra in her: controlling, and protective, yet passionate. There was a pain in her eyes that reminded me of his. Perhaps it was that memory of him that made me push back.

"I don't understand," I said, starting softly but growing bolder, remembering the arguments in front of the Greenshield. "Why should you get to decide what traditions they follow? That choice should be theirs to make."

Ishkara turned toward me sharply. Galva snorted and glared, while Velodik glanced nervously between the lot of us. The chancellor slowly rose to her feet. She loomed over the table, a striking and ominous figure.

"I do not need to explain myself to the likes of you," she hissed. "You have not been here long, urchin. You do not understand this nation like I do. You do not understand its people like I do. You do not understand what is best for Vsevora." She looked me up and down. "You should not bite the hand that feeds you." Her words were laced with venom. She turned from me over to Velodik. "You would do well to teach your pet, Senator."

I rose from my seat, straightened up, and stepped forward until we were practically eye-to-eye. Galva swiftly jumped to her feet with a harsh snort and Velodik started to stammer. Ishkara didn't back down; in fact a little smirk crossed her face as if she were excited to have riled me up.

Velodik hurriedly stepped up behind me and placed a hand upon my shoulder, gently guiding me away from the Chancellor. He expressed all kinds of apologies and tried to kindly laugh off the whole incident while hurriedly leading me out of the room.

Out in the hall, he let out a deep sigh, then glared at me and spoke in a harsh whisper: "You told me, Kalrevi. You told me you'd be on your best behaviour. Perhaps it's best if you didn't build a presence in the palace. You may do better operating out of the shadows."

"I'm sorry, Velodik, I honestly—"

He cut me off quickly. "Forget it. Let's head home. And hand me one of my vials."

Chapter Sixteen:
Slipping

The people of Vsevora are primitive. Their power sources? Wind and sunshine? Hah. If they knew how to harness real power, they would have no need for their petty politics.

— Oil, potentate of Mephistopolis

Velodik

Thankfully, Ishkara didn't bring up the dinner again. I considered telling Kalrevi to avoid the palace and the Grand Hall of the Senate; I didn't want her to run into Ishkara and create an awkward situation. However, Ishkara would soon be gone for the national tour. If everything went well, the stress caused by the Oksanans would wash away and the unpleasantness from the dinner would be forgotten.

On the day of Ishkara's departure, we walked through the palace together; Galva pulled a luggage cart just behind. I could tell Ishkara was quite tense: her shoulders were bunched up and she walked so briskly that Galva could barely keep up.

"You need to relax," I told her. She said nothing and picked up her pace—even I was having trouble keeping up. "At least avoid any unnecessary outbursts."

She came to an abrupt halt and swung around to face me. I nearly fell into her. "What's that supposed to mean?" she snarled.

I threw up my hands defensively. "That. That right there. That's what I mean." She glared at me furiously. "I'm surprised at you," I continued. "You're losing your composure more and more. Where's the woman from the gala all those years ago?"

Behind us, Galva grunted, perhaps unhappy that I was being so straightforward. It had taken us twenty years to get where we were; I couldn't let Ishkara throw it all away over some hot-headed Oksanans.

The flames in Ishkara's eyes quickly dwindled and she let out a low sigh. She turned and stared off thoughtfully. "I'm so close, Velodik. The golden age is nearly upon us." She looked back into my eyes. Even in a moment of turmoil or doubt, her eyes still held a kindling ferocity and determination. "I cannot let Vsevora fall to a group of withered old fools who refuse to move forward."

I studied the crow's feet around her eyes and thin lines around her lips. She certainly wasn't close to the "withered old fools" she derided, but I wondered if she still saw herself as the same young woman who met me in the café—who opened up to me in the library—so long ago.

"Your dream for Vsevora will not fall." I gave her a reassuring look, standing straight and with full attention to show her I was by her side and at her service. "Don't get impatient."

Ishkara stood quietly for a moment, before muttering softly: "I'm tired of saying you're right. I'm not going to let it happen anymore."

I smiled. There she was.

We started walking again until we reached the base of the stairs near the palace entrance. From above there came a loud banging sound. Siranna, the Oksanan artist, was clambering down the stairs bashing an easel against the railing as she went.

"What are you doing?" Galva barked.

"Sorry!" Siranna exclaimed. "I'm just,"—*bang!*— "bringing along," —*bang!*— "my easel! —*bang!*

"Why on earth would you need that?" Galva let out a harsh snort and her hairy face turned red.

"In case I need to paint anything while we're gone!" Siranna responded earnestly.

I stifled a laugh as the young woman clumsily made her way down the stairs and gasped for breath in front of us. She smiled awkwardly and stood up straight as she turned her attention toward Ishkara.

"All set, Chancellor!" She looked anxious and seemed like she might start hyperventilating as Ishkara scrutinized her. "I-it's all right if I bring this, isn't it?"

"Leave it," Galva snapped harshly. "You should travel light."

Siranna's face sank and I almost felt sorry for the poor girl. She was naive and sweet, but she clearly wasn't that sharp. Ishkara smiled, putting on a familiar show of warmth. She gently placed a hand on Siranna's cheek.

"My dear," she said, letting her hand linger, "this tour will go by so quickly. There will be no time for painting. You'll blink and it will be over!" Siranna's face sank even lower, but Ishkara's smile never faltered. Her hand moved to Siranna's shoulder. "But..." she paused thoughtfully and a little twinkle came into Ishkara's eye, "if the opportunity does present itself, we can get you whatever you need from a local supplier."

Siranna warmed up immediately. "That would be wonderful. Thank you, Chancellor. I'll just return this to my room!" She turned and immediately started to bang the easel back up the stairs.

"Wait!" I exclaimed. I had to hold in my laughter and maintain a semblance of authority. "We'll make sure one of the staff returns it. You need to go. The skyship awaits!"

In short order, Ishkara, Galva, and Siranna had left the palace. As I prepared to do the same, imagining I'd escape to my manse and enjoy a blissful evening with the pleasures of one of my vials, I was approached by a Public Security officer.

"Chief Minister!" he exclaimed with a wave as he made his approach. He stopped in front of me and gave a quick salute before he continued: "Sir, your presence has been requested at Station One by Commissioner Zradya."

I raised an eyebrow and looked at him quizzically. "What's going on that can't wait for the morning report?"

"I'm not sure, sir. I was just given the instructions. There's a carriage waiting for you."

I sighed. "Very well," I muttered and stomped by.

"What's all this about?" I asked, annoyed, as I marched into the Commissioner's office. Zradya sat behind her desk, poring over a handful of documents with a concerned look on her speckled face, framed by the horns that looped near her ears. Her black, curly hair didn't show a hint of grey.

There was always some satisfaction when I stepped into Zradya's office. She had done well for herself, but I still felt a certain smugness for having won out on that first promotion. "Surely there's nothing so important that it couldn't wait."

"I apologize, Senator," she replied. She could have been a politician. Her tone was well-practiced to give the air of sincerity and earnestness, but I could see through to the disdain she held for me. "I thought you'd want to see this before we took action. Please, have a seat."

I sat across from her and leaned back as she ruffled through a few folders on her desk. She selected a few papers from each and handed them to me for my inspection while she spoke:

"We've observed the recent activity in Agate Square: there have been larger and larger gatherings on a regular basis, ever since the new propaganda restrictions."

I threw the papers onto the desk and growled, "It's a night market, Zradya. Of course people are gathering there. This is a waste of my time!" I moved to stand but Zradya shot up and stared me down.

"Sir," she said firmly, "take a look at this." She produced a small stack of books and a pouch. I picked up a few of the books and flipped through them—storybooks and poetry— then tossed them haphazardly back on the desk. Next, I snatched up the pouch and peered inside. There were two little vials within, each filled with a familiar white powder. I stared, wide eyed, and then fought to regain my composure.

"Commissioner, exactly what is it you're trying to tell me?" I asked gruffly.

"These are just a few of the contents that we confiscated from a rowdy group of vandals. They procured these illicit goods from the night market. Radical, sectarian propaganda and drugs, sir. Based on our interrogations, it's not just one or two vendors. The whole market is rife with it." I tried to remain stoic and focus my thoughts, but she kept going: "We need to put a stop to it before it gets any worse. We're planning on sending in officers tonight."

"No," I shot back quickly.

She was startled. "But sir—"

"Not yet," I said, a bit more evenly this time. "Monitor the situation, but take no action. Let the night market continue."

"I don't understand, Senator. The laws are clear here. We should put a stop to this before it's allowed to spread."

"That's an order." We locked eyes. She was scrutinizing me carefully, waiting for me to let slip my motivations. "Situations like these need to be treated with care; we don't want anything to escalate. Leave the night market alone. Is that clear?"

"Yes, sir. Completely clear." I could tell she wasn't satisfied with my response, but I was confident she would obey. Zradya was more likely to stab me in the back than openly betray me.

"Good. Have all of this evidence sent to my office for my personal review. I will decide the next course of action after careful consideration." I stood. "You will not discuss this matter with anyone else." She nodded solemnly.

As I returned to the carriage, I clenched my teeth and cursed under my breath. If there were no more night markets, there were no more little vials. I needed to stall. But if I let them carry on for too long, undermining Ishkara's authority... I could lose everything.

Chapter Seventeen:
The Branching Path

As a child, I knew so little about our nation. People outside Oksana were like characters in a storybook—and often made out to be the villains. Now I've met so many different people. One thing is certain: there are no villains. Only different people, different walks of life, and different ways of thinking.

— Siranna Ankova

Siranna

A national tour! It was exhilarating. It was also exhausting.

Ishkara and I flew to every city-state. My artwork joined us, along with a few other select pieces from the gallery show that highlighted the exciting new path forward for Vsevora.

The importance of what I had created didn't dawn on me at the Gallery of Sophia, or as I was invited to serve as artist-in-residence, or even as we took to the skies on our grand tour. It wasn't until we arrived in Ksenya and I met Baba Raisa that I realized I was shaping history.

When we disembarked from the skyship, I was struck with a blast of cold wind. Ksenya was a frigid place—colder than even Sophia—high in the stony mountains. I wrapped a heavy fur coat tightly around me and shivered as we trudged through a well-worn path in the snow. My shoes were not appropriate for such weather; I winced as snow fell into them and stung my feet.

Ishkara showed no sign of trouble with the weather. She pulled up the fur-lined hood of her royal-blue cloak. It whipped about in the wind, but she was not slowed down by it. She moved with an ease and grace through the snowy path that I lacked as I clumsily stumbled behind.

We approached a great wooden building. It was unlike anything I had seen before. It had a great rectangular base and it arose in multiple levels with three tall steeples—each one rising higher than the next. Each level had a great, sloping gable roof with dark shingles. I gazed in wonder at the unique construction, then noticed that two of the steeples were not as worn or sun-bleached as the rest of the building. Much of the building must have been destroyed in the Scourging of Ksenya many years ago and reconstructed since then. The rebuilding had been done with great love and attention; I suspected that only an eye trained to detect subtle variation in colour and texture like mine would have noticed.

The entrance was flanked by a pair of young men in colourful, thick, woollen clothes. In front of them were two massive branches; at least, I thought they were branches at first. They were quite smooth and shaped like an elongated cone, and as we approached the young men lifted them up. They blew into them and as a powerful sound trumpeted into the air, I realized they were instruments. I marvelled at the unfamiliar tones as they echoed across the mountains.

We then entered the warmth of the building and I breathed a sigh of relief as I shook the snow off my shoes and loosened my coat. We were led through the halls to a large chamber where a group of Ksenyan delegates waited for us. They sat around a long table which was draped with intricately-patterned table runners.

A woman sat at the head of the table, and she was introduced to me as Baba Raisa. She was quite old—her face was covered in thick wrinkles, her skin was leathery, and I could see the thin bones of her arms as she raised a hand in greeting. What I marvelled at most, though, were her horns. I was amazed that she even had enough strength to hold her head up straight for how widely they branched around her. They climbed up and around her head, like a great bush, then extended downward in a gnarling path past her shoulders.

Ishkara and I were seated next to her on either side and she smiled warmly at each of us with her thin lips. Her eyes matched Ishkara's, although they seemed much more faded, almost like a thin sheen of white fabric was passed over them, but they were just as attentive.

As I marvelled at Baba Raisa, I noticed that Ishkara's countenance had changed. In all of my encounters with the chancellor, she had shown herself to be warm and kind, with a kindling intensity behind it all. As she looked at the old woman at the head of the table, Ishkara's warmth disappeared. She grew cold, distant, and perhaps even uncomfortable. I wondered at what the reason for the change could be, and then I thought of how difficult it must have been for her to be here at all. I knew that Ishkara was a refugee from the time of the Scourging. Could Baba Raisa have reminded her of someone she lost years ago?

As the question rolled about in my mind, I thought of our next stop in Oksana. I thought of my mother. I thought of her scowl. An uncomfortable feeling started up in my stomach and I tried to steady my breathing.

My thoughts were broken by the crackling voice of Baba Raisa as she spoke to me directly. "Your painting spoke to me, Siranna." I looked into her eyes and they seemed to glitter with fresh vibrance, as though the white sheet over them were being pulled away. "A Ksenyan woman's horns are her great pride. Each branch is a pathway in her life, extending and unbroken for all her days. To carry a crown of horns like mine is the greatest honour that one can bear, for it shows a long and storied life. It shows the wisdom that only comes from travelling through this life's many mountain paths."

She gingerly lifted a bony hand and gestured at one of the curling gnarls of her horn. "Sometimes," she said, "we do not know where these paths may take us, and sometimes they are not the correct path. Sometimes we become lost. But we still learn and follow the next path ever-forward." She lowered her hand and placed it on mine. She gave it a gentle squeeze.

"That is Vsevora now," she continued. "That is what your painting says. We became lost. We have been hurt and we have hurt one another. But that is not the path we need to carry on. There is wisdom that will carry us forward. Together." She turned her gaze toward Ishkara. "You will carry us forward, Chancellor."

Ishkara's discomfort immediately gave way to a bright and regal smile. "Thank you, Baba Raisa." She turned her gaze down the table toward the rest of the delegation. "And thank you all for your hospitality today. Indeed, we are embarking on a bright new future for Vsevora: one that shall break away from the paths that separated us and take us toward a single path together. Young Siranna here has captured that beautifully, and continues to serve as a beacon for Vsevora's bright future.

"Moreover, I want to thank everyone gathered here for their support in my recent initiatives to unite our culture together and move away from the divisiveness that we have seen in the art and literature of our past. We are forging a new Vsevora: one that celebrates the bold vision of artists like Siranna."

I felt my cheeks flush at Ishkara's words. As she continued, the conversation turned to politics, agreements, and other discussions.

I looked again at Baba Raisa and she was still looking back at me. She smiled again. Gazing into her eyes, I knew that what I was doing was shaping Vsevora for the better.

~ ~

Ksenya had left me hopeful and full of pride. Our stop in Oksana was not the same.

The closer we got to my homeland, the more my nervousness grew. By the time we docked at the skyport, I was doubled over in my seat, a hot fire rolling through my head. As much as I tried to push them away, thoughts of my mother kept flooding back. What if she came to see me? What would she say? What would I say?

"It's time to disembark." A heavy hand caught my shoulder and heaved me up straight. Galva glowered down.

"I-I'm sorry. I'm not feeling well. I just need a few more minutes," I stammered.

"No time," Galva grunted back. "You need to put on a good show for the Oksanan Council." She clasped my other shoulder and helped me to my feet—which was to say she dragged me up. I stumbled and felt queasy, the heat in my head radiating down my neck and into my shoulders. Galva gave me a not-so-gentle shove toward the exit. I felt like I might throw up.

Outside, a crowd had gathered. The dock was high above the city, overlooking the massive port where travellers, merchants, and citizens gathered. The area below was full of people, a sea of spiral horns that excitedly swayed about.

As I shakily stepped out of the skyship and onto the platform, people cheered. My knees trembled and quaked. I didn't understand. Why were they cheering? What was going on?

"Looks like you've become quite the local celebrity." Ishkara was standing far ahead, just outside of an elevator that would bring us down below. I couldn't quite read her expression. "Come on. Let's go greet them face to face."

As we went down the elevator, I felt like something was sinking down into my bowels at the same rate. *I should be happy,* I told myself. *This should be exciting. Everyone loves me. Why do I feel this way?*

As we maneuvered through the crowd, I tried to keep the growing discomfort at bay. I turned my thoughts outward.

There were bright, smiling faces. I saw massive posters on signposts and along the walls of buildings—posters with my artwork. There was Ishkara, looking boldly to the future, surrounded by sunflowers and amaranth. "Look to a future free of the violence from the past," the posters said.

I noticed something in the distance—something off. Ishkara was looking as well; a deep frown weighed heavily on her face. Some of the posters were painted over. I couldn't make out what had been done to them. I squinted and tried to focus, but a headache took shape.

We made our way toward a stage that had been set up for our arrival. I weakly stood to the side as the turmoil in my head and stomach continued. Ishkara clasped hands with a tall, stony Oksanan. They exchanged a few words that I couldn't hear and then Ishkara stepped forward, overlooking the crowd. The people grew quiet.

Ishkara wore an icy blue dress. It was far lighter than what she normally wore, probably to combat the heat of

Oksana. As she lifted a hand up in a gentle wave, I realized that she still wore her long gloves despite the heat. She started to speak.

I couldn't make out what Ishkara was saying as my focus turned to the crowd. I ran a finger along one of the medallions around my neck and I scanned the sea of faces to see if I could find my mother somewhere amongst them. Everywhere I looked, I thought I saw her familiar scowl. I thought I saw her glaring at me, judging me, hating me. I gripped my necklace, pressed it against me, and my breath quickened.

I felt dizzy. I closed my eyes in the hopes of keeping myself steady, but the dizziness only got worse and worse. Just as I was about to topple, someone grabbed my hand. My eyes shot open and I saw Ishkara next to me, grasping my hand and drawing me close. Had she noticed? She was helping me. The heat started to fade. Ishkara pulled me forward to the front of the stage.

She called out proudly: "This young artist is a shining example, not just for Oksana, but for all of Vsevora, of what we can accomplish when we work for the future of our united nation!" The crowd cheered in response.

I looked again at the mass of smiling faces, my free hand still following the strands of my necklace as my thoughts called out: *Mother... Are you out there? Where are you? Do you even care?*

After the speech, we were brought into the grand chamber of the Oksanan Council. I was thankful for a chance to sit. The dizziness and the heat in my head had finally subsided, and I pushed the intrusive thoughts away while Ishkara and the Council spoke.

"It appears you have a problem with vandals," Ishkara said. There was an unfamiliar harshness in her voice that caught my attention. I noticed that her expression had become stern and authoritative.

"What do you mean?" one of the councillors asked.

"There was graffiti on several of the posters. Harsh red lines stroked across my face and 'through flame' written on many of them."

The councillor had a bemused expression on their face. "Well, not everyone has taken kindly to the new laws that limit our ability to celebrate Oksanan culture. I don't blame anyone for that sentiment."

"So, you wish to nurture violent extremists?" Ishkara snapped. "'Through flames' certainly isn't a peaceful call."

"Come now, Chancellor, I thought you were familiar with Tibor's works.

> *'Carried up on phoenix wing*
> *Our hearts' music flies*
> *Call out, stand tall, and sing*
> *Through flames spirits rise.'*

"It is a poem about the indomitable nature of the Oksanan spirit, not a call to violence."

Ishkara narrowed her eyes. I saw a fierce burning in them that I had never seen before. "Excuses," she hissed. "You obfuscate the truth, Councillor, with pretty sentiments. The call to violence is clear, and no double entendre can hide it. This is exactly the kind of dangerous rhetoric that our new laws aim to put an end to.

"This council has an opportunity. Here and now. A chance to turn the tide and forge a new path in a united

Vsevora." Her tone became uplifting as Ishkara turned her attention away from the one councillor and addressed everyone in the hall. "Look at Siranna here. She is not held back by Oksana's past. She has embraced the new culture of our nation."

The adversarial councillor scoffed. "She's a puppet, not an artist. Those posters she makes for you—that's not culture; it's empty drivel that panders to your agenda." Their words cut deep and the headache came back with a vengeance.

I couldn't take it. I hurried to the exit. There was a clatter of voices behind me, but I couldn't hear what anyone was saying anymore. I thought, perhaps, that the other councillors had tried to defend me; Ishkara said something about a bold vision; someone questioning if I was truly Oksanan. It all blended together into a whirling echo that seared as it radiated through my skull.

I slammed the great doors behind me and leaned up against them, gasping for breath, tears streaming down my face. I doubled over; suddenly my necklace felt so heavy around my neck. The voices in the chamber were getting more heated. The only words that I could make out anymore were my mother's:

"You may think you are strong now, but the world is heavy and it will crush you beneath its weight. I do not think you are strong enough to carry it alone, Siranna."

~ ~

Things got better after we left Oksana; each stop on the tour was more akin to our visit in Ksenya. I got to see each and every corner of the nation, eat foods I had never tried before, and saw all kinds of clothing, architecture, and customs. By the time we got back to Sophia, I was thankful to have a chance to rest and get back to my work.

There was a problem, though. For all that I had seen, done, and experienced, I had no idea what I wanted to create next. I played around with a few more portraits of Ishkara, but I wanted to do something different. Something that spoke to my experiences across Vsevora. Something that spoke to all of the cultures I had encountered. Most of all, something that spoke to me.

I was frustrated, staring at a blank page in my sketchbook, wondering why I couldn't put anything onto the page. I thought of the beautiful architecture in Ksenya. I remembered the stunning coral beads that they made in Halyna. I tried drawing the sculpture of the ravenhart from the library of Lyudmila. But nothing felt right.

I sighed and tossed my sketchbook down next to me. I closed my eyes, hoping that something would dance through my mind and excite me enough that I had no choice but to create it.

I sat there in silence for some time, cozied up in an alcove in a deep corner of the palace. There were many such places here where no one went, and it allowed me a chance to be alone and to think.

The silence was broken by the sound of shuffling footsteps and hushed voices. I held my breath for a moment to listen better. There were two of them, and they came to a stop nearby. I could almost make out what they were saying. I peeked out of the alcove to listen better.

I saw them in a dim corner: a man and a woman. The man I recognized as Senator Velodik. The woman I didn't know. She stood with her back to me; all I could tell was that she wore red and her hair was black as pitch. Still, there was something familiar about her, as though I had caught glimpses of her from the corner of my eye at some point. I listened carefully as their tone became more urgent.

"I thought you were going to come up with a plan so I could stop doing this," the woman said.

"I know, I know," Velodik growled. "But I haven't. It doesn't matter."

"She's back. She'll find out soon and then it's all over."

"I've got it all under control."

"Then why do you seem so nervous?"

"I'm not nervous!" Velodik snapped, his voice echoing. I pulled back into the alcove as the two looked around to make sure the outburst hadn't caught someone's attention. No one heard them but me. I had never heard Velodik yell like that; it was unlike him. There was something primal about it that frightened me.

"It doesn't matter," the woman said. Her tone remained even and she seemed unfazed by Velodik's temperament. "I'll go shopping at the night market regardless. But if this keeps up, you'll get hurt."

"I told you, it's under control. Now quickly, off to Agate Square with you. I'm almost out."

"You've been going through them faster than usual. I'm concerned that—"

"Don't start lecturing me, Kalrevi. Just go to Agate Square and get it done," Velodik said in a cold, commanding tone.

The two separated. The woman, Kalrevi, hurried off silently and disappeared down the hall. Velodik remained behind for a moment, growling to himself before stamping away in the opposite direction.

I shuffled back into the alcove and leaned against the wall, thinking about what they had said. My curiosity was growing.

I remembered going into the city of Oksana with my family once and we visited the night market there. People were bustling around everywhere. It was so dark, I could barely see my hand outstretched in front of me. There were all kinds of wares strewn out on blankets that they showed off with candlelight.

We had stopped at a stall where an old man had an arrangement of watercolour pigments in neat little rows alongside little buckets filled with brushes. My father had bought me my first paintbrush and a few colours for me to explore.

The warm memories flooded through me and I shot up straight. I needed to go to Agate Square.

Chapter Eighteen:
The Night Market

Okay, okay, okay. I'll make you a deal. Three silver and your daughter's hand. Kidding! Kidding! Keep the silver.

— *Yeska the haggler*

Kalrevi

Velodik and I made for strange friends. The longer I served him, the more I questioned why I didn't leave and take my own path. Perhaps it was the support he offered: a position of authority as his guard, safe lodging within his mansion, and the freedom to do as I wished outside of my obliga-

tions. More than that, though, I think it was the companionship.

Velodik was crude and snakish, but he was the only person I had met since I left the Greenshield that wasn't disturbed by me. If ever any of Sophia's locals caught sight of my mask, they saw it as an unsettling and frightening visage. When I visited the halls of the Senate or the palace on official business, the guards and workers were uneasy around me. And, of course, Ishkara certainly didn't care for me—our recent dinner together had made that abundantly clear. I struggled to find any real connection with someone else in Sophia.

Velodik had brought me freedom and lifted me out of the darkest of my days. I felt I owed him something for that. Still, he found ways to try my patience.

"Kalrevi! Kalrevi! Come over here!" he exclaimed one night.

I stepped into the room to find a gaggle of Sophian elite, and Velodik standing in front of them, thoroughly intoxicated. He had them all on one side of the room to form an audience and he looked as though he was preparing to put on a show. When he saw me, he let out a joyful yip and waved for me to come closer.

"Kalrevi," he exclaimed, "I've been telling everyone about you. She's a real Feras, you see! A living legend!"

Tales of the "Feras vampires" hadn't made their way through much of Vsevora outside of Lyudmila. Velodik delighted in those tales and enjoyed regaling his guests about all of the twisted stories he had heard about us in his childhood.

This wasn't the first time that he had paraded me out for one of the dinner parties at his mansion. At first, I thought he wanted to give me an opportunity to meet others who would look past the mask. That was not the case.

He looked at me with a drunken grin and continued: "Tell them, tell them about the mask." Before I could speak, he blurted, "They never take it off, you see! Never! But I saw her without it!"

He laughed and I clenched my fists. To show your face or to look upon another Feras' face was a great taboo. Should such a sighting ever come to pass, the event should be kept silent. And Velodik was sharing my shame with the entire room. I told myself that he didn't understand our customs and tried to keep calm.

"Let's see, Kalrevi," he said mischievously. "Come on, be a dear, take it off to show everyone!"

Velodik reached toward my mask and my hands snapped into action before I could even think. I grabbed his outstretched hand and wrenched it behind his back. He let out a yelp, like a dog who had just been kicked, and the gathered elite let out a horrified gasp. I immediately released Velodik and stepped back, horrified at the thought of what might happen to me for my assault.

There was an eruption of laughter from Velodik. "Look at that!" he cried. "Lightning fast reflexes and the strength of an Olgan, all in that svelte little frame! Absolutely stunning, isn't she?" He hadn't missed a beat. Had that been his intention all along? Or had years in public office taught him how to fabricate a quick cover-up? Neither Velodik nor I discussed the incident after that, but he never tried touching my mask again.

While those kinds of incidents should very well have been enough to make me leave, he wasn't all selfishness. When we spoke together, just the two of us, I felt like he regarded me as an equal—as a friend. I didn't have that back in the Greenshield. My father never saw me as capable enough to manage on my own, and as the daughter of the chieftain, most others were wary around me.

"What shall you do today?" Velodik asked me one morning. He was lounging on a long sofa, relaxing in a sunbeam. I was sitting nearby.

"What do you mean?" I replied.

"What do you think I mean?" he laughed. "Certainly you're not just going to sit there all day."

"Well, what would you have me do?" I asked.

"Hah! Kalrevi, you may serve me but you're not my servant. I don't need you today. You're dismissed. Do whatever pleases you! Break some more radios or go visit the library. Something—anything! What do you want to do?"

I sat in silence for a moment. It felt like such a bizarre question. It had been so long since I had left my home that I had forgotten why I wanted to leave the Greenshield to begin with. I wanted to explore, to learn, to see, and to experience everything and anything that I could.

Velodik helped me with that. He showed me every corner of Sophia; he took me to all of the interesting places he had discovered during his days as a constable. He helped me to acquire engines and clockworks from across Vsevora so that I could tinker and learn. He tried to help me grow my status—and while the attempt hadn't worked out—he did it to afford me even more opportunities.

For all of Velodik's lechery, selfishness, and insensitivity, he was my friend. And I was growing more and more concerned for my friend.

I had a regular shopping trip to complete for Velodik. It had become one of my favourite duties, despite the unscrupulous nature of it. Under the cover of darkness, I would make for Agate Square in the heart of Sophia, and visit the night market.

I was told that night markets were an old custom that carried on throughout Vsevora. For the most part, they were quite above board: vendors of all sorts selling food, artwork, and oddities. There were, of course, others who sold much more objectionable goods. That was always my purpose for going there: to procure a few vials from a shifty-looking merchant selling "substances of pleasure."

Things had changed in recent weeks, though. The night market was getting busier and garnering more and more attention. Velodik had told me about Public Security's desire to shut it down, but that he had given them orders to leave it be. Public Security complied, but that only made matters worse.

With no sign of Public Security intervention, the night market had made way for the black market. The number of peddlers with illicit goods increased, and the night market had become a target for thieves and scoundrels. That didn't stop people from coming. In fact, it was busier than ever before.

I tried to warn Velodik that he needed to act soon or else something would go sour. He didn't care for my warnings, though. He was only concerned with his vials of powder— and he was consuming them at an ever-increasing rate.

I was becoming a frequent visitor to the night market, which raised concerns that I would be more and more likely to be recognized. No one else in Sophia wandered the streets in a white mask. Luckily, no one else in Sophia was familiar with the prowess of a Feras. In a strange way, my father might have been proud of me for the way I continued to employ the skills he had taught me. Usually I made it through without any trouble. That was not the case on this particular night.

The night was like any other. The market was bustling: dozens of little makeshift stalls surrounded a great stone angel that stood at the middle of the square. People were milling about and sifting through wares to find new treasures. They were all illuminated by the stars above and by little twinkling strings of light that stretched and crisscrossed from one end of the square to the other.

I crept through the crowd stealthily, the hood of a heavy cloak obscuring my mask. I passed some barker, who loudly offered to both buy and sell jewelry. I was reminded of Lucien, the merchant to whom I had sold most of my possessions after I left the Greenshield. There were so many like him at the night market, trading in precious heirlooms and dealing with the desperate. But I was desperate no longer. An unseen smile spread across my face at the thought.

I came upon a simple tent with an antlered man sitting cross-legged beneath it. He had a peculiar air about him; he seemed far more relaxed than anyone selling illegal goods ought to be. He was draped in all kinds of patterned fabric and he had various herbs and spices laid out on a blanket in front of him. He was serving a customer who was carefully choosing between two similar herbs. They went back and forth, taking big whiffs of each of them, and agonizing over the choice. I stared impatiently.

The shifty merchant caught sight of me and said quickly to his customer, "One time special—just for you. Buy one and get the other for free."

"Oh! How exciting!" the customer exclaimed. "Now which one should I buy so I can get the other free?"

I rolled my eyes and the merchant was caught off guard by the perplexing comment. He gave a sigh and pointed haphazardly at one. "Go with that one. It's the better choice."

"Ah, thank you, my friend!" There was an exchange of coin and goods, and then the customer slipped away to peruse some other stalls.

No one else was approaching. I leaned in closely to the merchant and dropped a small bag full of coins in front of him. "The usual," I whispered.

He grabbed a small box that sat next to him, partially obscured by all of the fabric he wore. He opened it gingerly and withdrew a small handful of the little vials filled with white powder. He held them aloft, although careful to keep them hidden from anyone but me. I swiftly pocketed them and turned away, hurrying back into the crowd.

I took some time to explore a little bit more of the market before I retreated out of the square. There was one stall that seemed to be garnering a fair bit of attention. There were a number of people gathered there, and all of them had the long, spiral horns of the Oksanans.

I was curious why so many were gathered. Was it another protest, or something more nefarious? I made my way over, squeezed through the tight crowd, and peeked curiously over shoulders to see what they were up to.

"Come along now, don't be shy. But not too much ruckus, now. Can't be telling everyone about this," the merchant called out in an even tone, just loud enough for those gathered around to hear. "This is a real treat! An illuminated volume containing a dozen poems by Tibor of Oksana!" There was an excited murmur. "That's right friends. Only a few copies to be had. But keep quiet about this; it is prohibited material after all. Can you believe that something as lovely as this is considered radical propaganda?"

The merchant pulled out a lantern and held it above his head. Dim yellow light spilled over him. He wore a shoddy brown cloak overtop of an embroidered tunic and baggy blue-grey pants. Each of his large ears had thick gold-coloured rings pierced through them and he gazed out at the gathering crowd with wild, excited eyes. In his other hand, he held an open book up to the light that he drew in close to his face. With a dramatic voice, he started to read:

"Upon the road of glass I tread
One foot before the other.
With every step I leave behind
The child that once I was.
With every step forward I shall become
The man I'm meant to be.

Within these graves, this land of dread

I bury my father and my mother.
Our fates once were so entwined
And I wonder what it does
To me to be left so numb.
The ones I ne'er again shall see."

There was a reverent hush from those who had gathered there as they listened to the poem and allowed its meaning to sink in. I was surprised to find that it had affected me as well. I couldn't help but think of my father and the uncomfortable knowledge that I would likely never see him again. I remained in still thought, letting the words hang and echo through my mind, until a voice finally broke the silence that we shared.

"I'd like to buy one," she said softly.

The merchant smiled. "Of course!"

A young Oksanan woman stepped forward. She had a soft face, bright eyes, and auburn hair; she wore a necklace of gold medallions. She was the artist-in-residence at the palace: Siranna. I drew back, pulling the hood of my cloak further over my mask, and slipped away from the stall to make sure I wasn't seen.

I kept watch from afar as she left the stall with the book clasped tightly against her chest. I wasn't about to report what had happened, of course. It would only serve to give light to my own illicit dealings. But I wondered if this Siranna was wise enough to keep her own vices hidden. I decided to follow, if only for a moment.

She made her way to a few other stalls, procuring a few innocent ornaments, fruits, and spices. When at last she began to make her leave and head back toward the palace, I noticed that I was not the only one who was paying attention to her. At the dark edge of the square, away from the bustling crowd, two young men slowly closed in on her.

"A beautiful necklace you have there," one said with false kindness. "I bet my girl would love it."

Siranna froze in her tracks. She stammered, "W-well, she'll need to find one of her own. Th-there are some Oksanan merchants; see if they have one!"

A laugh from both of them and they drew in close. "Nah. I think she wants that one."

"You can't have it!" she exclaimed. As she rose her voice, they took action. One grabbed hold of her arms while the other reached for the necklace. "Stop it!" She thrashed about and kicked up her feet into the stomach of the man in front of her. He was winded, but she wouldn't last much longer, and there was no one else in sight. She screamed: "Security! Help—" The one behind her clasped a hand over her mouth.

I leapt into action, running toward them as quickly as I could. I grabbed the man who held Siranna, pried him away from her, and threw him to the ground. I gave him a swift kick which sent him tumbling across the cobblestones.

The man that Siranna kicked had regained his composure and was now barrelling towards her. She let out a piercing scream. People were starting to pay attention now.

I rushed over to her as the man grabbed a hold of her blouse and tried to yank her to the ground. I snatched his wrist, then twisted it behind his back. I threw him down forcefully.

"Run!" I exclaimed, making sure to keep Siranna from seeing my mask.

She responded quickly. She grabbed the poetry book from the ground, blurted out a quick word of gratitude, and ran in the direction of the palace.

A few people were hurrying in my direction and there were more calls for Public Security. I shoved the thief to the ground again as he tried to pull himself back to his feet and then ran off as quickly as I could.

As I darted through the street, I worried how much longer this could last. Velodik had no plan to deal with the night market, and the cracks were forming faster.

Chapter Nineteen:

Haze

"The depth of Velodik's compassion and the quality of his character are unrivalled. There is no better person to oversee the protection of our citizens."

— Senator Ishkara at Velodik's vestiture as Chief Minister of Public Security

Velodik

I rolled the empty little vial in my hand, smiling quietly as it rocked back and forth. I set it down gently on my desk and let the vial's contents overtake me. I breathed out a happy sigh as I picked up the most recent report from Commissioner Zradya and threw it over my shoulder.

"Robbery! Theft! Battery! Assault!" I shouted in a mocking falsetto. "Whatever will we do!" I broke out into a fit of laughter. "Poor pathetic people: you're in a precarious position! How pernicious of me to pooh-pooh your pitiful predicament. Perhaps... *puh...puh...* periwinkle? *Puh...* pissants!" I lost myself in giggles and continued to pop my lips together for as long as the sensation delighted me.

I cheerfully made my way down one of the many halls of the palace, intending to make a little stop by Ishkara's office before retiring for the day. I was fairly sobered up, but I was still riding the delight of my high. Something caught my eye on the way and I paused at an open doorway: the studio of the artist-in-residence. I spied the young woman in front of a canvas streaked in vibrant red paint. Curious, I peeked my head inside.

The curtains were drawn, although the drapes were different here than in every other room of the palace. Rather than blue satin, they were made of a thin material and delicately white. It allowed the sunlight to diffuse throughout the room with a soft, natural glow.

The room was filled with canvases and easels. There were various portraits of Ishkara: she was with a group of playful children, or she was standing proudly outside the royal palace, or she was smiling between an Olgan and an Ostapan who were shaking hands. "Ishkara is Harmony" was written across many of the paintings. The Chancellor had become quite fond of the slogan and it had already started plastering the streets. In fact, the phrase was all over the room, as well: evidence of Siranna's repeated practice at calligraphy.

I had actually rather enjoyed looking at her progress when the opportunity presented itself. Her talents were not the primary purpose for her presence in the palace, but she really was quite skilled.

More than her prowess, it was Siranna's Oksanan heritage that Ishkara found particularly useful. The girl was so desperate to please that she'd paint anything asked of her —at an exceptional pace, too, based on all of the canvases sprawled about. Best of all, she kept the Oksanans pacified.

As I continued to gaze throughout the room, I noticed a collection of new paintings grouped together that were

quite unlike anything I had seen Siranna do before. I was perplexed. They all featured four-winged birds in all kinds of poses—wings outstretched or perched on mountain-tops—each in shades of vibrant red. Near the paintings were sketches and drawings pinned to the wall: practice pieces that highlighted the wings, feathers, and face of the bird.

I turned my focus back to the piece that originally caught my eye. With a procession of practiced brushstrokes, Siranna transformed an indistinct red mass into a stunning red wing attached to the body of another of these birds.

"What is it?" I asked, breaking the silence. Siranna jumped back and gasped. I turned on my charm. "My apologies; I didn't mean to intrude."

"Sorry! Sorry Senator Velodik!" Siranna began in a half-panic. "I didn't know you were there. I must have gotten lost in my work." She laughed nervously.

"It's all right," I laughed in kind. "But tell me, what is this you're puh-puh-painting? I've never seen anything like this before." I moved closer, angling my head to make out the detail in the wing. It was beautifully crafted.

"It's a phoenix: a bird that's important in Oksana. When it's done, it will be rising up from a backdrop of glass mountains."

I saw that she was quite excited and impassioned as she spoke. I smiled lightly. That was the kind of thing that must have served Ishkara well when they visited Oksana.

Siranna continued: "Back at home, we have a coming-of-age ceremony: the *Vinnya*. We climb Mount Zorya, and it is said that when we reach its peak and look into the mirror-glass, we see a vision of what we are to become. In that moment, we are transformed into our adult self, and reborn like the phoenix." Siranna spoke with a mix of humility and pride.

"What a story," I said in an airy whisper. I had never heard anyone speak of the *Vinnya* in such a way before. Ishkara only spoke of its dangers and its horrors. I stared at the drawings and at the unfinished painting. I started to imagine myself floating up above the mountains, gazing into the mirror-glass. "What did you see?"

"What do you mean?" she asked.

"When you reached the puh-peak of the mountain, what did you see?"

She paused for a moment. Her gaze shifted and she stared thoughtfully at the tip of her paintbrush. At last, she said softly, "I... I saw myself,"

"Just... you? No glorious vision of your life in the palace?" I asked, gesturing to the space around us.

"Oh! No. Nothing like that. It's just a story." She looked back up at me and smiled. "The mountain isn't some magical portal to the future. That's the beauty of it. When you reach the top and you look into the mirror-glass, you only see yourself. But you see yourself after the journey. Tired, sweaty, maybe a little dishevelled, but stronger for making the climb. The rebirth is the moment of realization that you have both changed but you also haven't. It's a moment of self-discovery that there was something stronger locked up inside you all along."

I looked back at the painting again and we stood in silence for a time as I got lost in the details of the elaborate feathers bursting with fire and life. I was amazed at what just a few brushstrokes could do.

"Do you think Ishkara will like it?" Siranna asked at last.

"What?"

"I want to incorporate something like this into my next painting of her. How Ishkara was able to unify us. The rebirth of Vsevora, as it were."

"Perhaps," I said. "I'll let you carry on. Good work, Siranna." I smiled weakly, she thanked me graciously, and I left. I felt uneasy and uncertain.

It felt as though I had wandered through the halls of the palace for a long time before finally making it to my destination. Galva stood outside of Ishkara's office. I tipped my hat to her and reached for the handle, but she quickly blocked me.

"She's in a meeting," she said in her familiar brutish fashion.

"A meeting?" I furrowed my brow. I tried to remember if Ishkara had mentioned any meetings today. Nothing came to mind, but the more I thought about it, almost nothing from this morning came to me—just the memory of colours, sounds, and feelings.

I didn't need to puzzle long, for a moment later, the door opened. Commissioner Zradya stood in the frame and as soon as she caught sight of me, a beaming smile spread across her speckled face.

"Ah, Senator, it's a good thing you're here. I suspect Ishkara would like to chat with you." Her voice was dripping with smug delight.

I growled low in my throat. "How dare you try to go above my head, you rotten—"

"Senator!" Ishkara's voice boomed from within the office.

"I'm sure we'll chat soon, Chief Minister." Zradya bowed her head and stepped aside.

I could see Ishkara sitting behind her mahogany desk, her expression furious. I said nothing else and hurried inside, shutting the door carefully behind me.

"How much longer were you planning to keep the night markets from me?" Ishkara demanded.

"Night markets, Chancellor? What do you mean?" I asked, feigning ignorance. I wished I hadn't, as Ishkara glared disapprovingly.

"Don't play dumb with me. The Commissioner brought me her report: night markets springing up all across the country, including here in Sophia, and you do nothing? You're my Chief Minister of Public Security!" Her voice had risen to a frightening high which she then brought down to a dull growl: "Have you been spending so much time sniffing tails that you can no longer manage your obligations?"

"No, no, you misunderstand!" I struggled to play this to my advantage somehow. "I just mean... there's nothing of consequence. Nothing to worry about! A few peddlers with illicit goods, a couple of cutpurses. This is the every day bustle of the city! Commissioner Zradya is overreacting."

Ishkara's intensity didn't falter as she continued to glower. My heart quickened and I felt a bead of sweat slide down my brow. For all of our years of friendship, for everything we had been through together, Ishkara could still shake me to my core.

Ishkara opened a drawer and grabbed something from within. She rose from her seat and began to wind around the desk. She wore a blue dress that extended all the way to her hooves. It was inlaid with intricate crystal beadwork at its base in a pattern that was reminiscent of her crown of horns. She had dozens of similar dresses; each one would be fit for the greatest balls held by the kings and queens of old, and she wore them as part of her daily attire.

"It is not the drugs or the thieves that concern me, Velodik," she said plainly. She held up her hand, displaying a small book. She threw it toward me. "Look at this. Someone found it within the very halls of this palace!" I inspected it closely: poems written by Tibor of Oksana and illustrations of a four-winged bird intermingled with them.

I frowned. For a moment, I felt like I had seen this bird before. The thought percolated in my mind and then popped out of existence. I paused. Nothing but colours and sounds and feelings. I focused instead on the poems, quickly reading a few of them over.

"You know, Ishkara, the poetry here seems rather harmless. Nothing like the unflattering one you had quoted to the Senate." I tried to downplay the situation. I looked up from the book at Ishkara, hoping that she might see some reason in my argument. She hadn't. She was fuming.

"The prohibition on radical, sectarian propaganda is necessary to preserve Vsevora's unity," she snapped. She stormed away from me and stopped when she reached the window. I could see her draw in a deep breath and slowly let it out. She traced a gloved hand down one of the blue satin drapes to a vase that sat on a small, circular table. She picked up a scarlet flower from it.

Her tone became cold and brittle: "People look at their culture and traditions with fondness, but they forget the pain that came with them: fragmentation, scarcity, and war." She crushed the flower in her hand and ripped the petals from the stem. She turned back to face me, moving slowly until she was only inches away, still clutching the petals in her fist.

"Now, Senator, I must ask you to fulfil your duty as Chief Minister of Public Security," she said, her voice low and serious. "For the protection of all of Vsevora's people, you are tasked with finding the night markets and stamping them out."

"Of course, Chancellor," I said quietly. I felt a tense tingle up my spine and a dull pain in my head that started to throb.

"Not just in Sophia. All of them. With enough force that they *never* return." The words hung there for a moment. Ishkara held up her fist before me. "I will be very disappointed if you fail. Understood?" She opened her hand and let the broken scarlet petals drop to the ground.

I swallowed hard. "Understood, Chancellor."

I burst into Zradya's office and slammed the door behind me.

"Chief Minister, good to see you. Assuming you're still the Chief Minister." Her smug smile hadn't faded since she left the palace.

"Shut up," I barked. "We need to act quickly."

"I suspected that would be the case," she said lazily as she reached into a cabinet, grabbed a bottle and a glass, and poured herself a drink. "The arrangements are ready. The night market in Sophia will be no more after tomorrow night." She swirled her drink and cockily took a sip.

"No," I growled. "Not just Sophia."

Zradya looked confused; she sat up straight. "What? What do you mean?"

I glared down at her and snarled: "Everywhere. Every night market in Vsevora. A coordinated strike."

Chapter Twenty:
Flame to Ashes

Look up! Look up into that golden sky!
With wings of cloud and fire red
The phoenix starts to fly.
With flaming crest upon its head
It climbs up and up on high!
Behind its tail a fiery thread,
A beauty none deny.
So it soars, the heavens spread,
Our spirit that cannot die!

— *"Phoenix XXVII" by Tibor of Oksana*

Siranna

My mother used to read me the poetry of Tibor of Oksana when I was a child. I sometimes thought back to those days when I sat in her lap as she read, her voice filled with energy and pride. I remembered the way her face lit up whenever she read one of his pieces about the phoenix rising over the mountains.

After I bought the poetry book at the night market, I spent hours reading it over again and again. Reading those poems brought me back to those memories of my mother—memories of warmth and tenderness. Slowly, as I read, the memories of my final parting with her faded and were replaced with those of love.

One night, after poring over poems and frantically scribbling new sketches, I took a long walk through the royal palace. I meandered through the halls and climbed many stairs until I found an unsuspecting door. It led to the roof.

There I stood, high atop the royal palace, gazing at all of Sophia stretched out below me. The city was dark, but flickering bits of lamplight illuminated the buildings, streets, and windows. I drew in a deep breath, letting the cool night air fill my lungs, and sending a burst of energy through my whole body. I beamed a wide smile.

A streak of light crossed the sky, arcing overtop the great square at the heart of the city, before stopping just above it and spreading out. Four majestic wings hung in the air followed by a great waving tail of feathers and flame. There was a high-pitched trill that echoed across the sky and then the phoenix flew toward me.

In a flash, the mother phoenix arrived and perched next to me atop the palace. I gazed up in awe and delight at her and I reached my hand out to touch her feathers. Despite the fire that burned within and upon her, she was warm and safe to touch. She nestled herself low next to me, invitingly.

I grinned and climbed up on her back, feeling the gentle warmth of her against my body. With a powerful wingbeat, she took to the air. I clung to her neck and we rose up together. We raced over the city, but soon went higher and higher, climbing over the mountains.

My eyes widened in wonder as we flew across Vsevora. We soared over snow-capped mountains, and I saw Ksenya down below. There were small flames dancing around the city like fireflies, offering light to travellers and night-hunters.

Onward we flew until the shape of the mountains changed. Moonlight glistened off the glass peaks and I soon gazed upon Oksana. I thought of my last visit there; it had all gone by so quickly. I thought of the heat. I thought of the worry and the dread that had loomed over me.

As I looked down upon the quiet streets far below, I was awash in disappointment. It had been such a waste. Returning home should have been something else—something joyful.

The phoenix dipped low. We were flying right over the port: right where the crowd had gathered. I wondered once again if my mother had been in that crowd. I wondered if she had heard Ishkara call me a shining example for the nation. I wondered if she cared.

My heart sank. The painful memories of my final parting with my
mother returned. I buried my head
into the back of the phoenix's neck
and started to cry.

"Take me away," I called out. "Take
me away from here. I never want to
come back!"

The mother phoenix turned and shot upward. I let out a
startled yelp with the suddenness of her ascent and I clung
hard to her feathers. I could feel myself slipping as we
climbed straight up.

I screamed: "Wait! What's happening?" There was no answer. She just kept rising higher and higher, faster and
faster. I held on as best as I could, but my grip continued to
slip. "Stop! Please!" She didn't listen. We were higher than
the mountains, reaching ever upward toward the stars.

I could hold on no longer. My hands slipped and I
screeched. My stomach hurled itself throughout my body,
every muscle tensed, and I fell. I hurtled back down toward
the ground.

With a shaking thud, I crashed into my bed. At least,
that's what it had felt like. I awoke with a gasp, gripping my
bedsheets with white-hot knuckles. As I regained my composure, I let out a sigh and let myself sink into the bed,
gradually relaxing the muscles through
my body.

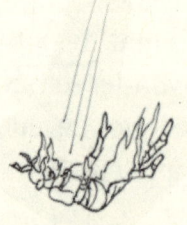

I turned toward my bedside table,
turned on the lamp, and reached into the
drawer. I wanted to escape into one of Tibor's poems, to push the feelings of sadness and fear from my mind, and bring

back the ones of warmth and love. I paused for a moment, puzzled. I pulled the drawer open as far as I could, then reached in and clawed my hand to its back edges. Empty.

My morning was a tizzy. I searched all over the palace for my misplaced book of poems. I often snuck it away with me to read in a quiet alcove or secluded part of the courtyard, but I couldn't find it anywhere.

I returned to my studio empty handed; there was no time to keep looking. I hurriedly began rearranging my artwork—I had to prepare for Ishkara's arrival.

Senator Velodik's visit the day before encouraged me; I made arrangements to see the Chancellor. Admittedly, I was a little deceptive. I told her attendants that I needed her for a sitting to complete an important composition. Instead, I would show her my vision: the phoenix of Oksana for all of Vsevora. I had made dozens of phoenixes—paintings and drawings—rising up from the ashes of the past and bursting through the air.

I had hoped to show her the poetry book at the same time. I knew that Tibor's poems were frowned upon, but they had inspired my idea. Once Ishkara understood how important they were to my vision, she would soften.

I was sure that she would commission a whole series of paintings. I envisioned one with Ishkara at its heart. She was standing proudly, the wings of the phoenix rising up behind her, and the sun's light shimmering in a halo that extended to the edge of the canvas. But even that idea paled in comparison to what I had already completed.

Carefully, I placed my latest painting on an easel in the middle of the room. I had stayed up late to finish it: *The Phoenix of Vsevora*. In it, a majestic phoenix rose, with fiery feathers of gold and red filling the sky. Below it, warmed by the glow of its flames, mountains of stone and glass stood tall, giving way to valleys and forest, all representing the varied lands of the nation. I loved it. It invigorated me. I knew that there was something special here that I needed to share with all of Vsevora. I had never felt so strongly about one of my paintings.

My mind raced. I was nervous and ecstatic. I imagined what other artists would think when they saw what I had created. What wonderful things would Ishkara say? I took a deep breath and quietly rehearsed what I would tell her:

"Paintings like this are more than a nod to my heritage. I want to encourage other artists to showcase their homelands and their traditions. Imagine a mosaic of art coming together to form Vsevora. Each tile will tell a story, adding up to a beautiful whole!"

I heard a sharp clacking sound echoing down the hall. It was time! I gasped and tried tidying the mess of paints and brushes that were ever-present within the space. I stood next to my painting, gripped a brush tightly in my hand, and took a deep, calming breath as the clacking sound drew closer. Turning to the door, I saw a woman in a blue dress.

Then she was gone. She had continued swiftly past the door, never adjusting her pace for a moment. Not her. I let out an exasperated groan and tossed the paintbrush to the floor. I turned back to the easel, looked at the clock, and back to the easel. Maybe she wouldn't come at all.

I picked up my sketchbook and sat down on the floor in the corner of the room. To calm my mind, I started to draw. Another beak, another tail, another wing. I paid careful attention to the details of the feathers. I didn't even notice when three figures had entered the room.

"Siranna," a commanding voice called and I looked up. There was Ishkara, a stern grimace on her face, along with Galva and another one of her attendants.

"Oh!" I exclaimed as I jumped to my feet. I dropped the sketchbook and pencil and dashed up to the attendant. "I'm so sorry. I didn't see you come in!" I hurried past and stood near the easel. I gave a nervous curtsy before I continued to speak:

"Chancellor Ishkara, it's such a pleasure and an honour to have you here. I wanted to introduce myself, no, not myself, you know who I am, I mean... I want to introduce you to my newest work." I started stumbling all over my prepared speech. Ishkara had a scowl on her face. I was losing her already. "You see, Chancellor, I have been creating new pieces based on my heritage. I think that by juxtaposing the images of the Phoenix of Mount Zorya alongside your message of a united Vsevora, that we can illustrate how you have—"

"Stop talking," Ishkara said coldly, raising up a gloved hand. She moved slowly past me and inspected the painting up close, the scowl still etched on her face. "Imagery of this kind is restricted," she said at last, turning back to face me. Her eyes burned.

"I'm sorry? I-I don't think I understand," I stammered.

"Depictions like these glorify the primitive customs and divisive nature of our past. This only serves to fray the fabric that holds Vsevora together." Her voice was direct and matter-of-fact, but I saw such an intense expression on her face. Was it anger? Hatred? What was it that I had sparked?

I was afraid, but I felt like I had to speak up: "With all due respect, I don't think you understand. That's not the intent of this work. You see, I was inspired by Tibor of Oksana, but I want to show how the phoenix can carry us to all parts of Vsevora. We are like a mosaic that—"

"I said stop talking." A cold silence hung in the air at her command and she slowly moved closer to me. She was shorter than I was, but her presence towered over me as she closed in. "Any content of this kind is restricted and will be destroyed. You will resume the work that my office commissions you or else your residency will be terminated. Consider this your only warning, and be happy that you have received any warning at all."

I stood there, slack-jawed. I tried to speak up, but I could only muster a few indiscernible squeaks and peeps. Ishkara ignored me and continued, "We will schedule another sitting in a few weeks. Until then, expect an attendant to be with you to monitor your work and ensure that there are not any more... errors in the work you create." Ishkara broke eye contact and made her way to the door without hesitation. "Galva." She gave a subtle gesture to her guard who nodded stoically in response. Ishkara and her attendant left, leaving Galva behind.

I looked up at her: a broad and hairy woman with rectangular eyes and short, pointed horns. She drew a dagger from her belt and began to advance.

"What? No! Please! Please don't hurt me! I-I'm sorry! I didn't realize what I was doing was wrong. Please, please, please, you have to realize—" I gasped and begged as she lifted the blade and then plunged it down—tearing apart the canvas next to me.

I stared in stupefied horror at the phoenix that was torn in two. I had been left untouched, but I felt as if I had been stabbed through the heart anyway. My gut sank, a wave of heat flooded up through the back of my head, and my knees buckled. I hit the ground.

Galva's blade rent the painting apart and with a grunt, she ripped part of the canvas off the frame. She dropped it to the ground and stamped on it with a heavy hoof. I felt like she had kicked me—hard. My breath quivered and my heart shook in my chest.

There were more phoenixes throughout the room, spread out on the walls and on easels. Galva moved to the next painting, lifting up her blade. I was paralyzed.

"Please. Please stop," I managed to choke out, barely able to speak. My throat was tight and I felt tears well up in my eyes.

She didn't even look back. She slid the blade into the canvas and dragged it mercilessly across the phoenix's body. Then she moved on and did the same to a third, then a fourth. Her eyes roamed across the room, looking for more of the four-winged birds.

My hand reached forward uselessly as she made her way around the room. She tore apart every phoenix, every glistening glass mountain, every single one of them.

As her carnage spread, I let out a guttural moan—a retching sound that didn't seem real. It was like every ounce of my being was forced out of me and vomiting out as a gurgling, wailing sob. It was over in a matter of minutes, but as I sat there trembling, it felt like hours—days. All of the time I had pored into those paintings played over in my mind, and each cut of Galva's blade was another jab into my flesh.

I sat there, gasping, my face drenched with tears, my throat aching from wailing so hard. Galva spotted a sketch of Ishkara on a canvas in the corner. She picked it up and then walked over to the easel that stood before me in the centre of the room. She carelessly knocked the torn painting to the floor and set the unfinished piece upon it. "You should finish this next," she said cruelly and left.

My hand mindlessly clawed at the ground in front of me, weakly stroking the floor. I looked around at my work, at my soul, torn to shreds around me. I turned my eyes up to the sketch above me. Ishkara stared back. Her eyes— meant to be warm and inviting—burned into me. I croaked, trying to find my breath. The words across the canvas called out to me: "Ishkara is Harmony."

Chapter Twenty-One:
The Raid

Broken bones and broken homes. We leave a trail of ash and death. I thought that we were better.

— from The Blight of War *by Kavya of Sophia*

Kalrevi

"You must be quick," Velodik said in a hushed tone as the carriage hurried through the streets. "There is only one chance at this."

"I understand," I replied stoically.

"You mustn't wear your badge, of course."

"Of course. I never do."

"But keep it with you, Kalrevi! I don't want you to get hurt!"

I stared at Velodik quietly for a moment. His expression was frantic and concerned. I wondered for a moment if he didn't want me to go. Frankly, I barely wanted to go. But I knew that when push came to shove, he was going to send me. It was just best to hurry.

"We should stop here. We don't want your carriage to be seen too close," I said plainly. He nodded and called up to the driver. We came to a jostling halt and I opened the carriage door.

"Wait," Velodik said and grabbed my wrist. "Your mask. Surely you'll be spotted if you wear it. Give it to me." He held out his hand.

I glared back at him and spoke firmly: "It hasn't been a problem for me before and it won't be one tonight. Trust me." We stared one another in the eye for a moment before he conceded and released my wrist. I stepped out of the carriage and it hurried off. I pulled up my hood and made my way to Agate Square.

There were a few dim stars flickering in the sky and no moon to be seen, but the streets of Sophia were bustling. The appeal and taboo of the night market had gripped its people, drawing in crowds larger than I had ever seen. They milled about, under the gaze of the stone angel, clad in bulky robes and scarves to disguise their identities. People spoke in hushed voices, but through sheer numbers they filled the square with a dull roar.

Overlooking the square were faint eyes gazing down and watching intently. Ishkara. Her posters hung all around the square, ever-vigilant but inert.

I kept to the outskirts at first, away from the strings of white light that illuminated the makeshift stalls. I looked up at the dimly lit face of a clock at the edge of the square. Nearly time. I thought I saw shadows gathering at the edges of my vision, just beyond the market, but I couldn't be sure. I needed to find the stall.

Draped in my dark blue cloak, I blended in with the throngs of people. I threaded my way through them as they bought up food, books, and other wares. A merchant held aloft a glowing amber orb that cast its light out toward me. I quickly turned my face downward, ensuring the white of my mask didn't catch its glow, and hurried deeper into the mass of people.

My mission was much the same as it always was at the night market: seek out the stall of the shifty seller. Market stalls were laid out by whoever put their goods there first, so he was never in the same place twice.

I scanned the area as I shoved my way through a thick throng of people that gathered in front of some purveyor of smut. As I pushed past, I saw menacing shapes close in from the streets. I looked around frantically. I spotted him!

I squeezed through another mass of the crowd as fast as I could. The shifty merchant was under his tent, chatting with a few interested parties and showing off the variety of herbs and spices laid before him. As I got closer, I could see the locked box beside him where the vials were kept. I was just a few feet away.

I hadn't made it in time.

A loud bang broke the rumble of the crowd and then smoke began to fill the middle of the market square. I looked at the surrounding streets and there they were: row upon row of Public Security officers pouring in, armed with heavy metal batons and shields emblazoned with the crest of Vsevora. The officers barked out orders, but as the crowd began to panic, their commands were lost. They shouted something about illicit activity and called for everyone to stand down. Vendors packed up what wares they could before taking flight, and people screamed as they tried to flee. Few were able to get by the barricade of shields.

There was no time to worry about any of that. I ran toward the drug peddler as he picked up the box next to him and darted toward the shadows. I grabbed a bolas from my belt, swung it above my head, and released it as the space between us became clear. The steel balls hurled through the air and then wound around the peddler's legs as the rope of the bolas caught his ankles. He stumbled forward and hit the ground, his body crunching against the box as he did.

A line of officers moved toward us, their batons striking down panicked people as they approached. I could tell they were delighting in this. I moved swiftly, putting my back to the officers and obscuring my actions as I knelt down by the peddler. He was groaning and moaning. I pried the box away from him and cracked it open. It was filled with vials of white powder. I swiftly deposited a few handfuls of them into a bag which I then secured in place, close to my heart. The officers closed in, the stamping of their boots coming up loudly behind me.

I spun around, now squatting on top of the peddler and pulling his arms behind his back, putting on a show. "You are under arrest for the sale and distribution of restricted materials and substances," I boomed.

"Hold up here," a gravelly voice called above me. "Who are you?" A rough hand pulled me to my feet.

Before I could react, another officer ordered, "Arrest her," and the rough hands clamped down on my arms. I struggled against them and my resistance was met with a powerful jolt of pain. A baton struck my shoulder with incredible force and brought me to my knees.

"I'm Public Security," I growled.

"Sure you are," the gravel-voiced officer scoffed.

"Confiscate the bag and take her away with the other ones," the leader barked. I felt bindings around my hands and the bag violently ripped from my body.

"What do you have in here anyway?" Gravel asked.

"I *am* Public Security," I hissed and pulled myself to my feet, turning to face Gravel. "Check the front pouch."

He eyed me suspiciously. I silently stared up at him. His eyes were a solid foot above mine and his shoulders twice as broad. Most of Public Security were muscled out beasts like this. Velodik told me there were two types: schoolyard bullies who never grew out of it—who only found strength in punishing the weak; and those who had been bullied— who now doled out their punishments indiscriminately. Gravel seemed more like the former than the latter.

Another crack to my shoulder forced me down. "Stay down, scum!" the lead officer hollered. "What have you got under that mask, anyway? What are you trying to hide?" I felt a hot hand reach for the clasp of my mask and I pulled my head away. Another crack from the baton threw me all the way to the ground. I writhed as I realized my shoulder popped out of its socket. I glanced up at Gravel who had a bemused smile on his face. I was like a worm to him, wriggling helplessly on the ground.

He looked curiously at the bag again now that I was subdued. If he looked in the main pouch first and saw all of the vials I had collected, there was no chance I was making it out of this.

I coughed out, "I am a member of Public Security in direct service to Senator Velodik. Look inside the front pouch." Gravel's eyes focused on mine. He was skeptical, but I could see a lingering hint of fear. He realized that if what I said were true, his head would be on a platter.

"Check it," the leader said at last. Gravel obeyed and opened the front pouch, revealing a silver badge that identified me as Public Security and as someone with far higher rank than any of the officers present. Gravel handed it over to the lead officer who eyed it with discerning horror. He grunted something affirmative and Gravel pulled me to my feet. As he quickly released the bindings, a shock of pain shot through my shoulder, but I grit my teeth through it.

"You should be in uniform if you're a part of the raid," the leader said unapologetically as Gravel shoved the bag back into my chest. I seethed for a moment, holding it close with my good arm, and then regained my composure.

"Take him," I said, gesturing to the peddler. "He was selling restricted goods back at the market stall over there." I kicked lightly at the box which still held a few vials of powder and calmly took my leave of the officers, clutching my bag tightly in hand.

The plan had been to swipe the goods in the first moment of confusion and then disappear in the shadows as the raid began. The ache in my arm that now hung limply by my side groaned at me. Not everything could go according to plan, but at least I made it.

I moved quickly toward the perimeter of the square. Smoke choked the air and the rumbling din of commerce had turned into fearful chaos and violence. I watched as officers continued to beat at people as

they fled. They threw vendors roughly to their stomachs and then ground their beefy knees into the vendors' backs while binding them.

A young man ran crying past me, his face drenched in blood and tears. An older woman was being roughly dragged away by an officer. Her body was limp; I hoped that she was just unconscious. An officer ran deeper into the fray, a wide grin stretched across his face as he readied his baton.

Behind me, overlooking the tumult and the pain, were the posters. She was still there. Watching. Smoke obscured the words. "Ishkara is Harm." I turned down an alleyway and into the darkness, leaving the screams and smoke to carry on throughout the night.

Chapter Twenty-Two:
Dagger's Edge

Selfishness is a wound upon the whole community. When you surrender your mind to desire, you think only of yourself and not of the suffering of your people.

— *Surrendra, Chieftain of the Feras*

Velodik

Thirteen little vials! I couldn't wipe the grin off my face as I counted them out again. Kalrevi had secured quite the supply!

Everything went perfectly: the night markets across Vsevora had been shut down with enough force to prevent their return. It was all far better than anything the damned Commissioner would have executed on her own. Ishkara would certainly be pleased.

I couldn't help but feel a twinge of pity for poor Kalrevi. In the days that followed the raid, I noticed she was quieter than usual. I didn't give it much mind. It was a shame about her arm, but wounds heal after all! Just a dislocated shoulder. While Kalrevi sulked, I took some well-deserved time for myself.

I embarked on a joyride of immeasurable highs as I dipped into my new supply with celebratory fervour. I drank! I feasted! I rolled around on my silk blankets just to feel them shimmer against my body!

The trouble with any high as exhilarating as that is always the crash. As I woke up one morning, I felt a dagger jabbed just above my left eye. My fingers were slightly numb and my mouth was like sandpaper.

I felt around the empty bed. Nothing. Nothing! I roared and threw the silk blankets as hard as I could. I sat up on all fours and darted to the nightstand. I tore through the drawers, throwing them to the floor, and then knocked the whole thing over. I was a feral animal.

Then I spotted it. I scrambled over to the dresser, crawled along my belly, and snatched up the small vial on the floor just underneath.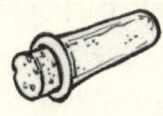

I pulled off the cap and greedily snorted up the little bit of dust that remained inside. My body relaxed and I lay sprawled out on the floor for what felt like hours upon hours, watching the shadows softly dance around the room.

The door opened and I remained motionless, waiting for the last of the aches to drain away. Out of the corner of my eye, I saw a Kalrevi-like shape. *Probably Kalrevi,* I thought, and started to giggle.

"You missed last night's session." I heard a Kalrevi-like voice from somewhere in the direction of the Kalrevi-like shape and my giggling turned into all-out laughter. She seemed unfazed by it. "I imagine that some people will be upset that you missed it, especially in light of how Public Security behaved during the night market raids." I rocked gently back and forth then left to right. I couldn't quite put together what the voice was telling me.

The shape moved across the room and opened the blinds. Dazzling white light tore apart the shadows and harshly burned a path on top of me. The dagger returned, just when I thought it might be gone; it slid back into my head and vibrated there.

The voice continued: "You have an audience with Ishkara in three hours. I assume you can put yourself back together by then, but if not, I can claim some kind of illness on your behalf again."

I gasped and suddenly remembered how parched my throat had become. The dagger drove itself in deeper and I moaned as it tore into my brain. I was stranded, now, in some vast desert. The sun beat down on me and the ground was coarse and stony.

"Water. Water!" I cried out in agony as the last drops of saliva were evaporated by the blazing of the sun.

"I'll get you something to drink." The Kalrevi-like voice was disgusted.

I tried to keep steady as I walked down the hallway of the royal palace. The dagger was firmly planted in my skull and refused to come out. I had tried smuggling another vial along with me—to ease my journey through the palace—but Kalrevi kept it from me.

"It's too dangerous to take it outside," she said. I hated her. She deserved what had happened to her at the night market.

There was a sudden surge of pain as the dagger twisted and sank in deeper. I yelped and stumbled, slamming into the wall. I looked around, hoping no one had seen me like this. I spotted a pair of startled onlookers and snarled at them. They turned abruptly and hurried away.

I groaned as I pushed myself off the wall and staggered onward once again. I couldn't face Ishkara like this. I stopped and focused on my breathing for a moment. *Inhale. Pause. Exhale. Pause. Inhale. Pause. Exhale. Pause. That's it. This is helping.*

"I need you to explain yourself, Senator," Ishkara's voice was measured and menacing. She kept control over her anger, but I could recognize her righteous fury, even as the dagger bored into me.

"I don't know if I understand, Ishkara," I replied uneasily, standing at attention.

"Chancellor Ishkara," she seethed, rising up. "Let me see if I can make you understand. Your Public Security officers raided night markets all over Vsevora, but they decided to take out their frustrations on people's skulls."

"But Chancellor, I thought this is what you wanted."

"I wanted definitive action, not blood in the streets!" Her fiery gaze was focused right on the blade—I could feel it growing hotter. "And then you disappear for over a week. A special session was called for an inquiry and you were nowhere to be found."

"I'm sorry, Chancellor. I was, uh, ill," I mumbled.

Ishkara slid past her desk and stepped toward me. I shrank before her unflinching gaze. "I don't care. I don't care if you're sick or gallivanting or high as a skyship." She clasped her hand on the side of my face and held tight. Her fingers dug in, right by the blade, and I cried out woefully. "I don't even care that a few filthy traders broke their bones and that Public Security got hot and heavy while they did it."

Her fingers were like talons now, digging into my skull. The dagger ignited with flame and I fell to my knees. *Inhale. Pause.*

"Do you know what I care about?" *Exhale. Pause.* "Answer me, Velodik!"

"It-it-it was Commissioner Zradya! She gave the orders!" I exclaimed, looking for some way to pull the fiery dagger out of my skull.

"Do you really think I'm that stupid, Velodik?" Her grip tightened and more and more daggers threw themselves into my head, twisting and turning, biting and burning. Ishkara seethed. "She was at the session, you fool! She told every senator in Vsevora that you gave the order—and that you did it to satisfy me. "

"I'm sorry, Chancellor!" I cried. "Please forgive me! I will set this right! I will!" I pulled myself away from her and held my head, unable to keep the daggers at bay.

"And how do you plan to do that?"

"I don't know, Chancellor. I don't know. I'm sorry!"

Ishkara stepped back. I looked up and I saw the contempt and disgust in her eyes. "Instead of the night markets coming to a swift end, people are calling into question my motives for disbanding them. Senators who voted to outlaw the propaganda that the night markets peddle are turning around and questioning my judgment! If we don't turn the tide on this, Velodik, then this is the first step toward our downfall—and Vsevora's descent into savagery and disorder."

"I can fix this. I'm certain that I can fix this," I gasped.

"You'll have to," Ishkara said with frigid resolve. She turned away from me. I silently nodded to her back, still panting as the daggers drove deeper and deeper into my head.

I staggered out of the palace, into my personal carriage, and returned home in constant suffering. My mind raced, but every turn it tried to take there was another dagger blocking the way. I was afraid of what Ishkara would do if I couldn't fix this blunder.

I thought that it had all been so perfect: no more problems with the night market and all of my little vials in hand... but now it was all problems.

I dragged myself out of the carriage and started wobbling toward my home. The daggers were everywhere now.

Where was Kalrevi? Why wasn't she helping me? I stumbled and hit the curb with a yelp. My legs were falling asleep. The world was unfocused and blurry around me. I squinted. *Inhale. Pause. Exhale. Pause.* Focus returned and I saw a light post. I gripped onto it and pulled myself up, my legs jiggling underneath me.

"Kalrevi," I cried out, my voice thin and trembling. "I need your help. Kalrevi!" She didn't come to my rescue.

I struggled to find my footing. I took a few steps forward before crashing back into the post. As I steadied myself again, I noticed there was something taped to it. I tried to focus on it, to discern what it was, but another dagger slid into the space just below my eyeball. I groaned and bashed a fist against the post.

Inhale. Pause. Exhale. Pause.

I could make out a few words: "Laws must serve the people. The people must unite." I stared at the words for some time. It was a poster. There was more. As my head spun, it all started blurring together. Agate Square. An angel. People rising. Soon.

Then all of the jumbled little pieces tumbled into place. I stared wide-eyed and I laughed. "Yes! This is it! Kalrevi, this is it!"

When the daggers were gone, I could spring into action. I knew how to fix everything.

Chapter Twenty-Three:
Broken

Do I have any regrets? Too many to count.

— *Siranna Ankova*

Siranna

I could barely pull myself out of bed. My throat ached and my eyes were exhausted from having cried so hard the night before. As I stared up at the ceiling, the only thing I felt was a dull emptiness inside of me—a void where something had been ripped out.

Somewhere, deep down, I thought I could continue my work; I thought I could remain at the palace and keep making paintings of Ishkara. But the moment I stepped into my studio, my heart broke. The tatters of my paintings had been removed, along with all of my sketches and practice drawings that I had pinned to the wall. No more glass mountains, no more phoenix—only a sorrow that sunk into my very being.

I stepped up to an empty canvas and picked up a brush and a container of red paint. My hands started to tremble. I couldn't do it.

I looked to my right and Ishkara's painted eyes were staring at me from across the room. "Ishkara is Harmony." I gripped my paintbrush hard and felt fresh tears well up. I ran over to her. My heart was beating faster and faster; I screamed and threw the container, spraying paint across the canvas and leaving a great bloody gash across her face. The paint dribbled down, washing out her name.

I drew in a deep breath and let out a laugh—not of joy or mirth—it was a hollow laugh. I didn't care. It was relief. I ran from painting to painting and spilled thick streams of paint over them. I hurried to each one, faster and faster. I screamed at her bloody visage and smeared paint across her vicious smile. One by one, I destroyed all of the work I had created; every last image of Ishkara was bathed in red.

Guards soon arrived, summoned by my screams. That moment of catharsis may have saved my sanity, but it destroyed my career.

I was ejected from the palace. They gave me a single bag to pack up my belongings and cast me out. Luckily, I was used to packing up my life in a single bag.

Everything will be alright, I told myself. *This is a setback. I'll find my way.*

As I walked the streets of Sophia, unsure of where I would go, I could not escape Ishkara's gaze. "Ishkara is Harmony." The words—my own artwork—haunted and mocked me from every corner.

Her eyes were everywhere. My eyes. I created those eyes. They were hers, but they were my own. And they ripped through me every time I saw them. My stomach churned like I was about to vomit and heat swelled up in my head. How could I paint anything again after painting those hateful eyes?

How can I ever paint again? The words rolled through my mind and then the reality of everything I lost came crashing over me. My breathing became heavy and erratic; I gasped uncontrollably. I crouched down and lowered my head. I was dizzy. The eyes kept spinning around me.

"Miss? Excuse me, miss, are you okay?" a kindly voice echoed in my ears. I felt something press onto my shoulder which sent another shockwave of heat through me.

"Get away! Don't touch me!" I gasped. My body felt like it was on fire and before I knew it I was drenched in sweat. Everything kept spinning. Spinning. Those eyes were swirling around me. I clenched my eyes shut, but they were still there. My stomach churned and I fell forward onto my hands and knees. I gagged. A cacophony rung through my head.

"Is that...?"

"It's Siranna Ankova..."

"You mean Ishkara's artist-in-residence...?"

"Is she okay...?"

"What's she doing here...?"

"I love her work..."

"I think we should find help..."

A thousand voices were chattering around me. I needed them to stop. I needed to get away. I forced myself back to my feet. Concerned faces leered at me. I groaned as I threw my bag over my back and tried to push myself forward. The sweat poured down my face and I felt another hand, this one holding me back.

"Wait; you need help."

"I said don't touch me!" my voice shrieked.

There was a worried murmur and then the faces backed away. I grit my teeth and strode forward. I started to run. I ran until my legs finally gave way beneath me and I collapsed on the street. I pulled myself up against the cold stone of a nearby building and tried pushing myself back to my feet, but I couldn't.

I just can't, I said to myself. I felt fresh tears well up in my eyes. *I can't do this. It's over. I've screwed it all up and I'll never get it back. I never should have left. I should have stayed in Oksana, married Sylchiv, learned to bake bread, and painted my children's cheeks instead. I should have. I should have.* The words echoed throughout my mind

I tried to get my bearings. I didn't recognize this street. Where was I? I looked for a sign and instead saw Ishkara standing on a poster announcing to passersby, "Together We Make Vsevora Strong." I jumped weakly to my feet and I threw myself at her. I bashed my fists uselessly against the paper, clawing at the edges until I ripped it in half. I tore Ishkara's face to shreds.

I crumbled to the ground again. I felt like the shreds of paper scattered around me. *What do I do from here?* I had no answers. I didn't want to feel anything anymore. I closed my eyes and let exhaustion take me.

"Dear, are you okay?" a soft voice broke my slumber.

"Don't talk to her. Just keep walking."

"Nonsense! We can't just leave her here. It's not safe— especially if Public Security finds her."

"Oskar, we're not bringing her home with us! Don't give me that look. Oskar. Oskar! ... Fine!"

My eyes opened slowly and I regained focus. There was a man leaning over me; his expression was warm and inviting. His face was furry, round, and gentle. But his eyes. He had her eyes. I tensed up.

"Good, you're awake. Nothing to worry about, miss. Are you well enough to stand? Here, let me help you up." His voice was like warm honey. He offered me a hand and as I looked up into his eyes, I realized they were not like hers. His were full of care and compassion. I graciously accepted his hand and he lifted me up to my feet. I groaned and stumbled against his much larger frame. He was about as tall as I, before the horns, but at least twice as wide. He continued: "You're lucky no one ran off with your bag. Here, Emil."

"I have to carry her bag now? If you want to bring her home, you have to carry it." The other voice snapped. The two of them looked quite similar, although Emil had a rigid scowl carved into his face. He was also a fair bit thinner than Oskar, the honey-voiced man.

"All right," Oskar said, without missing a beat. He picked up my bag and winced as he threw it over his shoulder.

"Stop! I'll carry it!" Emil was clearly at his wit's end. He took the bag from Oskar. "You're going to hurt yourself. Come on. Let's get going."

"Don't worry. We don't live far. Are you all right to walk?" Oskar asked.

I nodded softly and we started walking. I was in a bit of a daze as we went. Emil grumbled occasionally as we carried on down the street. Oskar explained that Emil loved to complain and suggested I ignore him. I kept my gaze low, avoiding Ishkara's gaze. As we came to an apartment building, Oskar announced our arrival in a jovial boom.

"Now, it's not much, but it's certainly better than the street. Make yourself at home," he said warmly.

"Not too at home," Emil grumbled.

"You're both Ksenyan, aren't you?" I asked.

"That's right," Oskar said.

"Why are you being so gracious, then? I'm not Ksenyan after all."

"We're all a part of one Vsevora, are we not? At least, that's the hope." He smiled and held the door open for me. I nodded softly, trying to find the strength to smile back, but the idea of *one Vsevora* brought Ishkara's visage whirring back into my mind.

Oskar continued, his expression becoming more serious, "Sometimes I wonder, though. I wonder if the powers that be would rather wipe the names Ksenya, Oksana, Sophia, and the rest off the map."

"Shush," hissed Emil in a worried whisper. "Let's just get inside."

Oskar and Emil were gracious hosts and spectacular conversationalists. They didn't ask many questions of me. I could tell that they knew who I was, but they chose not to pry. Instead, they told me about themselves. It was a much-needed distraction from the looming memories of my time in the palace.

Oskar regaled me with stories about his siblings. The whole clan was a fanciful bunch of tricksters. They would often do each other's makeup—sometimes for beauty, sometimes for fun, and sometimes for mischief. The most I ever laughed since arriving in Sophia was when Oskar told me about the time he and his siblings decked themselves out in war paint and tripped up a night-hunter, sending them rolling down the mountainside.

Emil warmed up to me too. He loved to cook and when I offered to help him in the kitchen, he taught me a thing or two about baking bread. My mother always told me, "It's impossible to bake bread with enemies." I thought the saying had to do with arguing in the kitchen, but perhaps it was about making fast friends over a shared undertaking.

We talked about Emil and Oskar's lives together. About how they met. How they fell in love. How neither one had proposed to the other, even after twenty years together.

"Why haven't you gotten married, anyway?" I asked over a cup of tea. The two looked at each other, then back to me.

"Maybe if he'd ever ask me," Oskar said with a laugh. Emil kicked him playfully.

"I thought that marriage was important for Ksenyans," I continued. "Your traditions have even influenced Oksanan weddings."

"Yes but..." Emil trailed off as he searched for the right words. "Will a ceremony change how we feel about each other? Will it change who we are? How strong is our relationship if it needs a ceremony to bind it? Tradition for the sake of tradition."

Oskar nodded, his eyes locked on Emil, full of warmth and admiration. Slowly, he turned toward me and said quietly, "Back home, our families would be quite upset that we haven't done the ceremony. I've seen families broken apart over it. That's not what a wedding is supposed to be. Who's it all for, if not for the couple?"

"For everyone else," I said softly.

"That's right," said Emil. "For the community. For Ksenya. All those traditions do is hurt people." Oskar looked at Emil with wide eyes and Emil nodded back knowingly. He continued: "Traditions don't decide the way that we feel about one another. But they are important. They're as much a part of us as anything else." Oskar's gaze softened. "Maybe one day." Emil placed a gentle hand upon Oskar's; Oskar winced and pulled it away.

"Careful!" he exclaimed.

"I told you it was worse than it seemed! You're going to the doctor first thing in the morning," Emil said sternly.

"It's fine. I'll be fine. Just calm down."

"What happened?" I asked.

"He had to get a book," Emil groaned.

"I was at the night market when the raid happened," Oskar explained.

"There was a raid on the night market? Why?"

"They say that Public Security shut it down because of the exchange of 'restricted material.' They made it sound like it was a place for sin and vice. That's not at all what it was about. All I wanted was a music book; it was full of folk songs from Ksenya. None of the sanctioned bookstores carry anything like that."

Emil growled under his breath, "Public Security became rowdy."

Oskar continued: "I got off easy compared to some. They got my arm something fierce, though." He gingerly pulled up the sleeve of his sweater to reveal deep purple, blue, and black bruising all along his forearm. I gazed at it in horror and clenched my fists.

"This has to stop," I said. "Ishkara can't be allowed to continue like this. We can't just lie here and take it."

"Siranna, it's okay. My arm will heal. Let's talk about something else," Oskar said warmly.

"I'm sorry. I think that maybe I should get some rest. Good night." I stood up abruptly and hurried to the makeshift room they had for me: a cot amongst their dry storage.

I sat down on the cot, frustrated. Public Security needed to be stopped. Ishkara needed to be stopped. But what could I do?

I reached into my bag and grabbed my sketchbook, a few pencils, and a pen. They were the only art supplies I brought with me from the royal palace. I started to draw, my hand working rapidly across the page.

As gracious as Oskar and Emil had been, I felt I was wearing out my welcome. Oskar had been nothing but pleasant and Emil had been exceptionally kind, but I noticed the uncomfortable stares he sometimes gave me from across the room. As much as I wished I could stay within the warmth and comfort of their home forever, I knew that I couldn't impose on them any longer.

The three of us were enjoying breakfast together. I had packed up my bag and was prepared to head out on my own again as soon as the meal was finished.

"I want to thank you both for letting me stay with you these last few days. I can't tell you how deeply I appreciate it. I'm going to miss you."

"Wait, Siranna," Oskar said softly. He paused and looked at Emil. Emil seemed to hesitate but he gave a firm nod. "You're welcome to stay with us as long as you need to get back on your feet. The streets of Sophia are more dangerous than ever. It would put our minds at ease to know you're safe with us here."

I looked from one to the other. Emil nodded his agreement. I smiled wide, stood up, and dashed over to Oskar, wrapping my arms around him. He yelped as I pressed myself too tightly against his injured arm.

"Thank you! Thank you! Sorry. Oh... I'm so sorry. Oh Oskar, Emil, thank you both so much." I beamed brightly and hurriedly hugged Emil next. He reciprocated, but in a stilted, somewhat awkward, way.

"Don't mention it. It was all Oskar's idea, anyway." There was something in Emil's tone that betrayed a tenderness and happiness just below the surface. I placed a hand on his shoulder, still grinning, as warmth washed over me. This time it was a kind of cozy warmth that came from happiness and relief.

I didn't realize just how much I needed this—to be with other people. My entire time in Sophia I had never made any real friends. I spent so much time alone in my tiny apartment, and even when I made it to the palace, I didn't really connect with anyone. The closest was Velodik for our little chats in my studio once or twice a week.

"Thank you both. And don't you worry! I'll earn my keep," I said, full of determination. "I'm going to the printing press today; hopefully I can get my old job back."

As I stood outside the doors of the old printing press, I couldn't help but feel nervous—even a little afraid. I tugged at the strands of my necklace as my thoughts raced. *What if Mr Pravda doesn't want me back? What if there's no openings? Even if I do get my job back, what will they think of me?* The questions fluttered through my mind and I had to take a quick, deep breath to silence them.

With steely resolve, I opened the door. There was a great wave of heat and noise; I had nearly forgotten about them both. I stepped inside and immediately made my way up the stairs to Mr Pravda's office.

Mr Pravda was there, just behind his desk. His chair was turned around and his back was facing me. He seemed to be rummaging for something.

"Excuse me, sir," I said softly as I nervously stepped inside the office.

"Now I told you not to disturb me right now, I'm just trying to—Siranna? Siranna Ankova! By the stars!" Mr Pravda jumped out of his chair and hurried over to me. We shared a tight hug. "Well, what brings Ishkara's official artist-in-residence to our humble printing press today? Here to see your art get pressed onto some new posters?"

Memories flashed before my eyes: Ishkara's visage hanging above me and the tattered remains of my work strewn around me. A heavy rock rolled through my stomach. I forced a hint of a smile.

"Actually, Mr Pravda, I'm..." I paused as I tried to summon up the courage. Part of me couldn't believe I was coming back. I thought of the long hours, the intense heat, and the back-breaking labour. I remembered how drained I was each day and how hard it was to get myself up in the morning. I took a breath and Mr Pravda waited patiently for me to finish. For all of the toil, nothing could be as bad as what I experienced in the palace.

I continued: "I'm hoping to get my old job back."

Mr Pravda stared incredulously for a moment, and then came a flood of curiosity. "But, what about the palace? Are you no longer the artist-in-residence? What happened?"

My heart sank. I immediately felt tears well up in my eyes. How could I tell him?

One look at my face told him everything he needed to know. He nodded softly and said in a kind, firm voice, "Don't worry, Siranna. You are more than welcome here."

~ ~

The work was dreary, but I used it to my advantage. I worked late and snuck some of my own work onto one of the presses. I was printing posters.

As the first one came off the press I stopped to check it. I beamed with pride. It showcased people from across Vsevora gathered around a statue of an angel rising from a ram's skull. The statue was located in Agate Square and was said to symbolize the founding of Sophia which had "risen from the ashes of tyranny." Across the poster I had added in large, bold letters: "Laws must serve the people. The people must unite." Beneath that, a call for a peaceful protest at Agate Square.

Satisfied with the results, I kept printing. I needed to work quickly. After each shift I'd set up the machine, make small batches, and then reset it. No one would know.

As I walked back home to Oskar and Emil's, I took a winding route so that I could get as many posters in prominent locations as I could. There was no way I could blanket the city alone, but if enough people saw them, maybe they'd start talking and maybe... maybe something would happen.

The next day was the same. Set up the press, print, and head out in the night to put up posters. I noticed, however, that one of my posters had been torn down and in its place

I found "Ishkara is Harmony." With an angry grunt I tore down the poster and put mine back up.

This went on, night after night. I'd put up my posters one night, and the next they were replaced—assumedly by Public Security. The Poster War, as I called it, had begun.

"Aha, my old foe!" I exclaimed as I came to a street corner. Ishkara stared back at me. "You think I'm going to give up don't you? You think I'm just going to lay down and let you stomp all over Vsevora? You destroyed my art. You hurt innocent people at the night market. You've taken away the heart and soul of our culture. No more!" I lunged forward, grabbed hold of her face, and ripped it right off. I laughed as I threw it to the ground and replaced it with the stone angel. "You won't stop me," I muttered softly and I ran a hand along the illustration, tracing it across the people gathered together. "You won't stop us."

As I finished for the night, another battle won, I breathed in the cool night air and let out a soft sigh. Deep down, with every poster I saw of her, I could still feel Galva's blade slicing through the wings of my phoenix. But it felt good to be doing something. It felt like I might just make a difference.

I returned home and made my way back to my cot. Emil was at the dining table. Oskar must have already been in bed.

"Another late night," Emil said quietly.

"Yes," I responded, a hint of uncertainty in my voice. There was something unusual about his tone. Something accusatory. I tried to walk past him.

"I found this," he said before I could get by. My sketchbook was on the table flipped open to one of my practice sketches of the statue of Agate Square.

"You were looking through my things?" I asked, incredulous.

"It was sitting out while I was getting flour. Siranna, this looks a lot like those posters that have been appearing through town." His eyes were locked on mine and they burned with a fierce intensity. They reminded me of hers, but weren't quite the same; behind the fire was a quiver of fear. "I don't want any trouble, Siranna. Public Security has been tearing down those posters. I don't like what's happening. What they did to Oskar." He stopped and looked away from me. He stared at the sketchbook. "I'm just... I'm just thankful he made it out without being arrested. Or worse." He paused for a long moment before looking back up at me. "Please. We don't need any more trouble."

I swallowed hard. "Emil," I began, trying to find the right words, "this is important. For me, you, Oskar. For Vsevora. We can't keep quiet while Ishkara and the Senate take away everything that we love. We can't let more people get hurt."

Emil shook his head. "If we just stay quiet, Siranna, this will all blow over. Things will take their course and... Well, nothing is ever perfect."

I sat down next to him and grabbed my sketchbook. I flipped through the pages and turned to a phoenix; it was one of the few I had left. It was perched atop a stony outcropping like I saw in my dreams.

"It won't blow over, Emil. The storm is only beginning. If we don't do something soon, it will get worse. They'll keep taking things away from us. She will keep taking away all that we love until only the memories remain. And I fear she'll take those as well."

We sat quietly together for a moment and then Emil let out a frustrated sigh. "He wants to go, you know. He wants to attend your little protest."

"That's good!" I exclaimed.

"It's not!" Emil caught my hand in his and he stared at me with a desperate intensity. "You saw how Public Security hurt him. You know what they're capable of. Imagine how they'll treat you at Agate Square. I told you, Siranna, I don't want him to get hurt. I don't want any more trouble."

I could feel his hand trembling in mine. I could see the fear in his eyes. And as much as I felt for him, it only stoked the fire within me. I gripped his hand tightly.

"You shouldn't have to be afraid, Emil. That's why this is so important." We looked into one another's eyes and then he broke away. He stared down at the table and shook his head softly.

"Good night, Emil." I stood up and went into the storage room. I let out a long sigh as I sat down on my cot and looked at the sketch of the mother phoenix.

I picked up a pencil and pressed it up against the paper. Slowly, I pushed the pencil along, creating a curve that mirrored her beak. My hand started shaking. I tried to continue. I finished the beak, but the lines were ragged and distorted. My hand struggled to move. I felt a tear slide down my cheek. I stopped.

I tucked my sketchbook into my bag, crawled under a blanket, then closed my eyes tight and fell into darkness.

Chapter Twenty-Four:
Loyalty

I was nervous as we left the Greenshield behind us. There was a foul smell in the air and an uneasy feeling in my gut. But I trusted Surrendra. He would never knowingly lead us astray.

— Lakira of the Feras

Kalrevi

For a day, Velodik holed himself up in the master bedroom where he "formulated his plan." He pinned a poster to the wall and he stared at it, contemplating how he would use the upcoming protest at Agate Square to his advantage.

I had never felt more like a maid. Every half hour or so, he beckoned for fresh tea or for a meal before sending me away so that he could "think." I was certain that most of his time was spent with one of his remaining vials.

He had brought me in one last time to prepare me for an errand to Station One of Public Security. I was concerned about the nature of the task, but he quickly dismissed me.

"It's going to be perfect," Velodik said with wide eyes and a manic grin. "When you return, I will have run through all of the possibilities. This is going to work."

His room had turned into the den of a madman. There were papers and photos scattered about. A pile of cushions and blankets had been stacked up in the corner. It wasn't unusual for Velodik's room to smell so strongly of sweat, especially after bringing one of his toys around, but the odour was far more foul than ever before.

"Velodik, I'm worried about you," I said at last.

Before I could continue, he stepped up close. "No, no, shh. Everything is fine. Agh!" He shouted and gripped his head. I moved in, instinctively, to help in some way but he pushed me back. He staggered and fell onto the bed.

Still wincing, he grasped blindly until he grabbed a folder from a pile near the headboard. He rolled over to the edge of the bed, sat up, and held it out to me. "Take this with you. It's going to be fine, Kalrevi. Everything will fall back into place."

"I know you're afraid," I said bluntly. "Ishkara can take all of this away from you. But this isn't the way to keep—"

"Shut up, Kalrevi!" he barked. "I don't think you realize. If I lose everything, so do you. Do you think you can make it out there without me? Some masked freak wandering the streets! You'll be worse than how I found you. This city will grind you up without me." Silence hung between us. His words cut through me, but I knew they weren't truly his. "Bring me a tea before you go," he growled, turning away. "Be quick. You are instrumental in this execution, Kalrevi!"

I sighed and slowly slipped out of the room. Somewhere along the way, my friend had disappeared. I wanted him back and I didn't know what I could do to get him.

As I prepared his tea, I closed my eyes. I could go. I could leave him behind and run. I thought back to the night we met. I remembered the cold rain falling on me in the alleyway hundreds of kilometres away. I remembered his curiosity and his cocky smile. I remembered him welcoming me into his home and leaving out a radio on the table for me to tinker. Somewhere, under the chaos of his little vials, my friend was still in there. I couldn't run. I couldn't leave him. If he was in there, somewhere still, then perhaps I could still trust him.

The sun hung low in the sky as I arrived at Station One. As Velodik's servant, I had all of the clearance required. I stepped inside and made my way to my destination. It was all so effortless—almost disturbingly so.

I walked down a lengthy hall, my badge displayed prominently. I got a few strange looks from some of the officers within, but no one took the time to stop me. I turned a corner and nearly bumped into someone coming the other way. I immediately recognized him.

Gravel loomed over me. "Watch where you're going," he barked gruffly before realizing who he was talking to. "You." He didn't really sound surprised and he certainly wasn't pleased to stumble into me again. "Finally wearing your badge." A snide smile drifted across his thin lips.

"Keep walking," I snapped. A twinge of pain struck my shoulder just looking at him. I had spent the better part of the week recovering from his assault at the raid.

"Your master Velodik must be in a panic. All the trouble in the Senate after the raid. He's not gonna be a senator much longer." He chortled smugly.

"If Velodik goes down, you'll be going with him for the way you behaved out there."

"Hah! They'd have to shut down all of Public Security. It'll be a rap on the knuckles and that's it. Those rats out in the market all got what they deserved. You be careful, though. Best keep wearing that badge. Don't want you to get hurt." With that, he stepped past me, shoving my shoulder roughly as he went. I winced, but stood tall and was otherwise unflinching—thankful that my pain could not be seen past my mask.

I slipped down the hall until I came to a metal door with multiple locks. Glancing around me to make sure there was no one in sight, I produced a ring of keys from my bag. Quietly, I tested them one by one until I had gotten through all of the door's defences, opened it, and slid inside.

The room was dimly lit. It was lined with cabinets and cages, each filled with various contraband and evidence. I stepped up to an imposing-looking cage, unlocked it, and made my way to a trunk in the corner, just where Velodik said it would be. I crouched down and drew in a deep breath before cautiously lifting the lid. Swiftly and gently, I slipped its contents into my bag.

I heard the door behind me. With a start, I let the trunk lid slam shut and stood up. I looked left and right but there was nowhere to hide. I adjusted my stance, ready for a fight. Perhaps Gravel had come back around and decided he wanted to test my strength. It was not his silhouette that filled the doorway. It was someone smaller, but one who I had expected to see nonetheless.

"Commissioner."

"I thought I might find Velodik down here, not his pet," Zradya replied, her tone full of bile. I was reminded of Ishkara's disdain for me. I didn't let it trouble me. "What does he possibly hope to accomplish here? Tampering with evidence, perhaps?"

"My actions and those of the senator are not your concern. Walk away."

She did no such thing. She came closer, opening the cage and stepping inside with me. Her curling horns caught the dim light and draped a bleak shadow across the tiny space. She came up close, looking right into my eyes.

"What are you?" she asked, her voice barely above a whisper. Her eyes showed curiosity but also a kindling hate —the kind of hate that's fed by the fear of the unknown and the misunderstood. "What's behind that mask? What are you and Velodik so keen to hide?"

I let out a soft sigh. "You should go."

"I should arrest you."

"Then do it."

We stood there in silence for some time. I could see the thoughts spinning through her mind as she considered the possibility. Then she took a step away and shook her head.

"No. I'll give Velodik all the rope he needs to hang himself," she said with a dark smile. "Now go." She stepped aside to give me a path out.

I walked past her out of the cage and to the door. I stopped as I grabbed hold of the handle, letting out a long, slow breath. I hated what I was doing. I turned back around to face the Commissioner.

"You should leave."

"What?" she asked, incredulous. "You think you can scare me out of my own station? That mask might frighten off the common folk, but you can't intimidate me."

"No. I'm not trying to intimidate you. You should leave. Not just the station. You should leave Sophia."

Her face contorted into a snarl and she stomped toward me. "How dare you—"

"Velodik means to frame you." She stopped and stared at me with wide, skeptical eyes. I continued: "He's doctored images to make it look like you've been stealing and con-suming... illicit materials. He's created documents showing that you not only gave the orders for the raids, but that you explicitly told the officers to 'make an example' of the people there. He'll destroy you. You need to go." The words came out quickly and with a solemn seriousness. I felt an ache in the pit of my stomach. I felt like I was betraying Velodik.

Zradya's eyes narrowed in on me and she responded hotly. "I told you, you can't intimidate me. And now that you've revealed his little plan, I can refute whatever evidence he's conjured up. He can't honestly think this will be enough to undermine me."

"No. Not on its own." Her face twisted in confusion. "First of all, the Senate will be thrilled to have another scapegoat; they'd love to tear you apart. After months of turmoil, even if you manage to clear your name, you will be tainted and your career in shambles. That's the best case scenario. At worst, you're hauled off to Kamin Prison for... years, perhaps? If you leave the city, your career is still lost, but you save yourself from the worst."

As I finished, I could see the anger rising up inside of her. She clenched her fists and bared her teeth in a harsh grimace. Before she could speak up, I opened the door.

"Velodik's scheme has already been put in motion. It doesn't matter to me if you believe me. But you have a chance to save yourself from the pain." I turned and hurried out without waiting for a response. I moved briskly down the hall. The door didn't open after me. She must have been considering everything I said.

I took a turn down another hall. I wasn't making my way to the exit. Not yet, at least. I slipped into the Commissioner's office and pulled an envelope out of my bag. I glanced inside at the sepia photographs Velodik had forged. I slid them into a cabinet, just where he had told me to put them, and quickly fled.

My stomach turned again. I didn't feel any better about following through than I did about telling her. I couldn't betray him completely. At least I gave Zradya a chance.

Darkness had fallen over Sophia as I stepped outside of the station. I tugged at the bag strapped across my chest and thought about the contents within. I didn't know what they were. I didn't know what else Velodik had planned.

I looked up at the sky and gazed at the twinkling lights above. I thought back to the stories of my ancestors and how they had once navigated by those stars. There weren't as many stars in Sophia as there were back home; the lamplight drowned so many out. I felt lost.

Chapter Twenty-Five:
The Patrol

Sometimes I wonder where I'd be if I never met her. Would I have stayed a simple officer? Maybe I'd have married Klim. Would it have been worth it... to give up all I've earned?

— from the diary of Velodik

Velodik

I screamed. I screamed as loud as I could and bashed my head against my pillow. The daggers wouldn't come out. Tears rushed down my face. I dug my nails into the mattress and kept screaming until my throat could no longer bear it.

I gasped and rolled onto my side. I took in a deep breath, held it, and slowly let it out. I kept it up until slowly the pain started to subside, if only a little bit.

Just as I started to relax, the walls of the room began closing in on me. I cursed. I needed to get out. I couldn't stay here any longer. I pulled myself up and warily got to my feet. As I put one foot in front of the other, I nearly fell over as my strength gave way. I stumbled into the wall and pressed myself against it, holding myself up shakily.

Gradually, I shuffled to the door, pausing at the poster I had pinned to the wall. I stared at the image of the statue and traced my hand along its wing. "Soon. It will fall into place soon."

I drew in a deep breath, feeling the strength return to my legs and shambled out of the room in a daze. The pain from the daggers lingered through my head but I managed to persevere despite it. I grabbed a long coat and wrapped the dark green fabric around me. I ran my fingers along the thick wool, but I could barely feel its texture. It was as though my whole body was turning numb.

Everything was still closing in. I was having trouble breathing. I hurried outside and gasped with relief as the cool air hit my lungs. I kept walking, moving briskly down the street. An ache started in my legs and slowly rolled up through my back. I grit my teeth and pushed forward. I didn't know where I was going—I just had to move.

The city hurried by. Rows of houses turned into taller buildings and I found myself walking down a familiar path with familiar turns. It was my old patrol.

As I walked, I remembered all of the little sights and stops along the way. There was an old woman who'd often be out for a walk this way. I'd lift my hat as we crossed paths and shared a warm smile. A few blocks down and I'd have to keep my eyes open for some mischievous youngsters; their schemes were innocent enough, but it was important to make my presence known to keep them in line. A few more houses along and there was a lavender bush. I'd stop there and smell the beautiful flowers throughout the spring. It was nowhere to be found though; the bush must have been dug up years ago.

It had, of course, been many years since I walked this path. It felt like centuries. I felt as ancient as the trees and the stones. I had been eroded, weathered by wind and storms and sand. My body ached as it continued down my well-worn path.

Back then, I had no idea what I would become. All I wanted was to make a difference for people like me. Had I? Was I making a difference now?

A new dagger found its way into my head and I growled. I shook my head and the questions all fell away, but the dagger remained. I kept walking.

Despite the pain that ached throughout my brain, my mind didn't stop racing. For days I had been carefully contemplating my schemes and even as I drifted through memories, my machinations kept bubbling to the forefront of my thoughts. Just as I walked along the old patrol, I walked through the plan. It was perfect; I knew it.

Soon I would be rid of Commissioner Zradya, burying her in scandal and blame. After that, I needed Ishkara back on my side.

Ishkara's shakedown had left me dizzy and raw, but I was determined to set things right with her once again. Kalrevi would be the key to that; the whole plan hinged on her.

When I told Ishkara about my intentions, she doubted me. "It's dangerous," she said. "You're playing with fire."

As I walked, I saw her staring at me. I stopped. "Trust me," I said. "The Senate will be firmly on your side when all is said and done."

She looked back at me silently and stoically. I narrowed my eyes and glared. "You don't believe me, do you? You don't think I can pull it off." Nothing. "It's going to work," I said sternly. "It has to," I quietly added.

She remained silent and I let out a frustrated grunt. Then I realized it wasn't her. Her poster looked back at me unblinking. I let out an exasperated sigh and rubbed my temples. *I'm going insane,* I thought.

I closed my eyes for a moment. I just wanted all of it to be over. I wanted the controversy to fade, for Ishkara to succeed, and to go back to my toys and my vials.

Patience. I told myself. *It won't be long. Kalrevi will succeed at Station One and then tomorrow everything will fall into place. It will be exactly as you planned. It will be exactly as Ishkara desires.*

I opened my eyes and smiled. For the first time in days, the daggers fell away and my mind became clear. I felt pleasantly refreshed. I started walking again.

Before long I came upon another familiar sight. I gasped as I looked upon the old building. It had been so long since I had been there and the place hadn't changed. It looked exactly as it had all of those years ago, back when I visited it every day.

I looked up at the old wooden sign hanging above the doorway: Brazen Bull Café. I couldn't help but grin as I stared at the sign, watching it sway lightly in the breeze. I felt a youthful spark shoot through me. I was excited. I wanted to go in, to have a bowl of homemade soup, and to see Klim again for the first time in years.

I could just imagine his face: his pale blue eyes would light up; he'd smile; his grey little ears would perk up on the top of his head.

I practically skipped up to the door. I grabbed hold of the knob, gave it a twist and then... It didn't budge. I was confused. I gave the door a push, then a pull, then a push again to be safe. It still didn't move.

As I stood there, my mind wandered back to the last time I had been to the Brazen Bull—the last time I saw Klim. I had just been promoted to Commissioner.

"Klim!" I exclaimed as I barged into the busy café.

"Well well, Sergeant Velodik! Good to see you. It's been a while!" Klim replied with a bright smile.

"Ah, not Sergeant. It's Commissioner now!" I said with a laugh. I staggered up to the counter. I had imbibed a great many celebratory drinks.

"Well, congratulations!" he exclaimed. As I came up close I saw him wrinkle up his nose and recoil a bit at my presence. He stammered, keeping up his politeness and customer service, "Were you, um, looking f-for some soup or a tea then, Commissioner?"

I leaned up over the counter and growled deep in my throat. "No, Klim. I'm looking for something hotter than soup!" I laughed lecherously. "Come on. Close up shop and come with me back to my place."

Klim's eyes grew wide and he staggered back, bumping into the back counter behind him. "V-Velodik. I uh... I'm sorry but..." He stumbled over his words and looked around nervously.

"Oh you sweet little thing. Don't be shy and don't be nervous! We can have plenty of fun, you and me!" I grinned widely and reached over the counter, trying to grab him and pull him over to me, but he was just beyond my reach.

"Please stay back!" he exclaimed suddenly. The café grew quiet and I froze in my tracks. All eyes in the room turned toward us. "I-I'm not i-interested."

I drew back and straightened up to my full height. I narrowed my gaze. "I'm the Commissioner, you know. It would be a shame if the constabulary found a problem with your little establishment, Klim."

His eyes grew even wider and he trembled with a mix of anger and fear. "Get out," he hissed. "Get out of here, Velodik, and don't you dare step foot in my café again."

I didn't retaliate, of course. I left. And I never returned. Or at least, I never intended to return. Perhaps after all this time he would have forgiven my drunken provocation. Not that it seemed to matter.

I sighed and let go of the door knob, then looked around at the old building. The lights were out. Surely old Klim hadn't closed yet. I took a step back and wondered at what could have happened. It didn't look like it had been abandoned or shut down. It was just as it should have been, except for the lights. I took a deep breath. There was no smell of soup in the air. What happened?

A young man happened by as I was staring at the building and I waved at him, stopping him in his path.

"Excuse me," I said, "but do you know why the café is closed?"

He turned around and looked up at the building. He shook his head thoughtfully and some jewelry dangling from his horns rocked gently to and fro. He turned back to me with a sad expression on his face.

"It was an unfortunate thing that happened to ol' Klim. Going to miss his soups," he said with a deep frown.

My heart jumped up and rattled through my chest. I stammered, "Wh-what do you mean? What happened to him?"

"He got caught up in that whole night market business. He was hurt. Badly."

I breathed a sigh of relief and the young man looked at me strangely. I realized how it must have seemed and I held up my hands apologetically. "No, no. I just—from what you said, I thought it was something worse."

He shook his head. "It was still pretty bad. I don't know the whole story, but people in the neighbourhood have been talking. I guess Klim used to get a lot of ingredients from the night market—spices and whatnot. Well, when the place got raided, he got caught up in it. I don't know if he was trying to help someone out and Public Security didn't take kindly to it, or if he just ended up in the wrong spot at the wrong time, but he got it bad."

I frowned and stepped up closer. "What do you mean?"

Something in my tone, the growing desperation perhaps, threw the young man off and he staggered away from me; but he continued: "Old Lady Jana says that Public Security really enjoyed themselves that night. They were acting more like a street gang than officers. They hurt Klim badly: a broken nose, broken arm, a couple ribs, and they messed up the poor guy's leg. I hear he barely got himself out of there."

I stood silently. My arms shook and my legs grew weak again.

"Brazen Bull is closed up until Klim is up and able again. Hope to see him well soon," the young man said. He looked toward the ground forlornly.

"I see," I said quietly. "Thank you."

"Good day to you, sir," he replied, quickly pulling himself out of the sadness he created. He turned and continued on his way.

I stumbled back up to the door and leaned against it as my legs surrendered. I remained there for some time, trying to process everything I had just been told.

Was it worth it? I wondered. I felt the daggers softly sliding back into their places, piercing through the thin membrane of my mind, and sending forth a surge of static through my brain.

I pulled my coat tighter around me as though it were the embrace of another person offering some small sliver of comfort. The feeling was empty. There was nothing there. I had no one.

My hand balled up into a fist and I bashed it against the door. I let out a harsh, barking shout and collapsed to the ground. The little outburst did nothing to assuage the painful feelings that wormed their way through me. I lifted my hands; they were shaking.

This shouldn't bother me, I thought. *I barely knew him. He wouldn't even recognize me now. He doesn't matter. He doesn't matter. He doesn't matter.* As I repeated the words in my head again and again, I felt hot tears fall onto my hands. I snarled at myself and hit the door again. I couldn't abide this weakness.

I took a handkerchief from my pocket and wiped it across my face. Even the little square of silk fabric felt dull against my skin. I stuffed it back into my pocket and looked down the street. There was no one nearby to see me at least.

I scrambled to my feet and fled. I took an unfamiliar turn, avoiding any more familiar paths. I pushed the Brazen Bull behind me; I forced the memories away. I didn't want to remember anymore—the patrol, the café, Klim, any of it! They were gone, and I didn't want anymore reminders of that old life ever again.

My thoughts turned toward the future and my inevitable victory. Tomorrow, Kalrevi would execute the plan. The day after, Ishkara would raise me to a new pinnacle. All of my machinations would fall into place. I wouldn't need anything else.

Chapter Twenty-Six:
The Protest

The Vsevoran spirit is unyielding. It is that sprit that shall guide our nation and uplift us higher than any other.

— *Ishkara*

Siranna

It was late as I stoked the fires. I was exhausted, but I couldn't stop. This was my last chance: my final print run. Tomorrow, as the sun set, the people of Sophia would gather together in protest.

The last of the posters came off the press. I quickly cut and stacked them into neat little bundles. I filled up my bag and hoisted it onto my back. It felt like I was carrying an entire tree, but I could manage; I was determined.

As I shut down the machine, I heard the clanking of the door followed by a voice: "Hello? Hello? Who's there?"

My heart jumped into my throat and my stomach knotted up. I darted behind the machine and crouched low as a harsh clacking sound echoed through the facility.

I remembered the sound of Ishkara's hooves as she strode through the palace. I closed my eyes and I saw her face. She loomed over me, smiling darkly. I could feel rough hands grabbing me as Public Security officers dragged me away. Everything grew dark. I heard the heavy clank of a metal door sealing me up. I would never see the light of day again.

I shook my head and snapped out of it. My breathing was heavy and erratic. I tried to steady it as I pressed myself against the still-warm printing press. Then I realized that the clacking sound had stopped.

Looking across, underneath the machine, I could see a set of hooves there. If I stayed in place, I risked getting caught, and so I crept away. I kept low and silent and as I rounded the corner, I prepared to make a dash toward the door. I didn't notice my bag had gotten caught on the machine and the moment I tried to hurry forward, I was yanked backwards. I hit the ground with a thud, the bag tore open, and posters spilled out. Frantically, I scrambled to pull myself back together. I tugged at my bag and struggled to get back to my feet. *Clack clack clack.* The hooves moved toward me. I wriggled free from the bag and left it and the scattered posters behind. I ran; I was too late.

I slammed into a broad frame and stumbled back. I turned and darted the other way. I hurried through the mess of papers and didn't look back, even as a voice boomed after me to stop. The broad frame clacked swiftly behind me. I made a quick turn and sped forward, only to realize that in my panic I had gone the wrong way. I had gotten myself caught in a dead end. I spun back around to the broad figure which now barred my path.

"I uh, I'm sorry," I stammered. I didn't know what else to say.

"Siranna, is that you? What on earth are you doing?" I finally recognized the voice: Mr Pravda.

No, no, no, I thought. I didn't want him to know. I couldn't face his disappointment and his wrath. I had abused my access to the facility. After he had welcomed me back with open arms, I betrayed his trust. I didn't know what he would do to me, but in that moment I wished it had been Public Security that stood before me instead.

He moved in closer. He was carrying my bag with a few of the posters still inside of it. "You shouldn't be here after hours. Is this what you've been up to?" he asked, lifting one of the posters from the bag.

"I'm so sorry, Mr Pravda. I can explain everything."

He unfurled the poster, revealing the angel and the call for protest. "I've seen these around Sophia," he said, inspecting it thoughtfully. "Public Security would not look kindly upon anyone printing and distributing materials like these. As a sanctioned printing press, the fact that these were even printed here puts us at risk of being shut down. You, your colleagues, all of us could be facing a lot of trouble."

Knots roiled about in my stomach. I hadn't thought about how my posters might affect the rest of the people at the press. I hadn't thought about the consequences for anyone outside of myself. I shrunk back in shame.

"Mr Pravda, this was all me," I said softly. "None of the other workers had any idea. Please. Turn me in if you must. I don't want anyone to get hurt."

He shot a smile back at me. "Well, let's not be so hasty. No need to rush to tell Public Security about this." I was dumbfounded. I couldn't even stammer a response. He continued: "I, for one, have welcomed the sight of these posters. In fact, I was thinking of going to Agate Square myself."

"I... You... Really?"

Mr Pravda laughed. "Siranna, come with me." He clacked away toward his office. I followed, still confused and spinning, although the knots were calming down.

He offered me a seat and a cup of water. Mr Pravda picked up a frame from the wall and placed it down in front of me. It was a grainy, sepia-tone photo of the outside of the facility. There was a trio of young men standing outside of it. The one in the middle had Mr Pravda's bullish horns, broad frame, and wide nose, but he must have been at least thirty years younger.

"Do you know why I opened the printing press?" he asked as he leaned back in his cushioned chair. I shook my head, staring back down at the photo. "Because I love books. I was a voracious reader as a child. My parents had a desperate time trying to keep me sated back then." He chuckled softly, leaning back in his chair as he reminisced.

"There was no printing press in Sophia. Can you imagine that? In the heart of Vsevora! The home of Kavya herself and we couldn't even print our own books. All of our books came out of Olga at that time. Our family was well-off and could afford them, but the same could not be said for many others. As I grew older, I wanted to share that love of reading with every other person in Sophia.

"I partnered with a few other lads and we built this place from the ground up. Over the years, we expanded, and as Ishkara unified the nation, we were soon distributing across Vsevora. You can imagine my delight at the opportunity to share my love, not just with Sophia, but every person in the nation." Mr Pravda had a warm smile on his face, but it faded to a saddened scowl.

"What happened?" I asked.

"We became an officially sanctioned printing press."

I thought back to the day of the celebration. I remembered Mr Pravda halting everything to gather us together for the announcement. "But I thought that was a good thing. Everyone was so excited!"

"That's what I thought, too. I thought we would have more opportunities and more resources to distribute a wealth of knowledge and stories. But no." He reached into his desk and pulled out a folder. He laid it open and I saw a variety of documents with bright red ink and Vsevora's crest sealed upon them. "The mandates changed. Once, we were able to print whatever we pleased. Not anymore. New books and manuscripts required approval. We needed to dedicate more of the facility to produce materials specifically for Ishkara. I pushed back and tried to loophole my way into printing the same kinds of works we always did, but they quickly put a stop to that."

He slid one of the papers toward me. I furrowed my brow at it and spoke its words with disdain: "The 'prohibition on radical, sectarian propaganda.' Why not withdraw sanctioned status?"

"Ishkara's new laws only allow sanctioned printing presses to operate. If we don't comply, then the whole facility is shuttered."

"I see," I replied, sadly. I put the paper back into the folder. "You don't want to hurt all of the families that rely on this place."

Mr Pravda nodded solemnly and reached into his desk again. He withdrew a few well-read books and gently set them down before him, then continued: "Some of my favourite books from my childhood: beautiful folktales from the Olgan countryside; the historical and political writings of Kavya of Sophia; collections of poetry from Lyudmila. I can't print these books. They are no longer sanctioned." He opened one of them and traced his hand along the words within. "'Vile propaganda that cannot be permitted for public consumption.' Imagine: a simple story being too dangerous for the nation."

"That's exactly why I want to protest," I said, feeling courage welling up inside me once again. "We need to show Ishkara and the Senate what we want."

"What is it that you want, Siranna?"

I paused and looked down. I stared at the books. I thought of my sketches and my paintings. I thought of Oskar's bruised arm. I thought about my mother. "I want them to understand what Vsevora really is. We aren't just one nation. We are a collection of communities. I want them to see that we are made whole by the things that make us unique. I want them to celebrate that instead of tearing it down."

"Well said," Mr Pravda replied with a smile. "I must say, Siranna, I'm quite proud that these posters were printed here. I think you'll find that there are more people like us who are ready to push back on these laws. I'll be sure to see you at Agate Square tomorrow night."

It was getting late. I was tired. Almost time.

As I approached Agate Square, my feet ached. I felt like I had walked across the entire city putting up the last of the posters. As weary as I was, I knew I had to keep going.

A small force of Public Security was scattered around the square. I froze as I caught sight of them. They seemed ready to intimidate and disperse any protestors that might appear. If they knew that I had created the posters... I didn't want to imagine what would happen to me. I ducked into an alley to keep out of sight. I tried to steady my breathing.

I thought back to Mr Pravda. He had such confidence—confidence that I wished for now as I felt my stomach churn. *What am I doing?* I asked myself. *What if no one comes? Will Oskar convince Emil to let him come? What if it's just Mr Pravda and me? We get dragged away by Public Security together, I guess.* My stomach ached more with every passing moment. I heard laughter: a pair of officers telling a joke and cackling. I tried to steady my breathing.

The sky became a yellow backdrop against the black outline of the square. The statue at its centre, a triumphant angel rising from a ram's skull, towered over everything else. The buildings seemed to lose their depth as they turned into silhouettes against the setting sun. In my mind, I broke down their shapes into little geometric tiles. I imagined adding more tiles, building them higher and higher, spreading them out and filling the square. I did this as I tried desperately to distract myself from the fear building up inside of me. I tried to steady my breathing.

The sun sank lower and the sky turned orange. I slumped to the ground. No one was coming. They were afraid. I couldn't blame them; I was afraid, too.

It's over, I told myself. *I should leave Sophia—go home to Oksana, to be forgotten, and to start over again.* I wiped a tear from my cheek and pulled myself back to my aching feet. I turned away from the angel and shuffled slowly down the alleyway.

That's when I heard something.

I turned around and ran into the square. Down the road were a dozen people, some of them holding signs, and all shouting together. They were marching toward the statue, calling for others to join them.

The officers stared them down and sauntered toward them, lifting up heavy shields that bore the crest of Vsevora. They rattled them intimidatingly.

There was more shouting—from behind us this time. Approaching from another road were at least two dozen, all chanting in unison: "Laws serve the people! The people don't serve the law!"

The officers stopped in their tracks and their posture became uncertain. They tried to disperse the chanters—

tried to shout them down—but the officers couldn't be heard over the gathering voices. Both groups of protestors came together around the statue, lifting their voices together. I couldn't help but smile as I ran to join them. An officer barked an order and two others ran down the street. I laughed. Running off with tails between their legs.

We chanted louder and soon more and more people joined us. There were people of all ages and all backgrounds: Oksanans, Ksenyans, Olgans, Lyudmilans, and more. They hoisted up my poster and our voices rose together, echoing throughout the square until it felt as though all of Sophia could hear us. As shades of red began to stretch into the sky, our number had grown immensely; I guessed that there were perhaps five hundred of us filling the square.

I climbed up onto the statue and grabbed hold of one of the angel's wings. I unfurled an orange flag with Vsevora's crest upon it and "For the People" written beneath. I waved it over the crowd and they cheered.

"Friends!" I called out to the sea of people before me. I watched as five hundred faces looked back, with even more coming, pouring in from every thoroughfare. The cheering and the chatter died down as they prepared to listen.

What in the world am I doing? I thought. *Who am I? I'm a girl from Oksana. A desperate artist. A printer. A fraud. A child.* I stood still and quiet. I thought of the crowd in Oksana... my mother... Ishkara. I stared at the faces in the crowd and I could feel the weight of the world. My hand trembled and my grip upon the stone wing started to slip. My legs shook. I was going to fall.

I stopped. I caught myself and held the statue tightly. I pushed my thoughts aside. I steadied my breathing.

"We have witnessed a dangerous turning of the tides," I began. My throat was already dry, but I couldn't stop. My heart burned and the words burst out of me. "We've stood idly by as the Chancellor and the Senate have violently stripped away the treasures that make us unique. Our literature, our music, and our traditions are being restricted in the name of one Vsevora. But as I look out at those who have gathered tonight... We have not gathered as Sophians or Oksanans or Ksenyans. We have gathered as Vsevorans. What is Vsevora without the Ksenyan piccolo? What is it without Oksanan tapestry? Who are we without the writings of Kavya of Sophia? Chancellor Ishkara would have us believe that these things divide us and turn us against one another. But we know that these are the very things that make Vsevora whole! We cannot stand by any longer as our culture is taken away. Tonight we stand up! Tonight we march forward! Tonight we tell the lawmakers that their laws must serve the people. Vsevora *is* the people. The people do not serve the laws!"

There was a glorious roar from the crowd. I waved the banner against the setting sun and the glittering strings of light that sparkled to life around the square. I shouted out as loudly as I could: "We march! To the Senate! To Ishkara! We will make our voices heard!" Another roar and the crowd turned its sights to the violet sky in the east and the silhouette of the royal palace.

My heart was beating with wild thrill. All of our voices as one. Everything coming together. Because of me. I had made all of this happen. The fear and doubt melted away as we chanted together: "The laws serve the people! The people are Vsevora!" I was brimming with strength. We were going to make a difference. I waved the flag from the statue as the crowd surged around me. The last fire-red ray of the sunset gleamed behind us and vanished behind the horizon.

Suddenly, a furious, ear-splitting crack of thunder broke through the chanting. Smoke poured out from the heart of the crowd and the crowd began to surge with fear. Row upon row of Public Security officers marched toward the protest. They were heavily armoured and their faces were consumed by shadow. Another crack of thunder! This time the sound came from behind us, and I saw another plume of smoke rise up. There were more officers marching in, closing off our escape. The euphoria melted away and I felt panic crawl like a slithering eel up from my stomach and into my throat.

There was silence for a moment and then the crowd rumbled to life again. "The laws serve the people! The people are Vsevora!" The crowd met the blockade and stood its ground, continuing its chant. I watched as the officers closed in behind. While everyone else was undeterred, my panic continued to slither and writhe inside of me. I gripped hard onto the flag and closed my eyes as I focused on driving these feelings out.

My eyes darted open when I heard a scream. Ahead of me I saw a ball of flame careening across the sky. *What was that?* It arced down, not onto the crowd, but onto the officers. I watched in horror as the ball impacted on a member of Public Security and erupted around them. I watched as the officer was immolated, crumpling to their knees, and burned to death before my eyes. The nearby officers tried to douse the flame, but instead, it spread.

A moment later, another fireball crashed down onto Public Security. *No, no, no, no, no,* I thought, *not this.* The chanting died, and in its place a roar of screams as officers charged in and the crowd tried helplessly to escape. More smoke rose up, enveloping the protestors. They coughed, choked, and flailed about blindly; pushing, shoving, and trampling over one another. I clung to the statue, frozen there, as if I had become a part of the stone. I screamed, begging for sanity, but no one could hear me any longer.

A war raged through the streets. The officers spun their batons and bludgeoned the protestors, battering them to the ground and dragging them into carts that lined the edge of the square. In the glittering lights I could make out their expressions: a mix of rage and excitement and mirth.

A third fireball rose up, but Public Security was ready this time. Officers raised their shields to the flame. This time, when the fire exploded out, it coated their shields. There was a triumphant cry from the officers as they brought the shields back down and turned them into fiery battering rams. They surged in quickly and the people tried to run from their burning fury.

I could barely keep track of all of the chaos. I gasped for breath and cried out hoarsely, begging for it all to stop. An officer leapt onto the statue with me. She had horns like mine. Eyes the same colour as mine. I never wanted a fight with Public Security. I wanted them to stand with us—to march with us—unified.

"Please," I said, my rasping voice barely carrying over the screams. "We have to work together. For Vsevora. For all people. We are all the same."

"I don't care." Her words pierced through me as she grabbed the flag and pushed me from my perch. I crashed to the ground, hard, and my head cracked against the cobblestone; everything spun around me. I saw blurry figures running and grappling; I heard more screams. The Oksanan officer shattered the flag staff in half and threw it to the ground. With a leap, she was on top of me. She lifted me up by the clasp of my cloak and dragged me across the square toward the carts.

There was an obstinate roar—more protestors, but these ones were fearless. The violence had put them into a frenzy; they swarmed us and the officer dropped me. There was a massive writhing of limbs as the protestors battered her to the ground. I screamed as I got caught in the cross-fire and their boots pounded into my side. Something got my leg and I was dragged out of the mob. I barely saw who saved me before they, too, joined the swarm around the screaming Oksanan officer.

I rolled onto my hands and knees, my head still spinning, and I crawled away. I could barely see anything beyond the smoke, the shadows, and the flame. As I crawled, I caught sight of someone else on the ground and I hurried toward them.

"We'll get through this together," I called out to the person on the ground. I winced at the aching of my head. *Keep going. Keep moving through the pain,* I told myself. "I'm almost there. It'll be all right!" I stopped as my hands splashed into thick, warm liquid. *No no no!* I waded through the pool of blood and followed it to its source: the man on the ground.

I pulled myself over to the man's broad frame. Tears welled up in my eyes as realization washed over me. His eyes were still open, but there was no life behind them; they had the same faded sepia colour as his photo.

"M-Mr Pravda," I whispered softly. "Oh no. Why did you come?" I crumbled into Mr Pravda's cold chest and sobbed. Everything else melted away. There were no other sounds.

The screaming faded. The smoke washed away. All that was left was my anguish echoing across the void.

I closed my eyes and held him tightly, begging for him to stand up. I wished for the nightmare to end. I wanted the phoenix to carry me away and to wake up in Oksana. I wanted to paint my face the way my mother wanted.

Reality came rushing back as a hand gripped my shoulder and flipped me onto to my back. The shouting and roar of the square pounded against my head and the smell of smoke and blood flooded my nose.

Everything looked hazy through my tears and I was still dizzy from the fall. Above me stood a black shadow against orange flame and violet sky. A porcelain-white visage wreathed in smoky wisps loomed in close.

My head ached. I was fading fast. The shadows, the fire, the visage, and everything else blurred together. Something grabbed hold of me, pulled me up, and then everything turned black.

Chapter Twenty-Seven:
The Snare

The city burnt like a torch in the night. I could see it all, up on
Ferma Hill. The flames grew higher. Then came the screams.
They echoed across the valley and filled the air like smoke.

— from the account of the shepherd Siemo,
on The Ransacking of Lyudmila

Kalrevi

"Kalrevi! Kalrevi!" Velodik's voice rang through the halls of his manse. I had only just returned from Station One. I sighed and hurried to his room.

I swung the door open, bathing the dim room in light. Velodik sat in the middle of his bed with a long, green coat wrapped around him. There were maps of Sophia, Agate Square in particular, laid out all around him, illuminated only by a few flickering candles. He must have been working out the last details of his plan for the protest tomorrow night.

He slowly turned his head toward me, his eyes narrowing sharply. "Did you find them?" he barked. His tone was vicious and impatient.

I stepped into the room, unfazed by his change in demeanour. I set my bag onto the bed and reached inside. I revealed a glass orb that fit neatly into the palm of my hand. I set it gently in front of Velodik and his eyes shone brightly.

"*Vohon*. The Ravager of Lyudmila. Perfect." He took the orb into his hands and pulled it close to his face, inspecting it gleefully. He was smiling from ear to ear. He looked back to me with a piercing gaze. The beam of light from the hallway and the creeping shadows of the room turned his face into that of a distorted clown.

After an uncomfortable silence, he said softly, "I'm ready." He inched closer, holding the orb in one hand and gathering up one of his maps in the other. "I've laid it out perfectly, just as Ishkara wanted." His voice was quiet and his tone conspiratorial. He waved me closer, leaned in, and laid out his plan.

I walked steadily toward Agate Square, focused on the path ahead. The sun had started its descent and so I quickened my pace. I needed to find a place to keep hidden until the time was right. I tugged at the cloak that enveloped me, pulling it far over my face to conceal the mask, and taking care to obscure the three glass spheres strung to my belt. I couldn't be conspicuous.

I silently lamented the task that had been thrust upon me. When I first donned my mask it was because I had succeeded in my apprenticeship as a builder and tinker. It was in picking up a tool and repairing that which was broken that I had found my passion and my joy. Yet all Velodik cared about was my strength and my stealth. To him, I was a tool to destroy all that stood in his path.

As thoughts of the task ahead simmered in my mind, I wondered if I really was any freer now than I had been behind the Greenshield. Perhaps this, the wide world beyond, was the prison cell instead. I shook the uneasy feelings away and turned my attention to the square.

A handful of officers from Public Security were gathered around the statue. Their faces were young and eager. They nattered on about how they would put a stop to any protestors and joked about the violent ways in which they would do it. This was a game to them, but they didn't realize that they were the pawns.

I lingered longer than I should. One of them caught sight of me and looked at me suspiciously. I thought of Gravel; he'd have loved the opportunity to cross paths with me once more. Thankfully, he wasn't amongst this crew.

I hurried away before the officer could take any action and found a quiet corner just outside Agate Square that I could sink into. I was a shadow.

As the sun set, the empty square quickly filled with dozens and then suddenly hundreds of people. It was easy to blend into the growing throng as the protest began. They didn't care whether or not I was chanting along with them; I was just another body amongst hundreds.

I recognized the ringleader. It was the same young woman that I protected from thieves at the night market: Ishkara's propaganda machine, Siranna. She must have become dissatisfied at the palace. As the square filled, I watched her confidence grow. She lifted her orange flag high above her spiral horns and rallied the crowd. As she spoke, I questioned my mission.

I had questioned Velodik when he revealed his plan the night before. He snapped back, refusing to listen to me. I had never seen him so incensed. Everything in the square seemed to melt away and his words rang through my mind:

"I don't care what you think! I can send you back to the squalor that you came from! I can have Public Security take you away from here and you won't see the light of day ever again!"

"I don't understand this," I stammered back. "You're advocating murder."

He calmed as suddenly as he had exploded. "It's the only way the Senate will understand. Vsevora doesn't know how much it needs us. For protection. For harmony." Velodik's tone was void of emotion and more measured than anything I had heard him say since the night market raid.

"Velodik. This is evil."

"It is a necessary evil," he said. "A small evil when you compare it to what would happen otherwise. If we don't see this through, the unity of Vsevora will crumble. The city-states will revert to local control and bit by bit the fighting starts again. As the years roll by, the wars begin. Thousands will be impoverished and displaced. Hundreds will die. Think about how you had suffered before I found you. Imagine that suffering amplified across the entire nation!"

A sudden cry broke through my memories: "We march!" I was thrust back into reality. Siranna was waving her flag vigorously and a roar erupted from the crowd. The sun drifted away and the unrelenting dark crept over the square. "We march to the royal palace! We will make our voices heard!" Siranna exclaimed. The crowd called out in ecstasy and rage all around me and began their chanting anew. They turned their sights to the palace and began their march.

I kept pace with the crowd, preparing myself for what would happen next. As if on cue, Public Security arrived in terrifying force and formed a blockade. I placed a hand on one of the spheres, staring at the officers.

I still don't think I can do this. The words rolled through my mind. They were just as uncertain and fearful as when I said them back at the mansion. Even as smoke rose up through the square, more memories returned to haunt me:

"I don't care what you think!" Velodik screamed. All measure and reason had vanished from his voice. He leapt to his feet and stood tall and imposing before me. I shifted my weight and held my ground. His yellow eyes flickered with wild fury and he grabbed my throat. A sudden shock of pain struck me as he clamped down hard. I drew a gasping breath, but barely any air passed through my throat.

"Velodik! Stop!" I choked, but he kept constricting. His claws dug into my flesh, intensifying the pain. I reached for his hand and tried to pull him away, but my strength was fading fast. "Velodik! I can't breathe!" I managed to gasp.

"You would be lost on the streets without me! You would be dead!" he continued, ignoring my pleas. "Whose life will it be, Kalrevi? Yours or theirs?" I choked and gurgled in response. I tried to bash at his wrist and elbow but he held firm with a strength I didn't know he possessed. "Yours or theirs, Kalrevi?" His voice was unrecognizable as he screamed. I couldn't manage to make a sound anymore. I felt my body going limp.

He threw me to the ground. I drew breath into my empty lungs and coughed. I struggled to catch my breath; for the first time my mask felt like it was suffocating me. After a few strenuous gasps, my breathing evened out. I clutched at my throat and felt thin lines of wet blood.

"Whose life will it be, Kalrevi?" he asked again, looming over me.

I touched my throat and ran my fingers over the dried scabs. The crowd's panic grew as Public Security closed in on them. I shook the visions of Velodik out of my mind once again, and I grabbed one of the spheres from my belt.

I lifted up the sphere, the *vohon*, to the level of my eyes, and activated it; a fire came to life inside of the glass. I gazed at the onslaught of officers.

Then I spotted him. Velodik was there amongst Public Security. He was staring right back at me—menacing at me with wild, yellow eyes.

With a cry of anger, I hurled the sphere with all my strength. I aimed it right for him. It arced through the sky, and as it did, I grabbed the two other spheres, ready to follow up my volley. The fire struck its target.

As the *vohon* crashed open and erupted with flame, I realized too late that those yellow eyes were not Velodik's. Velodik was nowhere to be seen. I froze, horrified at what I had just done.

My victim's eyes filled with terror. I could tell he was still a young boy—barely old enough to be an officer. Had he joined with dreams of keeping the streets of Sophia safe? Or was he like Gravel, and only wanted to dominate those around him? Did it really matter?

He screamed as fire rapidly engulfed his body, leaving his visage, wreathed in flame, seared into my mind. I was shaken. I stumbled to my knees and dropped the remaining spheres; they rolled away from me. I was unable to move—unable to recover them.

The crowd roared with fear and rage. Many were horrified as they watched the fire spread from officer to officer, but others drank it up, thrilled at the chance to punish Public Security at last. A scream pierced through the cacophony and I saw another ball of fire arcing overhead. I looked around frantically, but the spheres had disappeared. Someone had gotten a hold of them.

As chaos broke across the streets, I tried to push my way back into the shadows. Instead, I was caught up in a wave of panic, and dragged along by the force of the crowd.

Public Security stormed through, without even an illusion of restraint. They were out to avenge their comrades and stamp out the flame of rebellion.

A group of officers surged in my direction. I, and the others around me, started to run. A baton crashed down on a young woman next to me and she dropped to the ground. I kept going. Another one fell. There was hot breath behind me.

I saw my chance—a break in the line. I pushed my way against the current of the crowd. The batons came down like a crashing wave that I narrowly avoided. I broke free just as the officers closed the gap. They forced the rest of the crowd back, rounding them up and caging them in.

I ran into the shadows and then I paused. I looked back at the churning crowd of screams and smoke. I felt sick for what I had done. And then I saw her: the instigator. Siranna was crawling on hands and knees.

She's the one who started this, I told myself. I closed in on her. *She should carry the blame. Not me.*

I stood over her. She was sobbing over a body in a puddle of blood. I turned her over. She was disoriented and afraid.

What am I doing? I asked myself. I looked around at the chaos. *This isn't who I am. This isn't what I want to be.*

I had caused this, and nothing could absolve me of that. This wasn't the life I had dreamed of beyond the Greenshield. It was time for change.

I picked up the girl and lifted her into my arms with a groan, as my shoulder reminded me of its recent injury. I hurried out of the square and back into the shadows.

I laid Siranna down in my bed. I watched the gentle rise and fall of her chest before stepping back out the door and closing it carefully.

"I trust everything went according to plan." A cruel voice spoke behind me. I whipped around and looked at Velodik. His hair was matted and he wore only a loose-fitting robe. I noticed a few grains of white powder lining his nose. His wide, yellow eyes were searing. "Did you do what needed to be done?"

"Yes," I replied, defeated. "I didn't even have to do it alone. Two of the *vohon* got away from me; the protestors used them against Public Security as well."

"Perfect. The filthy lot of them. So hungry for violence and retribution." Velodik lifted a hand gently toward my mask and I flinched away. He let it rest on my shoulder. As he pressed down, the gesture felt like a mixture of reassurance and dominance. "Well done, Kalrevi. You've assured us that our stature is secure. Rest now. Forget about today. Tomorrow we celebrate."

He staggered away from me and I forced back the desire to lash out and strike him down. I wanted to scream and thrash and destroy. But I had already destroyed so much. It had to stop. Vengeance would beget vengeance until there was nothing left.

I pressed my back up against my door. *I need to start doing what I am meant to do,* I told myself. *I need to repair the damage I have done.*

Chapter Twenty-Eight:
Absolute Authority

When we clasp hands with one another, we are stronger than when we grasp a weapon. Forget what Hekar has taught us. Join hands and make way for a new beginning.

— from The Blight of War *by Kavya of Sophia*

Velodik

The Grand Hall of the Vsevoran Senate inspired awe and wonder. It was larger and more elaborate than even the royal palace. It bustled with hope and ambition between dual spires at its northern and southern walls. Constructed from marble and alabaster, it stood as a monument of the might of Vsevora. Within, massive rose windows illuminated pristine corridors, vaulting archways, and violet carpet.

I bounded happily up the stairs leading to the Grand Hall's entrance. A row of Public Security enforcers stood vigilantly along the steps, brandishing their crest-emblazoned shields, and protecting those within from the rabble without. They were strong, proud, and noble.

I felt rejuvenated. Perhaps it was the sight of the building, perhaps it was the little vial I consumed before my arrival, or perhaps it was the knowledge that this meeting would finally put our troubles to rest.

I made my way to the Senate chamber which slowly filled with a hundred other representatives from across Vsevora. The air within was heavy with concern. Before last night, they were outraged about the night market affair. They cried out for checks and balances against the Chancellor and the forces of Public Security. Now, they were fearful—afraid of a violent public that had gone too far at the protests the night before. They worried that they, themselves, would be the next to burn.

I wouldn't even have to worry about Commissioner Zradya any longer. The evidence of her misdeeds had been discovered and she was, conveniently, nowhere to be found. Quite suspicious indeed.

I smiled warmly as I took my seat. My snare had worked better than anticipated—perhaps perfectly. Ishkara would take the reins and make a show of force to assure the Senate that Vsevora's unity would remain intact. She would rise up as the hero, and my place at the table would be firmly set. Everything would continue as it had been, just as if the whole mess of the night markets had never occurred. I leaned back in my chair, revelling at my success, and waited for the Chancellor's arrival.

"Stand ready!" a booming voice rang out across the chamber followed by the creaking of chairs as all in attendance rose to their feet at once. "The Chancellor of Vsevora!" There was a solemn and dignified silence as Ishkara entered and made her away down the centre aisle. She took each step with purpose. Her expression was serious, stoic, and sober. There were no beads in her crown of horns, no ornate earrings dangling from her ears, no gemstone necklace around her neck. Her dress was a similar cut to what she often wore, but it was not accented with fur or fine embroidery. It was very nearly black, and would have seemed plain, but for an amethyst sheen that glinted from it when caught in the light. She tugged gently at her black gloves, ensuring they touched her elbow, as she reached the end of the aisle. She started up the short stairway that led to a raised pulpit overlooking the assembly.

"My friends," Ishkara began solemnly, a look of sorrow in her eyes. "The events and horrors of last night linger fresh in our hearts and minds. We find ourselves in the midst of a nation in crisis."

A young, antlered man sat nearby, hurriedly adjusting controls on a spinning machine in front of him; Ishkara's address was being broadcast live to every radio across the continent. She paused for a moment, looking at him as he worked, making certain that her words would be heard. He looked back reassuringly.

"But it is not a nation that is beyond healing. The series of events that led up to this moment—the abuse of power, the violence of citizen against citizen—these tragedies have been eye-opening.

"When I became Chancellor, I promised to bring Vsevora together. Regardless of birth and blood, I knew we were capable through the bonds of memories and love. I still believe in that promise. I have served in this Senate for decades with the hope to create a stronger Vsevora: one that stands for unity, one that rejects the pettiness that once defined it, one that can withstand anything that would try to destroy it. I believe that is the Vsevora that exists today.

"Look at what we have accomplished when we worked together. We ended age-old disputes. We produced more for our families. We built a better place for our children and our children's children. For a blissful moment, we had pulled Vsevora into the light and cast out the shadows of our past.

"But the shadows never left. They crept in from every coastline, through every forest, and over every mountain. The shadows lurked in the alleyways of our cities and even hid in our homes. I toiled to keep the shadows at bay. Sectarianism. Ostracism. Isolationism. These are the shadows that threaten Vsevora.

"There are those who cling to these shadows of the past. They conspire to tear apart what we have built and drag us back to a time of division and distrust. Their memories are filled with hate.

"So I sought out the dangers that threatened our unity and I fought to defeat them. While I toiled, this senate hall became complacent. You sat on your laurels and grew fat while the hard work needed to be done. You abandoned Vsevora and left it to drown in darkness."

A murmur started up throughout the assembly. I leaned forward, concerned and curious what angle Ishkara was trying to take.

"Where do we find ourselves now? Our people are tearing one another apart. And who is there to defend them? The protectors have become the oppressors. And as hard as I have fought, as much as I have toiled, I had trusted you to toil alongside me. I trusted you, Senators, to stand vigilant with me and defend the people of Vsevora with the same dedication and fervour. Instead, there is corruption, bloodshed, violence, and death. Vsevora has been betrayed."

The murmur grew louder and angrier. Any bit of energy and optimism had washed out of me. I felt the dagger slide back into place. I stood up, glowering at Ishkara.

"Senator Velodik," she said, raising a hand toward me, "a man I have known and respected for years. Look no further for a shining example of one who has grown fat and lazy. He has allowed corruption to enter the ranks of Public Security as they harm the very people they are meant to protect."

"How dare you," I screamed. "How dare you, Ishkara!" There was a rousing of voices along with mine, and senators began pounding on their desks. Curses and slurs hurled across the room.

Ishkara raised her hands. "Silence!" The cacophony abated and Ishkara's tone turned to a low rumble. "Look at you. Petty squabblers and power-hungry rats. You do not represent the will of the people. Did the people choose you to sit in this hall? No. You were chosen by familial elders, academic cabals, and wealthy plutocrats. Even I, the elected Chancellor, was not chosen by the people. I was chosen by you. Does that make me any better? How can we claim that we represent the people of this nation? Where is the voice of Vsevora?

"We heard it out there, on the streets and in the square. For all of the tragedy and atrocity that occurred last night, that voice will not fall on deaf ears. Vsevora is the people. And the laws are meant to serve the people." She paused and a cautious hush washed over the hall.

Her dark eyes looked to me as she continued: "Effective immediately, I am disbanding the office of Public Security. A full investigation shall be conducted and all hints of corruption will be purged. To ensure that peace and order are maintained, control of Public Security forces shall be in the hands of the People's Army of Vsevora whose authority runs through me."

I fell back into my chair. Each word she spoke thrust another dagger into my skull. The room erupted around me, at first a roar, but then a dull ringing sound that circled my head. My vision blurred. I saw a misty vision of Ishkara, her eyes on fire. My head spun and the room went with it. I fell forward on the desk and pounded it with my fist. *Inhale. Pause. Exhale. Pause. Inhale. Pause. Exhale. Pause.*

I stopped spinning and the ringing stopped with me. I looked up and saw that people were on their feet. Some were applauding while others gnashed their teeth and bashed their fists.

Ishkara looked out over the crowd, lifted her hands in a call for order, and continued: "Three generations ago, Vsevora was torn apart by the last dynast-king, and since that time, the city-states have dictated the distribution of power. As the city-states put forward their Senators, the true interests of the people of Vsevora have never been considered. Until now." A hint of a smile crossed her face.

"From this moment onward, the Senate of Vsevora and the Office of the Chancellor are hereby dissolved."

The tone in the room shifted as a fearful stillness overtook us. I looked around and I realized that military personnel had filled into the hall. I sank into my chair, the dagger turning.

"In six months' time, the first free and open election of a unified Vsevora will be held. For the first time the people, and the people alone, will choose a new Senate and a new Chancellor. Until that time, to ensure that power is squarely in the hands of Vsevora's citizens, the authority of the Senate and the Chancellorship shall be transferred to the High Regent of Vsevora, an office in which I will serve as protector of our sovereign unity.

"The laws shall serve the people. Vsevora shall know harmony again. Through unity, Vsevora is strong!" Ishkara called out to thunderous applause from the soldiers that lined the room. The Senate sat in shocked silence. I felt the dagger bore deeper and deeper into agony.

Chapter Twenty-Nine:
Aftermath

As she approached the pulpit, I felt a knot in the pit of my stomach. But what could I do? I'm just one person.

— Ivas Fedkov, chief technician of the regency

Siranna

Thick smoke spread out in every direction while screams echoed around me. I choked and gagged as I staggered about, trying to get my bearings. I was in Agate Square. I saw heavy black batons rising up through smoke. They crashed down and then a body came tumbling out of the mist. A young woman, no older than I, lay still before me. Her eyes were rolled up into the back of her skull and a red pool formed behind her head.

I screamed and backed away. A terrible heat rose up from behind me and I turned to see a column of flame. The column shifted, expanded, and grew four whirling tendrils. No. Not tendrils.

Four wings took shape and the column of flame revealed itself as the phoenix. Her wings created a great gust of wind, blowing away the smoke. Everything was laid bare: the desperation, the violence, and the cruelty.

"Please!" I cried up to the phoenix. "Please make it stop!" The mother phoenix looked back at me and replied with a sharp shriek. She seemed to understand.

She climbed up and circled the statue of the angel in the centre of the square. Her tail had three long feathers that stretched out like thin strings and ended with bursts of flame, like the fire of a candle upon a wick. As she circled the statue, a stream of flame formed behind her, creating a fiery halo. Everyone in the square grew quiet and watched.

Then, something silver-black streaked across the sky. The phoenix let out a hideous screech and convulsed in the air. I looked around frantically as the shouting started once again. Another silver-black streak—an arrow or a harpoon—flew into the air and struck the phoenix. She screamed again and sputtered, barely keeping herself up. A third arced across the sky and when it hit, she crashed to the ground. I charged toward her.

She landed on her back at the base of the statue in front of the ram's skull. Three long shafts of metal stuck out of her chest and stomach, and molten blood poured out of her. I hurried next to her, weeping uncontrollably. I fell to my knees by her head as she gasped and croaked.

I looked into her yellow-red eyes as they faded to empty black. I no longer saw myself reflected in her eyes. I wrapped my arms around her neck.

"Please! You have to help us! Please don't die!" It was, of course, too late. Her whole body went limp. I watched through teary eyes as the fire went out and her feathers turned a dull brown before fading to ashen grey.

The smoke crept back up through the square and blotted out everything else. I was lost in the darkness.

I opened my eyes. Everything still felt like a black fog as I awoke. Once it cleared, I found I was in an unfamiliar place. My head hurt, my throat ached, and my memories were a blur of images.

Was it all a horrible nightmare? I remembered fire streaming across the sky, people shouting all around me, and the dying cries of the phoenix. What was real? I thought of the woman in the pool of blood, and then I saw Mr Pravda's lifeless face. I shook my head, trying to push the images from my mind, which instead sent a jab of pain through my skull.

No! It was a dream. All of it was a dream, I told myself. I sat up and pulled my legs in close. Then I screamed as I looked down at my blouse: it was caked in dry blood. The aching grew and I knew that the worst of it was real. My eyes filled with tears and I allowed the truth to sink in.

As my breath shuddered through the tears, I knew that I couldn't let the pain overtake me. I turned my attention to my present situation.

I was in a soft bed in the middle of a bright room; it was sparsely decorated with a few simple furnishings. Birdsong fluttered through the window, and there was the hint of something in the air. I breathed in deeply through my nose, trying to place the scent. Bread.

I shifted, feeling smooth, lush fabric beneath me: the bedsheets. They were seafoam green and matched the sheer curtains. As more light poured into the room, every-thing took on the gentle colour. It was all unusually calm. For the moment it appeared as though I was safe, but I wondered how long.

I slowly pulled myself up, gripping my head lightly as the room gave a quick spin. I waited for everything to settle be-fore I swung my feet off the edge of the bed.

I stood up and made my way to a full-length mirror. My hair was a matted and tangled mess. My cloak had been badly torn, but not beyond repair. My blouse was ruined; it had been soaked in Mr Pravda's blood. A pang of sorrow hit my stomach and I felt fresh tears in my eyes. Once more, I forced the thoughts out.

I focused on the mirror and drew in a deep breath, con-tinuing my self-examination. I reached up to the back of my head, the source of its aching, and I could feel a tender spot that made me wince as I touched it.

I leaned in to look more closely at my face. Despite the violence, I had made it out with just a few scratches and a bit of a bruise near my neck. That's when I realized my necklace was gone. My family necklace! I grasped at the empty space at my neck and looked around frantically.

"If you're looking for your necklace, it broke off. Don't worry, I recovered it," a voice said from behind me. I whipped around and I saw her. I remembered, now, the last thing I saw before I blacked out. The white visage with raven hair was standing in the doorway. My throat was so dry, all I could do was croak fearfully.

A voice from behind the mask responded calmly: "Everything is alright. I'm not going to hurt you. I've hurt too many already. Here's the necklace." She moved closer and held out the gold medallions. I reached forward carefully, took the necklace, and held it close.

"Why am I here?" I asked, managing a hoarse whisper.

"I brought you here so you wouldn't get hurt or carted off to prison," she responded plainly.

I stared at her, thinking over her answer and trying to sort through the memories and the images. She just looked back at me, her mask unchanging. It made her seem menacing, despite her otherwise kind demeanour. There was something familiar about her.

She continued: "You can get changed with something out of the wardrobe. If nothing fits, I can find something of Velodik's. He won't notice if anything goes missing."

"What?" I gasped, a sudden panic overtaking me. "Velodik? As in Senator Velodik? This is his house? And you brought me here so I wouldn't be carted off to prison?"

"Don't worry," the masked woman said nonchalantly as she turned to leave the room. "He's at the Grand Hall. Ishkara has called a special session after what happened last night. He'll be gone for a while. There's a wash closet down the hall so you can get cleaned up. Afterward I can get you some food." With that, she slipped out of the room.

I stood there in frozen fear. *I have to get out of here,* I told myself. There was no telling what would happen to me if I stayed. I looked down at the necklace in my hand. The clasp was broken, but all three strings were still intact and not a single medallion was out of place. *If she wanted to hurt me, she could have done so easily by now. If she wanted me arrested, I would have woken up in a prison cell. She could have just left me on the street last night.* I was uneasy about it, but I felt like I could trust her.

I washed up and changed my clothes, then found my way through the mansion to a large kitchen where the masked woman was cutting fruits and laying them into a bowl. I was wearing a dress that matched hers, although it was an awkward fit on me, as I was several inches taller than she was. I took a seat at the island in the middle of the kitchen.

"My name's Kalrevi, by the way," the voice behind the mask said, never looking up from her task at hand.

I had heard that name before. My mind slowly worked past the ache and I began to put it together. I saw her in the palace talking to Velodik about the night market. That hadn't been the only time I saw her, I realized.

"You've helped me before," I said uncertainly. "You saved me from the thieves at the night market, didn't you?"

She nodded. "You should probably stay out of Agate Square; you keep getting into trouble there." Something about her tone suggested she was trying to bring levity to the situation, but the expressionless gaze of the mask cut through that and left only uncomfortable silence behind.

"I'm, uh, my name is Siranna," I said at last.

"I know who you are."

"Oh. I suppose you would if you're Velodik's um... wife?"

She laughed. "Certainly not. No, I'm his..." she trailed off and paused her knife work, then continued, "servant, I suppose, is the right word for it." She turned around and slid the bowl of fruit in front of me.

"Thank you," I said and popped a wedge of citrus in my mouth. "For everything, I mean." Kalrevi nodded, silently staring back at me behind her mask. Uncomfortably, I looked down at the colourful contents of my bowl. I grabbed a few berries and ate them. The only sound in the room was my chewing. I was about to bite into another citrus wedge when I stopped and looked back up at her. "Why did you save me?"

Kalrevi turned her head slightly as if she hadn't considered it before. She moved in closer and sat down next to me. "I've made a lot of mistakes, Siranna. Costly ones." She looked away and became quiet. "It was my fault that people died last night. I started the attack on Public Security."

I held my breath and my hands started to tremble in fear and anger. I could see the fires in the street. I could hear the dying shriek of the mother phoenix intermingled with the screams of the crowds. I could see Mr Pravda. My mouth grew dry, but I managed to rasp, "H-how could you?"

"I didn't want to. I had no choice... No. That's not right. I did have a choice. But I was too afraid to make it. I'm sorry, Siranna." She locked eyes with me. Beyond her cold visage there was warmth in her eyes. I knew, immediately, that what she said was true. "I saved you because I knew I had to make right what I had done. It's time to make a change."

As we looked into each other's eyes, I thought of my own mistakes. The wounds of them cut deep, but as I sat there with Kalrevi, the pain they left behind seemed to dull. I wasn't alone.

"Do you really think things can change?" I asked. "A lot of people got hurt last night. How do we come back from that?"

"I hope," Kalrevi began quietly, "that there's still some way to get through to Velodik. I have to believe that there is. He saved me when I was at my worst and in my hour of need. He may yet do the same for Vsevora."

"Do you really think so?" I asked.

"I'm not certain, but—" She stopped suddenly and got to her feet. She hurried over to the window.

"What is it?" I stood and started after her, but she gestured at me to stop.

"Siranna, head for the back door. It's just down the hall." Her voice was concerned and serious.

My heart immediately began to race. "What do you mean? What's going on?"

"Soldiers. From the People's Army. I don't like this." She turned to face me. "Quick. Go!"

There was a heavy pounding at the door and my heart leapt up into my throat. I stood and dashed down the hall as Kalrevi rushed to the door. I glanced back as I heard it open, but I was, thankfully, out of sight.

"You're coming with us," a sharp voice commanded.

"What? Let go of me!" Kalrevi exclaimed and I heard the sounds of a struggle. I bounded away as fast as I could while still keeping as quiet as possible. "You have no authority here!"

"We have all of the authority," the sharp voice replied. "The People's Army of Vsevora keeps the peace now. And that includes locking up Velodik's pet."

I quietly slid out the door and gingerly closed it behind me. I whispered a silent thank you to Kalrevi for saving me once again, and then I ran as quickly as I could.

As I rushed back to Oskar and Emil's, I could tell that something had changed within the city. There was an uneasy stillness in the air. Even in the busy market streets, the bustle felt off. People moved with caution. There was no din of friendly banter or routine pleasantries. Everyone was on edge—suspicious—as though another riot might break out at any moment.

I noticed a small gathering. I stopped and checked for any sign of Public Security or the People's Army. No one of concern. I decided to investigate. The group was huddled around a radio and they had become deathly quiet. Ishkara's voice rang out, harsh and clear:

"The authority of the Senate and the Chancellorship shall be transferred to the High Regent of Vsevora, an office in which I will serve as protector of our sovereign unity. The laws shall serve the people. Vsevora shall know harmony again. Through unity, Vsevora is strong!"

I staggered back, hearing my own words turned against me. The gathering began chattering, voicing their approval:

"Damn right!"

"I never cared for those fuddy-duddy senators."

"About time Ishkara rooted out the power-hungry rats."

"Power straight back in the hands of the people. That's what it's all about!"

"No!" I exclaimed. "Ishkara's vision of unity would destroy everything that makes Vsevora special. Can't you see that?" I shouldn't have said anything.

Some of them began shouting me down and defending Ishkara. Then one sneered, "Wait... Weren't you the Oksanan that started the riot?" There was a cold murmur from the gathering.

I backed away and then saw two soldiers from the People's Army approach. I didn't wait—I fled. There was a command to stop, but I didn't heed it, and within a few moments I could hear them coming up behind me.

I wanted the nightmare to be over. I wanted the mother phoenix to be real—to rise up, alive again, and take me far away from Sophia, from Ishkara, from everything. I looked up, grasping at some faint hope that she would appear, but of course there was no phoenix there to save me. But I did spot something else.

There was a tall fence to my right and an apothecary's cart in front of it. I made a wild dash, clambering up the side of the cart. Someone started shouting, probably the apothecary. I looked to the fence; the gap was further than expected, but there was no time to hesitate. I drew a deep breath, shifted my weight back and forth, then leapt with all my might. There was a great crash behind me as the cart toppled over and dozens of glass tinctures shattered on the cobblestones. I had made it, though!

I scrambled and pulled myself over the fence. There was more shouting and a loud ruckus on the other side, but my pursuers couldn't make it over. I ran all the way to Oskar and Emil's apartment, desperate to escape the unravelling of the world around me.

"Siranna! You're safe!" Oskar exclaimed as I burst breathlessly through the door. "I assumed the worst when you didn't come back last night. I heard... I heard people were killed."

Oskar reached out and pulled me into a warm embrace. Emil stared at me sternly from behind Oskar. I could see the relief in his eyes, but his posture revealed his tension.

"Yes. I'm... okay..." I gasped, thankful to be back. "And you. You're safe, too."

"He didn't go last night," Emil snapped.

Oskar nodded, ignoring his partner's tone. "That's right. I wanted to support you, but Emil insisted I stay."

"And it's a good thing I did." He stepped forward and took Oskar's arm. "Siranna, I'm very glad you're safe, but you can't stay with us any longer." His words hit like a slap across the face, but I couldn't blame him.

"What? We didn't talk about this!" Oskar exclaimed.

"It's too dangerous. She instigated the incident. They could come for her!"

"All the more reason she needs to stay here."

"I can't keep on like this, living on the edge of a knife!"

"I know it's hard, but we can't abandon someone in need."

"Please, stop," I said and the two paused to look at me. "You're right. I should go."

A worried look crossed Oskar's face, but Emil was awash in relief. I slid past them to gather up my things, but a heavy hand caught my wrist. I looked up at Oskar.

"No. You're staying," he said firmly, but with gentle care. "Emil, I know you're worried. That's why I stayed last night. But we need to help her, now more than ever."

Emil stepped in close and pulled Oskar away. "Why? Why do we need to do this?" His voice quivered.

"I feel it. I feel it in my gut. Same as I felt it that night you first asked me to dance. Same as the day I said we needed to leave for Sophia. It's the same now. She needs us, and we've got to help her."

They gazed into one another's eyes. Through all of the fear and upset, their love for one another still shone through. Oskar wrapped his hands around Emil's and held on tight. Emil faltered and looked at the ground.

"Stay, Siranna," Emil said with a deep sigh. He looked up at me and I could see tears forming in his eyes. "But please... No more. It's time to stay quiet."

Chapter Thirty:
Caged

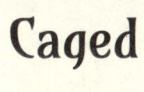

Chains.
Not of metal, but of mind.
Bound by the weight
of the World
of the Heart

Chains.
That cannot be broken
without Will
without Hope
without Action.

— *The Forgotten Bard*

Kalrevi

When I saw the soldiers coming, part of me thought for a moment that Siranna and I could stand our ground and fight. Or perhaps both of us could escape together. But I knew that if she had any chance at all, she would need to go alone. And for all that I had done, I deserved whatever happened next.

They weren't particularly kind or gentle. As Siranna made her escape, they bound my wrists roughly behind my back. I struggled long enough to buy her some time, but after a heavy fist to the stomach pushed the wind out of me, I didn't put up any more of a fight. They shoved me out the door into an armoured carriage that took me out of the city.

There were mountains all around Sophia, but none loomed so harshly as those to the east. There, built into the grim stone, stood Kamin Prison. It was a cruel-looking fortress where people were sent to be forgotten.

The skies were clear and blue as they carted me up the mountain. It was unfitting, given the bleak fog I felt I was wading in. There were about half a dozen carriages heading up to Kamin, all filled with those like me: members of the Senate or Public Security who were deemed too "dangerous" or "disruptive" to act freely.

There was no trial or due process. In the wake of the Senate's dissolution, Ishkara put forward a number of decrees in the name of security. Only a few had been spared from her culling, and I was obviously not amongst their number.

The air grew colder as we gradually made our way up the winding slopes. The further we went, the more the melancholy sunk in. I looked out the tiny window of the carriage and I caught sight of Kamin Prison as we drew near. Its high walls menaced over the mountainside and cast a great black shadow over us.

I thought about home; I had fled one prison just to be taken to another. I thought about Velodik; I wondered if he had escaped Ishkara's ire, or if he had ended up in a situation like mine. I thought about my father; his disappointment would have overshadowed even Kamin's walls.

"All personal effects into the box," a cold voice said again and again as we filed in. I looked down at the plain, brown box in front of me. My name and a number were scrawled on it and there was a dingy, grey jumpsuit next to it. "Your uniform. Get changed." I did as they said. The jumpsuit was bulky and itchy, but it was fine. As I laid my bracers on top of my dress, I wondered if I would ever see them again, or if the guards would pilfer them. I closed the box and moved along, but a baton swiftly blocked my path.

"I said all personal effects in the box," the voice boomed again. It belonged to a woman in a People's Army uniform; the word WARDEN was proudly emblazoned upon her lapel. She was a glorified babysitter.

I spoke softly, carefully avoiding an adversarial tone, "You don't understand. I can't take off this mask." She didn't look impressed. I wasn't sure how to explain. "It's a part of who I am."

"It's a mask," she replied sardonically. "Put it in the box."

"No, it's a part of our customs and—"

"I don't care," she barked. "Your customs aren't a part of my prison."

She reached for the mask, and my hands moved of their own accord. I gripped her arm and wrenched it away, twisting it behind her as I had done to Velodik at the dinner party. She yelped, probably more from surprise than pain.

In a moment, I came crashing down. There was a bright flash of light and a surge of vibrating electricity that coursed through my body. A thousand painful needles stabbed into me and my muscles contracted hard. I dropped to the ground. My body twitched and ached as my muscles tried to relax. A guard loomed over me; he gripped a short black staff in his hand that crackled with blue lightning. The warden came into view now. She stepped over me and crouched down, putting her face close to mine.

"I suggest you do as you're told the first time; otherwise, you're going to find it quite difficult in here." She reached her clawing fingers under my mask and ripped it from my face. I lashed out weakly, but there was another flash of lightning and my body convulsed. I screamed, unable to control myself as the barrage of needles thrust through my body again. The warden laughed as consciousness faded. She walked away from me, still holding my mask, and everything went dark.

A shudder rolled throughout my entire body as I felt a warm, unfamiliar, horrifying feeling. Hot breath pulsed along my cheek and made my skin crawl. I writhed about and my eyes shot open to see a strange face hovering directly above me. The face screeched and staggered back as I shot up, gasping.

I found myself in a dim, grey cell and there was another woman in there with me. She slowly drew closer after being scared off. She looked at me with curious green eyes. She reminded me a bit of the people I encountered when I first left the Greenshield. She had long, thin, whisker-like strands that came from her eyebrows and bounced as she bobbed her head to and fro.

"Mornin'!" she said, her tone unusually chipper given our shared situation. "Who're you?" She came up close, right to the edge of the bed. I pulled back and turned away from her. In any other situation I might have found myself drawn to her kindly demeanour.

"It doesn't matter. Just leave me alone," I said with a mix of vehemence and despair.

There was a lull of silence as she considered my request, then she crawled over the bed and sat next to me. "My name's Katchya," she said, as though I had said nothing at all.

I leaned forward and buried my face in my hands. "Go," I whispered, my voice trembling. I thought I might break down, then and there, but I held myself together. I couldn't let her see.

Katchya apparently had a hearing problem. She leaned onto my shoulder and kicked her legs. "Well, that's not really my name, but it's what they call me. My gang used to say 'They'll never catch ya!'" She paused for a long moment. "Guess they were wrong though." She let out a half-hearted laugh. "So what's your story? Never seen anyone like you. Your face is a little funny-lookin'."

My whole body tensed and a fire erupted within me. I stood up and glowered down at Katchya. "Leave me!" I screamed. "Don't look at me! *Never* look at me. I don't want to be here. I don't want to be your friend. I don't want... I don't want anything. Just to be left alone and to never be seen again." As I yelled, my voice buckled and started to break. I fell to my knees. I looked down to the stone floor and shut my eyes tight, holding my arm in front of my face.

Silence was my only response. There was a quiet rustling and when I looked back up, Katchya had climbed up to the top bunk of the bed and turned away from me.

My breath came in staggered, quivering gasps. I crawled onto the lower bunk and tried to pull myself back together. The thin mattress offered little comfort, and the more I relaxed, the more I could feel the uncomfortable metal beneath it. I stared listlessly at the bunk overhead.

I felt sick. I was completely exposed. I covered my face with my hair. Each strand felt like a cold spider crawling across my eyes and mouth. I shuddered and grit my teeth, searching desperately for some small comfort to reveal itself to me.

There was no revelation, but eventually, the tension in my body settled. I closed my eyes. My cellmate remained quiet above. There was a distant rattle of metal and the din of harsh, commanding voices beyond the bars of the cell.

My thoughts swam through murky waters. I wanted to be alone. I wanted to be forgotten. Did my father still remember me? The thought struck my heart and caused me to recoil. I curled up in the middle of the bed.

I wondered what my father would say if he saw me. I imagined him standing in front of my bunk. He stood there with crossed arms and a stern posture. My thoughts of him became more vivid as he crouched down to look at me and see what had become of me. Slowly, he shifted over and sat down next to me, and then with three powerful arms, he pulled me up into his embrace. I was surprised at him—at myself and my imagination. I had expected judgment. Instead, he held me tight. I felt like a child again, wrapped up in his arms.

"Kalrevi," he said. His voice was distant in my mind. It had been so long since I had heard him. Did his voice have a deeper timbre? I looked him over and his bracers seemed fuzzy. What did the etchings look like? The thought that this image may be all I had left of him hit me with a sudden panic. My mind raced to rebuild him and preserve him perfectly in my memory.

"Kalrevi, this is why I wanted you to stay. I knew that the outsiders would hurt you." His voice sounded right. He placed a hand on my cheek. The delicate etchings of his bracers became clear. I sighed and gently faded into his arms.

"Did I not teach you well enough about the dangers?" he asked. I looked up into his eyes; they trembled behind the mask. "Or maybe I never gave you enough reason to stay." He placed a hand on mine and held tight. I had forgotten how strong his grip was. "I didn't want to lose you, like I lost her."

My thoughts turned to my mother. I had no vivid image of her like I did for my father.

"I didn't protect her. I put all of my strength into protecting you instead. I wanted to keep you safe forever. But that was selfishness. If I had given you more freedom—trusted you—then maybe you would have stayed. Or at least... if you had left... maybe you would come back."

I knew it was a waking dream, but it was so real. I could feel the warmth in his arms. I could hear the beating of his heart. I could smell the fresh, minty leaves that he loved to cook with. Tears welled up in my eyes. I couldn't do this. Not here. Without even a mask to hide behind.

"It's all right, Kalrevi. It's all right."

Hot tears streamed down my face and I buried it into him. I cursed my foolishness. "I wanted to be free," I gasped, "but look at me now."

He placed a hand under my chin and gently wiped away the tears with another, just as he had done when I was a child and I scraped my knee. He looked at me with a familiar gentleness and warmth, but something kindled in his eyes.

"Think for a moment, Kalrevi. If I couldn't stop you from escaping..." He leaned his head right down against mine and pulled me close. I closed my eyes. He spoke with a smiling whisper: "...What makes you think they can?"

My eyes snapped open. He was gone. My cellmate hadn't stirred. I wondered if I had been dreaming or if it had been something more.

I stepped over to the bars of the cell and pressed my hands against the cold steel. He was right. I had escaped the great Surrendra, chief of all Feras. I had repaired a skyship on my own. I was the first Feras to fly cross the Greenshield in over a hundred years. This was just a cage with a lock—something I could easily overcome.

Chapter Thirty-One:
Deeper Into Shadow

He had everything. Wealth. Power.
Why would he have torn the nation asunder?
What did he lack that he sought to gain?

Love.

—*from* The Fall of Vsevora *by Orianna, knowledge keeper*

Velodik

I seethed as I burst into my office at the Grand Hall. In my rage, I threw a chair across the room and bashed a fist against a cabinet. I howled in response as pain shot through my arm.

She would have nothing without me, I thought. *After everything I've done to assure her power, she strips me of mine? The dissolution of the Senate! What does she hope to accomplish?*

My mind was still racing from Ishkara's stunt no more than an hour before. I contemplated how I could dismantle her, but every new thought only caused the daggers to sink in deeper, and so I turned to a vial for relief. I paused for a moment as I pulled it out of my inner breast pocket. It was the last of my vials. I didn't care. I popped in open.

In a few minutes, the agony subsided into a dull ache and I breathed a sigh of relief. I turned down the lights and stumbled to the corner of the room, slumping to the floor. I stared numbly at the darkness as the ache faded further and further until it felt just as listless as I was.

"Puh...puh... pathetic..." I murmured. My head rolled back and it thudded against the wall. As I gently pursed my lips, there was no joy in the feeling—only an empty breath. "Everything had been so perfect and now it's fallen a-puh-part."

A sudden flash of light filled the room and stung my eyes. I recoiled, closing them tightly, and pulled myself further into the corner. I let out some kind of half-sentence, half-moan as I tried to discern what was happening.

"Oh my. You're not looking well, Senator. Oh, I suppose I shouldn't be calling you that anymore." The voice was snide and familiar, and I was surprised to hear it: Commissioner Zradya. I squinted my eyes open and held up a hand to the light. Her silhouette loomed in the doorway.

"You!" I growled. "I thought I got rid of you."

"It was a good effort, Velodik," she said with a laugh. She stepped into the room and sat on the desk with her back to me, kicking up one leg over the other. She placed her hands on the desk and leaned back. "Turns out that the High Regent cares more about loyalty than doctored photographs."

I struggled to pull myself to my feet; I pressed my back against the wall and dragged myself up. As I pushed myself forward, I immediately felt a wave of dizziness and I fell back. I leaned against the wall for support.

"It doesn't matter," I barked. "Public Security has been disbanded! You're as puh-powerless as I am." I regained my balance and staggered over to the desk.

Zradya laughed again. "Oh dear. Didn't you notice my new uniform?" I stepped past her silhouette and turned to look at her in the light. Instead of green, she wore dark blue. Her lapels were emblazoned with new, glistening pins. "I serve the People's Army now. Lieutenant-Colonel! I'd say I'm quite potent, Velodik. Unlike some."

I snarled. "Get out of my office!"

"Ah, you see, that's the thing," she said, still smiling. She pushed herself off the desk and strutted towards me. "You don't have an office anymore. You'd best tidy it up for its next owner." She glanced at the chair lying on the floor and the detritus that had toppled over with it. "And you really should take better care of your things."

I shook and clenched my fists, and stormed up to Zradya's speckled face. I wanted to knot my fingers into her curly, black hair and thrust her cocky little smile right down upon the desk. I lifted my arms, but they trembled weakly and fell to my side. I opened my mouth to shout, but she quickly placed a finger over my lips.

"Shh shh shh. It's okay. I know; you're frustrated. But you should be happy. Ishkara took pity on you." She stepped over to the fallen chair, picked it up, and slid it back into place behind the desk. "Had it been up to me, you'd have been arrested and taken in for questioning over the incident at the protest. It's not easy to get your hands on *vohon* and your masked friend was seen rummaging through a weapons locker at Station One."

Zradya sat down confidently in the chair and ran her fingers along the edge of the desk. She grinned and leaned back. "But, the High Regent says you're a free man. Count your lucky stars, Velodik. That privilege didn't extend to your little lap dog. You'll need to find yourself a new pet."

I snarled: "This will all come crashing down, Zradya." My legs shuddered beneath me. I leaned over the desk, both to keep my balance and also to glower over her. "I'll make sure of it."

"I admire your confidence," she replied in a patronizing tone, unaffected by my threat. "You should go." Her smile never faded.

As I struggled to keep my wobbly limbs from giving out, I realized just how empty my threat really was. I had no authority to lord over her, no officers to command, and no servant to undermine her. I just glared uselessly at her; there was nothing more I could do. I was defeated.

"So you've gotten everything you wanted," I growled. "You get my office, and now you're in charge of Vsevora's security?"

The delight on her face made me want to wretch. "No, actually," she said sweetly, "I just came to watch you squirm. Ishkara has placed me in a much more important position."

I returned home to an empty mansion. Kalrevi was gone. Everything I had built for myself was gone. I stood alone in a dark and quiet room. I was hollow.

Was it all my fault? Was it Ishkara? I stumbled to a cabinet, withdrew a bottle of brandy, popped it open, and took a generous swig. The liquid felt hot down my throat and immediately filled the void inside of me. I breathed a long sigh and collapsed into a plush chair. I gently pet the cushioned arm as I guzzled down another mouthful. The room began to pleasantly sway.

I walked through everything that brought me to that moment. I had lived a lifetime of corruption. *Had Ishkara infected me, or was I born with the disease?* I walked through every moment. I thought about the night at the gala, promotion after promotion, our efforts to take down Dazbov, Ishkara's rise through the Senate, and then the night she became Chancellor.

I remembered the tremble of my hands as I confirmed the ballots and the knot in my throat when I told the officiants that Ishkara had won.

It was a lie. But I had been lying for a long time before that moment. Was it Ishkara's fault I found myself on that path? Or would I have found myself on it regardless?

As I guzzled down more brandy, my memories sunk deeper and deeper. I recalled the first time I acquired one of my little vials. It was long before I was Chief Minister; even before I was Commissioner. We had arrested a drug peddler and confiscated his entire supply. As I stacked it all neatly into a box and prepared to lock it away, I hesitated. How easy it would be to take just one vial. Just to experience it. It wouldn't be missed. And it wasn't. I slid it into my pocket; no one was troubled and no one was the wiser.

I took another swig from the bottle, savouring the precious drink as the memories subsided. I put the bottle aside and got out of the chair with a groan.

I felt the blades tracing their way across every bone in my body up towards my skull. There was a great throbbing in my ears that sloshed up into my brain and my body ached. My muscles were weak and sore, begging for rest. I was worn and wasted.

"Kalrevi!" I cried, but there was no answer. Of course there was no answer. I cursed under my breath. I wanted her back.

I fumbled around until I found a candle, lit it, and staggered down the hall into a small office where I rummaged around in the dim light. I snarled, searching through drawers and recklessly throwing their contents aside until I found what a sought: an intricately-crafted pendant.

I fell back into a chair and pressed the pendant against my chest. Zradya's shrill laugh pierced my mind. She was off celebrating—gloating—as I crumbled away into nothingness. I wanted to snuff her out and destroy her.

My grip on the pendant tightened. I stared up at a map on the wall. All of Vsevora was laid out before me in the flickering candlelight. I could see Ishkara's growing shadow crossing over it, choking it out. She wouldn't stop. She had worked too long and fought too hard to let Vsevora slip through her grasp.

I ran my fingers along the pendant, tracing the swirling pattern over its surface. "No matter its source," I mumbled thoughtfully, "I need to stop it. Before it continues its spread—before Ishkara goes any further. The disease must be cleansed."

Chapter Thirty-Two:
Unity

Vsevora has come so far. Let us not falter now. I beseech you to consider the path before us. Let us meet as allies and friends. Let us build the nation together, not tear it apart.

— Senator Ishkara to the delegates of the 10th Summit

Siranna

Sophia transformed. The tension from the day after the protest was only the beginning.

Ishkara sought to dismantle the corruption within Public Security, and so she gutted them. With the resources meant to "protect the people" stretched so thin, a curfew was put in place and strictly enforced by the People's Army.

Citizens were called upon to do their part as well. Suspicion and surveillance were the new Sophia. There was always someone watching, listening, waiting. Breaking curfew, possessing restricted literature, and even tearing down the High Regent's posters were enough to warrant a report; and it was every citizen's "duty" to maintain the peace and keep the People's Army informed.

"KEEP WATCH," the posters said while displaying alterations of my paintings. "OUR UNITY RELIES ON YOU," they claimed. "REPORT THE UNLAWFUL. THE LAWS ARE FOR THE PEOPLE." My artwork and my words had become twisted—I had been used.

I wasn't safe. I was known, after all. I feared that it was only a matter of time before I would be taken away like Kalrevi, so I took care to cover myself with a scarf and keep an eye over my shoulder as I walked the streets.

I returned to the printing press. I had to, if only so I could pay my fair share to Oskar and Emil. Mr Pravda was the only person at the facility who knew about my involvement in the protest, so I felt I was safer returning there than risking the unknown. But the changes at Pravda Press were the worst of all.

When I arrived for my shift, the building looked dark in the dim morning light. It leered over me—a bleak reminder of Mr Pravda's fate. There was an air of uncertainty as I stepped inside. There was something cold and grey about even being there at all. Word of Mr Pravda's death had spread quickly and everyone could immediately feel the void that he left behind. No one knew what to expect. Would the press be shut down? What would happen to us?

A uniformed woman stepped out from the offices above. Her presence was a grim cloak over the already-uneasy atmosphere. She looked down upon us with an arrogant smirk. She had thick horns that coiled near her ears and black hair that curled up even tighter. Her skin was a mix of brown and pale stretches like drops of light ink blotted on dark paper.

"Good morning," she said, her voice dripping with delight. "I am Lieutenant-Colonel Zradya. I've been sent here on behalf of High Regent Ishkara herself."

There was a murmur across the floor and I felt my stomach lurch. I looked around at my colleagues' worried expressions—an all-too-common reaction in Sophia of late.

Zradya continued: "The work you do here is pivotal to Vsevora's unity. With the newly-announced election coming, it is more important than ever that we keep the nation informed and protect it from the spread of radical, sectarian propaganda. That's why I have been chosen to oversee the efforts of our sanctioned printing presses. Pravda Press has a rich history and stands as one of the most robust and productive facilities in Vsevora. You should all be proud of the work that you do."

She gradually made her way down the stairs as she spoke. I suspected that she thought it would endear us to her if we were on the level of equals. Instead, she seemed condescending, as though she were coming down to speak to a gathering of children.

"With Mr Pravda's tragic death, it is important that this facility has strong leadership, and so I will be personally overseeing it." There was another murmur. Zradya's smile was unfaltering. "There will be some changes, of course. Some big. Some small. Your cooperation is necessary. If you do not wish to participate in the new Vsevora, then there is no place for you here." That statement bore a vicious menace—it was a promise, not a warning—it hung in the air and she inspected the reactions of those present. For a moment, her gaze locked with mine and I felt a shiver run down my spine. I looked away.

"You will notice a shift in the types of material that we print. Many of our orders will come directly from the Office of the Regency of Vsevora. Our task is to inform and unify the nation."

I winced at the thought of being forced to print and cut the propaganda that I saw plastered out on the streets. Ishkara's painted face loomed over me in my mind; she was laughing at me. I tried to steady my breathing.

"We will, of course, continue to publish other works—certified works." Lieutenant-Colonel Zradya looked across the floor. She smiled and gestured at a group of supervisors who nervously chittered amongst themselves.

"I know what you're thinking. It was already a daunting task to ensure that you were conforming to the laws that prevent the spread of propaganda. Fear not. You will have more freedom than ever to publish works of art, literature, and scholarly discourse."

A murmur rose up through the facility: the first bit of optimism of the morning. I scrutinized Zradya and waited for the caveat to drop.

"To ensure we only publish certified works of the highest quality, High Regent Ishkara has assembled the Council of Vsevora. They have made certification quite simple and streamlined, opening the way for new writers and artists to share their perspectives in the new Vsevora."

The grim churning in my stomach continued and Zradya clapped her hands together. "This is an exciting time, my friends. We are a part of history in the making! Let's get to work!"

~ ~

The weeks dragged by. The misery of working in the printing press was made worse when Zradya decided to install a radio system that blared its nonsense loudly over the din.

The broadcasts were always sponsored by the Office of the Regency and they spoke of the upcoming election: important notices for registration, information on the candidates, and empty platitudes from Ishkara.

At first, Ishkara said she was not going to run. "My duty is to preserve our unity and ensure that the election proceeds freely and fairly," she said. She was seen as making a noble sacrifice for the good of the nation, and that it was only right that she stood aside and kept her name off the ballot. As time wore on, the dialogue changed.

More and more, the discourse shifted, and people began to ask why Ishkara wouldn't run. Everything that she was doing for Vsevora seemed to make her a natural choice as leader.

One day, while I toiled away next to the heat of a printing press, the radio broadcast a public forum. Ishkara answered questions from a string of sycophants who cooed and fawned over her. Finally, a question came from a child from the city of Ostap.

"High Regent Ishkara," the child began with a nervous quiver. "When I was born, my parents had to leave Ostap. They left because... because..." They stammered. I could practically see a gentle hand urging them to continue. "Because everyone was fighting with Olga. And ever since you came, the fighting stopped. We got to go back home and we don't fight with Olga anymore. Why can't you stay our leader?" I clenched my teeth at the blatant manipulation.

"My child, I am so happy that you could return home safely with your family," Ishkara began with a false tenderness. "It's a difficult question to answer. There are some misguided people who don't want us to choose a leader. My role, as High Regent, is to make sure that the people of Vsevora are allowed to choose, and that they get to make that choice freely and fairly. I have to protect that choice and ensure that whoever is chosen to lead is not stopped by those misguided few. My job is to put power into the hands of the people of Vsevora."

Lies! I thought. *You don't care about us or our choices.*

Ishkara continued: "Since I called the election, I have heard many stories like yours, my child. I have said time and again that the people have the right to choose their leaders, but I have been blind to the reality that so many people want to choose me." My hands stopped working. "It's only right that I give Vsevora the opportunity to make that choice." I froze completely and held my breath, paralyzed by dread.

"Effective immediately, I will put myself forward as a candidate. If Vsevora wants me to lead, then I will happily continue forward on our path to unity."

That was it. I started shaking. There was no one else with greater resources, reach, or authority. With Ishkara's name on the ballot, there was no question who would rise to the top.

Chapter Thirty-Three:
Behind the Mask

I wear this mask to remind me of who I am—of who I swore I would be. On the Cerah Night, the night I first put on this mask, I promised that I would help my community. I can't forget that.

— *Kalrevi of the Feras*

Kalrevi

Kamin Prison was bleak. Day by day, I sat in my cramped little cell and day by day, I plotted my escape. I made an ally of my cell-mate, Katchya, and warmed up to her chipper demeanour. Mostly, though, I observed the workings of the prison around me: the prisoners, the guards, and the warden. I believed that I could escape, and I had determined the key to do it: the black staff.

The black staff was a powerful tool for keeping the prisoners of Kamin in line. It had certainly been effective against me when I first arrived. If I could get my hands on one, it would also be a powerful weapon in securing my freedom. It would be no simple task to acquire one, but I had a plan.

It hinged on a woman that I quietly referred to as Spitfire. I met her my first morning in Kamin at the mess hall. It was not a pleasant meeting.

I uncomfortably shuffled through the hall, down the line of long tables and benches where the prisoners sat and ate their gruel. The room was filled with the dull roar of the prisoners' chatter and the disgusting squelch of slathering mouths as they chewed their slop.

I sat down at a bench, my hair over my face, and stared at the bowl of light brown sludge in my hands. I glanced up as others filed onto the bench next to me. I felt sick. I couldn't possibly eat here.

That's when Spitfire sat down. She was a beast of muscle and anger. She hunched over her bowl of gruel, which appeared tiny in her thick hands. Her hair was shaved short and two stumps of horns came out from the sides of her head. I couldn't tell if the tips of her horns had broken off through some past deed, or if the warden had done it as a safety precaution.

Spitfire slammed her bowl down roughly with a heavy grunt and immediately began shovelling gruel in her mouth. There was a thick, slopping sound as it rolled around her teeth, then a sickening glorp as she gulped it down her meaty gullet. My stomach churned, but I couldn't look away.

She stopped when she noticed me staring. She narrowed her dark eyes and slammed a fist on the table, sending a reverberation throughout. Everyone at the table stopped eating and looked at us. Spitfire glowered at me as bits of food slowly dribbled down from her lip and onto her chin.

"You have a problem?" she growled, her voice an explosive burst of disdain. As the puh of problem popped, a chunk of gruel flew from her mouth. I watched in frozen horror as it soared across the table in a perfect arc. It splattered against my cheek and oozed across my skin. The vulgar slop slid down my face, crawling like a slug down my cheek toward the corner of my mouth.

I opened my mouth slightly as if to speak, but there were no words. Instead, there was a great heave in my belly followed by an involuntary contraction in my throat. I wretched and gurgled, and then my mouth opened up wide. A spew of vomit erupted from within and onto Spitfire.

Needless to say, she was unhappy. Her breakfast now ruined, and finding herself covered in warm bile, she roared with anger. I couldn't blame her, even as she reached across the table, deftly grabbed me by the jumpsuit and pulled me over for a beating. Her burly fists pounded into my stomach, chest, and face. I struggled against her, but was no match for her strength.

A guard came as quickly as he could and applied the black staff to Spitfire. There was a flash of blue light and a crackle of electricity that washed over her. Much to my surprise, though, it barely slowed her assault. Again and again he struck her with the full force of the black staff's fury. The guard cursed as his smouldering staff refused to do anything any longer; apparently he had drained it dry.

Reinforcements came and applied their own staves until finally, with a roar, Spitfire staggered back and hit the ground. There was a lingering smell of burnt hair and an uproar from the mess hall that the guards now worked to quell. I weakly rolled off the table to my feet; every part of me radiated with pain.

The experience provided me with an idea on how I might acquire a black staff. I just hoped that I wouldn't get pulverized again in the attempt.

It was time for dinner and everyone was gathered in the mess hall. Even after spending weeks in Kamin, I hadn't grown used to eating there, but I did what was necessary to survive.

I surveyed the guards that lined the hall with black staves in hand then scanned the crowd of prisoners. Spitfire was already sitting and eating, slurping up her gruel with abandon. For days I had been waiting for the perfect moment.

I stood awkwardly with my bowl of food in hand. I needed a catalyst—something to start the engine and put everything in motion—but my moment hadn't come. I couldn't wait long; the guards would get suspicious if I didn't sit down and eat. I held my breath, sweeping the mess hall one last time, looking for—

My opportunity arrived!

A wiry Lyudmilan woman with frazzled grey hair turned and made her way down the aisle in my direction, a large, hot bowl in hand. She would be my catalyst. I shot forward, moving briskly but not so fast as to draw attention to myself. I timed my strides so that I was right behind Spitfire as the Lyudmilan and I crossed paths.

With careful agility, I bumped the Lyudmilan and tripped her. She stumbled right into Spitfire, spilling her hot food all over the violent woman's head. I darted aside as Spitfire stood up and locked eyes with the poor, unfortunate soul that I had sent stumbling to her doom. I went unnoticed and Spitfire unleashed her fury.

There was a cheer from the hall as their thirst for blood and sport was quenched, but the fighting quickly spread. Another Lyudmilan rushed to aid her compatriot, which encouraged others to stand up for Spitfire. Soon, the whole mess hall erupted in riotous violence.

The guards charged in with black staves to quell the roaring crowd. One of them charged at Spitfire and cracked her with a bolt of blue lightning. Spitfire bellowed, but did not fall, just like before. Instead, she turned on the guard and punched him in the face. Another crack from the staff. Another and then another. Finally, Spitfire was brought to her knees. She was dizzy and sluggish, but she would be back into the heat of it soon. The black staff flickered for a moment and then smouldered; its life had run out. The guard tossed it aside and restrained Spitfire with a set of manacles.

Amidst the chaos, I slipped in and grabbed the discarded weapon. I smuggled it into my jumpsuit and hurried away. In the confusion, I brought it back to my cell and hid it.

I suspected that the guards in Kamin were much like Public Security. They wouldn't readily admit that they had made a grievous mistake like losing a black staff. I was correct.

With the black staff in my possession, I needed to devise a way to restore it. Several of its components had been reduced to a blackened crisp. Over time, I replaced them with makeshift substitutes. Forks and nails were probably not intended for it, but they would have to do. I felt confident enough in my skill that the staff would work at least once.

There was just a question of how to power the device. There had been some kind of battery inside of it, but in the struggle against Spitfire, it had been thoroughly burnt. There was no chance I could make use of it again.

I sat in my cell and stared at the wall, trying to think of how I could get a hold of a new battery. I could risk trying to get another black staff—one that hadn't been drained. As I thought, my vision blurred and I thought I saw stars glittering softly in the wall. I wondered if they would guide me to where I needed to go.

"Whatcha starin' at, Kalrevi?" my cellmate asked as she popped into view from the bunk above me. The strands from Katchya's eyebrows bounced playfully around her head.

"Stars," I replied softly, letting my vision shift focus.

She laughed. "Oh, you see the faestone, too!"

"What?" I asked. I focused on her directly.

She smiled widely, which looked awkward from upside down. "Faestone. It's all through these mountains. I like it! When you squint just right, you can see it glowin' in the walls—like glitter! Have you never seen it before?" she asked quizzically. I shook my head. "My mom told me that way up north, beyond the ocean, they have these big pieces of faestone. I mean massive! As big as a building! They use it to power their cities!"

I listened in amazement. "And you say that's faestone I see in these walls?"

"Yup!" She hopped down from the bunk in a swift motion then sat down next to me on the thin mattress. "It's just tiny little bits, though."

I frowned in disappointment. "So they're not big enough to power anything."

"No," she replied solemnly, but quickly perked up. "But! There's bigger pieces deeper in! If they ever send you to solitary, you can see 'em. It actually makes solitary kind of nice. Just starin' at the faestone—great big glowy chunks of it!"

That was it. That was my power source. "Thank you," I said with a smile and started formulating the next step of my escape.

Getting into solitary confinement was a straightforward task. I just needed to upset someone enough to send me there. I found the perfect opportunity while we were afforded some time outside for exercise.

The warden was pacing the grounds and surveying the prisoners with a pompous smirk. A gentle euphoria filled me up as I picked up a small stone and took aim. I loved the look on her face as the stone cracked into it. Her lips and eyebrows contorted with rage and she started shouting. It almost made the jolts from the black staves worthwhile.

Once in solitary, it was just as my cellmate had said. I could see a faint pink glow in the walls; it was far more pronounced than in my cell. I withdrew a tiny pick that I had fashioned and smuggled with me. I had plenty of time to work and carefully picked away at the faestone until I had freed a whole crystal. It was warm in the palm of my hand. I spent the rest of my time in confinement quietly dreaming of my escape.

The dream was cut short when I was returned to my cell. As I reached under my mattress to acquire the smuggled staff, I panicked to find nothing there. I looked at Katchya with wide eyes.

"They raided the cell while you were gone. They took it, Kalrevi."

I beat my fists into the mattress and screamed. I had been so close. I dropped onto the floor, a useless, crumpled lump, gripping the warm faestone tightly in hand. I had been so close, and I couldn't believe it had all fallen apart. The cage had bested me.

"Hey," a deep bellow shook me. "Warden wants to see you. She didn't take kindly to your contraband."

I was dragged through to the warden's office and shoved into a chair. The warden had a deep scowl on her face as she paced before me, holding my black staff in hand. She shot a look to the guard and he slipped out.

"I warned you that if you didn't keep in line, you'd have a hard time here," she began. "What did you hope to accomplish with this, huh? Did you think you could electrocute every guard on the way out?" She took the end of the staff and pushed it into my throat. "I'm going to make sure that from here on out, every one of your days is misery."

She shoved her face close to mine, pressing harder with the staff. I hated the way she looked at my face. As I gasped against the pressure of the staff on my neck, I averted my eyes. That's when I spotted it—my mask. It was placed like a trophy on the wall. I seethed. *Does she really want to see what's behind my mask?*

I stared at her venomously; my quick shift in demeanour seemed to startle her for a moment and she eased off the pressure. I opened my mouth wide, exposing canines that slid out of pockets in my gums and revealed themselves as lengthy serpent's fangs. She staggered back and I opened my mouth wider. I unhinged my jaw completely, and my mouth sprawled open. Her eyes grew wide in fear and they reflected my dripping fangs and the gorging depth of my maw that could have swallowed her whole. My thick, rolling tongue poured out and curled through the air toward her, fully extending out of my mouth as if it were a hand reaching out to grab her. She was so taken aback, she dropped the staff and stumbled. I leapt on top of her, my mouth still stretched wide over her face. I could have slid her whole head into mine. Instead, I gripped her head into my hands and cracked it against the ground.

She was dazed, but not out. I needed to be swift. I jumped off of her and grabbed the black staff. I opened a compartment, slid the faestone inside, and jabbed a fork that I had wired inside up against the stone. It wasn't pretty, but hopefully it was enough to work. The warden rose back to her feet.

"You freak," she groaned as she drew a sabre. She leapt at me, thrusting the blade to run me through. I slid to my left and extended the black staff, flicking its switch. The whole thing felt suddenly hot in my hand. A crackle of red lightning burst out of it and into the warden's chest. She screamed, convulsed, and hit the floor in a heap.

The guard outside hurried in to see what the commotion was. I turned around, my fangs still visible and my jaw unhinged. He gasped and staggered back as he reached for a whistle around his neck. His hand trembled violently as he lifted it towards his lips. I lunged and pressed the black staff against his arm, letting loose another crack of red lightning. He dropped to the ground before he could let out a breath and I turned back around.

I snatched up my mask and delicately put it back into place. It felt so comforting on my face, like being wrapped in a warm blanket. For so long I felt naked and exposed; at last I was protected. Alas, there was no time to savour the sensation.

I grabbed the warden's keys off her belt and exchanged my clothes for hers. I hurried to the room where my personal belongings were kept, gathered them up, and fled.

I swore I would never be imprisoned again.

Chapter Thirty-Four:
The Dagger Falls

Death is certain. The question isn't how you want to die.
It's how you want to live.

— *Omen*

Velodik

"Pravda Press," I muttered under my breath as I stared at the building before me. A cart had just pulled up and a pack of Ishkara's goons scuttled out and into the facility. They'd be back shortly, hauling boxes upon boxes of Ishkara's own *radical propaganda*.

"Ishkara is harmony. Ishkara is unity." I took a hearty swig of my flask. "Ishkara is death."

I had spent a long time thinking about how I might tear her down. Weeks. I reached out to my contacts to get an edge, some information—anything—but it turned out that the most useful amongst them had been carted off to Kamin Prison. I missed Kalrevi. There wasn't a day that passed that I didn't miss her.

"Ishkara has placed me in a much more important position," Zradya had told me. I snarled as I thought of her smug face and took another drink. The liquid scalded my throat, and not because of its temperature. "I'm in charge of every sanctioned printing press. I shall ensure that all of Vsevora knows the truth."

I had come to Pravda Press many times. To watch. To plan. To drink. This place seemed to me to be the key. As I fondled the pendant around my neck, I wondered how to use the facility—or Zradya—to my advantage against Ishkara. For how often I sat here, nothing ever came to me.

Zradya stepped out of the building. She stood tall and proud. An involuntary growl hung low in my throat and I took a fast gulp from my flask. I considered pursuing her.

Perhaps I could jump her in an alleyway and force her to turn against Ishkara. She started down the street and I took a few steps after her before grinding to a halt.

I cursed under my breath. It was a senseless plan that would only get me sent to Kamin with the others. I groaned softly and stumbled back into my place in the shadows. I took another drink.

With bleary eyes, I caught sight of another woman slipping out of the building. I had seen her once or twice before. It was an Oksanan woman. As she stepped into the light, she wrapped a dark red scarf around her head. I hadn't noticed before—the auburn waves of hair, the nervous eyes, the tentative steps. There was no mistaking her. It was Siranna: Ishkara's former artist-in-residence.

I grinned as an idea immediately sprung to life. I followed her through the streets, careful to keep my distance, until she approached an old apartment building. I caught up as she reached for the door.

"It's been a while, Siranna," I said softly, grabbing the handle and holding the door open for her.

"Senator Velodik!" she exclaimed, a bit too loudly for my taste. I glanced around, but no one seemed to have noticed.

"Not anymore," I replied soberly. My fingers wrapped around the flask in my pocket and I yearned to take a drink, but I thought better of it for the moment. "Come, let's go inside and talk."

She hesitated for a moment as she scrutinized me. I looked quite plain compared to any time she had seen me before. Even in clothes of high quality, I looked slovenly without my uniform.

"What do you want?" she asked at last, understandably suspicious.

"I suspect it's the same as you," I replied. "To put an end to Ishkara and her delusions of grandeur."

She paused, considering my response. I saw her eyes drift through the door, but I could tell she wasn't ready to invite me in. "How do I know I can trust you?"

"You can't." I shrugged. "But consider, what could I possibly do to you? I have no power or authority left in this world. Ishkara saw to that."

"You could betray me to get back in her good graces."

She was smart. Very smart. And, admittedly, I had considered doing exactly that.

I shook my head. "It's a fair point. But I don't want to get back into her good graces. I mean to dismantle her—along with your new boss, the Lieutenant-Colonel."

"Zradya?" she asked, and as she did, it was her turn to scout the area for unwanted eyes and ears. "How do you hope to accomplish this?"

"Let's discuss. Shall we?" I gestured through the door. She hesitated again and finally gave a begrudging nod before hurrying up the stairs.

I slipped in after her, snuck a sip from my flask, and followed her up into a cozy apartment. Siranna wasted little time; she sat down and gestured to a chair across from her. "Be quick. What are you plotting?"

I ignored her offer and continued deeper into the apartment until I found the dining table. "I have information," I said, calling back over my shoulder. I pushed aside some newspapers and an open jam jar to make some space. "Information that would be quite harmful to Ishkara if it were to get out." I pulled a pen and a few slips of paper from my pocket and began writing.

Siranna stepped up behind me. "I fail to see why you need to talk to me about this. There are any number of outlets you could go to."

"Yes, but they are all under her control. You've heard the broadcasts; you've read the papers. They won't stop singing her praises. They're not about to share the kind of information that I have." I continued writing, scribbling rapidly. "Nor can I just throw it out into the aether and hope that it manifests in Ishkara's destruction. Now, if this information were to come from a sanctioned press, that would raise some eyebrows."

Siranna sat down next to me. "And of course, if this comes from the sanctioned press that Lieutenant-Colonel Zradya personally oversees..."

"It would reflect quite poorly on her, wouldn't it?" I chuckled softly and finished writing. I inspected the papers once again and slid them over to Siranna.

"I'm not sure about this," she said in a hushed voice. She reached toward the papers, but seemed nervous to pick them up. "What kind of information could you possibly have that could be so impactful?"

I laughed boisterously. "Are you serious? I did Ishkara's dirty work for over twenty years." I leaned in close. "But let's start with something recent. The violence at the protest was no accident; she authorized the entire operation."

Her eyes widened and for a moment I thought she might cry. She spoke with a trembling voice: "What? But-but I thought that was Kalrevi..."

I froze. "How do you know that name? Where is she?" Some small part of me hoped beyond hope that perhaps Kalrevi had escaped. Perhaps Siranna knew where she was.

I grasped her arm tightly, pressing it tight against the table and drawing her close.

She squirmed and pulled away fearfully before stammering, "She... she rescued me. But she was captured. Taken by the People's Army."

I sighed deeply as my hopes were so quickly dashed away. I returned to the matter at hand and pushed the papers closer to Siranna. "It's all there. Take it. Find a way to publish it. Let's put an end to Ishkara's dominion."

She picked up the pages and glanced over what I had written. Her hands were shaking. She glanced around the room. "I don't know," she said.

I let out a frustrated huff and wrapped my hand around the flask in my pocket once again. An ache surfaced just below my left eye. *Inhale. Pause. Exhale. Pause.*

"Think about it. You can turn the tide, Siranna." I stood up and abruptly left, guzzling down the rest of the flask as soon as I was outside the door.

I stormed out of the building. The sun was sinking and filled the sky with pale yellow light. The ache was growing. I couldn't trust Siranna to follow through, but I knew I was now on the right path. I just needed something more. A guarantee.

I arrived at the royal palace as night fell. Four soldiers of the People's Army of Vsevora, clad in dark blue, stood at the sealed gates. I stopped for a moment, expecting them to open. Nothing but stares from the soldiers.

I barked, "Open the gates! I need to see Ishkara. I'm a Senator and Chief Minister of Public Security!" Even after so long, the words came out so naturally.

"Not anymore, sir," one of them replied with a snigger. "Or did they not tell you that they were both disbanded?"

"I know that!" I snarled, my temper rose and the ache in my skull bit hard. "It doesn't matter. I need to see her. It's Velodik!"

"A bit late for an appointment, Mr. Velodik." The contempt with which he called me "Mr" was cutting.

I growled and spat daggers right back: "Tell her I need to see her. That's an ord—just do it!"

"It's all right, Velodik," a familiar voice said from somewhere behind the group. "I can escort you to see the High Regent." It was Galva. She emerged into view and stepped up to the gate. She was filled with smug delight as she gazed down at me. She gestured; the soldier opened the gate, and Galva stepped up close to me.

I tensed as she made her approach; she somehow seemed bigger and more brutish than ever. She grinned. It was unsettling to see her smile. She moved her head in the direction of the palace and I started walking; she followed closely behind.

The air in the palace was different. Servants traversed the corridors in anxious silence. They looked over at us as we passed, but any time I looked toward them, they averted their gaze. In each corridor, there was a soldier from the People's Army vigilantly keeping watch.

We stopped outside of Ishkara's office. "Sit and wait," Galva ordered. There was a guard stationed at the door and he gave a quick knock with the back of his fist as Galva approached. I heard Ishkara's voice call back an affirmative; the guard opened the door and Galva slipped inside.

I sat on an ornate, uncomfortable couch and leaned forward. I rubbed my temples and questioned why I had come here. I reached into my pocket. The flask was empty. I wished desperately for one of my vials.

I looked down at the intricate pendant that hung around my neck. I lifted it up and inspected its whirling pattern. The metal shapes curled about like Ishkara's horns, branching about in all directions. I heard something behind the door and I gently pressed the pendant before letting it drop back into place.

The door swung open and Galva emerged. "Leave us," she grunted and the guard marched down the hall. She looked at me with steely eyes; they bore the same intensity as her master's. "You've been granted an audience. You have ten minutes." She stepped aside.

I made my way to the door, but paused at the threshold. Nervously, I ran my hand along the gold chain around my neck. *Inhale. Pause. Exhale. Pause.* I stepped inside with Galva close behind. She gently closed the door and stood next to it.

Ishkara was behind her desk with a cup of tea in hand. She stared at me like she always had. I thought back to when we first locked eyes and wondered, still, what had been running through her mind that day. Had she chosen me? Had she planned each step from the moment she saw me? Her schemes were a branching pathway.

"Ishkara," I began.

She raised a hand to silence me and lowered her teacup into its saucer. "I'm surprised it took you so long to come see me. I was expecting gratitude."

I was incredulous. All thoughts of anything I might have prepared to say vanished. "Gratitude?" I exclaimed. "Gratitude for tearing away everything I had earned? Gratitude for destroying all that I had built?"

Ishkara scoffed. "Be honest with yourself. Was anything you were given really earned? It was me, Velodik. I was the one who lifted you up, gave you pretty titles and empty responsibilities while you played with your toys. And while you played, I built a nation. You should be thankful I didn't send you to Kamin with the rest."

Fire bellowed within me. "You couldn't have done any of it without me! You can't just cast me aside, Ishkara. I've done too much. I know too much. You need me!"

Ishkara stood. Her dress was far more lavish and bright than anything before; she wore amethysts from top to bottom. "I don't," she said coldly, evenly. "You lost control. You can't be trusted anymore."

I hissed, "You're the one who pushed me!"

"And you played your part well, but it was time that I took the reins." She curved slowly from behind the desk toward me. She stood straight and firm, and her tone grew ominous. "Step aside, disappear, and be happy that you still have your freedom."

I clenched my fists and ground my teeth as daggers cascaded into my skull. "Y-you can't keep this up! The people won't stand for it!"

"Have you not been listening?" She smiled now. "For the first time, Vsevora is following the people's will. The people love me."

"The people's will?" I jeered. "The dissolution of the Senate, the erosion of our checks and balances, the destruction of Vsevoran culture? That is the people's will?"

Ishkara's smile didn't falter. "They have become complacent. The protests, Public Security, and the Senate are all being forgotten. All they'll know is that the High Regent brought order from the chaos and kept them safe. They will see that I was the one who rid us of the relics of the past that tore our nation apart." She spoke with a sinister edge. "When the election comes, they will ask for me with a single voice."

"What if you're wrong? What if they don't ask for you?" One by one, I pulled the daggers out of my skull and threw them at her with every biting question.

"My will shall guide them. Ballots can be made to say whatever they need to." A cruel smile crossed her lips. "As you well know."

My voice grew weak, but I had a few daggers left to throw: "You won't have my help this time. Do you think the people won't notice? Do you think they'll stand idly by?"

"They will stand where I tell them to stand," Ishkara said, raising her voice in anger. "The people are worthless dogs. They are ignorant farmers and miners. Not twenty years ago, they were spilling each other's blood over dirt. The people of Vsevora are blind and stupid. They need someone else's will to guide them from their squalid existence and lift them up from mediocrity. They need me to survive."

A cold silence hung in the room. I thought back to everything I had ever done for her. How I helped her—uplifted her—only to bring down ruin. Daggers.

"You are no different than the dynasties that you denounce," I gasped, my voice a whisper.

"Hekar was the problem," Ishkara snapped. "Hekar—the last dynast-king—a rapacious fool at the end of a noble line. He killed his mother and started a war that shattered Vsevora. Before him, the monarchy understood the power of memories and love. Vsevora will understand it once again. I shall be as Queen Vekara was, before she was cut down. I shall continue her legacy and extend the might of

Vsevora. Imagine, Velodik, an empire with a mighty Empress at its head. Do not speak to me of dynasties past. I shall ascend them all."

Her eyes were burning as they looked into mine—burning with a flame that would never be extinguished. I felt trapped within her eyes, unable to escape the fire.

"I'll tell them," I whispered at last; she laughed. "I'll tell them the truth. That I had set up the attack on our own officers. That I had tampered with the ballots to make you Chancellor. All of it. Everything."

Her laughter quieted. "You would only destroy yourself."

"What do I have left to lose?"

"No one would believe you."

My voice grew stronger. "They don't have to. I only need to plant the seed of doubt. Enough doubt to keep the people from becoming complacent. Enough doubt to keep the army in check. Enough doubt to ensure that your election is just. Do you think that you can win without lies?" My chest heaved, I felt hot under my collar, and I started to gasp. I pulled the daggers from my skull and cast each one into the flames.

Ishkara stood silent, her eyes unchanged. Gingerly, she removed her right glove and clutched it tightly in hand. I winced at the sight: thick, mangled scars and burns laced her hand and forearm. She lifted her scar-etched hand before my eyes; her nails were long and painted with a clear varnish. I stood aghast as she placed her hand upon her face and then dug her nails into her cheek. Blood spilled silently down her face as she continued to stare into my eyes. She carefully slid her hand back into the glove and pulled it tightly back into place. Then she screamed.

"Velodik! Stop!" she cried. "My face!"

"What?" I gasped.

"Get off me! He's trying to kill me!" she shrieked. "Stop him, please! Help!"

I didn't know what to do or what was going on. Everything was daggers.

"Wait, hold on," I stammered.

Galva's heavy hand grabbed hold of me. "He has a weapon!" she exclaimed.

I pulled myself away from her and turned around to see that she had drawn a dagger from her belt. I cried out and turned to Ishkara, stumbling over my words, begging her to stop. She looked back at me with a smile painted in blood.

"He won't stand down!" Galva cried.

A cold burning cut into my back and cascaded through my entire body. My legs shook as the pain coursed up and down my spine and into my abdomen. I gurgled and coughed, blood sputtering from my mouth. My hands felt numb and I grew dizzy.

I moaned Ishkara's name and staggered toward her. I stumbled and fell to my knees. I reached toward the fire with a trembling hand. *Inhale.* I gasped out in pain; it hurt to breathe.

She watched me as I struggled. The room faded away. Everything else dimmed around me.

Amethysts, blood, teeth, fire, a crown—

Chapter Thirty-Five:
Dismantling the Oppressor

When we write, we seal onto the page our ideas and our ideals. When we read, we transform our way of thinking. There is no greater responsibility than choosing what is written and what is read.

— Mr Pravda

Siranna

"It's all there. Take it. Find a way to publish it. Let's put an end to Ishkara's dominion." Velodik stared at me intently as he spoke. He slid the papers over to me and I tentatively picked them up. I hadn't asked for this. I tried once already to take a stand against Ishkara, and it only resulted in bloodshed.

I looked over the pages. There were details about the protest, about past operations he had completed for Ishkara, and about her election as Chancellor. They were damning allegations.

I started shaking. I saw Mr Pravda's blood spilled on the page. How many more people would die if I released this? I remembered what Emil had said; maybe it was time to stay quiet and be happy with what little I had. I closed my eyes for a moment, and when I reopened them, the blood was gone.

"I don't know," I said softly.

Velodik snorted angrily and his eye twitched. I sunk back in my chair, worried that he was about to burst.

"Think about it. You can turn the tide, Siranna," he said. He got up and left without another word.

I looked over everything Velodik had written again and threw the papers onto the table. *I can't,* I thought. *Not again. I can't let anyone get hurt again.*

I hurried to the door and locked it. I leaned up against it as I took a deep breath; I was still shaking. I needed a distraction—something to push the thoughts out of my head.

I retired to my cot and picked up my sketchbook. The warm, familiar feeling of working my pencil across the page started to relax my hands.

"You can turn the tide."

The words echoed through my mind. I tried to tune them out. I let my mind wander and my hand went with it. I scratched random lines and arcs across the page.

Do I sit back and watch our world slip away? I paused, took a breath, and let the thought go. I kept sketching. A broad wing-like shape started to form. *People need to know what kind of monster she is.* Little feathers filled in the space around the wing. I started another. *She doesn't care about the things that make Vsevora beautiful.* Little strands flowed out from the wings, ending in fiery bursts. *I have what I need. I could tell everyone what she's done.* More wings. More feathers. They all started to come together. *Imagine what she will do next.* A phoenix took flight across the page.

I stopped. A phoenix. I thought I'd never draw one again.

Setting down the sketchbook, I returned to the table, picked up the slips of paper, then meandered to the window. An uncomfortable feeling stirred within me—not fear or dread. It was an anxious desire to act.

I looked up from the papers and focused on calming my mind. I gazed at the sky as it filled up with warm reds and yellows, concentrated on my breath, and felt a sense of calm overtake me.

Without warning, a white visage suddenly flashed into the window and I screamed. The surprise threw me backwards and I fell, wincing as I hit my tailbone. The visage jumped through the window and hovered over me.

"Siranna." I recognized the voice.

"Kalrevi?!" I was struck by a flood of shock, surprise, relief, and joy. As the wave of it crashed over me, all I could do was blurt out: "There is a door! You can knock on it!"

"I couldn't risk being seen," Kalrevi said plainly.

"Kalrevi! You were arrested. What happened? Were you released? Did you escape? How did you find me?"

"In due time. Let's be brief. What did Velodik want?"

"You knew he was here?"

She sighed impatiently. "I followed him from the rooftops and saw him talking to you. He's on his way to the palace now. There's too many soldiers; it's too dangerous to confront him, so I decided to check on you."

"What about the arrest? The People's Army? Did you escape?" She glowered in response, her impatience growing. "Right. Later. Oskar and Emil should be home soon, anyway." I shook my head and handed her the papers with Velodik's notes. "He gave me this. He wants me to disseminate this information across Vsevora through Pravda Press."

She looked over the papers. "The accusations are strong, but do you really think that accusations alone are enough?"

I shook my head uncertainly. "I'm not sure. But maybe," I said. I thought about the drawing of the phoenix and my confidence rose. "It would be enough to make people ask questions... maybe even push back against Ishkara's regime."

"I think you're right, Siranna. If this can help bring the truth to light, then there's a chance that Ishkara will fall." Kalrevi's eyes locked on mine; they were filled with determination.

I turned away. My breath got caught up in my throat and I felt warm. "I can't. I can't do this alone." The panic surged through my body, but it came to an abrupt end when I felt a gentle hand on my shoulder. I looked back at Kalrevi. Her face was a void, but I could feel her compassion and her confidence.

"You're not alone, Siranna. I'm here to help."

I took a deep breath and placed my hand on hers. Ishkara needed to be stopped, and this was our best hope. A trembling seed of courage rose up inside of me.

"All right," I said. "Let's start tonight. There's no time to waste."

It was late, I was tired, and it felt all too familiar. It had been both an eternity and a blink of an eye since I was secretly printing posters through the night.

I quietly worried as I made my way through the empty facility. The air was still warm and humid from a long day: residue from the steam-powered machines that were, for the moment, quiet and calm. There were stacks of posters, pamphlets, and booklets—all propaganda espousing Ishkara's strength and character.

I climbed the stairs up to the offices that overlooked the facility and made my way to a window. It was stiff, but with a heave I managed to pry it open. Within a few moments, Kalrevi popped through and stood next to me.

"You're sure this was better than just coming through the door with me?" I asked.

"Absolutely," she replied stoically. "Later, I'll show you how to travel by rooftop."

I shrugged and led the way. "I'll have to set the machines with the new text. It will need to be subtle. When we're done, though, everything will blend in with the other pamphlets; they'll fire up the machine, and they won't even know that they're distributing Velodik's truth."

I got to work changing the contents of one of the pamphlets, instructing Kalrevi as I went so she could assist. Before long, the machine was rolling and we printed a test run of our revised propaganda.

Kalrevi carefully scrutinized the finished product and nodded approvingly. "It looks good. And you're certain that no one will notice the contents have changed?"

I chuckled softly and placed a reassuring hand on her elbow. "Trust me. No one who works here gives a damn about anything that we print. Everyone down here is too tired from stoking the fires and the managers are too busy slacking off upstairs. Even the Lieutenant-Colonel spends more time trying to look important than actually supervising the facility."

Kalrevi laughed in response and looked back down at the pamphlet. Her fingers gently moved across the inner fold. "But what's this?" she asked, gesturing to a stamp in the corner.

"A phoenix," I replied with a smile. "A call to Vsevora that it's time we rise up against Ishkara's lies." Kalrevi nodded her approval. "Now let's get going. We'll come back tomorrow and make alterations to one of Ishkara's booklets next. We need to make every print count."

The next day, hundreds of our altered pamphlets quietly made their way out across Vsevora, and the next evening, Kalrevi met me at the apartment. True to her word, she offered to show me how to travel by rooftop. I barely had a chance to say anything before she pulled me out the window and helped me scale the apartment. When we reached the top, Kalrevi gestured for me to join her at the edge of the roof.

I looked down nervously at first, but was relieved to see it was an easy jump to the next building; I had managed worse while climbing in Oksana. As I prepared to jump, I noticed that Kalrevi was hesitating.

"What's wrong?" I asked. "I hope you're not scared; this was your idea!"

"No. I'm just distracted," she said quietly. "I went back to the mansion after we finished last night. Velodik wasn't there. He never came home."

"What happened?"

She shook her head. "It's nothing. Another bender. A one-night escapade. Nothing to worry about. Let's go." With that, she jumped gracefully down to the next roof.

I followed suit and we were soon dashing along the rooftops and jumping from building to building. I had to stifle a yell from the sheer exhilaration of it all.

I was winded when we arrived at the printing press and slipped in through the open window. There was no time to catch my breath though; we had to get to work.

It was faster preparing the next round of pamphlets. We had just fired up the machine for our test prints, when the sound of a slamming door echoed throughout the facility. It was the entrance. We weren't alone.

"Damn! Hurry! Turn off the machine!" I exclaimed and Kalrevi jumped into action. The machine screeched to a halt and I waved for her to follow so that we could hide.

There were voices chattering loudly to one another. At first, I couldn't quite make out what they were saying, but then one cut through loud and clear. It was Zradya.

"Enough complaining!" she shouted. "I know it's late, but we just received the materials from the High Regent's office. They're breaking the story tomorrow, and we need to distribute the evidence."

Kalrevi and I huddled together behind a machine and I peered out to see the Lieutenant-Colonel along with a few of my beleaguered colleagues. They began setting up a machine while Zradya watched impatiently. She had a folder in hand.

"Come on, pick up the pace."

"It's not like he's going anywhere," one of my colleagues mumbled.

"Shut up. We've had enough delays already," she snapped. With a groan, they continued their preparations.

Zradya opened the folder and flipped through its contents. "Poor Velodik," she muttered. Kalrevi perked up. "You sure picked a hell of a way to go. You deserved it, though. In a strange way, I think I'm going to miss you."

"What does she mean?" Kalrevi seethed.

"I don't know," I whispered. Kalrevi crept up and I grabbed her hand. "Hold up. You can't just—" Before I could finish, she had slipped out of my grasp and was creeping over to Zradya. "—just... no... dammit." I considered for a moment following after her, but feared I'd be caught immediately. Instead, I just watched, my heart pounding in my chest.

Kalrevi moved with practised precision, gracefully sliding closer than I would have dared. Eventually, I could only make out a faint silhouette and the glint of the edge of her mask. She had climbed up on one of the machines to survey from above and her shadow loomed over Zradya. Slowly, the shadow leaned forward and Kalrevi dipped into the light. I could see horror in her eyes.

"No!" she gasped aloud—loud enough for everyone to hear. Zradya whipped around and looked up.

"What on—what the hell are you doing here? It doesn't matter!" Zradya snarled and she drew a sabre. Kalrevi jumped off the machine and ran. "Time for you to meet the same fate as your master!" Zradya cried as she gave chase.

My heart was beating faster and panic clawed its way up my throat. I ran after them. I couldn't let Kalrevi get hurt. No one else could get hurt.

I caught up to them. Pale moonlight shone down in thin beams from the windows, washing them in a mix of light and shadow. Kalrevi was cornered and Zradya was ready to strike with her blade. That's when I noticed something in Kalrevi's hand; it was a long black stick or a metal bar—perhaps a part of a machine she had managed to grab. It would surely be no match against Zradya's blade.

The Lieutenant-Colonel's muscles tensed as she readied a strike. I screamed and Zradya glanced over her shoulder—enough of a distraction for Kalrevi to use to her advantage. She leapt at Zradya. I cursed; she was supposed to run.

An eruption of bright red light flashed out from the bar in Kalrevi's hand. Crackling, jagged lines of light streamed out at Zradya and cascaded across her body. She screamed in agony, her body convulsed violently, and the sabre fell to the ground.

"What was that?" I exclaimed.

"Worry about it later. Run!" Kalrevi exclaimed. Before she could take more than a few steps toward me, Zradya reached out and tripped her. The bar clattered out of Kalrevi's hands.

"Insolent dog!" Zradya spat. "You're dead. You're dead!" She jumped on top of Kalrevi and the two rolled about on the floor. With a kick, Kalrevi thrust Zradya off of her and sent her clambering across the ground—right toward the black bar. The two were quick to get back to their feet, but Zradya had managed to pick up the weapon. She grinned darkly as she stalked toward Kalrevi.

"Your master was a worthless excuse of a man. Selfish, useless, and despicable. The world is better off without him in it." Zradya's words were vicious and cruel. She slowly drew closer; the red lightning crackled threateningly in her hands, waiting to be unleashed.

"Velodik was an awful person in many ways," Kalrevi said, her voice quivering. "He was selfish. He was despicable. He hurt me and he destroyed our friendship. But that doesn't mean he deserved to die."

Kalrevi charged at Zradya, ducked past a flash of lightning, and grabbed hold of her wrists. They stumbled back and forth until Kalrevi shoved Zradya. I took that as my moment. Adrenaline took over and I tackled Zradya. I couldn't believe what I was doing. A blast of red lighting arced over my head and sparked in all directions. As the lightning crackled around us, it struck rolls of paper and stacks of pamphlets, igniting them.

Zradya and I hit the ground and we tumbled together. I kicked and thrashed, knocking her head into a piece of machinery. The bar rolled out of her hand and I scrambled over to pick it up. Panting, I got to my feet and looked for Kalrevi so I could throw the weapon back over to her. Instead, I was frozen in horror. The fire had picked up, spreading fast and erupting swiftly around us. My arms trembled and I almost dropped the black bar as I staggered away from the flame.

"Come on!" Kalrevi exclaimed. She pointed toward safety and ran. I followed quickly behind.

As the fire spread, it soon formed a maze that led us away from the main entrance and plunged us deeper inside of the facility. I looked around desperately as the flames grew higher and the smoke thicker.

"Siranna, how do we get out?" Kalrevi asked. Fear had crept into her voice by now. If she was afraid, what hope did I have? The two of us searched the area as the heat built up. The stairs. We could get out through the office window. I could make out a clear path, but it wouldn't last long.

"This way!" I exclaimed and darted forward.

"Wait!" Kalrevi turned and ran in the opposite direction, right toward the flames.

"What are you doing?" I screamed. Kalrevi skidded to a halt and picked something up. Fire crawled up a nearby support pillar. It wouldn't be long before the whole facility collapsed. I called to her frantically and I ran to the stairs.

She was finally following; I waited for her at the base, watching the fire continue its spread.

A blade swung out from the smoke in front of Kalrevi and she stumbled back. Zradya appeared, swinging the blade once again and narrowly missing Kalrevi.

"There's no escape for you," Zradya growled. "Except death." An obsession had overwhelmed her, as though killing Kalrevi would bring solace as the world burned around her. She moved in on her quarry, her body looming black against the growing flames. She raised her blade and brought it down in a swift, powerful stroke. Kalrevi expertly weaved aside, but Zradya readjusted and swung hard a second time. The blade connected and Kalrevi fell to the ground in a heap.

I held my breath. The crackle and roar of the fire died down around me and everything became quiet except for the pounding of my heart in my ears. I was overwhelmed by heat. I started to choke.

Zradya laughed. "Good riddance." She turned and pointed her sabre toward me as the fire rose higher. Smoke filled the air between us, and she began to close the gap. For a moment, she disappeared in the haze.

I trembled and held on tight to—the weapon! I realized I was still holding Kalrevi's weapon. I lifted it up and activated it; the black device came to life with crackling electricity.

Zradya emerged from the smoke. "Put it down. Now." She spoke with cold authority and eyed me cautiously. "You don't want to die like your little friend, do you?" Slowly, she drew closer, her sabre still pointed at me. She shifted the blade left and right, preparing her moment to strike.

"You should know," a confident voice said from behind her, "I'm exceedingly well-versed at escape." Kalrevi rose up and kicked Zradya in the back of the leg, bringing her down to her knees. "Siranna, the black staff!"

I threw the weapon to her and Kalrevi swiftly applied it, but it didn't last long. With the one final burst, Zradya shook, but then the black staff dwindled and ceased to spark. Zradya was dazed, but not defeated.

"Go! Go!" Kalrevi exclaimed. We ran up the stairs as quickly as we could. I glanced back and saw that Zradya was back on her feet. She screamed and chased after us.

I wanted this all to be over. I forced myself up the stairs, pushing my legs with all the strength I could muster. I gasped for breath, the smoke and heat overwhelming my lungs. I coughed. And then I couldn't stop. I collapsed on the stairs, coughing uncontrollably.

"Siranna, keep going!" Kalrevi had stopped up ahead. I followed her gaze and looked back as Zradya scrambled up behind me. She was only a few stairs away.

Crack! The furious sound blasted through the facility and the ground quaked. A support pillar, consumed by flame, gave way and collapsed. It tumbled down right toward us. I screamed and clambered to my feet. I leapt up and the pillar crashed down behind me. Everything shook violently and the stairs crumbled away.

I stumbled, falling backward, and started slipping back into the inferno below. I reached forward in vain, but the handrail broke away and out of my grasp. I lost myself to the heat.

A sudden jolt. I stopped moving. Kalrevi's hand wrapped tightly around my wrist. She pulled me forward and into her arms. I gasped, feeling solid ground beneath me. It wouldn't be solid for long.

"Let's go!" she said. Without hesitation, we charged up the rest of the stairs, ran through the office, and dashed out the window.

We didn't stop. We darted across the rooftops until we were safely away from the smoke and flame. When at last we stopped running, I collapsed and rolled onto my side. I coughed and gasped until I started gagging. Kalrevi knelt down and pulled me up to sit. She patted my back reassuringly and with a few more coughs, it felt as though my body had expelled the last of the smoke from my lungs.

Gradually, I steadied myself and could start to think again. *Zradya didn't make it out,* I thought. *I didn't want anyone getting hurt—even someone like her.* No *more.* No *more pain. No more death. It has to stop.*

Kalrevi and I sat together and watched as Pravda Press burned—a great bonfire that sent our hopes for change up in smoke.

Chapter Thirty-Six:
Farewell

In death, you are alone.

— Eternity

Kalrevi

I stood on the rooftop and watched the printing press burn. I had enough of fire.

Siranna was slumped nearby, coughing so hard I thought she'd break her ribs. She trembled weakly between each coughing fit. I sat down next to her and tentatively lifted my hand. I was not familiar with or even particularly good at comforting others, but I thought of how safe I felt in my father's arms; I wrapped mine around Siranna's shoulder and pulled her next to me. After a few moments, she began to breathe normally. We sat together in silence, and gradually, she stopped shaking.

I gingerly touched my mask. I could feel a mark across it, left by Zradya's blade. I thanked the stars that it saved me. Every Feras forges their own mask, and I was relieved that I had made mine so strong.

There was a commotion in the streets below as onlookers gathered and a fire brigade arrived to quell the flames. We weren't very conspicuous, but we weren't completely hidden either. I certainly didn't want to answer any questions about what had just transpired.

"We should go," I said.

There was fear in Siranna's eyes. I couldn't blame her. Every step forward seemed to get worse and worse for her. I gave a reassuring squeeze around her shoulder and offered her a hand as I stood. She took it and rose up.

"What are we supposed to do?" she asked.

"For now, get home safely and rest. After that... we'll figure it out."

We hurried back across the rooftops. Siranna returned safely to her home and I went to my own—at least, what I was using for now. It seemed unwise to return to the mansion, so I made a little home for myself in the attic of a shuttered horologist's shop.

I slid through the window, lit a lantern, and a warm glow filled the space. The light glinted off a host of old, broken down clocks and dusty old crates. There were little boxes scattered about, each filled with cogs, timepieces, pendulums, and more, all in different sizes and varying levels of disrepair.

It had been a fortuitous find and I had, admittedly, spent more time rummaging than planning after my escape from Kamin Prison. There were a few old tools, an assortment of clockwork assemblies and mechanisms, and even a few faestones packed away in a forgotten lockbox. I had marvelled at just how much had been abandoned; it had been enough to improve the black staff. Although, that wasn't saying much—it wasn't difficult to improve on forks.

I sat down at the makeshift workbench I had set up for myself: a crate next to the window. It was a mess of tools and discarded components. I pushed them aside and laid down the black staff. I would need to revitalize it yet again. But that wasn't what I was interested in at the moment.

I placed Zradya's folder down in front of me—the one I risked my life to rescue from the fire. I ran my hand along the cover and took a deep breath, preparing myself. I knew what awaited me inside. I quietly wished I had been mistaken—that I didn't really see what I thought I saw over Zradya's shoulder... that Velodik was still alive and well.

My hand quivered as I opened the folder. I expected to see Velodik, dead. I shut my eyes. I felt a lump in my throat. Another deep breath. I needed to review all of the folder's contents. I needed to hold myself together.

I looked inside and breathed a sigh of relief. I was met with pages of text: information on the circumstances of Velodik's death and instructions on how to break the news. The contents claimed Velodik had met with Ishkara and attempted to assassinate her. Submitted as proof was a photograph of the deep gash along her face where he had struck her. It went on to praise the heroics of Galva who saved the High Regent and "unfortunately needed to resort to lethal methods to protect her. Velodik made it clear that he would stop at nothing to kill High Regent Ishkara."

I didn't trust what I read, but at the same time, I couldn't forget Velodik's assault on me on the night of the protest. Was he capable of killing Ishkara? Would he have done it? I certainly believed he would have killed me.

I was about to close the folder when I noticed one more photograph at the back. I held my breath and slipped it out. Just as I feared. Velodik: pale, lifeless, gone. I felt a sick thud in my stomach and thought I was about to wretch. This photo wasn't meant to be shared with Vsevora; it was Zradya's trophy.

I stared at his face. I didn't want to. I wanted to close the folder and pretend it was all a lie—another scheme that Ishkara had invented to secure her power. I wanted to believe that I could track Velodik down, and find him alive and well. But as I gazed at him, I knew how real it all was.

The image was crisp and detailed. The warm, sepia tone made him look peaceful... calm. Perhaps he was finally at rest.

The name of a funeral parlour was scrawled in the bottom corner. I sighed, knowing that I wouldn't be able to attend his funeral. Would there even be a funeral for the would-be assassin of the chancellor?

"I wish it had gone differently," I said softly. "I wish..." I trailed off as I gazed down at the photo and finally took notice of the pendant around Velodik's neck. I was puzzled; I never saw him wear anything like that before. There was something strange about it.

I stepped away and hurried into the back corner of the attic. I frantically sifted through a crate of tools until I found what I sought. It was an unusual apparatus: it had a strap so one could wear it on their head and it featured a series of lenses, large to small, connected by brass arms. It was quite old. The arms didn't move very fluidly and some of the lenses were scratched, but it would be useful enough.

I polished the lenses as best I could, put the apparatus on awkwardly over my mask, and returned to the photograph. I adjusted the lenses, one in front of another, and squinted, taking in as much detail as I could. The pendant had a beautiful pattern, but there was something underneath. The pattern left a window that revealed intricate layers of gears and cogs. It wasn't just a simple clock movement; I had certainly seen enough of those in this shop. There was something familiar about it—something I recognized from disassembling and reassembling all of Velodik's radios.

I stood up quickly. I was weary, but there was no time to waste. That pendant wasn't just a piece of jewelry.

The curfew ensured the streets were quiet, save for patrols from the People's Army. I patiently lurked above as one such patrol marched past the funeral parlour from the photograph. Once they were out of sight, I climbed down to the street below and crept over to the parlour's door.

I crouched low and fumbled at the lock, working as quickly as I could. It wasn't cooperating. I looked over my shoulder to make sure the area was still clear. I noticed a pair of dark shapes down the street. I grit my teeth and focused on the lock, my fingers working rapidly to open it. Voices. They were getting close. I held my breath and kept my hands steady. Finally! A satisfying click.

The heavy oak door creaked open and I slipped inside; I closed it quickly before anyone could notice something was amiss. It thudded louder than I expected as it shut and I gasped. I paused for a moment, pressing my ear against the door. Nothing changed outside. I breathed a sigh of relief.

The funeral parlour was dark and unsettlingly still. I lit my lantern and began my search of the building, sweeping through room after room. I wasn't entirely sure what to look for, but as I picked my way into a locked room, the smell suggested I had found what I sought.

There was a pungent odour in the air: a wretched mix of pickle and lavender that made me gag. As I worked to regain my composure, I held my lantern high and scanned the area. I found him!

Velodik's body was lying across a table, mostly covered by a thin sheet. There was no sign of the pendant. His clothes had been removed and I couldn't see them nearby.

I stepped up close, looked down at his empty face, and lingered. I thought of the wildness in his eyes the last time I saw him and the ferocity with which he had grabbed my throat. I pushed the image away.

Instead, I remembered his smile as he returned home after a trip; he set some new contraption in front of me and beamed as he invited me to explore it. I recalled his laughter when I tried on a hat at the market. I thought back to our first meeting and of the long hours we spent sharing stories on the boat to Vsevora.

I placed a hand on his fuzzy cheek. It was cold. Tears welled up in my eyes and I closed them tightly to keep the pain at bay.

"Farewell," I said softly, my voice trembling.

I took a deep breath to try to hold myself together, but the wretched smell filled my lungs and made my stomach heave. I gasped loudly.

"Hello?"

I swallowed hard and shot up straight. The voice was distant, but it wouldn't be for long.

I frantically searched the room, pulling open cabinets and drawers. Then I spotted a plain box on a shelf with Velodik's name written on it in a tiny handwritten scrawl. Inside, resting on top of his clothes, was the pendant. I grabbed it.

There were footsteps approaching. I turned off my lantern and ducked behind the table where Velodik's body lay just as the door opened. I held my breath.

A beam of light shone and flashed overhead, scouring the area. "Is anyone here?" I wondered if they really expected someone to respond. The light lingered, drifting around the room, and I heard the floor creak as the footsteps drew closer.

There was a half-hearted chuckle. "Oh, Maksim. You need some more sleep. The dead don't wake up at this hour and neither should you." The light shifted away and wandered out of the room. I silently slid out from behind the table and moved as quickly and quietly as I could until I was out of the building and on the street. I breathed out a deep sigh of relief and returned to the rooftops.

Back in my attic, I had the pendant laid out before me, my tools in hand, and the magnifying apparatus secured on my head. I found a thin seam along the pendant's edge which I carefully pried open. I marvelled at the intricacy of the mechanism inside. On one side, it had what looked like a spinning wheel connected to a tiny, cracked faestone. On the other was a flat, black disc with small, circular etchings. The mechanism appeared to have been damaged during the skirmish that killed Velodik. But I wasn't deterred.

I started to tinker. With gentle precision, I disassembled the pendant. I began adjusting, bending, and replacing pieces as best I could. Once I was satisfied, I reassembled the mechanism and inserted a new faestone into it. Finally, I took a flat, thin piece of brass and fashioned it into a hollow horn. I measured and shaped it, then snapped it into place, closing the pendant around its thin tip: a perfect fit.

I held my breath as I twisted the little knob that connected the pendant to its chain. The mechanism came to life. It was a recording device, and with my repairs and the addition of the brass horn, it was able to play what was recorded. I trembled as I heard what I thought I would never hear again: Velodik's voice.

Chapter Thirty-Seven:
A Message for Vsevora

If you want to stay out of the grave,
don't go digging any holes.

—old saying in Yelena

Velodik

"The Ransacking of Lyudmila... My parents and I barely escaped the fires of the *vohon*. I was so young, I didn't really understand what had happened or why. Even as I grew older and I learned more, I didn't understand.

"How could anyone hate someone so much that death and destruction is their only course? Were the Yuliyans truly so monstrous? No. They were taught to hate. Hate became the fuel that justified their leaders' heinous acts. Lyudmila burned so the corrupt could live in opulence.

"When I arrived in Sophia, I was a scorned refugee. Our people were not looked upon with kindness. Their mockery fuelled my ambitions. I wanted to prove that I was every bit as quick and strong as any Sophian. I would outperform them. I would overcome them.

"The moment that I could apply, I joined the constabulary, and I put everything of myself into my training. Not only would I overcome the others, I was going to protect those like me—protect them from the bullying, the violence, and the hatred.

"Somewhere along the way, that changed. When I discovered that I could use the power I acquired to help myself. At first, they were small allowances: a little lie, a tiny cheat, a small theft. Corruption is a disease that comes on slowly. A few questionable decisions are easy enough to reason away. But as the disease takes hold... Soon you're acting in ways you would have never condoned before.

"As I look back, I realize that at any time, I could have stopped, but I chose not to. That's the worst part. Corruption is not a disease that you are powerless against; it is a disease that you choose to succumb to. Instead of asking how to stop it, you ask, why would I stop it?

"I was selfish and I was hungry. I stopped caring, stopped helping, and stopped protecting. Instead, power was everything. Power meant control. Power assured my domination. And domination brought with it euphoria. I wasn't so unlike those that destroyed my home. But I didn't realize it. Not until now, at least. With the disease firmly in place, I forsook my duties and allowed corruption to overtake Public Security. It became fuelled by hate.

"I am responsible for the tragedy at Agate Square. I gave the order for a Public Security operative to launch an attack that ultimately killed another Public Security officer. And like the Ransacking of Lyudmila, hatred was allowed to rise up and fuel the violence in the square.

"I was not alone in setting this tragedy in motion. Ishkara believed this would allow her to secure more authority over the Senate and over the Vsevoran people. I never imagined she would use this as an opportunity to impose herself as a dictator.

"I wonder when Ishkara first became infected. Her ideals inspired me just as she has inspired all of Vsevora. She lifted us up and showed us the power of unity. She told us that violence and hatred were the enemy. But her words do not match her actions.

"Ishkara's path to unity has been tainted with corruption. It's clear that she lusts for power as much as I do. Our corruption runs deeper than the tragedy at Agate Square. It stems from the very beginning of Ishkara's reign as Chancellor. Perhaps earlier still.

"Ishkara has no right to serve as Chancellor. I used my position as Minister of Public Security to tamper with the Senate election and ensure Ishkara's victory. She would have lost if not for me. She claims that she will rule until a free and democratic election supplants her, but that will not be the case. I am certain that any election held will be neither free nor democratic.

"There was a time when I believed that we were doing the right thing for Vsevora. We fought for change in the Senate. I admired Ishkara for her dedication to righteousness, truth, and order. Not anymore.

"To Ishkara, hers is the only righteousness; hers is the only truth; hers is the only order. She is infected. She is filled—body, mind, and soul—with rot. She does not care about harmony, peace, or unity. Look no further than her purge of Vsevora's cultural uniqueness. She will not stop there. She will do whatever it takes to ensure that absolute power rests with her and her vision of a perfect nation is achieved.

"I hope that it isn't too late. Truth is the only cure for this disease, now. While I cannot be absolved of my sins, I can hope that Vsevora can still be saved.

"If anyone is listening to this, I hope it's because of a celebration. I hope it's because I was able to get out the truth. Perhaps Ishkara even saw reason and turned to a better path.

"I fear, though, it's more likely that I was locked away and this was found as some piece of evidence against me. It means that it's up to you now.

"Ishkara promises us a nation built on memories and love, but if left unchecked, Vsevora will be dictated by lies and hate. Go. We are, all of us, infected. But we cannot give in to the disease. Do not allow it to take hold. Do not be tempted by the allure of power. I beg of you. Be stronger than I was. Stand up and share the truth."

Chapter Thirty-Eight:
Defiance and Dominion

The sun is blotted out
By grey-thick clouds.
Smoke wrings Mount Zorya,
Chokes the crystal path.
Its sheen, muted and marred
Scarred by the encroaching gloom.
Passing into grey void
A lone pinion drifts down
From o'erhead upon my crown.
The final light
The smothered flame
The broken wing.
Will Phoenix Fire
Be seen again?

— "Phoenix CLIII"
the final poem of Tibor of Oksana

Siranna

I sat in stunned silence as Velodik's words rung out through the attic of the shuttered shop. Kalrevi stood quietly in the corner; she had clearly listened to this many times already.

I hunched over the device on the crate and winced in horror as the final conversation between Velodik and Ishkara played out. The brutal sounds of the former-senator's murder shook me.

I turned to Kalrevi with wide eyes. Her posture told me that no matter how many times she had heard it, it was still painful to hear. She pointed gingerly at the pendant: a gesture to keep listening.

"One last time." It was Ishkara. Her voice was barely audible. There was a sweetness in it, but it was marred with a selfish cruelty that made my skin crawl. "You'll help me one last time."

"They were going to frame him: claim that he tried to kill Ishkara and then spread that lie across Vsevora," Kalrevi said quietly as she picked up the recording device. She fiddled absentmindedly with it as she paced across the attic. "Some attempt to garner pity... or to silence her opponents. But you heard him! They..." She trailed off and shook her head. "I don't know what to do."

"We need more people to hear this," I replied. "We need everyone to know what Ishkara plans to do: rig the election, assume absolute authority, and unleash an imperialist invasion." I rose to my feet, a fire building up inside of me. I couldn't take it any longer. Ishkara would do anything—even murder—the recording proved that without a doubt.

"I don't suppose you have the keys to another printing press?" While Kalrevi's mask was as stoic as ever, her tone clearly betrayed her doubt and her defeat.

I sighed. "Even with that one run, we had made an impact. There was talk at the market this morning; some people even think that Ishkara had the printing press burned down to prevent more information getting out."

Kalrevi was silent for a moment, but then a hopeful fire began to kindle in her as well. "We have a start, then. You're right, Siranna. We need more people to hear this."

I paced about. "We could start small, spread information to a few others... But can we act quickly enough? Ishkara has the power to address the entire nation all at once." Then it struck me. "The radio!" I exclaimed.

Kalrevi's eyes lit up. "We could bring this to the broadcasters and get them to play it," she said.

My excitement dwindled. "They're Ishkara's puppets. They would turn us in rather than share the truth." I looked at the pendant in Kalrevi's hands and marvelled at her ability to repair it. "But what if they didn't know? Could you make something, like a transmitter, that could jack the radio signal?"

Kalrevi hurried over to me. "Yes! Not a transmitter, per se. But I think I could connect the pendant to their equipment and override a broadcast." Her eyes were alight for a moment, but doubt soon crept back in. "The local station will only reach Sophia. We still can't compete with her reach."

"Surely there's a way to amplify the signal?" I asked.

Kalrevi sat down at the workbench and tapped her fingers thoughtfully. "Maybe? But the equipment we'd need for that..." She stared forlornly around the attic at the boxes full of mismatched clockworks. "Maybe we could find a different way."

I knelt down next to her. "What if..." I wracked my brain. "Not a way, but a place. A place that connects every broadcast station across the continent: the Grand Hall of Vsevoran Senate."

"Of course. We use Ishkara's power against her." The sparkle returned to her eyes.

"That's right. We should move quickly. They've announced that Ishkara will make a statement tomorrow."

"To frame Velodik," Kalrevi seethed.

"And to use the fire at Pravda Press to her advantage, I suspect. More restrictions. Tighter control." I sighed, feeling a heavy weight as I imagined the possibilities. "If we can get this out quickly enough after that statement, maybe we can throw her into doubt."

"No. Not after. We override that broadcast. We stop her before she can get any further." Kalrevi had become deathly serious. I nodded solemnly.

"All right," I said. "Let's do this. Do you have what you need?"

"Yes, I believe so. I've seen the equipment at the Grand Hall before and know how to interface with it. I can get the override done in time. Then it's just a matter of getting in."

We hurriedly discussed our plans—a flood of ideas that quickly built upon one another. We worked together, preparing everything that we could. I grew more and more confident. For all of the pain I had caused, this was my chance to set things right. I felt warm. It wasn't a sickening, dread-filled heat; I felt energized! It was phoenix fire.

"Just a few more preparations to make. I'll meet you back here at dawn," I said with a smile. I wrapped my arms around Kalrevi, pulling her into a tight embrace. She hesitated, but returned the hug. I climbed out the window to visit the market while there was still time.

I climbed down from the roof and into the window, returning to Oskar and Emil's. Clambering down was a challenge, given the bag of supplies I was also carrying with me, but I had noticed a few soldiers from the People's Army lurking outside. I thought it best to keep my distance and avoid them as much as possible. I slipped inside and immediately realized something was off. There were agitated voices coming from the entrance.

"There's no use denying it," a gruff voice rumbled. "Your neighbours have seen a young Oksanan woman coming and going from here for weeks. They told us they saw her speaking with Velodik and invited him inside."

"I told you, I don't know who you're talking about," Oskar exclaimed. I heard the sounds of a struggle.

"We're taking you in for conspiracy and treason!"

I crept quickly down the hall and peered out to see two bulking brutes clad in the deep blue of the People's Army. One of them was handling Oskar roughly and pulling his arms behind his back while Emil panicked.

I felt a tug in my stomach and a wriggling eel in my throat. My breathing became erratic. *I should run for it while I still can,* I thought. *I'll get back to Kalrevi, we'll broadcast the message, and then Oskar and Emil will be free. It will all be over soon.*

The soldier yanked Oskar towards the door and he let out a painful yelp.

"No! Stop it!" Emil screamed.

The second soldier punched Emil and sent him staggering back. Blood flowed out from his lip and nose. Oskar cried out and tried to pull away to help his partner but couldn't escape the soldier's grasp.

"You've got one last chance," the first one growled. "Where's Siranna Ankova."

I saw Oskar and Emil trading glances, and then Oskar's focus shifted and locked with mine. His eyes widened as he saw me, first with shock, then with painful uncertainty as he looked back at Emil. His face became stern and determined. He shook his head subtly at Emil. He wasn't backing down; he wasn't going to give me up.

They had done so much for me. They offered me safety when everything had collapsed around me. I couldn't leave them now. I couldn't let it get any worse. I drew in a breath and let it out slowly. I stepped into the hallway.

"Leave them alone," I said with as much authority as I could muster. My bravado grew as the words came out: "I'm the one you want. If you let them go, then I'll come with you peacefully."

I sat in a dimly lit room, fastened to a cold metal chair. I wasn't sure what to expect next, but whatever it was, I would face it head on. I could withstand Ishkara's goons.

"Siranna Ankova," a familiar voice filled the room with disdain. My pulse started to race. "You've certainly caused me a lot of trouble recently." The sharp clack of her footsteps came next. I lost control of my breath. "And I think it's time we put an end to this nonsense." A crown of horns slowly entered the light, casting long shadows across Ishkara's face as she leaned in. I shut my eyes and said nothing.

"I am weary of you Oksanans. You're a pox upon Vsevora." I heard a slip of paper slide across the table before me and I opened my eyes. It was one of the pamphlets that we put out. "Did you think I wouldn't recognize your phoenix?"

I conjured up every ounce of my resolve to steady my breath and I glared right into Ishkara's eyes. "What are you going to do to me? Lock me away? It doesn't matter! Vsevora will see through you!"

She ignored my questions and kept speaking: "You're such a naive little girl. You'd have been the most famous Oksanan in all of Vsevora—greater than Tibor; your works would have lived for generations as the most celebrated artist of our time. All you needed to do was obey."

"I could never be your puppet." I snarled.

"Are you certain?" A chilling smile flashed out of the shadow. It hinted at dark machinations.

I knew that whatever happened to me didn't matter. Kalrevi would override the broadcast and Ishkara would fall. I bit back. "The seeds of doubt have been planted," I said, looking at the pamphlet before me. "You can't stop it. You can lock me away, but what I have to say can't be silenced."

"That's just what I'm counting on. Galva." Ishkara faded into the darkness and a broad, hairy woman shifted into the light. I drew in a deep, measured breath and let it out. There was a glint of metal in Galva's hand and as I saw it, I felt myself teleported back: the blade coming down and one by one, rending my work asunder. I gasped for breath and returned to the dark room, the icy chair biting me, the restraints digging into my flesh. Galva crept closer, lifting the metal to the level of her eyes. I saw a squirt of liquid. A syringe.

I writhed against my restraints, bashing my arms and kicking my legs, but unable to break free. The point of the needle drew closer and closer. I tried to pull away as far as I could. Galva's strong hand clamped down firmly on my shoulder, holding me in place, and she pressed in. I screamed.

A stabbing pain. Whirring lights. Tumbling. Voices. A cacophony of voices.

"Lies!" they said. "Vandal!" They blurred together in a cold, droning tone that echoed through my brain and shook my mind apart.

"Who are you?" I gasped. More lights. Spinning. I wondered... "Where am I?" I cried. My throat was so parched. The light was so bright. I tried to close my eyes, but I could feel it burning behind my eyelids. "It burns!" I screamed.

The stabbing pain grew stronger, starting from my shoulder and shooting through my arm. I let out a raspy cry and opened my eyes. Amidst the light I could see a dagger sticking out of my shoulder. I panicked and grabbed the hilt. I tried to pull it out, but a powerful hand reached out and wrapped around my own. I followed the hand up to an arm then further and further until I saw a wicked smile.

Galva loomed over me, gripping my hand tightly, keeping the dagger in place. She slowly lowered her face down next to my ear. Her breath was as cold as her voice as she whispered, "Shh... it will all be over soon."

I shook and my breath grew ragged. She stepped back, taking the dagger with her. Blood flowed out of the open wound, drenching my arm, and Galva laughed. She narrowed her wide eyes into tight slits. Only her black pupils, stretched out across her eyes, were still visible. She shifted, preparing to strike. I held up my hands defensively as she leapt toward me, holding the dagger up high. I screamed and shut my eyes as she brought it down and I heard it tearing through the fabric of my blouse.

There was no pain. I was fine. I opened my eyes again—they still stung in the intense light around us. An easel with a painting had appeared before me; Galva had plunged the blade into the canvas. I stared, wide-eyed and quivering, at the painting: my self portrait.

It was a lifetime ago. I thought of the little portrait on my wall, of the childish brushstrokes I painted when I was twelve, of the hopeful visage I had made for myself. The dagger cut through my painted chest.

"No," I gasped, trembling, "not again."

Galva's cruel laugh rose up and she lifted the blade again, ready to bring it down for a finishing blow. My muscles tensed, I clenched my fists, and I jumped between Galva and the canvas. This time, as she brought down the dagger, it plunged into me instead. As it tore into my chest, there was no pain. I felt release.

Galva's eyes widened with disbelief. She stared down at the dagger; it started to dissolve, dissipating into crackling sparks. We both watched in awe as Galva's hand was next to go, then her arm, all breaking away into glittering sparks that rose up and vanished. Within moments, Galva was gone.

I blinked. I couldn't fathom what was happening. I looked around to take in my surroundings as the last remnants of Galva disappeared. My eyes finally adjusted to the intense light around me.

There were massive glass walls rising up in all directions, refracting light all around me. I was in the mountains of Oksana. Home. I wondered which mountain path I was on and how I would get back. This place was unfamiliar to me.

"Where am... wait—" I did recognize this place. From my dreams. This was the mountain basin where I found the phoenix nest.

I took a few steps forward and smoke seethed up from below, clouding the basin. I felt suddenly dizzy and cold. I tried to push through, coughing and gasping as I staggered onward.

"What's going on?" I called out.

A soft droning reverberated off the mountainside. "Come forward," the voices said. The words were foreboding, and yet I felt compelled by them.

"What's happening?" I called back. Only silence and smoke answered me now. I carried on until I bumped into something—someone actually. I tried to push the smoke away with my hands, to see who it was. I could barely see their outline in the thick smoke. "Who's there?"

The smoke parted and a bloody face stared back at me.

"No. No, Mr Pravda!" I exclaimed.

Mr Pravda said nothing. He just stared at me, a saddened expression chiselled on his blood-smeared face.

I placed a trembling hand on his shoulder and whimpered. "I'm so sorry. It was all my fault. It was all my fault!" I fell down to my knees in a lump, tears streaming down my face. "I didn't want anyone to get hurt."

He silently knelt down next to me and cupped my hand in his. It was warm. Gently, he wiped away the tears and lifted my face to his. A calm smile slowly crossed his kind face.

"You didn't do this to me, Siranna." Mr Pravda said gently. I looked up into his soft eyes, fighting back more tears.

"If it weren't for me, you wouldn't have died. It was my fault. If I had never called for the protest, if—"

He gently shushed me, his smile unfaltering. "I regret nothing," he said quietly. "To stand up for something you believe in... To stand up for the people around you... To stand up for freedom... It's worth any cost."

I held my breath, nodded firmly, and gripped his hand tightly. Slowly, he pulled me to my feet and drew me into a warm embrace. I held him close; I didn't want to lose him again.

He continued: "You need to keep going. March forward, Siranna. Make your voice heard."

"I will," I said softly.

The smoke around us began to float away and in a moment Mr Pravda was gone. I reached through the drifting cloud, grasping in vain that I might pull him back. Nothing. I stood alone amongst the few, thin wisps that remained.

I looked up. The outcropping stood before me—the one that overlooked the nest. I took a deep breath and placed my hands against the rugged surface until I found a sturdy grip. I pulled myself up.

The lingering smoke grew thicker as I reached the top of the outcropping. I turned in the direction of the nest. A dark figure stood at the edge of the precipice, looming over the nest below.

"Just like we practised," a voice called. Was it the figure? Was it the cacophony? The voice called again, firmer now. "Come on. Again!" The voice echoed off the mountain glass. "It's not working."

Suddenly, another stabbing pain ricocheted throughout my body, and I fell onto my hands and knees. I winced and clenched every muscle. Had Galva returned? When the pain subsided, I looked up. The dark figure now loomed over me.

"What did I tell you, child?" The voice reverberated around me and chilled me to my bones. "I told you that you weren't strong enough."

"Mother?" I gasped. The smoke pulled back like a curtain and my mother stood before me. Her eyes burned with cold malice and her perpetual frown was etched into a deep scowl.

"You had a responsibility, Siranna," she began. Her words were sharp and pointed, and they cut deeper than Galva's dagger ever could. "To your traditions. To your village. To your family. To me." As she said those final words, her voice shifted; there was a sadness there that I had never heard before.

Slowly, my mother leaned down and she took hold of the gold medallions around my neck. She gingerly ran her fingers along them, one by one.

"My mother gave me this necklace. And my grandmother gave it to her. An unbroken strand from mother to daughter for seven generations." She turned her gaze from the medallions to look me in the eye. There was no sadness there. Her tone grew harsh and bitter. "You would break the strand to feed your own selfishness." With a quick movement, she snapped the necklace off and took it.

I winced, shut my eyes, and drew in a sharp breath. I felt as though a piece of me was being torn away. I shook my head. She was wrong. Or was she? My heart sank and I began to question myself.

When I opened my eyes again, my mother was towering over me and dangling the necklace above my head. Once again, she spoke with viciousness and malice: "You are not the only one to dream of a life beyond the village. You are not the only one who wanted something else! But some things matter more than dreams." She let the words linger there for a moment. The necklace gently swayed in her tight grip. "I gave up my life for you, Siranna."

A mix of feelings swelled through me as she spoke. With her final words, the strongest of them bubbled up and I stood up tall. I shook with anger.

"No," I said firmly, my voice a harsh whisper that quickly grew louder. "Your life is your own, mother, and you can't blame me for your choices! You can't take your hurt out on me." As I looked at my mother, I could see she was shaking as well. The necklace trembled in her hand and my anger gave way to pity. My voice softened. "It must have been hard to give up on your dreams. But that was your choice. Not mine."

Thick smoke climbed up around us, obscuring my mother from my view. I reached out toward her, but she was gone. I breathed a gentle sigh of relief and stepped past the smoke toward the edge of the outcropping. The nest was below and the yellow-orange phoenix egg sat in its centre.

I climbed down into the nest and carefully examined the egg. I could see the line of where it had cracked a thousand dreams ago—where it had been sealed shut by the mother phoenix. I placed my hand upon the seal and as I did, fiery smoke rose up from the egg, sending forth a flash of heat that shot through my body and up into my head. My breathing quickened and my heart pounded.

"Try it again. One more time!" The voice echoed around me once again. I looked up, but I saw nothing amongst the smoke and refracted light. I looked back to the egg, which continued to spark and plume.

"Come on," I called to the egg. "It's time. You've got to get out of there." I pressed my hands against the seal and tried to force it apart. The heat struck back, an eruption of flame that threw me against the wall of the nest with a powerful force. The heat radiated through my entire body and I shook from its fury. I felt suddenly weak, like I couldn't go on, and struggled to stay up on my feet.

"You failed, Siranna. You failed in everything that you set out to do. It's time to give up." My mother's cruel voice returned. She stood before me once again, between me and the egg. Fire sparked out from behind her and she seemed a powerful demon menacing overtop of me. "The world has crushed you."

I gazed up at her and steeled myself. I steadied my breath. "It hasn't," I said, my voice a mixture of defiance and sadness. "You were right; the world is heavy. It is heavier than anything that I could have ever imagined. But it has not crushed me."

She seemed taken aback by this. I continued: "You were right about my responsibility as well. I do have a responsibility to our village, to our family, to you... And so much more: to Oksana, to Sophia, to all of Vsevora!" I reached toward her and put her hands in mine. She still held my necklace. Gingerly, I took it from her hands and held it in front of her. "Without my help, there are no more traditions—all of the strands will be broken."

We stood in silence for a moment. My mother's eyes seemed to be holding back tears. I placed the medallions back around my neck and I gently moved my mother aside to return my focus to the egg.

"Do you really think that you can do anything? It's hopeless." My mother's voice was there, but something about it had changed. I felt a sudden grip on my wrist and I looked over my shoulder. Her pupils shifted into two rectangular slits and her spiral horns grew out in black branches, gnarling around her head. As smoke flooded around us, her cruel words clawed into me: "There's nothing that you can do. You're hopeless." My mother's voice had faded away completely. It had morphed into the same voice that had been calling out around me, the same as the cacophony that reverberated off the mountains: it was Ishkara's voice.

Ishkara tightened her grip around my wrist and pulled me close. Her breath was a chill wind against my ear. "You will do as I command," she hissed.

"Never again," I bit back. I pushed Ishkara away and she broke apart in a cloud of smoke.

I looked down at the egg as it shook and sputtered, sparks flying out of it in bright streaks. I placed my hands upon the egg; they burned.

Ishkara's voice echoed out again, coming from all directions: "Who are you?"

"I am Siranna Ankova," I said firmly. I pressed my hands against the shell, prying at the seal. It started to crack open. "I am Siranna Ankova. I will stand beneath the weight of the world and I will overcome!" I cried out, my own voice now echoing throughout the mountain basin. The egg broke open and the heat burst out of it. It shuddered and quaked and broke apart.

The phoenix burst out of the egg with a streak of fire. It rose up above me, fully formed, flapping its four powerful wings and circling overhead. I cheered as it rose higher and higher. Then I stumbled back and fell.

I fell a hundred feet through a torrent of smoke and haze. When I landed and my vision cleared, I found myself in the seat of a carriage. The world whipped past me.

"Where are we going?" I asked, my voice hoarse.

Ishkara's voice responded: "Never mind that." I tried to find her in my daze. I couldn't focus. I leaned forward and I could make out her silhouette in the carriage. "Give her another one, Galva, just to be safe." A firm hand grasped me and a sharp pinch struck my arm.

Ishkara's silhouette stretched and grew; her horns spiralled up higher and higher, stretching up and out of the carriage. Smoke seeped up from below. I shook my head to clear the haze from my mind, but the attempt only sent the carriage spinning around me.

The silhouette kept growing. Ishkara's voice boomed: "Let's try again. Who are you?" The words echoed through my head. At first, I wondered what they wanted me to say. Then the words came to me from out of the smoke and I started to panic.

"No!" I gasped. I looked around, desperate for someone to help me. I tried to find the phoenix, but it was nowhere to be seen; everything had turned to smoke and shadow.

"Who are you?" Ishkara repeated, more forcefully now. I looked up and she towered higher than ever. She had become the mountain. At its peak was a barren tree.

Then I saw it, flying up to the peak of the mountain: the phoenix was climbing higher and higher, its bright wings cutting through the smoke and casting out the shadows with its fiery light. I fought against the words as they filled my lungs.

The tree's gnarled and twisted branches stretched and grew, curling round and round, forming a black crown around the peak of the mountain. They reached out, grasped the phoenix, and pulled it into the shadow and the smoke. I cried out voicelessly as the branches closed in around the phoenix. I could no longer fight against the smoke in my lungs.

"My name is Siranna Ankova," I said. The words flowed out of me like foul water and there was nothing I could do to stop them. "I have come forward to you tonight with a confession of my misdeeds. I am the one who propagated lies about the High Regent. I am the vandal that burned down the printing press. And I am the one who conspired with Velodik to assassinate Ishkara."

Chapter Thirty-Nine:
Amaranthine

She is dead.
I anoint myself in her blood.
My reign is absolute.

— King Hekar

Kalrevi

Dawn had passed. I paced across the roof, looking back and forth from one of my pilfered clocks to the palace in the east. The sun hid behind the clouds, searing rose-red streaks across an amethyst sky. It was calm and vibrant and grim.

Siranna was late—worryingly late. It had been over an hour. Something must have happened to her, and I could only imagine how dire it was.

I raced from building to building until I made it to hers. I quickly scaled the side and jumped through the window as I had on the night of our reunion. I heard voices in another room. I crept silently through the flat and pressed myself next to the closed door. It appeared to be Oskar and Emil; Siranna had talked about them frequently.

"Oskar, please. There was nothing we could do," said a distressed voice from within; Emil's I assumed. "Can we stop talking about this and just be thankful that we're safe?"

Oskar responded; he sounded emotional—angry, fearful, and discouraged: "No, we can't just stop talking about it. I barely slept. Who knows what those goons are doing to her right now! We need to help her."

"We don't owe her anything! In fact, doing what she did was the kindest way to repay us."

I didn't like what I was hearing. I opened the door and stepped inside. The two leapt to their feet and stared at me in fear. They were Ksenyan; the smaller of the two looked rough—likely punched in the face—but he stood defensively in front of his partner despite his injuries.

"Who are you?" he exclaimed; this was Emil. He didn't wait for an answer. "Get out of our home!"

I held up my hands. "Please, don't be alarmed," I said, although it seemed a futile sentiment given the situation. "I'm a friend of Siranna's. If she's in danger, please tell me what happened. I need to help her."

It took entirely too long to explain who I was and what was happening, but when it was over, they seemed amenable. At least Oskar was. Emil was still highly distrustful, and I couldn't blame him.

"Did the soldiers indicate where they were taking Siranna?" I asked. Oskar shook his head sadly.

"She could be in Kamin by now," I murmured quietly. "There's nothing I can do for her. I need to go forward with the plan."

"Good, you can get going then," Emil sneered.

"Emil!" Oskar scolded.

"What? You're not thinking of helping her, are you?" Before Oskar could respond, Emil turned to face me. I could see the desperation in his eyes. "Please, just go. We don't want to have anything else to do with this." Oskar grabbed hold of Emil's hand and pulled him close. They exchanged concentrated glances. Emil's voice became quiet and quavering as he spoke. "Why can't we just forget all of this and go back to living our lives?"

"We're living in fear, Emil. We can't live like that." Oskar turned to me. "Kalrevi, what were you two planning, exactly? I want to help."

"It's dangerous," I replied. "There's no guarantee of making it out alive."

Emil put his arms around the larger man. "No! I don't want to lose you." Oskar remained silent, but his expression was thoughtful and certain.

I decided to explain the plan: "We were going to the Grand Hall of the Senate to override the broadcast system. Siranna forged some documents so that we could get into the Grand Hall under the guise of completing a delivery. I'd be easily recognized, so I planned to hide in the delivery cart. She said that she could forge a disguise for herself with some supplies from the market."

"We found a bag that Siranna had left behind; it had makeup, a wig, that kind of thing," Oskar said. "I'm pretty good with makeup. I could disguise myself instead!" Emil's face contorted with an uneasy expression as he struggled not to shout.

"I can't ask you to come with me. You've been through too much already." I paused to think. Going on my own would be a challenge—there weren't any masked couriers in Sophia. That thought lingered in my mind for a moment. I drew a deep breath, mentally preparing myself for what I was about to do. "Oskar, you can help me. Get that makeup. I have to look convincing." I reached back and undid the clasp of my mask.

I approached the spires of the Grand Hall of the Vsevoran Senate. Sun beat down on my face and it scalded my flesh. Every inch of my face felt disgusting and violated. *This is necessary suffering*, I told myself. I paused before a clear pool of water that rested in front of the imposing, white building. The water reflected the cheerful light blue of the sky and formed a gently rippling mirror.

I winced as I saw my reflection. The wig that Siranna had procured was made of bouncing blonde curls that framed my face. My cheeks were rosy, alive, and sharply contoured to "make my cheekbones pop" as Oskar had put it. Thin black lines curved over my eyes giving the façade of eyebrows where none existed before. I tried to look calm and natural. I pushed my red-painted lips into a smile. My fangs started to slide into view. No. That wouldn't do.

If it had been another's face, I would have admired Oskar's skill with the transformation. He had mentioned how much he loved applying makeup to his brothers and sisters when he was young and that I squirmed more than any of them ever had. As I stared at my clownish reflection, I wanted to throw my head into the pool and wash everything off. I sighed and looked away. *This is necessary suffering,* I repeated and continued my march up the steps to the Grand Hall.

Soldiers in blue stood at the ready. I confidently made my approach and produced the courier's licence that Siranna had created. "Delivery for the Ministry of Agriculture," I said, indicating the small package clasped tightly in my hands.

The woman in front of me scowled. "All deliveries are supposed to go through the west entrance. We have receivers there."

"Oh, I'm so sorry," I replied, my voice creaking up two or three octaves higher than where it would normally rest. "Oh dear. That's over on the other side of the building, isn't it? I still have other deliveries to make," I nodded toward the bag on my shoulder. "I don't suppose one of you could just take me through to receiving?"

"You'll need to go around," the woman said sternly.

"Please! I'm still quite new at this and I don't want to get in trouble for being late with my deliveries." I batted my long, fake eyelashes.

I caught the hint of a blush in the guard's cheeks and a brief flash of a smile, but she forced a scowl back onto her face. "All right," she said at last. "Come with me." I smiled sweetly, making sure I kept my lips closed, and I thanked her profusely as she bid me to follow her through the threshold.

We travelled down the corridors that I knew all too well. When we reached the right point I came to an abrupt halt. "I'm so sorry!" I called out, shaking my head to let the blonde curls bounce around. "I really need to use the restroom. Is there one nearby? Please! I'll just be a second, I promise!" Another flicker of eyelashes. My eye twitched with hatred for every moment that I drew attention to my face.

The woman eyed me suspiciously and considered my request. "Come on, over here," she conceded.

We turned down an uninteresting corridor. A few janitorial closets, storage facilities, and a single wash closet. We were the only two around. She gestured to the door. "There," she said. "Leave the packages outside with me."

"Oh, it's no trouble, I'll just bring them in," I replied, my voice still sweet and pitchy.

"No unauthorized equipment allowed out of my sight," she barked back.

I tried to conjure up an excuse, but I wasn't getting very far. She stepped up and forcefully pulled the bag over my head, and in doing so, got it caught up in my yellow curls—which promptly dropped to the ground. I looked up at the guard with a nervous smile, while her face contorted into a mixture of shock and rage.

"You know," I said, "I didn't want to have to do it this way, but here we are." As she grasped forward to restrain me, I reached inside of the delivery package and withdrew the freshly-repaired black staff. I ducked down and pressed it into her abdomen. With a flash and a crack she stumbled back.

Unexpectedly, she was still standing. She must have had a thick hide like Spitfire. She charged me, knocked me to the ground, and held on tight. The black staff slid from my hands and I scrambled to get out of the guard's grip to no avail. She punched me—hard—and I felt the wind driven out of me. She reached out and pulled at my hair, loosing the wig cap that kept my black tendrils in place. As her hand fumbled with the wig cap, I snarled at her, revealing my fangs. Surprised, she let me go long enough that I scrambled over to the black staff, grabbed hold of it, and jabbed it into her again. This time she dropped unconscious. I dragged her into the bathroom with me and locked the door.

I gave my face a quick rinse, withdrew my mask from the bag, and clasped it back into place. I gently lifted the pendant up from its hiding place under my shirt; it was undamaged in the scuffle. I secured the bag back over my shoulder, looked up at the ventilation grate above me, and in a few moments opened it up and made my way inside.

It was a tight fit, but I managed to snake my way through the ducts. The air was hot and humid. I was sweating heavily and gasping behind my mask, but at least I was wearing my mask again. I managed to get past a number of guard postings and other personnel in the building. I was close. I kicked open a grate and jumped down into an empty office.

Creeping out of the office, I peered up and down the hall. Thankfully empty, but I could hear footsteps approaching. I wasn't far from the Senate Chamber. I ran down the hall and ducked around a corner, then took a moment to peek back. I saw Ishkara and an entourage with her. I didn't take any more time to examine the group; I needed to act quickly.

I hurried into the empty Senate Chamber and spotted the broadcast controls. I had prepared for this, but I had hoped that I would have more time. Stepping up to the controls, I set down my bag and took out an intricate device made of copper and brass clockworks: the override. I took off the pendant next and carefully connected the two together.

The plan was simple. As soon as the broadcast started, it would trigger the override and the recording from Velodik's pendant would start to play. Then Vsevora would know the truth. I took my tools from the bag and got to work connecting the override device to the main controls.

The doors to the Senate Chamber swung open and I ducked behind the machine. I heard Ishkara and her entourage make their way down the main aisle. So long as I stayed there, I would be out of sight. I only had a few moments, though, before the technician would come to take their place, and I'd have nowhere to hide.

I could barely see what I was doing from my low angle and I was primarily working by feel. There was a satisfying click as I locked the pendant into place. *One more connection,* I thought, as I traced my hands along the override.

"Galva, make sure she's ready," Ishkara spoke with cold authority, "I can't afford to have her ruin this for me."

I was curious what she was talking about, but kept working. It was a tight fit; I could barely get my tools in. But it was so close. Just a few more twists and it would click into place.

"Go on," I heard Galva next. "Say it."

"My name is Siranna Ankova." I froze. "I have come forward to you tonight with a confession of my misdeeds. I am the one who propagated lies about the High Regent. I am the vandal that burned down the printing press. And I am the one who conspired with Velodik to assassinate Ishkara." My fingers stopped moving; I stopped breathing. I slowly looked up, peering over the controls. There she was: Siranna was standing amidst the entourage, Galva's hairy hand grasping her tightly by the arm. I lost sight of everything else.

"Excellent," Ishkara said smugly. "Prepare for the address, then." She gestured to an antlered man; he had a defeated look about him, as though he had accepted his place as a cog in Ishkara's machinations. He nodded solemnly and made his way toward the controls. He locked eyes with me. I realized what I was doing and ducked.

"Damn," I hissed under my breath.

"Who's there?" I heard the man blurt out.

"What? Someone's here?" Another voice and suddenly footsteps hurrying toward me.

I kept low, silent, and leapt through the shadows from empty desk to empty desk. I was almost at the door, almost out of there, but a powerful grip caught me before I could get any further. I swung out a leg to trip up my captor, but instead it flailed out uselessly as I was lifted off the ground by a thick, powerful arm. Face to face with Galva, I reached with my one free hand for the black staff. It crackled to life with bright red lightning and I thrust it at the arm that held me aloft, but it was swiftly bashed out of my hands. Galva swung me around and thrust my face into a desk. She pinned me in place and I looked up to see the pulpit in the middle of the chamber.

Ishkara stood there overlooking the room. She was amaranthine. Her floor-length dress and elbow-length gloves were the colour of the flower: a vibrant purple-red. Beautiful gems hung from her crown of horns. The crown had grown since I last saw her, continuing to curl and gnarl around her head. A scar marred her cheek, but it did not mar her vicious smile. Her rectangular eyes blazed victoriously as she gazed at me.

"Velodik's pet," Ishkara gloated. "I was informed of your escape and knew it was only a matter of time before you came here to avenge your master. Looks like another assassination attempt was foiled." I stared daggers silently back at her. "Don't worry," she continued, "you can stay for the address. Perhaps I can convince you that I'm not so bad. Galva, bind her and show her to a seat."

Galva restrained my hands behind my back and then threw me roughly into the chair next to us. I felt her hand pressed firmly on my shoulder.

I turned my attention to Siranna. She was flanked by another guard. She looked dazed, her eyes glazed over. I thought back to the words Galva had her say. Ishkara was going to undo everything that we did at the printing press. Even worse, it would be enough to galvanize the people behind her and secure her victory. But maybe that didn't matter, I reasoned. The pendant was in place, the override was ready, and as soon as Ishkara started her address, her schemes would come crashing down.

I waited in silence and smiled softly beneath my mask as Ishkara gestured to the technician. He began the broadcast. I looked up at the curved brass horns that trumpeted out from each corner of the room. Velodik's voice would soon fill the hall and spread across Vsevora.

But then it didn't. The second click. I hadn't heard the second click. The device was in place, the recording would play, but the automatic trigger hadn't been connected. But it could still be manually activated. I tried to leap to my feet, hoping I could get to the controls, but Galva instantly shoved me down. I slumped in the chair as wave after wave of anger, frustration, sorrow, and then despair came over me.

Ishkara spoke with a sickening smile. "Vsevora, my friends, I speak to you tonight as we encroach upon a new age for our nation. We are about to embark on the first truly democratic election that we have ever known. Generations ago, we were ruled by monarchs and power was doled out through blood. Since then, we have been subjugated by systems and politicians that have been ruined by corruption.

"The power to rule is not one person's to wield. Not even I, in the seat of the High Regent, can wield it. That power is yours. For the first time, Vsevora's future is in the hands of its citizens. This is your time. And it is imperative that you wield your power with thoughtfulness and care.

"Cruel forces are looming that would take your power away from you. It was only a few short days ago that a man I once respected tried to take my life. Velodik, a former senator and minister, came into my office and assaulted me with the intent to kill me. He attempted this atrocious act because he believed that your power, the power of the people of Vsevora, is unearned and should be surrendered. Men like Velodik would rip the power from your hands so that we could return to tyranny and corruption. And he did not act alone."

Ishkara shot a wicked glance at me as she continued, "Some of you may still doubt me. And I would not blame you. Many have stood before you spouting falsehoods. Now it is time that you hear the truth. Listen carefully, Vsevora, as I bring before you the traitor who tries to deceive you and who tries to take away your free choice. She offers her confession to the nation tonight so that she may be absolved."

Ishkara raised a hand and beckoned Siranna forward. "Now," she hissed. A guard escorted Siranna up the pulpit.

I felt tears rolling down my cheeks. It was over. It was all over. We had tried so hard, but had failed. As I sobbed, I felt a deep loathing fill me. There was no stopping the impenetrable shield that Ishkara had built around her. I looked up at her smiling face, then past it to the shadow she cast on the wall behind. The entire chamber seemed to be filling up with the growing branches of Ishkara's crown of horns—an ever expanding shadow that had begun to devour everything. We had failed.

I looked from the looming shadow of horns to the amaranthine form of Ishkara at the pulpit, and then at Siranna and her glazed-over eyes. *If I can just get through to her,* I thought. As Siranna tentatively approached, I called out as loudly as I could, "Vsevora is for the people!" Galva reacted quickly and slammed my head into the desk. Stars spun around me, but I shouted again, "The laws serve the people! People don't serve the laws!"

Ishkara stepped away from the microphone and pointed at me. "Shut her up." The other guard made her way over to help Galva.

Siranna stood at the pulpit, quiet.

"Just like we rehearsed now," Ishkara hissed quietly. "Speak, puppet."

"M-my name is Siranna... Ankova," she stammered nervously. "I.. I have..."

"Together we rise, Siranna! For Vsevora!" I screamed. Galva threw me backwards in the chair and the other guard arrived to kick me in the stomach, knocking the wind out of me. I was pulled back up again, Galva holding me in place, while the other pummelled me. I kept my eyes on Siranna.

"I have come forward..." Something in her eyes changed; they seemed to light up with a glimmering flame. She glanced about the room frantically and her breathing became sharp and irregular.

"Siranna," I gasped, barely audible. "You can do this."

"I have come forward tonight with a confession..." She paused. She took a breath and steeled her gaze. She gripped the microphone tightly in hand. "A confession... Not of my own actions, but a confession from the Senate. A confession from Ishkara herself. She bares no right to serve as High Regent! Do not listen to her lies. Vsevora is the people!"

Ishkara was enraged. She threw herself at Siranna, pulling her back from the microphone. The guard that had been pummelling me hurried to Ishkara and Siranna. In the confusion I threw my head back and cracked it into Galva's nose. Galva staggered back and I shouted, "The device is in place, but it needs a manual override!" I barrelled toward the other guard and threw myself at her, knocking her to the ground. I staggered back to my feet.

Siranna acted without hesitation. She grabbed a hold of Ishkara's crown of horns and wrenched her to the ground. She jumped over the pulpit and dashed over to the broadcast controls. The antlered man was in a panicked tizzy. "Excuse me," she said as she put herself between him and the controls.

Ishkara rose back to her feet. The gems in her horns were tangled and her hair dishevelled. Her eyes flared with rage. She gripped the microphone, "People of Vsevora, the villains are taking hold. Do not listen to their lies. Stand up for what is right and honest and true. Believe in the words that I speak to you!"

As if on cue, Siranna triggered the override and the gears inside of the clockwork device sprung to life. "The people are worthless dogs," Ishkara's words blared from the trumpets; they filled the room and would echo across the entire nation. "They are ignorant farmers and miners. Not twenty years ago, they were spilling each other's blood over dirt. The people of Vsevora are blind and stupid. They need someone else's will to guide them from their squalid existence and lift them up from mediocrity. They need me to survive."

Ishkara was stupefied. She stood in stunned silence as her own words crashed down around her. Next, Velodik's voice spoke up, revealing that he had tampered with the Senate election that put her in power.

"Turn it off!" Ishkara screamed. The technician put on a look of confusion and behaved as if he had no idea what had happened. She shrieked again. "Turn it off!"

Galva hurried over to the broadcast controls. She shoved Siranna to the ground and looked over the machine in confusion. "Turn it off!" Galva commanded as if the third time would make a difference.

The technician cocked an ear towards Velodik's confession. "No. Vsevora is for the people," he replied obstinately.

Galva snarled and cracked him hard over the head, and he fell limply to the ground. She bashed uselessly against the machine.

I searched rapidly for some way to help while my hands were still bound. I spotted the black staff on the ground. I hurried to it and kicked it toward the broadcast controls. "Siranna, grab it!" Siranna, still on the ground, leapt to pick it up. She stood, turned it on, and jabbed it into the back of Galva's neck. Electricity crackled through the air and there was a sudden blast of lightning and flame as the black staff exploded. Galva collapsed and the black staff tumbled to the ground, smouldering.

The recording was nearly done. We had done it. We won!

"Kill her," Ishkara seethed. She pointed a trembling finger at Siranna. The other guard strode forward. I tensed, looking at Siranna. Her gaze was still steadfast and steely, but I could tell she barely had any strength left. I, too, could feel my strength waning as pain coursed through me. There were certain to be more guards on the way. We couldn't keep fighting our way through like this.

The guard drew a sabre from her belt. "No," she said. "We are the People's Army. Our duty should be to them first. 'We are, all of us, infected. But we cannot give in to the disease.'" She echoed Velodik's words and she turned to face Ishkara, pointing the sabre at her. Ishkara's eyes burned.

"It's over," I said, adamantly. "It's all over, Ishkara."

"You don't understand what you've done," she said. Her voice was a thin whisper, but it bore all of the hatred and anger that shone in her eyes. "Without me, Vsevora will collapse into dissidence and chaos once again. Without me, the nation is nothing. It was all up to me to bring us together. To create unity." The fire in her eyes was slowly dying out and she muttered softly, speaking to neither of us directly any longer. "Memories and love. I am memories and love."

"No," Siranna said softly. Her voice was tired, but steadfast. "Memories and love celebrate our differences. Unity will come when each of us shares in that truth."

Epilogue:
Ishkara Eternal

*Hold your hands together and place this cord between them.
This cord is ishkara: memories and love. As we wrap the cord
around your wrists, we bind together the memories you will
share. As we tie this cord in place, we unite your love forever.
Go forward, bound hand in hand and heart to heart:
ishkara eternal.*

— Ksenyan wedding proclamation

Ishkara

Oksana was a miserable place.
Its winter should have been a
respite after the summer's heat,
but each frigid day brought either
rain, sleet, or snow.

I pulled a tattered grey cloak
tightly around me as a blast of icy
wind struck my face. It pushed
back my hood, revealing my
gnarled and tangled horns. I pressed myself against a nearby wall, hoping the wind would die down as I struggled to
pull the hood back up.

"Hey there," a voice called over the wind. I followed the
sound and saw two figures amidst the blowing snow. I desperately tried to pull the hood up, but it was caught amidst
the tangle.

"We need to see some identification," another voice
commanded as the figures moved closer. They started to
take on shape. Glinting badges, pressed uniforms, and spiralling horns.

I ran.

I pushed myself as hard and as fast as I could go, dashing
down the snowy street. The voices called behind me, urged
me to stop, and the clatter of boots followed. I darted
around a corner, skidding in the ice, but not giving in.

I pressed onward, gasping as I did. I glanced down an
alleyway and hesitated for a moment. I already felt the
muscles in my legs burning. I couldn't jump like I used to.

I slipped into the alley, tore a strip off my cloak, and
caught it onto a bit of exposed pipe, then doubled back. I

jumped into a bin and pulled the lid overtop. The figures were right behind. I peeked out as they hurried past.

"We lost her," said one. "You sure it's Ishkara?"

"Did you see those horns? Besides, innocent people don't just run like that," the other replied.

"I'll make you a bet. If it's her, I'll buy your drinks for a month."

They both laughed and then the first exclaimed: "Hey! A bit of her cloak. I think she went down this way." They hurried off.

Ah, how you've fallen, Velodik's voice mocked me in the back of my mind. I groaned as I pulled myself out from the trash and shook off a putrid-smelling slime from my cloak. I stepped out of the alley and tried to get my bearings. There was an inn a few blocks away. I pulled up my hood and made my way there as quickly and surreptitiously as I could.

The warmth of the inn welcomed me. I adjusted my gloves, pulling them tightly over my elbows as I approached the counter where a well-rounded innkeeper sat writing on a ledger. I stepped in front of him, dropped some coins on the counter, and silently waited to be acknowledged.

He appeared to notice the smell before anything else and he furrowed his nose. His voice was warm but uncertain as he looked me over: "Good evening, ma'am. Are you looking for a room then?"

I pushed the coins forward without a word. He cocked his head to the side as he counted them and said, "Just one night?"

"Yes," I replied with gravel in my voice.

He broke into a chipper conversational tone as he started writing on the ledger. "Travelling are we? Here to see the sights or maybe taking a longer journey? I've always wanted to fly on a skyship, myself. Oh, boats are fine, but you just have to be more wary of seasickness!" He laughed.

"Just the room," I hissed and glared at him.

"You know," the innkeeper said softly, leaning in and leering at my face beneath the hood, "You look awfully familiar. Something about the eyes I think."

"I'm sure you've met plenty of Ksenyans," I said slowly, my patience wearing thin. "Now please. The room."

"Right! Right! Of course!" He looked behind at a row of keys on pegs. I looked past him and spotted a poster that was pinned up next to them. It featured Vsevora's crest at the bottom. Rising above the crest's mountains, there was a four-winged bird. Beams of light and fire spread out from its wings to the edge of the poster, and across the top it read, "VOTE For A New Future." My fingers dug into the wooden countertop as I saw the artist signature "Siranna Ankova" scrawled in the corner.

The innkeeper traced his hand along the row of keys, tenderly lifted one of them, and then placed it down in front of me. He noticed my gaze affixed to the poster. "Ah, pretty striking, isn't it? The artist who made it, she grew up in a village near here," he beamed. "Siranna's the very one who uncovered all that corruption in the capital. Quite the hero!"

My fingers trembled as they raked across the countertop. The innkeeper looked down and then back up. "Well, people react differently to art, I guess. Room Seven is just up the stairs and to the left. Has a decent view. It's uh... got a hot shower too." He stared down at my clenched hand again. "You should find it relaxing." I snatched up the key and stormed up the stairs.

Once inside my room I quietly pressed the door shut, locked it, and dropped my travel pack to the floor. I breathed in through gritted teeth and stepped over to the bed, then proceeded to tear a pillow apart. I ripped off my gloves, exposing the unhealed scars from a lifetime ago and shredded the pillow with talon-like nails.

I drew a few deep breaths as I looked at the calamity of feathers around me. I seethed. I hated every waking moment of the last thirteen months. I sat on the edge of the bed in front of a chest of drawers and slowly raised my face to the mirror.

I gazed into dead eyes. I took off the hood and cloak, and looked at my twisting horns, my wrinkled face, and my scarred cheek. I lifted a scarred hand and pressed it up to the face of the old crone in the mirror.

My hands traced from her face and up the path of her horns, across the entire crown. I pulled my hands off the glass and placed them on the horn itself, moving up and down the branching paths once again, locking eyes with the crone. She stared back at me, relentlessly, but her eyes were bereft of fire. She opened her mouth in a silent scream as a tear slid down her withered cheek.

I stepped away from the mirror and grabbed my pack. I reached inside, withdrawing a small bottle and a bundle of white cloth. I set them both by the mirror and drew a breath as I tentatively reached back in and revealed a small saw; it was a medical device capable of rending bone.

I drew a deep breath as I looked down at the saw. My fingers carefully tapped the sharp teeth of the instrument.

Fleeting visions of the last thirteen months raced through my mind, and as I looked back at the mirror, they seemed to play out upon the glass. Angry faces and mobs, betrayers and villains, and so much senseless death. I saw Galva, her eyes fading into lifeless nothing. She gave everything so I could have one last chance at freedom. This wasn't freedom: scuttling through alleys, hiding in trash, feeding on sewer rats to survive.

I lifted the bone saw to the level of my eyes.

I saw the witch, Kalrevi, who rallied my armies behind her mask and ripped them away from me. I saw Siranna Ankova and her phoenix leading the masses. The Oksanan phoenix rose over the mountains of glass and spread its wings over Vsevora. My Vsevora. After a lifetime of rebuilding the nation, it was ripped away from me in an instant. I had nothing.

My knuckles were white hot as I placed the saw near the base of my left horn. I reached my other hand into the tangle and grabbed hold. I drew in a deep breath as I stared at the crone and pulled back the teeth. Shockwaves of pain overwhelmed me as I rocked my hand back and forth. As the pain increased, I clenched my eyes shut. I tried not to yell, but I couldn't keep the agony contained. Back and forth the teeth ground into me, each time a new wave of pain. My hand kept moving until there was no more resistance and the blade came through the other side.

My hands fell limply to my sides and I dropped both the horn and the blade. They clattered to the ground and I panted heavily. My hair was wet with fresh blood. I reached weakly for the bottle and the cloth. I clumsily splashed the liquid onto the stump and winced at the burning sting. I wrapped up the stump, looked down at the gnarled mass on the floor next to me, then back into the mirror.

My head and face were streamed in blood, as were the crone's. Like me, she was now missing half of her crown. I gripped the saw again and got to work on the other side. This time I watched. I watched as the old crone's face contorted in pain. My vision started to dim. She looked dizzy from the suffering. But I continued until the other horn was gone and fresh blood flowed down the side of her withered face. I disinfected and bandaged the other stump.

I looked at myself. I was dressed in filthy grey rags. I was doused in blood. My skin was wrinkled and pale. My eyes were two lifeless, stretched beads. They held no passion, no ambition, no hope. Two stumps sat atop my matted, grey hair. My crown was gone. It lay in two broken halves on the floor beside me.

I trembled and quivered, growing rapidly colder. I fell back onto the bed, pulled the heavy blankets around me, and succumbed to darkness.

As I left the inn the next morning, I spoke to no one. It was dark and the streets were blanketed with fresh snow. I had broken down the rest of the gnarled horns, stuffed them into my pack, and cast it all into an alleyway trash bin. I pulled the hood tight against my barren head and made my way for the harbour.

Oksana's harbour was both a seaport and a skyport. As I made my approach, I could see a few boats on the water and a few skyships docked on high towers along with a small, diffuse crowd of others who were preparing to travel. As I made my way closer to the water, everything became a din of chattering voices.

A dim, yellow light peeked out from the dark, grey sky. I looked up at a massive, ballooning airship docked above and wished that I could escape into the clouds. I stared for a long time, the chill wind biting my face. Then a familiar sound broke through the chatter and brought me back to reality.

"That's the one," an energetic voice exclaimed. "It'll take me across the sea to the City of Oil. I've heard the greatest mechanical minds in the world go there. Should be quite the adventure."

I stopped and looked from left to right, trying to find the source of the voice. I knew that voice. Then I saw it: the mask glided toward me, wreathed with raven hair that fluttered in the wind.

A gust blew back my hood as she approached, revealing the great nothingness atop my head and exposing my face. I choked as Kalrevi approached, grasping uselessly at the hood. She narrowed her eyes at me and I braced myself as I prepared for her to strike. But her eyes weren't focused on me. She whisked on by as if I were nothing to her. I was un-recognizable. I turned around, and watched her red dress as it moved toward one of the towers and disappeared.

I hurried away in search of the vessel that would carry me away from Vsevora. As I approached the pier, I felt as though I were being watched. I froze, looked around, but found no one in pursuit. Still, I felt someone's eyes on me.

My mind raced. I wasn't about to be dragged away just as I had reached the brink of escape. I spun about in desperate search for my pursuers. Someone bumped into me or per-haps I bumped into them, and I fell. And then I saw two ra-diant eyes staring down at me.

I held my breath, silent, staring back up at the eyes—her eyes—Siranna Ankova. Her auburn curls bounced vibrantly around the horns that spiralled up from the top of her head. She wore glistening, golden medallions around her throat and bore a fiery paintbrush in her hand. Phoenix wings rose up behind her with beams of light that shattered the clouds. With red-painted lips, she smiled down at me full of smug delight. She mocked me in my destitution, pleased to be looking down upon a fallen queen. I stared up, dumbfound-ed.

"See *The Phoenix of Vsevora*, the newest exhibit from Ok-sana's own Siranna Ankova at The Mirror Gallery!" The words were drawn in vibrant yellow below Siranna's bust.

I exploded with rage and jumped to my feet. I lunged forward and bashed my fists against Siranna's face. Her smile never faltered as I clawed at her eyes and her hair. She stared me down as I ripped off the phoenix wings. With a scream, I tore the poster off the wall.

I stood still, catching my breath, waiting for the anger to pass. I looked at what had been left in the wake of my destruction: "Ishkara is Harmony."

My knees quaked and I fell forward. I pressed myself up against another familiar face. Familiar eyes looked down on me. They were strong, proud, and resilient. I remembered those eyes. It had been so long since I had seen them.

An exquisite crown of horns wreathed her head. I reached up with a wavering hand; my fingers shook as they pressed against the horns, but felt only the weakness of the paper. I caressed them for a moment uselessly until I let my arm drop limply to my side. I wished with every part of my being that I could be her. A few wet drops formed on the visage's cheek. Gone.

I felt new eyes on me—passersby who had stopped to stare. I pulled my hood up tightly around my face as I staggered back and composed myself. After a breath, I quickly trudged away.

I silently queued up to board a rusty old boat. I produced a ticket from my pocket and looked back. Pink-yellow light had broken through the clouds and reflected off the glassy tops of the mountains. Oksana burgeoned with life as more and more people began a new day. Above me, a skyship spat out clouds of steam and glided northward. And just beyond the dock, I could still make out the words, "Ishkara is Harmony." Her fiery eyes locked onto my own and we stared at one another.

"Name?"

I looked away. I was standing in front of a woman in a blue uniform; she wore the crest of Vsevora on her lapel. But the crest had changed. A tiny phoenix surrounded the crest.

"Name?" I saw that she held a manifest in one hand and a pen in the other. Her tone grew impatient as we stared at one another. "What is your name?" she asked again.

"My name? My name." My mouth was dry. I felt the air seize up in me. I glanced over my shoulder. I felt the stubs atop my head ache. My heart pounded. I could feel Ishkara's eyes on me.

The woman with the manifest stared at me suspiciously. She tapped her pen and leaned in closer. She began to scrutinize me and as she did, I feared she would recognize me for who I was.

"Iryna," I gasped out at last. Speaking it burnt my throat like bile. I swallowed and continued raggedly, "My name is Iryna Trembatya."

The woman leaned back, stared at me, then looked down. She scribbled onto the manifest, and quietly waved me forward.

I stepped onto the deck and held my throat. I clenched my eyes shut and staggered to the guardrail. As I steadied myself against it, I drew in a deep breath, and the boat crept out across the water. I hoped for everything that once was to fade away.

I opened my eyes and looked back. All the beauty of Vsevora was back there: the great snowy mountains, the intricate architecture, and the nation I had created. It was the last time I would ever look upon them again.

As we slowly drifted further and further across the water, I looked back to the docks. I could still see her there. She was staring at me from the pier. And her eyes burned and melted everything else away. As Vsevora disappeared forever, all I could see were Ishkara's eyes and her twisting crown of horns.

Glossary of Places and Names

The nation of Vsevora, its places, and its people bear a strong resemblance to that of Ukraine. This is by no accident, as the world's creator, Audra Balion, is of Ukrainian heritage. As such, many of the names within this book aim to honour that heritage with either direct translation or etymological resemblance to Ukrainian names and words.

This glossary serves as a memory aid for places and people along with a pronunciation guide using the International Phonetic Alphabet. Items within the glossary are approximately in order of their appearance.

Places

Vsevora [vsɛ'vɔrɑ] - Vsevora is an entire continent and is made up of many city-states that are often in conflict with one another. These city-states consist of a main city and the surrounding area, including farms and villages.

Oksana [ɔk'sɑnɑ] - A city-state located on the northern shores and surrounded by mountains of glass. It's Siranna's home and where Iryna/Ishkara grew up as a refugee.

Mount Zorya [zoʊrjɑ] - The tallest mountain amongst the glass mountains of Oksana.

The Vinnya ['vɪnjə] - Not a place, but a right of passage observed by the people of Oksana where youths climb Mount Zorya to prove themselves and enter into adulthood.

Ksenya ['ksɛnjə] - The city-state that Iryna/Ishkara was forced to flee during a time of war. It is located amidst snowy mountains south-west of Oksana.

Sophia [soʊ'fijə] - The capital city of Vsevora. Nestled between mountains and centrally located within the nation, Sophia was the traditional home of the dynast-kings and queens of old, and is where the Vsevoran Senate presides.

Lyudmila [ljʊd'mɪlɑ] - The southernmost city-state where Velodik is from. During a conflict, much of the city was burned in an event known as The Ransacking of Lyudmila.

Yuliya ['julijɑ] - A city-state near Lyudmila that was responsible for its Ransacking.

Olga and Ostap ['oʊlgə & oʊs'tɑp] - Two city-states that have long had a close relationship, but for many decades they have had a series of conflicts with one another and surrounding city-states.

The Greenshield ['grinʃild] - Located on another continent away from Vsevora, The Greenshield is a massive field of grass that grows as tall as trees. This grass protects the enclave of Feras people that live there. It is where Kalrevi and Surrendra are from.

People

Iryna Trembatya [ɪˈrɪnɑ trɛmˈbatjɑ] - A young woman from Ksenya who fled to Oksana as a refugee during conflict and war. Her name means peace. Like all Ksenyans, she has elongated "goat-like" pupils and like many Ksenyan women, she has horns that twist and branch.

Ishkara [ɪʃˈkɑrɑ] - Originally a Ksenyan word that translates to "memories and love," it is the name that Iryna took for herself when she left Oksana for Sophia.

Vitaliya [viˈtɑlijɑ] - Iryna's closest Oksanan friend.

Velodik [vɛˈlɔdɪk] - A constable in Sophia, originally from Lyudmila. When his city was set on fire, he and his family fled to Sophia. Like most Lyudmilans, he has many wolf-like features: grey skin and hair, a tail, pointed ears atop his head, and a rounded nose (although not a dog-like muzzle).

Siranna Ankova [sɪˈrɑnɑ ˈænkoʊvɑ] - An artist from Oksana, she leaves for Sophia so that she might pursue her dreams. Like most Oksanans, she is thin, tall, and bears a set of tall spiralling horns (they look much like the real-world horns of the kudu).

Sylchiv [ˈsɪltʃɪv] - The man that Siranna's mother wishes her to marry following her completion of the *Vinnya*.

Feras [feɪˈrɑs] - The name of the people that live in isolation in the Greenshield. Outside, they are only known in stories where they are often described as mystical vampires and ghostly pirates. They wear white masks and it is their custom to never remove them.

Kalrevi [kæl'rɛvi] - A Feras woman who chooses to leave the protection of The Greenshield. Her passion is tinkering and building, but she is also adept in the art of subterfuge.

Surrendra [sʊ'rɛndrɑ] - Kalrevi's father and chieftain of the Feras. He is one of the few who lived in a time of direct contact—and conflict—with outsiders. While most Feras men have four arms, he has six.

Lakira [lə'kirɑ] - A well-respected doctor amongst the Feras. She is the only Feras woman to possess four arms.

Zradya ['zrɑdjɑ] - Sophia's Commissioner of Public Security (the highest position in the city, but not the nation like Velodik). She is Yuliyan and has sheep-like horns.

Mr Pravda ['prɑvdɑ] - The head of the printing press located in Sophia. He is sympathetic to Siranna and gives her a job. He has bull-like horns and hooves.

Galva ['gælvə] - Ishkara's chief bodyguard. She is menacing, cruel, and loyal. She is quite goat-like in her features and comes from Halyna.

Oskar and Emil ['ɔskɑr & ɛ'mil] - Two men from Ksenya that live in Sophia. They are a kindly couple who wish for peace in Vsevora.

Aid for Artists

At its core, *Crown of Horns* explores the importance of art, culture, and creativity in the face of tyranny. Because the nation of Vsevora is so inspired by Ukrainian heritage, it was important for us to give back to a nation that endures through many hardships.

The Canada-Ukraine Foundation's Aid for Artists project was a clear choice when we sought out a charity to support. A portion of the sale of this book helps fund Ukrainian artists and organizations that preserve and promote the arts in Ukraine.

Learn more and consider making a donation by visiting www.cufoundation.ca/aid-for-artists

Flight Nineteen – Where It All Begins

Go beyond Vsevora and step into the story that gave birth to the world. Travel to the city of Mephistopolis: a steampunk melting pot of mutants, hybrids, and the world's greatest mechanical minds. The Bio-Mechanical Revolution is in full swing thanks to the city's revered potentate, known simply as Oil. People come from all corners of the globe to augment themselves, but they have no idea what dark truths and wicked acts fuel the revolution.

After a terrible accident blinds her father, Andromache makes for the city to find a way to heal him. As she is pulled into Oil's mysterious Medusa Project, she learns that not all is as it seems. She is left with a choice: flee and save herself, or stay and save everyone else.

Flight Nineteen is a silent graphic novel by Audra Balion. It is a story told without dialogue or narration—only pictures and your own interpretation.

Learn more at **audra.balion.ca**

About the Author

F. David Schultz is a life-long creator. He has brought works to life on stage performing in theatres throughout his home province of Saskatchewan and delighted imaginations with his eclectic roleplaying games. In his debut novel, *Crown of Horns*, Schultz worked with his partner of fifteen years to create an imaginative world and thrilling story to delight both long-time fantasy fans and newcomers to the genre alike.

About the Illustrator

Audra Balion is a multidisciplinary artist. She primarily paints, illustrates, and creates comics, but she has also been known to sculpt, design for theatre and film, and perform on stage through acting and dance. She teaches art classes at her Saskatoon studio where she helps others fall in love with creating. She enjoys starting new projects and spending cozy evenings with her two cats.